At first, the whistling tones were indistinguishable from the random, hollow sounds of the windswept reeds. Then the sounds quickened and became higher in pitch, tumbling together into a dancelike melody that set the reeds ahead quivering merrily. There was something oddly like speech in the music, Danilo noted. A moment later, the song was echoed back from the far side of the marsh.

Then the largest reeds began to sound. A deep, resonant call rang out over the marsh in macabre counterpoint to the lilting dance tune. Despite his rising fear, Danilo listened to the marsh music as objectively as he could. The sound was very like that of an enormous hunting horn.

"A call to battle," Wyn said softly, echoing Danilo's disconcerting thoughts.

Elaith wrapped his reins around the pommel of the saddle and readied his bow. "What are we fighting?"

"I don't know," Wyn replied in a tense voice, "but whatever they are, they have us surrounded."

THE HARPERS

A semi-secret organization for Good, the H̲ freedom and justice in a world populated mages, and dread concerns beyond imaginati

Each novel in the Harpers Series is a complet detailing some of the most unusual and com the magical world known as the Forgotten Re

THE HARPERS

THE PARCHED SEA
Troy Denning

ELFSHADOW
Elaine Cunningham

RED MAGIC
Jean Rabe

THE NIGHT PARADE
Scott Ciencin

THE RING OF WINTER
James Lowder

CRYPT OF THE SHADOWKING
Mark Anthony

SOLDIERS OF ICE
David Cook

FORGOTTEN REALMS

FANTASY ADVENTURE

ELFSONG

Elaine Cunningham

TSR Inc.

ELFSONG

First Printing: January 1994
Printed in the United States of America.
Library of Congress Catalog Card Number: 93-61432
9 8 7 6 5 4 3 2 1

ISBN: 1-56076-679-4

TSR, Inc.
P.O. Box 756
Lake Geneva, WI
53147 U.S.A.

TSR Ltd.
120 Church End, Cherry Hinton
Cambridge CB1 3LB
United Kingdom

To Volo, who guided me
through Waterdeep.
When next we meet,
the ale's on me!

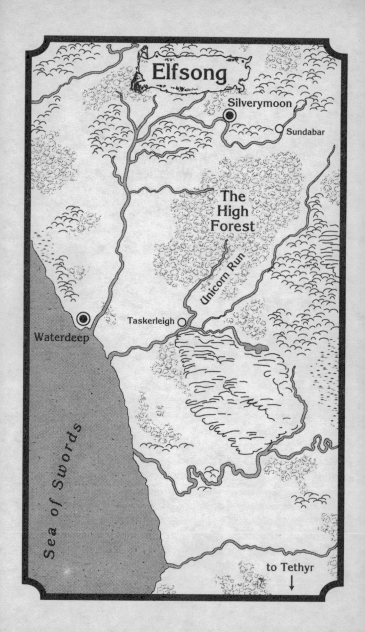

Prelude

In the heart of the Northlands, a few days' travel from the great city of Waterdeep, lay a vast, primeval wood known as the High Forest. The adventurous few who braved the forest brought back tales of strange sights and magical beasts, and many were the legends and songs that told of the land's beauty and its dangers. One tale, however, did not find its way into fireside boasting or bardic lore.

The villain of the untold tale was a green dragon named Grimnoshtadrano—Grimnosh, to his friends and victims—and this lack of notoriety hampered the dragon in his pursuit of his favorite pastime. Grimnosh collected riddles as avidly as he hoarded treasure. He waylaid and challenged all those who passed near his woodland lair, offering them their lives in exchange for a new riddle. Travelers were scarce, and none had offered a riddle that Grimnosh could not answer. The dragon had let two or three go free regardless, in hope that their stories might lure more worthy challengers to the forest: riddlemasters and bards in search of fame and adventure. Of course, in accordance with his nature, the dragon intended to eat these learned men and women as soon as he separated them from their riddles.

Unfortunately for the dragon, the travelers he'd set free had scuttled away into grateful anonymity, and more than a century had passed since the dragon's last riddle challenge. He was therefore surprised when a lone traveler came to the forest with a challenge of her own, a magical summons powerful enough to reach into his labyrinth of caves and shatter his winter sleep.

Grimnosh emerged into a world of stark contrast and icy brilliance. It was the morning of the winter solstice, and the forest was shrouded with a deep, unblemished blanket of snow. Except for the small clearing directly in front of the cave's mouth and the narrow road that lay beyond, the trees grew so close that even in winter they all but blotted out the sky. Their entwined dark branches were glossy with ice, and draped with so many icicles that the forest resembled a cave carved from diamond and obsidian.

The dragon's hooded eyes narrowed into golden slits as he studied the woman who'd ventured into this forbidding land. Swathed in a gray cloak and bent with age, she was seated upon a small, fine-boned white mare. Little of her was visible—a deep cowl covered her head and obscured her face—but the dragon's keen nose caught the tantalizing scent of elven blood. His first impulse was to devour the foolish elfwoman who had summoned him out into the snow and the cold, but he remembered the force of the spell that had wakened him. Grimnosh had been without diversion for too long, and the elven sorceress seemed promising.

So the dragon listened to her, all the while padding in slow circles around her, weaving his sinuous green tail in patterns as deft and ominous as a wizard's arcane gestures —taking her measure. When she finished her outrageous request, Grimnosh sat back on his haunches and let out a burst of derisive laughter. The thunderous roar sent a tremor through a stand of ancient oak trees. Like harps reverberating to a plucked string, the living wood echoed the deep, thrumming sound of the forest dragon's voice. Winter-bare branches shook, sending icicles crashing down around the elfwoman like so many descending fangs.

"The great Grimnoshtadrano does not bargain with elves," the wyrm said, malevolent humor in his golden eyes. "I *eat* them."

"Do you think that the best I can offer you is a light lunch?" she demanded in a voice worn thin by the passing of years. "In my time I have been a bard and a riddlemaster, and I am a sorceress still." A tiny, ironic smile deepened the wrinkles that creased her face, and she added in a wry tone, "And, lest you spoil your digestion, you should know that I am a *half*-elf."

"Is that so?" rumbled the dragon, taking a step closer. He was both annoyed and intrigued by this woman who showed no fear. "Which half of you should I eat?" The tip of his tail whipped forward, and with a flick he tossed back her cowl so that he might take a better look.

As a snack, the woman was not at all appealing. Elves at best were tasty but insubstantial, and centuries of life had nearly picked this one's bones clean. She was old, even by the dragon's reckoning, and her angular face had the hue and texture of aged parchment. Wispy strands of smoke-colored hair clung to her skull, and her eyes were so faded as to be almost colorless. Yet power surrounded her like morning mist on a woodland pond.

The dragon stopped toying with the sorceress and got down to business. "You want me to give you the

Morninglark. What do you offer in exchange?" Grimnosh asked bluntly.

"A riddle that no one can answer."

"Considering the number and caliber of humans who've passed this way of late, that shouldn't be too difficult," the dragon observed, casually inspecting the talons of a green forepaw.

"That will change. An ancient ballad about the great Grimnoshtadrano will inspire ambitious bards to seek you out."

"Oh? It hasn't yet."

"It hasn't been *written* yet," she said with a touch of asperity. "For that, I need the Morninglark."

For a long, ominous moment, the dragon glared down at the presumptuous half-elf. "Strange though this may seem, I'm in no mood for riddles. Explain yourself, and speak plainly."

"To you, the Morninglark is just another elven harp, a magic trinket lying atop your hoard." The sorceress held up her hands, which were long and elegant. "With these I can wield a rare type of elven magic known as spellsong. When my power is combined with that of the harp, I can cast a spell that will weave this new ballad into the memory of every bard within the city walls. Every enspelled bard will believe he has always known about the mighty Grimnoshtadrano. Every enspelled bard will aspire to meet your riddle challenge. These bards will spread the ballad throughout the land. Many will know your name, and the best and bravest of these will come."

"Hmmm." The dragon nodded thoughtfully. "And what will this ballad say?"

"It will send out a challenge to those who are both Harpers and bards. These must pass three tests: answer a riddle, read a scroll, and sing a song."

"And what will this ballad offer these bards, should they

succeed? The usual fame and fortune, I suppose?"

"That hardly matters."

Grimnosh snorted, sending a puff of foul-smelling steam toward the half-elven woman. "You're quick to give away treasure that isn't yours!"

"Your hoard is secure," she said firmly. "The riddle will be one of your choosing, and how many have answered such a riddle correctly?"

"In all modesty, none."

"Whoever passes this first test—which is most unlikely—will proceed to the second. The scroll I shall give you will be a many-layered riddle. I can say with reasonable assurance that no Harper could answer every layer of the riddle. I can say with absolute certainty that none wields the magic of spellsong. This magic is needed to truly *read* the scroll and to sing the song."

Grimnosh thought this over, and his sinuous tail wandered toward the half-elf's horse. The dragon absently twirled the horse's braided tail as a child might worry a lock of hair. The mare whuffled nervously but held her ground. At length the dragon said, "If all you say is true, how did you come by this knowledge?"

The woman pushed aside the folds of her cloak, revealing a small silver pin on her coat: a tiny harp cradled in the curve of a new moon. "I have been with the Harpers for over three centuries, and I know what they have become." Her face hardened, and her chest rose and fell in a long, measured breath. "The Harpers of today are likely to come against you with steel, not song. Eat as many of them as pleases you."

"Treachery!" Grimnosh exclaimed, regarding the ancient Harper with surprise and pleasure.

She shrugged and lifted her colorless eyes to meet the intent gaze of the great wyrm. "That depends entirely upon your perspective."

"A good answer." The dragon fell silent for a long, speculative moment. "It seems to me that you could accomplish a great deal with such a spell. Apart from sending me an occasional afternoon's entertainment, what do you hope to achieve?"

"What does any Harper hope to achieve?" This time her smile held a touch of bitterness. "In all things, there must be a balance."

* * * * *

Winter was hard and slow to pass. Twice the moon waxed and waned over the Northlands, but drifted snow still piled high against the walls of Silverymoon. Within the wondrous city, however, the Spring Faire was in full flower.

From her tower window, the half-elven sorceress looked down at the living tapestry of color and sound. Directly below her lay the courtyards of Utrumm's Music Conservatory, and bards from many lands crowded into the outdoor theater to share and celebrate their art. Snatches of melody drifted up to her, borne on breezes that were warmed by powerful enchantments and scented with flowers. Beyond the music school stretched the teeming marketplace, which offered all the goods and treasures of any such faire, as well as the specialties of Silverymoon: rare books and scrolls, spell components, and all manner of musical and magical devices. Equally on display were the people of Silverymoon. Brightly garbed in their best finery, they celebrated the ageless rites of spring with laughter, dancing, and whispered promises of joys to come.

She watched the merry crowd for a long time. The Spring Faire was a scene of such color and celebration, such pageantry and promise, that it could not fail to gladden the heart. Even hers quickened, although it had risen with the tides of over three hundred springs. Again that painful joy tugged at her, as it did every year when the dying winter yielded to a season of renewal. She felt it all, as keenly as did any youth or maid.

Soon the people of Silverymoon would dance to a different music, and all the bards in the city would sing only the songs that she herself had written. It pleased her that these songs would spring from a Harper's silent silver strings.

Her withered fingers sought the Harper pin on the shoulder of her gown, the once-cherished badge that she had worn—despite everything—for so many years. She tore it free and clenched it in her fist, as if to imprint every tiny curve and line of the harp-and-moon talisman upon the flesh of her hand.

With a sigh, she turned to the enspelled brazier that glowed in the center of the tower room. Steeling herself against the intense heat, she went as close as she dared and tossed her Harper pin into the brazier's dish. She watched in silence as the pin collapsed into a tiny, gleaming puddle.

Only one preparation remained for the casting of her greatest spell: the years had stolen the song from her voice, and song she must have. The last of her family's wealth had gone to purchase a potion to restore the beauty of her voice and her person. She drew the flagon from her sleeve and stood before the tower room's mirror. Closing her eyes, she whispered the words of enchantment and then drank deeply. The potion's warmth coursed through her, burning away the years and leaving her gasping with unexpected pain. She clutched the mirror's frame for support, and when the red haze was spent, she opened her eyes and gazed in dismay at what the spell had done.

The mirror reflected the image of a woman in her late middle years. A once-willowy figure was plump and

matronly. Her brilliant red hair, which in her youth had
been flame and silk, was reduced to a dull brown streaked
with gray. At least her ancient and faded eyes had regained
their youthful color, for they were again the brilliant blue
that her lovers had often likened to fine sapphires. After
the first stab of disappointment, she realized that she
couldn't have chosen a better guise. The beautiful woman
who had inspired comparison to rubies and sapphires
would draw too much attention, and no one alive remembered her as she now appeared. The true test of the spell
was her voice. She drew a deep breath and sang a verse of
an elven lament. The notes rang out clear and true, the
bell-like soprano for which she had once been celebrated.
Satisfied, she studied her reflection anew, and a little smile
curved her lips. The Harpers knew her as Iriador, a name
taken from the Elvish word for ruby. Now she was merely
garnet, a jewel still, but a dim shadow of a ruby's luster
and fire. She was content with image of the darker gem.
Garnet would serve for her new name.

She turned to study the harp that stood near the tower
window. At first glance, it too seemed unremarkable. Small
and light enough to carry with ease, it had but twenty
strings. It was fashioned of dark wood, and its curving
lines and subtle carvings proclaimed its elven origin. But
when the harp was played, a tiny morninglark carved into
the wood moved as if singing in time to the music. This
was not easy to discern, for the harp's magical namesake
was carved on the soundboard where only the harpist
could see it, and only then if she knew precisely where to
look.

Garnet seated herself before the Morninglark harp
and flexed her fingers, rejoicing in their renewed agility,
and then played a few silver notes. Finally she began to
sing, and voice and harp blended into a spell of great
power. The music reached out with invisible hands for

the last component of the spell: the melted silver bubbling in the enspelled brazier. As Garnet sang, the remains of the Harper pin rose into the air like a tiny vortex and spun itself into a long, slender ribbon. Unerringly it flew toward Garnet's harp, wrapping itself around one harp string. It bonded as tightly as if it had been absorbed into the very metal, and the spell was complete. The ancient melody ceased, and the last rippled chord faded into silence.

Exultant now, the sorceress again began to play and sing. Her songs floated over the city, carrying a corrosive, insidious magic on the breath of the wind. Throughout the night she played, until her voice was reduced to a whimper and her fingertips bled. When the first colors of morning stole through the tower window, Garnet shouldered the harp and ventured forth to see what she had created.

* * * * *

A heavy blow landed on Wyn Ashgrove's back, knocking his magical lyre off his shoulder. The elven minstrel's first impulse was to reach for the fallen instrument, but years of adventuring had trained him otherwise. He whirled to face his assailant, his fingers tight on his long sword's grip.

Wyn relaxed when he looked up—way up—into the beaming, brown-whiskered face of Kerigan the Bold.

Kerigan, a Northman skald and pirate, had befriended Wyn some ten years earlier, after stripping and scuttling the merchant ship that carried Wyn east from the Moonshae Isles. Northmen hold bards in high regard, so Kerigan had spared the elf and had even offered to deliver him to the port of his choice. Wyn had suggested a better plan. Always eager to learn more of humans and their music— even the crude and earthy music of the Northmen skalds —the elf had offered himself as apprentice to Kerigan.

Their time together had been one of rowdy adventure and
tall-told tales, and the elven scholar regarded Kerigan as
one of his more interesting studies.

"Wyn, lad! Late to come, but no less the welcome for it!"
The greeting rang out above the din of the street, and Kerigan punctuated his words with another hearty swat.

"It's good to see you again, Kerigan," Wyn said sincerely
as he stooped to recover his lyre.

"Trouble on the road, was it?" asked the skald. His eyes
gleamed, anticipating a new tale of adventure.

Wyn shrugged an apology. "Ice on the river. We were
held up for days."

"Too bad," Kerigan said. "Well, at least you're here for
the big show. That's not to be missed, if it means putting
off your own funeral. Hurry, now."

Wyn nodded his agreement and fell into step beside his
friend. Silverymoon's Spring Faire always culminated in an
open-air concert on the vast grounds of Utrumm's Music
Conservatory. The school was a fine one and justly famed,
built as it was upon the remnants of an elder barding college. All the finest bards had trained at the conservatory at
one point or another in their careers, and the spring pil-
grimage brought back most of them from all over Faerun
and beyond. Other entertainers came as well, to perform,
to pick up new songs, or to purchase instruments. The
final concert of ballads yielded an excellence and variety
that was exceptional even for Silverymoon.

The skald and the elf made a strange pair as they
elbowed their way through the milling crowds. Kerigan
was heavily muscled and broad of chest, and he stood
nearly seven feet tall on incongruously thin, bandy legs.
His helm was decorated with a broad pair of antlers; that,
his bulbous nose, and his whisker-draped jowls brought to
mind an image of a two-legged moose. The skald sang to
himself as he walked, and his voice was a fog-shattering

bellow that harmonized perfectly with his uncouth appearance. Wyn's progress through the crowd was silent and graceful, and his manner so refined that to all appearances he did not notice the stares leveled at his rough companion, nor did he seem aware of the admiring gazes his elven beauty elicited. Wyn possessed the golden skin and black hair common to the high elf people, and his large, almond-shaped eyes were the deep green of an ancient forest. His ebony curls were cropped short, and he was elegantly turned out in butter-soft leathers and a quilted silk shirt the color of new leaves. Even his instruments were exceptional. In addition to his silver lyre, he carried a small flute of deep green crystal, which hung from his belt in a bag fashioned of silvery mesh.

The two ill-matched musicians squeezed into the courtyard just as the herald's horn announced the concert's beginning.

"Where'd you like to sit?" boomed Kerigan, his voice clearly audible above the crumhorn's blast.

Wyn glanced around. Not an empty seat remained, and precious little standing room. He knew that this would not deter the brash skald. "An aisle seat, perhaps a few rows from the front?" he suggested, naming the area that Kerigan would have chosen regardless.

The Northman grinned and plowed forward through the crowd. He bent over two half-elven bards and whispered a threat. The bards obligingly abandoned their seats, their faces showing relief to have escaped so easily. With a sigh, Wyn made his way toward the beckoning Northman. At least Kerigan had acquired the seats without drawing steel—probably a first for the Northman, noted Wyn with a touch of wry amusement.

Wyn's face lit up when the first selection was announced: a gypsy ballad about a long-ago alliance between the Harpers and the witches of Rashemen. The tale was told entirely in music and dance, and few were the artists who could master the intricate steps and gestures that spoke as plainly as words.

Applause rang through the courtyard as the musicians filed onto the platform—small, swarthy people carrying fiddles, simple percussion instruments, and the triangular lutes known as balalaikas. The storyteller was a young Rashemite woman, tiny and fey, dressed as was customary in a wide black skirt and embroidered white blouse. Her feet were bare, and her dark hair had been tightly braided and wrapped crownlike around her head. She stood immobile in the platform's center as the music began with a rhythmic, low-pitched plinking from the huge bass balalaika. At first the storyteller spoke only with compelling dark eyes and small gestures of her hands, but one by one the instruments joined in, and her movements quickened as she danced the tale of magic and intrigue, battle and death. The story-dancing of the Rashemite gypsies held a unique magic, and this woman was among the best Wyn had seen. Yet something about the performance struck him as not quite right.

The problems were subtle at first: a misplaced gesture of the hand, a sinister note in the wailing of the fiddle. Wyn could not guess how this had occurred; the faire's ballad performers were carefully screened, and only the best, most authentic storytellers were selected.

Within moments, Wyn realized that the classic tale had been significantly altered. The Harper theme, a wandering arpeggio that was usually played by the soprano balalaika, had been eliminated entirely, and the roguish bass tune that represented Elminster, the Sage of Shadowdale, had been twisted into a halting tune that suggested a doddering and inept menace. As the appalled elf watched, the dancer's steps faltered, then picked up the thread of the story. Faster and faster she whirled, her bare feet flashing as she followed the new telling.

Wyn tore his gaze from the stage and glanced up at Kerigan. If the skald noticed anything other than twirling skirts and bare legs, it didn't show in his broad leer. The troubled elf searched the crowd, expecting to see outrage on the faces of more discerning bards. To his astonishment, every member of the audience watched the ballad with smiles that spoke of enjoyment and, even more disturbing, recognition. When the gypsy dance ended, the assembly burst into huzzahs and enthusiastic applause. Beside Wyn, Kerigan whooped and stomped in loud approval.

The elf sank low in his seat, too stunned to join in the applause or to notice when it ended. A sharp jab from the skald's elbow brought Wyn's attention back to the stage, where a chorus of beautiful priestesses sang a ballad extolling Sune, goddess of love. Wyn noted that this ballad had also been altered.

On and on the storytelling went, and each ballad was vastly different from the ones Wyn had learned in the bardic tradition, passed down unchanged throughout generations of bards. Yet not once did Wyn see any other bard display the slightest sign of distress. The rest of the concert passed like a dream from which he could not awaken. Either he had gone mad, or the past had been rewritten in the minds and memories of hundreds of the Northland's most skilled and influential bards.

Wyn Ashgrove was not sure which prospect frightened him more.

One

In the very heart of Waterdeep, in a tavern renowned for its ale and its secrets, six old friends gathered about a supper table in a cozy, private room. Thick walls of fieldstone and ancient beams muffled the sounds coming from the tavern kitchen and the taproom beyond, and in the center of each of the four walls stood a stout oak door. On each door was a lamp that glowed with faint blue light. The lamps, magical devices that kept any sound from leaving the room, also barred inquisitive mages from scrying in. In the center of the chamber was a round table of polished Chultan teak, and the deeply cushioned and well-worn chairs around it spoke of many long, comfortable visits. A dome of pale, incandescent azure surrounded the supper table, ensuring that no words would pass the magical barrier. In a city whose lifeblood was equal parts gold and intrigue, multiple privacy spells were not unusual. In all, the scene was common enough; the friends were not.

14

"I learned of this just last evening," said Larissa Neathal, a striking red-haired woman who, despite the early hour, was draped in white silk and ropes of pearls. She circled the rim of her wine glass with one slender finger as she spoke, idly coaxing a clear, ghostly note from the singing crystal. "I was entertaining Wynead ap Gawyn—a prince of one of those lesser Moonshae kingdoms—and he spoke at length about crop failures on one of the islands. The fields and meadows for miles around Caer Callidyrr withered mysteriously, almost overnight!"

"That's a misfortune and no mistake, but if it doesn't touch Waterdeep, we haven't spare tears to shed," observed Mirt the Moneylender, folding his arms over his food-stained tunic in a gesture of finality.

Kitten, a sell-sword whose hair was a tousled brown mop and whose leathers were cut to reveal abundant cleavage, leaned forward to poke playfully at Mirt's vast midsection. "So say *you*, Sir Beer-Belly. Those of us with more refined tastes—" here she paused to cast a coy, hooded glance around the table "—we know this news bodes ill for Waterdeep in more ways than Elminster has pipes." She began to tick off concerns on her red-taloned fingers. "First, the famous herb gardens near the old college. The woodruff there goes to make the Moonshae spring wine that sells so well at our Summer Faire. No woodruff, no wine, eh? Our finest wools come from those parts, too, and the spring shearing will be scant if the sheep lack grazing. You just try to tell Waterdeep's weavers, tailors, and cloak-makers that *that* isn't any of our concern. And what of the merchant guilds? You can't empty a chamber pot in the Moonshaes without hitting a handful of petty royals, and all of them strive to outdo each other buying our fancier goods. *If* they have the money, mind. With crops failing, they won't." She raised one painted eyebrow. "I could go on."

"And you usually do," grumbled Mirt, but he softened his words with a good-natured wink.

"Problems in the South Ward, too," said Brian quietly, folding his callused hands on the table. Brian the Swordmaster was the only one of their number who lived and labored among Waterdeep's working folk, and his practical voice and keen eye made him the most down-to-earth of the secret Lords of Waterdeep. "Caravans are losing goods to brigands. Outside the city walls, travelers and whole farm families have been found torn to bits with never a sword drawn in their own defense. Looks like monsters at work, and monsters with magic. Game has fled the woods to the south, and there's too many empty stew pots. The fisherfolk have troubles, too: nets slashed, catches looted, trap lines cut. What say you about that, Blackstaff? Are the merfolk falling off the job, and letting those murdering sahuagin too close to the harbor?"

All eyes turned to Khelben "Blackstaff" Arunsun, the most powerful—and the least secret—of the Lords of Waterdeep. His age was impossible to guess, but his black hair and full dark beard were shot through with silver, and his hairline was definitely in retreat. There was a distinctive streak of gray in the middle of his beard that emphasized his learned, distinguished air. Tall and heavily muscled, he was an imposing man, even seated. Tonight the archmage seemed oddly preoccupied. His goblet sat untouched before him, and he gave scant attention to the concerns of his fellow Lords. "Sahuagin? Not to my knowledge, Brian. No sahuagin have been reported," Khelben replied in a distracted voice.

"What's stuck in your craw tonight, wizard?" demanded Mirt. "We've troubles enough already, but you might as well put yours on the table along with the rest."

"I have a most disturbing story," Khelben began slowly. "A young elven minstrel stumbled upon a mystery at the

Silverymoon Spring Faire, and he has been traveling these three months trying to find someone who would listen to his tale. It seems that the ancient ballads performed at the Spring Faire, especially those written by or about Harpers, have all been changed."

Larissa let out a peal of silvery laughter. "Now, there's news indeed! Every street and tavern singer changes a story, adapting the tune and words to suit his own whim and the tastes of the listeners."

"That is so," the archmage agreed. "At least, that is the custom of street and tavern performers. True bards are another matter entirely. Part of a bard's training is memorizing the traditions and lore, which are passed down, precise and immutable, for generations. That's why so many Harpers are bards: to preserve a knowledge of our past."

"I don't often disagree with you, Blackstaff." Durnan, a retired adventurer and the owner of the tavern in which they met, spoke for the first time. "Seems like we've got enough to concern ourselves with in the here and today. Let the past take care of itself." The other Lords of Waterdeep murmured agreement.

"Would that it were so simple," Khelben said. "It appears that the bards themselves have fallen under some sort of powerful enchantment. Magic that far-reaching can only mean trouble to come. We need to know who cast the spell, why, and to what end."

"That's your end of the ox, wizard," Mirt pointed out. "The rest of us know little enough about magic."

"Magic can't provide the answer," Khelben admitted. "I've examined several afflicted bards. They are telling the truth as they know it, and magical inquiry yields no answers. As far as the bards are concerned, the ballads are as they've always been."

Kitten yawned widely. "So? The bards are the only ones who care about such things, and as long as they're happy, what's the harm in it?"

"Many bards may *die* happy," Khelben said. "Not only have the old ballads been changed, but new ones have somehow been grafted into the bards' memories. The elf minstrel brought to my attention a new ballad that could lure many Harpers to their deaths. It urges Harper bards to seek out Grimnoshtadrano for some insane riddle challenge."

"Old Grimnosh? The green dragon?" Mirt grimaced. "So this is more than a fancy prank; it's a fancy trap. Any idea who's behind it?"

"I'm afraid not," the archmage admitted. "But the ballad mentions a scroll. If a bard can retrieve it from the dragon, I may be able to trace the spell's creator."

"Well, there you go," Kitten said. "Bards are easy enough to come by."

Khelben shook his head. "Believe me, I've tried. Every available Harper bard in the Northlands seems to be afflicted, and therefore any one of them could be an unwitting tool of the spellcaster. Therein lies the problem. Who's to say that an enspelled bard won't take the scroll to his hidden master? No, we need a bard whose wits and memories are his own."

"What of the elf, the one who brought you this tale?" Larissa suggested.

"For one thing, he's not a Harper," the archmage said. "But more important, to succeed in this quest, a bard must understand both music and magic. The scroll mentioned in the ballad is most likely a spell scroll, and if that is so, reading the scroll means casting a spell. The elven minstrel has had no wizard training. And you know what would likely occur if I sent an elf to face a green dragon."

"Breakfast, lunch, or dinner would occur," Kitten said flatly, "depending on the time of day. So what *are* you going to do?"

"I've sent out inquiries, hoping to find someone farther afield whose gifts are unchanged." The archmage's frustration was almost palpable.

The friends sat in silence for a long moment. Brian stroked his chin thoughtfully before he spoke. "Seems to me you'll have to do like the rest of us, Blackstaff; make do with what you can get. Maybe there's a mage among the Harpers who could pass as a bard. Know you anyone like that?"

Khelben Arunsun stared at the swordmaster for a long moment. Then he dropped his head into his hands, slowly shaking his head as if in denial. "Lady Mystra preserve us, I'm afraid I do."

* * * * *

Far to the south of Waterdeep, a young man strode whistling into the entrance hall of the Purple Minotaur, the finest inn in Tethyr's royal city. He nodded to the beaming innkeeper and made his way through the crowded gaming hall on the inn's opulent first floor.

Many pairs of dark eyes marked his passing, for Danilo Thann was something of an oddity in the insular and sometimes xenophobic southern city. His manner and appearance clearly proclaimed his northern heritage: he was tall and lean, and his blond hair fell in thick waves to his shoulders. Mischief lurked in his gray eyes, and his face wore a perpetual smile and an expression of open friendship and guileless youth. Despite his callow appearance, Danilo had recently established himself as a successful and popular member of the wine merchants' guild. He was also vastly wealthy, and not at all loathe to spend money. Many of the regular patrons glanced up from their cards or dice and greeted him with genuine pleasure, and a few called out invitations to join in the gaming. But this evening Danilo's

arms were piled high with neatly wrapped packages, and
he seemed particularly eager to examine his newly
acquired treasures. Tossing back greetings and banter as
he went, he hurried toward the curving marble staircase
near the back of the gaming hall, and he bounded up the
stairs three at a time.

When Danilo reached his bedchamber, he tossed his
purchases onto the embroidered pillows that were heaped
on the Calimshan carpet. He snatched up a long, slender
package and unwrapped it, revealing a gleaming sword.
After admiring the sheen and workmanship for a moment,
he snapped into a guard stance and made a few flamboyant
lunges at an invisible adversary. A nasal, droning voice
immediately filled the room as the magic sword broke into
a Turmish battle song. The young man dropped the sword
as if it had burned his fingers.

"Egad! I pay two thousand gold pieces for a singing
sword, and it has a voice like Deneir's donkey! Or should
that be Milil's mother-in-law?" he mused, scratching his
chin as he considered which bardic god might best be
invoked under such circumstances. After a moment, he
shrugged.

"Well, you get the general idea," he said, whimsically
addressing the discarded sword. "So. What am I to do with
you?"

The sword had no opinion on the matter. It had been
fashioned to sing when wielded, inspiring fighters to new
levels of courage and ferocity. It also warded off the magic
of creatures that do mischief through music, such as
sirens and harpies. Conversation was not among the
sword's talents.

Danilo crossed the room to a reading table piled with
books. He took up a slender volume bound in crimson
leather and leafed through it. "This one is worth a try,"
he murmured, scanning a spell he had devised to add

additional tunes to the repertoire of an enspelled music box. With a brisk nod, he set down the book and his hands flashed through the gestures of the spell. That done, he fetched his lute down from its wall peg and settled down cross-legged on the carpet near the sword. He began to play and sing a ribald ballad. After a few minutes of silence, the sword began to hum along. When it joined in, it imitated not only the words and tune, but the ringing, resonant tones of Danilo's well-trained tenor.

"You're a baritone, but I suppose that can't be helped," the young mage commented, but he was vastly pleased with the success of his spell. Danilo had studied magic since the age of twelve, under the stern eye of his uncle Khelben Arunsun. At first Dan studied in secret to avoid a public outcry—his early attempts to learn the craft had resulted in a number of colorful mishaps—but he showed remarkable talent, and Khelben soon wished to make the apprenticeship official. Danilo had demurred. Even then, he'd had the notion that he might accomplish more if the full extent of his abilities were kept secret. His wealth and social position—the Thann family was among the merchant nobility of Waterdeep—gave him access to places denied most Harpers. Few suspected that he was anything more than what he appeared to be: a dilettante and dandy, an amusing dabbler in music and magic, a fop and a bit of a fool.

Seated on the intricate carpet amid heaps of embroidered pillows, Danilo Thann looked the part he had chosen to play, and quite at home in his luxurious surroundings. He was even dressed to match the rich purple shades that filled the chamber. His leggings, silk shirt, and velvet jerkin were all a deep shade of violet, and his knee-high suede boots had been dyed to match. The outfit, according to his Harper companion, made him look like a walking grape, but Danilo was well satisfied. Upon joining the guild of wine merchants, he had ordered an entire new wardrobe made up in shades of purple, for this was the favored color of the land. Wearing purple was a sign of goodwill, and it pleased the many tailors, cobblers, and jewelers Danilo patronized. All told, a new wardrobe and a small hoard of amethyst jewelry was a small price to pay for the popularity he enjoyed in Tethyr.

Danilo sang until the sliver of new moon rose high into the sky. After the magical sword had learned the ballad to Danilo's satisfaction, the mage returned the weapon to its scabbard, which he attached to his weapon belt. That done, Danilo again picked up the lute and began to play and sing. He was known among the Waterdhavian nobility for the amusing songs he composed, but since no one was around to hear and wonder, he played the music that pleased him best: airs and ballads by the great bards of ages past.

A magical alarm sent an insistent pulse sounding through the room, shattering Danilo's reverie and drowning out his song. The shrill warning of danger seemed strangely out of place, but Danilo immediately set aside his lute and rose to his feet. One of the magical wards he'd placed around the inn had been triggered by an intruder. He strode to a table near the open window and picked up the small globe. At his touch, the alarm stilled and a picture formed in the heart of the crystal. The scene it showed him brought an involuntary smile to the young mage's face.

A slender, feminine form stalked the roof two stories above him, a length of rope in her hands. She made no sound and was barely discernible against the dark sky; only the crystal's magic enabled him to see his potential assailant. With his free hand, Danilo reached for the decanter of elverquisst he kept for just such occasions.

He poured generous portions of the ruby-colored elven

liqueur into two goblets, keeping his eyes on the magical crystal. As he watched, the tiny figure reflected therein leaped far out into the night. The rope she held snapped taut, and she swung like a pendulum toward his open window. Danilo set down the alarm and picked up the full goblets.

A half-elven woman landed before him in a crouch, quiet and nimble as a cat. Her blue eyes swept the room, and a ready dagger flashed in one slender hand. Satisfied that all was safe, she tucked the dagger in her boot and rose to her full height, just three inches shorter than Danilo's six feet.

Arilyn Moonblade had been his friend and partner for almost three years now, yet Danilo never ceased to marvel at her talents—or her effortless beauty. Her raven curls had been tossed by the night wind, and she was dressed for concealment: her pale oval face had been darkened with ointment, and she wore leggings and a loose shirt of an indistinct dark hue that seemed to absorb shadow. To Danilo's eyes, though, the half-elf outshone every over-dressed Waterdhavian noblewoman he'd ever met. Once again Danilo had to remind himself of the importance of their working relationship.

"Lovely night for second-story work," he observed in a casual tone, and handed her a goblet. "That jump was most impressive. But tell me, have you ever miscalculated the rope's length?"

Arilyn shook her head, then absently tossed back the contents of the goblet. Danilo's eyes widened. The elven spirits had a kick more powerful than that of a paladin's mount, but his delicate-looking companion might as well have been drinking water.

"We're leaving Tethyr," she stated, plunking her empty goblet on Danilo's table.

The Harper mage placed his own goblet beside hers. "Oh?" he asked warily.

"Someone has placed a bounty on your head," she said in a grim tone, giving him a heavy gold coin. "These were given to any assassin willing to take on the job. One hundred more to whoever makes the kill."

Danilo hefted the coin in a practiced hand and then let out a long, low whistle. The coin felt to be about three times the normal trade weight; the amount Arilyn named was a substantial sum. He glanced at the markings on the coin's face; it was artfully embossed with an unfamiliar pattern of runes and symbols. "It would seem I'm attracting a better class of enemies these days," he observed wryly.

"Listen to me!" Arilyn clasped both his forearms and gave him a little shake. The intensity in her blue eyes drove the last bit of mirth from the young man's face. "I heard someone singing your ballad about the Harper assassin."

"Merciful Milil," he swore softly, at last understanding the situation. He'd written the ballad—an appalling bit of doggerel—about their first adventure together. The facts were well and truly disguised, and although it did not identify either Arilyn or him as Harpers, the very mention of that society of "meddling Northern barbarians" could create a good deal of resentment in the troubled land of Tethyr. For months he and Arilyn had worked to undermine a plot to replace the ruling pasha with a guild alliance, he from within the wine merchants' guild, and she in the dark underworld of the assassins' guild. All this he had undone with an ill-considered ballad. Danilo silently cursed his own stupidity, but out of habit he hid his emotions behind a frivolous quip.

"The locals express their musical preferences rather forcefully, wouldn't you say?" He cut off Arilyn's exasperated rejoinder with an upraised hand. "I'm sorry, my dear. Force of habit. You're right, of course. We must ride north at once."

"No." She reached out and touched one of his rings—a magical gift from Danilo's uncle, Khelben Arunsun, that could teleport up to three people back to the safety of Blackstaff Tower, or elsewhere if the wielder so chose.

Danilo knew from experience how much Arilyn hated magical travel. If she was willing to resort to it, the situation must be grave indeed. He snatched up his swordbelt and affixed to it the magic bag that held his wardrobe and travel supplies, and he quickly thrust his three spellbooks into the bag. He absently dropped in the assassin's coin and then reached for her hand.

The half-elf took a step backward and shook her head. "I'm not coming with you."

"Arilyn, this is no time to be squeamish!"

"It's not that." She took a deep breath as if to steady herself. "Word came from Waterdeep today. I've been assigned another mission. I leave in the morning." The magical alarm began to pulse again. Arilyn snatched up the magical globe and peered into it. Three shadowy figures moved toward the edge of the roof, just two stories above them. Arilyn tossed the alarm aside and cast a glance toward the open window. "There's no time to explain. Go!"

"And leave you to face them alone? Not bloody likely."

Her answering smile didn't reach her eyes, and she touched the gray silk sash at her waist that proclaimed her rank in Tethyr's assassins' guild. "I'm one of them, remember? I'll say you were gone. No one will challenge me."

"Of course they will," he snapped. Assassins in Tethyr rose through the ranks by killing someone with a higher-ranked sash. Arilyn had been forced to defend her reluctantly worn sash more than once.

The rope she'd left hanging outside his window began to sway as someone inched down it toward his room. "Go," Arilyn pleaded.

"Come with me," he demanded. She shook her head,

implacable. Danilo snatched the stubborn half-elf into his arms. "If you think I'd leave you, you're a bigger fool than I am," he said, his words racing against the approaching danger. "This is hardly the moment I'd have chosen to mention this, but damn it, woman, I love you."

"I know," she replied softly, clinging to him in turn and searching his face for an intense second, as if to commit it to memory.

Arilyn eased out of his arms and lifted one slender hand to stroke his cheek. Then she doubled her other fist and drove it into his midsection. Danilo went down like a felled oak.

As he struggled to draw breath, he felt her fingers on his hand, twisting the ring of teleportation that would send him back to Waterdeep. He lunged for her wrist, intending to drag her along to safety, but the teleportation spell engulfed him, and his fingers closed on a whirl of white emptiness.

* * * * *

When Danilo arrived in the safety of Blackstaff Tower's reception hall, his first impulse was to return to Tethyr immediately. His magic ring, however, would not grant him that power again until daybreak. Khelben could send him back, Danilo realized, and when he could muster enough breath to move, he lurched up the curving stone stairway to the archmage's private chambers. Khelben was not at home, nor was his lady, the mage Laeral. Danilo made a quick search of the tower, with the same result. He was alone, and thoroughly stuck in Waterdeep.

The Harper hurried back down to the reception hall and flung himself into the chair at the small writing table. He scratched a quick note to his uncle telling him what had occurred in Tethyr. Danilo cast a spell that made the paper float at eye level near the room's entrance. For good measure, he placed an aureole of sparkling pink lights around the parchment, so that Khelben could not fail to see it upon his return. Meanwhile, Arilyn was alone in Tethyr, and there was not a thing Danilo could to do to help.

Helplessness gave birth to frustration, and suddenly the Harper could no longer abide the symbolic purple he wore. He stripped off his amethyst rings and thrust them into the magic bag on his belt, but the fact remained that he was still dressed like a "walking grape." He strode out of the tower and through the second invisible door that allowed passage out of the polished black stone wall surrounding it. At a brisk pace he headed toward the townhouse he'd recently purchased. There he could discard the purple reminders of his mission in Tethyr and await his uncle's summons. For the last two years, both Danilo and Arilyn had received their missions directly from Khelben Arunsun; surely the archmage could tell Danilo where Arilyn had been assigned to go.

As he walked, Dan mentally kicked himself for leaving his magical globe behind in Tethyr. It was a small scrying crystal that he'd adapted into an alarm, but with it he could probably discover how Arilyn fared. Just before the ring of teleportation had carried him away from Tethyr, Danilo had caught one last glimpse of her. Sword drawn, the half-elf had faced the window in a battle stance, limned in the magical blue light of her sword as she stood to confront his enemies. Danilo could not dismiss that image from his mind, or stop wondering about the outcome of the battle that had surely followed.

Danilo was so preoccupied with his thoughts that he gave scant attention to others on the crowded street. He hurried past an alley and bumped heavily into a solid frame. Strong hands caught the Harper's shoulders and held him out at arm's length. Danilo focused his attention

on the smiling face of his friend and fellow nobleman, Caladorn Cassalanter. The man was several years older that
Dan's eight-and-twenty, also taller and broader. He wore
his dark red hair cropped short, and he had a warrior's callused hands. Caladorn had long been city champion in
fighting arts and horsemanship. Of late he'd taken to bouts
of seafaring adventure, even dropping his family name
until he had "done something do prove himself worthy of
it." With difficulty, Danilo summoned the inane grin his
friend would expect and pasted it firmly in place.

"Well met, Caladorn. Fancy bumping into you, as they
say."

The nobleman chuckled and released his grip. "Steady
as you go, Dan. The taverns have not been long open, and
already you walk as though tacking to a changing wind."
Caladorn's eyes narrowed. "Or are you ill? You don't look
yourself."

"Sad to say, all I'm suffering from is a bit of a headache,"
Dan lied, pressing his fingertips delicately to his temple.
"You know you're getting old when you feel this bad the
day after you've had no fun the night before." He paused,
as if slightly dizzied by his own observation. "Or words to
that effect."

Caladorn laughed and clapped Danilo on the shoulder.
"That's my lad. You know the Lady Thione, do you not?
Lucia, my dear, I am remiss. Allow me to present my old
friend, Danilo Thann. Despite appearance, he is harmless!"

Danilo turned his attention to the woman at Caladorn's
side. Tiny and slight, she was dressed in a gown of rich
purple and crowned by gleaming chestnut hair arranged
in thick coils about her shapely head. Her dark eyes
observed Dan with a touch of amusement, and her delicately aquiline features held the unmistakable stamp of the
Southlands. Dan stifled a sigh: he was not going to escape

his memories of Tethyr tonight. Lucia Thione was a prominent member of Waterdeep society, and as a distant relative of Tethyr's ousted royal family, she often wore the traditional purple to flaunt her exotic and royal background. Danilo disliked this sort of posturing, but he knew the rules of court behavior and could follow them as well as any. He took Lucia Thione's hand and bowed deeply.

"Caladorn is a fool, dear lady. Where a beautiful woman is concerned, no man should be considered harmless." He smiled at his friend, taking the threat from the words and leaving behind only the compliment.

"In that case, I'll consider myself forewarned, and we'll take our leave," Caladorn said in a jovial tone, encircling Lucia's shoulder with one massive arm.

Dan watched them go, noting the solicitous manner in which Caladorn bent over the tiny noblewoman. So that's why Caladorn was lingering in Waterdeep rather than going off to pursue adventure somewhere, Dan noted. Although Danilo was not exactly envious, he was in no mood to be confronted with other people's happiness. Feeling very alone and in sudden need of a stiff drink, Danilo ducked into the nearest tavern.

He regretted his choice immediately. The scent of a rain-washed forest greeted him, and the taproom's roof soared up at least five stories to accommodate the live trees that grew here and there in the room. Gentle, floating motes of blue light drifted among the clientele, who were almost exclusively elven. The reason for this was immediately apparent: a pair of well-armed gold elf sentinels guarded the door like a pair of glowering bookends. They looked him over, considering.

"I know you," one of them finally said. "You're that . . . *mage* that was discussed in the last innkeepers' guild meeting."

Dan smiled at them in his most engaging fashion.

"You've obviously heard about that unfortunate incident at the Fiery Flagon. Rest assured, I've paid for the damage in full. Except for the dwarf's beard, of course—hard to determine a market rate on those, don't you know—but it should grow back in, say, another decade or two. Not that the spell would affect any of your clients, of course; no one here appears to be bearded, so having ale suddenly turn to flame couldn't set anyone's beard afire. *If* I cast that spell, that is, which of course I won't."

The elven guards seized Danilo by his elbows and spun him toward the door. From the corner of his eye, the Harper saw an ancient elf lift one long-fingered hand in a peremptory gesture. Immediately the guards halted. The elf—marked by his fine white robes and platinum torque as a personage of some importance—whispered a few words to his hostess, Yaereene Ilbaereth. Her delicate face lit in a smile of genuine pleasure, and she came to meet Dan with outstretched hands. The door guards melted away at her approach. Dan noted this development with puzzlement. He had fully expected to be thrown out of the tavern, and indeed he had no wish to linger, but he could hardly ignore the regal elven woman who approached him.

Yaereene was tall and slender, with the silvery hair and eyes common to moon elves. She wore a sparkling gown that was alternately blue or green, for it changed color to match the whim and color of the tiny faerie dragon perched on her shoulder. The creature grinned and flapped its gossamer wings as the pair approached, and its jeweled scales were echoed by the fine blue topaz woven into the intricate silver mesh of the elf's necklace.

"Welcome to Elfstone Tavern," Yaereene said, holding out both hands to Danilo in a manner common to ladies of the Waterdhavian court. It was a gracious gesture, accepting the human by his own custom. Danilo took her hands and kissed the slender fingers, and then responded in kind. Holding both hands, palms up, before him, he bowed low to her in a uniquely elven gesture of respect. Yaereene's smile widened and then turned into a delighted laugh when Dan addressed the faerie dragon with a few words in its own tongue. In response, the tiny creature graciously craned its jeweled head to one side, allowing Dan to scratch its neck as he would that of a house cat.

Yaereene claimed Danilo's arm and led him deeper into the taproom. "Tonight you are the guest of Evindal Duirsar, patriarch priest of Corellion Lathanian," she said, indicating the aged elf who had interceded in Dan's behalf. "May we call on you later, after you have supped and shared a drink?"

"Of course," Danilo replied graciously, although he hadn't the slightest notion of what he might be called upon to do.

The elven priest rose when the Harper approached, and after the rituals of greeting were accomplished the two settled down before a crystal decanter. "Do you drink elverquisst?" the priest asked.

"Only when it's available," Danilo replied in a droll tone.

Evindal Duirsar smiled and signaled for another goblet, which was immediately supplied by an elven servant. The priest's mood abruptly sobered, and he leaned forward and spoke in a quiet voice. "My son is Erlan Duirsar, lord of Evereska. He has told me of your service to the elven people."

"I see." Dan settled back in his chair, uncertain of how to proceed. Two years earlier, he had helped to secure Evermeet, the island homeland and last retreat of the elves, by moving a magical gate from the elven settlement known as Evereska to a more secure, secret location. He had no idea how widespread this knowledge was, but, judging from Yaereene's reception and the number of gracious nods the elven patrons had sent his way, it was a secret poorly kept. "I suppose that would explain my welcome here," Danilo concluded.

"Not at all." Evindal shook his head adamantly. "Few know what transpired in Evereska. You are welcome here for other, more obvious reasons."

"Define 'obvious,' " Dan requested.

The elven priest chuckled and gestured toward the middle of the taproom. There sat a flaxen-haired elfmaid, playing upon a gilded harp and singing. Danilo recognized the tune as *The Gray-Mist Maiden*, an air that he himself had written. The song likened the magical mist that surrounded and protected Evereska to an elusive lover, and although it was popular with Dan's friends among the Waterdhavian nobility, to Dan's ear the words were trite and overly sentimental. He had deliberately written it so. Why would such a thing be sung by the music-loving elves, even translated as it was into Elvish?

"That is a lovely song," Evindal said admiringly.

"It must have gained something in the translation," Dan murmured.

Evindal smiled. "Such modesty in a bard is refreshing." He rose from the table. "I'm afraid my duties call me back to the temple, but please stay as long as you will. Call on me any time, for the People owe you a great debt."

Danilo lifted his goblet. "At the price of elverquisst, we should be even before the night is over."

The priest chuckled as he walked out of the tavern. Danilo watched him go, a puzzled frown on his face.

"What are you doing here, besides marinating in elven spirits?"

Danilo jumped. He looked up into the stern face of Khelben Arunsun. As usual, the archmage was clad in simple, dark clothing, and wrapped in a fur-lined coat against the sea breezes that chilled Waterdeep's nights, even now, in the midst of summer. Khelben's silver-streaked black hair was uncharacteristically rumpled, and his bearded visage looked a shade grimmer than usual. Danilo was one of the few persons in Waterdeep not cowed by the powerful wizard, and he gestured cheerfully with his full goblet.

"Sit down, Uncle. I'd ask you to join me in a glass—"

"But you doubt that we'd both fit." The archmage completed the jest in a sour tone. "Save the nonsense, Dan. We've more important matters to discuss."

"Indeed." The Harper spoke softly and met Khelben's glare with a measured gaze of his own. "Let's start with the most important matter: Where is Arilyn?"

The archmage was silent for a moment, then he nodded toward the decanter of elverquisst. "A mage of your potential has no business drinking anything so powerful. Magic demands keen wits and a clear mind. Or have you forgotten what happened last time you imbibed too freely? I hear that the butler at the Stalwarts' Club still resembles something from the Abyss."

Danilo's eyes narrowed. "I am in full possession of my senses—such as they are—and I was that evening in Cormyr, also. I regret changing the butler's appearance so drastically, but might I remind you that the episode occurred during the Time of Troubles? Mine was not the only spell to go awry in those days!"

"Defending your art." Khelben leaned back in his seat and nodded approvingly. "That's a good sign. May I infer that you're taking your magical studies more seriously, or would that be hoping for too much?"

The young mage's jaw tightened, and he ran a hand through his thick blond hair. "While in Tethyr, I memorized the spells in the book you lent me, as well as several more from a tome of southern magic I purchased there. Beyond my Harper duties, I have acquired over twenty new spells and researched several of my own. Just because

I study in secret does not mean I lack purpose," he concluded in a terse, quiet voice. "Likewise, although I play
the fool, I am not so easily distracted as you seem to think.
I left my partner alone and in danger, and I demand to
know where she is and how she fares."

"Fair enough," Khelben conceded, a touch of apology in
his voice. "Arilyn is safe, and on her way to her new task."

"Where is she? And why must she go alone?"

"The task requires someone who can pass as an elf.
Where she's going, you would be too conspicuous. I can
tell you no more."

Danilo received this news in silence. Although he was
relieved to learn that Arilyn was safe, he feared that this
mysterious assignment would take her far beyond his
reach. Always more elven than human, Arilyn would be
less likely to consider a human lover when she returned
from her time among the elves.

"And I'm human," Danilo concluded aloud.

"Don't flatter yourself," his uncle said tartly. "Fortu-
nately the dragon in question doesn't know you as I do."

Suddenly Khelben had Danilo's full attention. "Dragon,
you say?"

Again the archmage paused, and he studied the wall
opposite him. "You were trained in music, if I'm not mistaken. Well trained."

"Many years ago," Dan said absently, puzzled by the
abrupt turn the discussion had taken. "Why?"

"The Harpers require the services of a bard. At present,
not one seems to be available."

"I don't like where this is leading. I'm supposed to pass
myself off as a bard, is that it? On the strength of what?"

Khelben nodded to the elven singer. "That, for example."

Danilo marshaled his befuddled senses and focused on
the ballad. It had a lovely, vaguely familiar melody. He
knew just enough Elvish to make out something about

Khelben's lady, the mage Laeral, and the healing power of love.

"That's very nice. Whose is it?"

The archmage looked at him keenly. "You're sure you don't recognize it?" When Danilo shook his head, Khelben gave a grim smile. "Well, that settles that question. The ballad is yours. Very popular tune these days, I'm sorry to say."

"But—"

"Yes, I know. You didn't write it that way. There's a great deal of that going around."

Danilo listened to the singer for a few moments. "By Oghma, I'm not bad!"

Khelben's face darkened at the young man's flippant oath to the patron of letters. "This is serious, boy! Your songs are not the only ones that have been changed."

The Harper put a solicitous hand on Khelben's arm. "You may not have noticed this, Uncle, but there's usually ample room for improvement. Whatever do you wish me to do: change them back?"

"Precisely," the archmage said, tossing some coins onto the table and rising to his feet. "You start tomorrow at sunrise, and there's much to do. You'll need travel supplies, an instrument or two—what is it you play, zither?"

"Lute," Danilo replied absently. He had little choice but to follow his uncle out of the tavern. It finally occurred to him what Yaereene had asked him to do; it was common practice for a bard to play at any tavern or inn he visited. On the way out Danilo bowed to the proprietress, spreading his hands in a gesture of helplessness as he indicated the glowering archmage. Yaereene forgave him with a gracious nod, and Danilo hurried to match Khelben's long stride.

"The first order of business is meeting your partner," Khelben paused and raised one salt-and-pepper brow, "and your apprentice."

"I have an apprentice?" he said in a dazed tone.

"So she thinks, and I see no merit in convincing her otherwise. You would do well to have a skilled fighter at your side. Whatever her limitations as a bard might be, her credentials as a warrior are most impressive."

Danilo thrust his fingers into his hair and rubbed his scalp briskly, on the dim chance that he might be able to shake loose the mental cobwebs that kept him from understanding what was apparently crystalline to the archmage. "For argument's sake, let's say I'm a bard, apprentice, zither, and all. Who am I supposed to entertain?"

"Grimnoshtadrano," Khelben replied as he strode toward Blackstaff Tower.

"But isn't he—"

"A green dragon? Yes, I'm afraid so."

Danilo realized that he was gaping like a beached carp. He closed his mouth and gave himself a brisk shake. "You mentioned something about a dragon earlier, but I'd assumed you were jesting." He cast a sidelong glance at his uncle's severe expression, then he sighed heavily. "I suppose I should have known better."

"This mission requires someone with a knowledge of both magic and music," Khelben continued. "First thing tomorrow morning, you will set out for the High Forest, challenge the dragon, convince him you're the bard he's been waiting for, and get from him by whatever means necessary a scroll that is now in his possession."

The Harper flashed a rueful smile at the archmage. "If you say so, Uncle Khelben. Now tell me, what would you like me to do *after* breakfast?"

Two

When Khelben ushered his nephew into the reception chamber of Blackstaff Tower, a young male elf rose to greet them. "This is Wyn Ashgrove. He'll be traveling with you," the archmage said by way of introduction.

Danilo struggled to conceal his dismay as he surveyed his new partner. Fully six inches shorter than the Harper and as slender as an aspen tree, the elf had the serious mien of a scholar. He also possessed in generous measure the beauty of the gold elf people, an elegance of form and feature unmatched by any other race. Slung over Wyn's back was a delicate silver lyre, and the crystal flute that hung from his belt was closer to hand than his long sword. All told, the elf struck Danilo as a being better suited to charming the ladies with poetry and song than to the rigors of travel.

Wyn greeted Danilo politely, then, at Khelben's request, he seated himself and sang a ballad about the dragon Grimnoshtadrano. Danilo remained standing, arms

crossed, as he listened to the music with trained detachment. He noted that the song was written well, but in the
style of a time several centuries past. The words of the ballad were compelling, a stirring call to action, and Danilo
was drawn into the story despite himself. He began to see
the reason for his uncle's concern.

As soon as the ballad ended, Danilo got down to business. "How many Harpers have answered this challenge?"

"To the best of my knowledge, none," Khelben
responded.

"Really? That seems odd."

"Apparently, this ballad is not widely sung. Wyn has
long studied ballads by and about the Harpers, and he tells
me that although most bards know this ballad, they are
reluctant to sing it."

Danilo nodded slowly. "Very responsible of them. If this
ballad is no real threat to the Harpers, why do you think
that I should answer this summons?"

"You're armed with something the other bards did not
have: your memory," the archmage said, motioning Danilo
toward a chair. "It's time you heard the rest of Wyn Ashgrove's tale."

The Harper settled down and listened as Wyn related
the events of Silverymoon's Spring Faire, and the strange
spell upon the bards there.

When the elf had finished, Danilo massaged his aching
temples and tried to sort through the tale. "So you're saying that this ballad is newly composed, but the finest bards
in the land believe it to be nearly as old as the dragon himself."

"That's correct," Wyn said.

"I don't see the point."

The elf looked at him strangely. "A powerful mage has
devised a way to lure Harpers to their deaths."

"With very little success," Dan pointed out.

"True. The spellcaster works against the Harpers in another, more subtle manner. As I understand Harper philosophy, your purpose is, in part, to help preserve a knowledge of the past. By changing the Harper ballads, the spellcaster is undermining the society's work."

Danilo thought that over. On the surface, the elf's evaluation of the problem seemed accurate enough. But why was the dragon ballad so little sung? There seemed to be another motive at work, one Danilo could not quite grasp. Obviously Khelben thought this as well, for the archmage was not normally one to concern himself with music. Danilo tucked this thought away for future consideration and turned his attention to more immediate concerns.

"How are we to acquire this scroll?"

"According to the ballad," Wyn replied in a didactic tone, as if they were discussing nothing more pressing than dry theory, "you must answer a riddle, read a scroll, and sing a song. That is clear enough. When you have accomplished these tasks, you may demand from the dragon whatever treasure you wish. Obviously, you will ask for the scroll itself. Since it is mentioned in the ballad, and since the ballad first appeared when the bards were enspelled, it is reasonable to assume that the scroll was devised by the spellcaster we seek. If this is so, the archmage can use it to discern the spellcaster's identity."

Dan cast his gaze toward the ceiling, but he spoke patiently. "Let's say, just for argument's sake, that after we answer the riddle the dragon will keep his word and hand over the scroll. Ignoring the unlikeliness of that possibility, ponder this: What happens if we guess wrong?"

"I imagine the beast will attack," Wyn said, no concern at all in his voice.

"Yes, I imagine that, too," Dan said with exaggerated patience. He turned to Khelben and said in a low tone, "Before I run screaming from this tower, perhaps I should meet that other bardic adventurer you spoke of? The fighter?"

"I left her in the kitchen," Khelben said and sighed. "If she's typical of her kind, she's no doubt emptied the pantry cupboards and started in on my spell components."

Danilo blinked. "Don't tell me: our peerless fighter is a halfling?"

"No. She's a dwarf."

To Danilo, this new revelation was as great a surprise as any other of the evening's oddities. Dwarf females were but rarely encountered away from clan and hearth, and those who did travel often let their beards grow so that they might pass as males. "A dwarven bard," he mused, shaking his head. "What brings this most unusual person to us?"

Khelben stood and took a piece of rolled parchment from his belt. He handed it to Danilo. "This is all I know. Come; I'll introduce you."

The archmage asked Wyn to wait for their return, then he opened the door leading into a chamber that served double duty for dining and giving audience. Danilo rose and followed the archmage, scanning the parchment as he went. It was a letter from the wizard Vangerdahast, court advisor to King Azoun of Cormyr.

"Vangerdahast says that he located a bard of sorts whose gifts, such as they are, remained unchanged by this mysterious spell." Danilo sniffed. "Well, that's a rousing endorsement if ever I heard one."

He turned back to the parchment and read aloud. " 'A dwarven entertainer, known as Morgalla the Mirthful, she is a veteran of the Alliance War and a native of the Earthfast Mountains, where she met and befriended the Princess Alusair. The dwarf has been plying her trade in Cormyr for nearly three years. In King Azoun's name, I request that you show his daughter's friend all courtesy, and add the dwarf to your number for this most appropriate quest. Morgalla is, in my opinion, precisely what the Harpers require.'"

Danilo raised skeptical eyes to his uncle. "Isn't it nice of Vangerdahast to be so helpful. At the risk of sounding petty, I have to say the good wizard's motives strike me as being just a bit suspect."

"For once we agree." Khelben paused, his hand on the latch of the kitchen door. "I haven't had much time to speak with the dwarf. Let's see what my colleague has sent us."

Khelben swung open the door. His kitchen was as unique as the rest of Blackstaff Tower. One side of the room was taken up by several shelves of rare potted herbs. These were bathed by a faint green light that came from no apparent source, and they filled the room with a woody, pungent aroma. Some of the cupboards held the usual array of dishes and pans, but a few doors were gates into far places. As a boy, Danilo had been especially fond of the cupboard that brought an everbearing pomegranate tree within easy reach, but he admitted that the door that led into a small ice cave was the more practical device. At the moment, however, his attention was focused on the dwarf seated behind the kitchen table.

Morgalla the Mirthful perched on a stool, swinging her small, booted feet and wielding a hunting knife as she intently carved the last of the meat from a roasted chicken. The well-picked bones on the serving platter before her attested to a typically dwarven appetite, as did the thick wedge missing from a wheel of cheese and the crumbled remains of a barley loaf.

Then Danilo noticed that she had layered the meat and cheese between slices of bread, and arranged the hearty snack on a platter along with pickles and small dishes of condiments. Apparently she intended to share, for the table was neatly laid with plates and mugs for four, and a foaming pitcher of ale stood ready. When the two men entered the room, Morgalla laid down the carving knife and affixed Danilo with a long solemn stare. Then she hopped down from her perch and stuck out a stubby hand in greeting.

"Well met, bard. I be Morgalla of Clan Chistlesmith, darl of Olam Chistlesmith and Thendara Spearsinger, of the dwarves of Earthfast. It's proud I am to be entering your service."

Danilo was familiar enough with dwarven custom to know himself honored by this detailed introduction. Even in cordial situations, the naturally cautious dwarves usually gave only first and sometimes clan names. If she had wished to insult him, she would have been "Morgalla of the dwarves," delivered with a firm undertone of "Wanna make something of it?"

He grasped the dwarf's wrist in a brief salute and shot a venomous glance at Khelben. The young Harper had never yet refused a mission assigned him, but he resented his uncle for leaving him no choice in the matter. This evening was very like being swept downstream on a white-water flood. Even worse, the archmage had led Morgalla to believe that he, Danilo, was a bard worth following.

"When I am called upon to describe you," Khelben pointed out, divining the source of his nephew's ire, "*bard* is not the first word that comes to mind. That title is of Morgalla's own choosing."

"Aye." The dwarf's head bobbed in agreement. "And yer more cut to the cloth than most who wear the mantle." Dan looked at her with a question in his eyes, so she explained, "A traveling bard sang yer songs at Azoun's court. They're better'n most. My favorite's the tale of the magic sword."

"Not the *Ballad of the Harper Assassin*?" Dan slumped

against the kitchen wall. First the damnable ballad showed up in Tethyr, and now far to the east in the courts of Cormyr?

"That's the one. Good story. Little on the short side, though."

"Short?" Danilo's look of befuddlement deepened. "But it has nine-and-twenty stanzas!"

"Like I said," Morgalla agreed.

Danilo gave up that line of inquiry and looked more closely at the dwarf. Morgalla appeared to be quite young, for she was still beardless. Large, liquid brown eyes reminded Dan of his favorite hunting hound; the earnest, doleful expressions were almost identical. Her face was broad, with high cheekbones, full lips, and a small nose with an insouciant tip. Thick russet hair was tightly plaited into two long braids, and an impressive amount of muscle and curve was packed onto her four-foot frame. Morgalla was dressed for the road in a simple brown kirtle that fell to her knees, brown leggings bound with leather thongs, and iron-tipped leather boots. A small axe was tucked into her weapon belt, and leaning against the kitchen table was a staff of battle-scarred stout oak. The latter was capped by the grinning head of a jester doll, complete with the traditional floppy cap of yellow and green motley. Danilo was no judge of dwarven beauty, but Morgalla struck him as cute and rather harmless, despite her weapons. Or, perhaps, he amended with another glance at the jester doll's head, *because* of them. Dan noted that she carried no musical instruments, and that struck him as another odd note.

"I've never before met a dwarven bard," he commented lightly, hoping to draw her out.

The comment seemed to touch a nerve, for Morgalla's face hardened. "And you haven't yet."

Khelben and Danilo exchanged glances. "If you're not a bard, why you were sent here?" the archmage asked.

In response, the dwarf handed him a large, folded piece of paper. Khelben smoothed out the paper on the kitchen table and studied it for a long moment. His mustache twitched, and a low chuckle escaped him. Danilo leaned in to look over his uncle's shoulder, and he let out a long, admiring whistle. He lifted his gaze to Morgalla, and his gray eyes held both amusement and respect.

"You drew this?" he asked.

"I'm here, ain't I?" she replied gruffly, folding her arms over her chest.

Danilo nodded, understanding completely. On the paper was a deft sketch of a wizard, robed in a star-and-moon-studded gown. A tall cone hat rested on an oversized thicket of white eyebrows, and the features, although comically exaggerated, were unmistakably those of Vangerdahast. The wizard wielded a baton at an orchestra of glowing, levitating instruments. King Azoun sat in the background, enjoying the concert with a vague smile of pleasure lifting the corners of his mustache. The caption was simply, "The Musicians' Guild."

The sketch, Danilo knew, poked at the wizard in two vulnerable spots. Many years earlier, in his more frivolous youth, Vangerdahast had devised an enchantment that caused instruments to play alone. The spell amused Azoun, who, to his court wizard's vast chagrin, often requested it to be cast as entertainment. Morgalla's artwork embarrassed Vangerdahast, but it also posed a problem for his king. Many people in Cormyr and the surrounding lands were leery of Azoun's desire to unite the heartlands of Faerun under one rule: his. To depict the king and his court wizard as sole members of the musicians' guild was a deft reminder of the king's drive to centralize authority. Morgalla's work teetered dangerously on the line between satire and sedition. To make matters worse, the sketch had been stamped onto the paper, which indicated that many more copies could be in circulation.

"I can see why Vangy sent her on a dragon hunt," Danilo murmured to his uncle. He glanced over at Morgalla, who was tactfully giving the two men room to discuss the drawing. Again seated at the table, she was busily sketching. Her stubby fist flew over the paper, and her brow was creased with concentration.

"On the other hand, he may have taken a sudden dislike to dragons," Khelben commented, staring with narrowed eyes at the dwarf's artwork.

The Harper leaned in for a closer look. Rapidly taking shape on the page was Khelben himself, standing before an easel and painting stick-figures on a canvas. A circle of black-robed, helmed Lords of Waterdeep stood obediently near, holding his palettes and brushes for him.

Danilo chuckled. On the most basic level, the sketch deftly skewered the archmage's artistic pretensions. It also captured perfectly the commonly held belief that the archmage was a power—perhaps *the* power—behind the secret Lords of Waterdeep. The sketch provided Danilo with yet another explanation for Morgalla's presence. "As I recall, Vangy doesn't care much for the Harpers, either."

"Now yer catching on, bard," said Morgalla. She looked up from her work. "Vangerdahast ast me to draw yer likeness, Lord Khelben. I mean no offense."

"I should hate to be around when you do," Danilo said, his gray eyes dancing.

The dwarf beamed, taking Dan's teasing as a high compliment. "If'n you like this, it's yers." She folded the sketch and handed it to Danilo.

He thanked her and absently stuck it into his money pouch. "But what of Vangerdahast? If he commissioned this, I imagine he expects to receive it."

"Nah," Morgalla said with a demure smile. "He's got plenty o' his own, believe you me."

"I can see that you two will get along fine," Khelben noted dryly.

"Indeed we shall," his nephew agreed. "But if I might speak frankly, Morgalla, why do you consider yourself my apprentice? I am no artist."

The dwarf shrugged. "Bards tell stories. I just come at the task from a different tunnel. You tell good tales, and I'm here to learn. And to fight, if it comes to that. I'm looking to do plenty o' both." She grabbed her oaken staff and waggled it as if to emphasize the point. The jester doll's green and yellow motley cap flopped about. The effect did not exactly inspire fear.

Danilo drew a steadying breath. Despite her fighting credentials and her quirky charm, Morgalla seemed little more prepared for the task ahead than did the elven scholar waiting in the reception chamber. "I don't suppose the Harpers would like to diverge from common practice just this once and hire a small regiment?" Danilo asked the archmage. "No, I thought not. Then I suppose we'd better bring a riddlemaster along. That might improve our chances considerably."

Khelben nodded thoughtfully. "Good thinking. You handle that and get your own mount; Wyn and I will see to the other horses and the supplies."

Morgalla hopped down from her perch. "I'm comin' with you, bard," she announced eagerly. "Too much magic in this place for my comfort."

Danilo raised one eyebrow. "Do you have any objection to music shops?"

The gleam in the dwarf's brown eyes faded. She climbed back onto the stool and gave Danilo a long, considering look. "Tell you what, bard; I'll draw yer likeness while yer gone." She took out a new piece of paper and immediately began to sketch.

"I've never had a portrait done," Danilo mused. The

dark humor in Morgalla's art appealed to him, and since he'd developed a remarkable tolerance for mockery, he rather looked forward to seeing how she might depict him. "I'm sure I'll be delighted with it," he concluded with a smile.

"Maybe, but you'd be the first," Morgalla announced.

Khelben shrugged and led the way back to the front hall. "Do you have a riddlemaster in mind?" he asked the Harper.

"Vartain of Calimport," Danilo said firmly. "He's quite astounding. His services are as much in demand by adventuring parties as they are by those desiring an entertainer. He was in Waterdeep when I left the city several months ago. I'll check the register at Halambar's to see if he's available."

"Good thinking," Khelben conceded. Kriios Halambar, widely and secretly known as "Old Leatherlungs," was the head of Waterdeep's musicians' guild. Entertainers of all kinds registered at his shop, and employers in need of these services usually began their search there. If Vartain was available for hire, he would be listed, and if he were already employed, the name of his employer would be there as well. Either way, Danilo could seek the riddlemaster out.

The archmage walked out into the courtyard with Danilo. After a moment's silence, he placed a hand briefly on the young man's shoulder. "I know all this has come upon you suddenly, and I realize what you have left behind. I'm sorry that I have to ask this of you."

For a moment, the two men stood in silence. Although he was touched by his uncle's concern, Danilo could not bear to acknowledge Khelben's oblique reference to Arilyn. He sidestepped his own raw pain by deliberately misreading the archmage. "As usual, your confidence sustains and inspires me," Danilo quipped.

"That's not what I meant, and you know it!" Khelben snapped. "You can handle this assignment well enough. What you lack as a bard, you more than make up for as a mage." He withdrew a small, slender volume from a pocket of his coat. "This book is for you. I've copied in it spells that will hold you in good stead, should the dragon prove less than cooperative."

Danilo took the book gratefully and slipped it into the magic bag at his belt. The spellbook disappeared without adding a lump or wrinkle. Promising to return before sunrise, Danilo slipped through the invisible door in the tower's outer wall and disappeared into the night.

* * * * *

Like most of Waterdeep, the affluent district known as the Castle Ward stayed awake throughout most of the night. The Street of Swords was crowded with well-to-do Waterdhavians on their way to private parties, or seeking out the taverns, festhalls, and shops that made the city famous throughout Faerun.

It was often said that one could buy virtually anything in Waterdeep. While this was true, shopping was also a form of entertainment. Musicians performed in the streets and courtyards, setting a festive mood. The warmly lit shops and bazaars offered every comfort and inducement. Servants circulated trays laden with delicacies and tiny wine goblets. Beautiful shop attendants, wearing samples of the clothing and jewels available, mingled with the customers, offering advice and flattery. These were skilled in the art of making patrons believe that similar beauty could be theirs, for the price of a few gold coins.

In one of these shops, Rebeleigh's Elegant Headwear, a tall, silver-haired woman stood before a mirror and considered her reflection with a mixture of wry humor and resignation. As Lady Arunsun, Laeral faced a number of social obligations. With the Midsummer festivities right around the corner, these seemed as persistent and endless as the heads of a hydra.

"This will be perfect for Lady Raventree's masquerade ball," gushed the shopkeeper, standing on tiptoe to adjust Laeral's headdress of delicate links and tiny coral beads. "It's authentic, you know. It once belonged to a Moonshae princess who died more than two hundred years ago."

"I can see why," Laeral quipped. "If she could afford decent chain mail, she'd probably still be alive."

"Oh, yes, quite," Rebeleigh said agreeably, whisking off the headdress. The shopkeeper was a slight, middle-aged woman, a weather vane for the winds of fashion and a walking calendar of social events. She knew nothing of Laeral's years of adventure, intrigue, and combat. All that Rebeleigh gleaned from her customer's comment was that the headdress was not pleasing, and that was enough. She snatched up a fanciful confection of ice-blue velvet and silver ribbon. "This would suit you well, my lady. Stoop down a bit, if you please."

Laeral did as she was bid. She glanced at her reflection and burst out laughing.

"You seem to have singularly bad luck with headwear," commented a sweetly venomous voice to her side.

Laeral turned and look down into the lovely, insincerely smiling face of Lucia Thione. A scion of Tethyrian royalty, Lady Thione was a powerful figure in Waterdeep society. She was a popular hostess and a much-sought-after beauty, and she was widely acclaimed for her business acumen and her charm. She never wasted this charm on Laeral, much to the mage's secret amusement.

Lucia Thione bristled at the glint of humor in Laeral's silver eyes. Lady Thione despised the mage, whose birth and early life were swathed in mystery, and she envied her role as Lady Arunsun, a position to which she herself had unsuccessfully applied. The diminutive noblewoman also felt insubstantial next to the six-foot mage and completely eclipsed by Laeral's unearthly beauty.

"At least *that* hat is not enchanted," Lady Thione continued, since Laeral was apparently too dense to recognize a well-bred insult. She smiled again. "I suppose you'd hate to go through all that unpleasantness again."

The noblewoman was finally rewarded with a reaction: Laeral's face became very still.

"A street musician was just singing about you. Come, hear for yourself," Lucia said softly. "I'm sure you'll find it fascinating."

Without waiting for a response, she glided out of the shop and rejoined the small crowd clustered around a street singer. The minstrel was a jolly-looking man of middle years, and although his voice was mellow and pleasant, the people shifted uneasily as they listened. Lucia made her way over to Caladorn and gave his arm a sympathetic squeeze.

"He is singing that dreadful ballad *again*?"

"Yes," Caladorn said through gritted teeth. "I thought all the bards in town had been officially cautioned against singing it."

Lucia looked sharply at her young lover. Handsome and entertaining he undoubtedly was, but she had never known him to take an interest in political matters. More importantly, this warning had come down from the Lords of Waterdeep just this morning. Lucia knew about such things because she made it her business to know, but how had Caladorn learned of it? She drew him away from the crowd so that they might talk privately. "Surely there is no truth in this ballad?"

"I'm afraid there is. Lady Laeral once traveled with an adventuring group known as the Nine. She discovered a powerful artifact, a crown of some sort, and it twisted her into a madwoman and a menace."

"This was not widely known, I take it," she prodded gently, taking great care to hide both her curiosity and her delight.

"Until now," he agreed. "Such things should not be sung on every street corner, for the entertainment of the common people. Laeral's fall and the intercession of Khelben Arunsun are matters for lords and wizards of power."

Lucia's dark eyes narrowed with speculation. That was a strange sentiment for Caladorn, who at a young age had severed ties with his noble family to live a life of adventure. "I agree, my love, but what could you or I do to stop it?"

"Nothing. You're right." Caladorn forced a smile onto his face, but his eyes kept drifting back to the gathering crowd. He shifted restlessly, and he absently twisted the silver ring on his left hand. Lucia watched in fascination.

"You know, I'm not really in the mood to sit through a performance at the Three Pearls tonight," she said in a casual tone. "The party at my Sea Ward villa is just days away, and I have so much shopping yet to do. Would you mind if I finish it now, love?"

"Not at all," Caladorn replied, just a bit too quickly. He kissed his lady and hurried off through the crowds.

After she checked the hat shop and ascertained that Laeral was nowhere to be found, Lucia crossed the street to an elegant little tavern. She took a seat near the open window, ordered spiced wine, and waited.

She hadn't long to wait. A watch patrol hurried into the crowd, sending the people on their way by order of the Lords of Waterdeep. Lucia leaned back in her chair, her smile one of supreme satisfaction. Caladorn, her handsome and chivalrous love, might be the connection she had long sought! Of course, the timing of the watch's intervention could well be a coincidence. She glanced over at the Neverwinter water clock on the tavern's wall. No, the watch was not due on this street for almost ten more minutes. Lucia had made a study of patrol routes, and she knew how much time elapsed between patrols in any given area of Waterdeep. Not, of course, that she would boast of this knowledge in most social circles. She leaned forward and watched the scene eagerly. If Caladorn truly was behind this, he had a great deal to learn about the people he governed. He was a dear, but he was too pure of heart and blue of blood to realize how his actions would appear to most of the people in the crowd. Waterdhavians were an independent lot, and she doubted they would take kindly to this type of meddling.

Lucia's instincts proved impeccable. The minstrel took loud exception to the order and began to argue the matter with the watch captain. He turned to the dispersing crowd and ordered the people to protest such tyranny, demanding that truth be heard unhindered. It was a far better show than his songs had been, Lucia noted cynically, and the rapidly growing crowd indicated that she was not alone in this opinion.

She watched with amusement as the minstrel leaped onto a bench, the better to vilify the presumptuous behavior of the watch and the Lords of Waterdeep. He even produced a short sword, which he brandished as a counterpoint to his expostulation. He was not sufficiently powerdrunk to challenge the watch captain directly, Lucia noticed. Yet the ridiculous gesture galvanized the crowd and a few people began to pelt the watch patrol first with insults and then with goods from nearby shops. Others ran for cover, knocking over vendors' booths and trampling merchandise underfoot.

The guard, Waterdeep's more heavily armed militia, arrived promptly to aid the watch patrol. The street was soon cleared of troublemakers and order restored. Lady

Thione chuckled as the minstrel was dragged off by two of
the guard, singing lusty protests all the while. Shop-
keepers and vendors began sorting through the debris,
salvaging what had not been trampled or stolen by the
thieves and pickpockets who thrived even in the best-run
cities.

Lady Thione was ever one to grasp an opportunity. She
slipped out of the tavern and quietly approached an elderly
woman who stood weeping among her crushed and scattered flowers. Lucia commiserated with the flower vendor
for a few moments and then handed her a small purse.
Laying a finger to her lips, Lucia Thione slipped away. As
subtly as she could, she worked her way down the street,
passing out silver coins along with a subtle mixture of sympathy and sedition.

* * * * *

Danilo hurried toward Halambar's Lute Shop, absently
noting that the shopping district on the Street of Swords
seemed rather quiet for the hour. Perhaps it was the
weather. The night was cool, for a stiff sea breeze set the
street lanterns swaying and flickering. Danilo's purple finery, although well-suited to the hot, dry climate of Tethyr,
left him shivering in the damp chill. He ducked into a shop
that offered ready-made clothing, and purchased a traveling cloak in deep forest green, a full change of clothing,
and a pair of practical leather boots. He gave the shopkeeper an extra coin and bade him burn the discarded
purple garments.

Within minutes Danilo could see the elegant townhouse
he sought. Like many buildings on the street, it was three
stories tall, with whitewashed plaster gleaming between
thick dark beams. The large windows on either side of the
door had many tiny diamond-shaped panes of leaded glass,

and the door itself was constructed of thick, broad-planked oak. The brass hinges and locks on the doors and window shutters were fashioned like small harps—a bit of whimsy with a purpose: any attempt to disturb the locks triggered a powerful magical ward. The nature of this guardian was not widely known, since none of the thieves who'd challenged it had lived to discuss the details.

As Danilo swung open the door, his arrival was announced by the gentle plinking of the door harp. He stepped in, handing his cloak to the servant who greeted him.

The shop was a single room that took up the entire lower floor of the building. To Danilo's right were displayed an array of instruments for sale, ranging from the justly famed lutes made by the proprietor, to the inexpensive tin whistles of the western Moonshaes. To the left of the entrance was the workshop area, where master instrument builders and apprentices fashioned and repaired the finest instruments in Waterdeep. Kriios Halambar himself was there this evening, bent over a large bass lute known as a theorbo and patiently fitting it with newly carved tuning pegs. Halambar raised heavy-lidded eyes to the door, and his thin face lit up in what Dan took to be a smile. The guildmaster gently laid the theorbo aside and rose to his feet.

"Welcome, Lord Thann! You've returned to Waterdeep at last. You of course are here to register, but may we serve you in some other way?"

Danilo blinked. He'd been in Halambar's shop two dozen times at least, but never had he been invited to add his name to the registry of bards. Nor had he—or anyone else, for that matter—been greeted so effusively by the usually haughty guildmaster.

"I require a new lute," Dan said. "In my recent travels, I was forced to leave mine behind."

The guildmaster shook his head in silent commiseration over such a loss. "You play a seven-course lute, if I recall. I've one you might find suitable." He strode to the far side of the room and took an instrument of exceptional beauty down from its hook on the wall.

The lute was fashioned of cream-colored maple wood. An intricate rosette of inlaid rosewood, teak, and ebony surrounded the sound hole. Danilo took the instrument, stripped off his gloves, and seated himself on the stool provided. He played a few notes. The sound carried well, and the action of the strings felt about right.

He looked up with a smile. "The tone and workmanship mark this as one of your own, Master Halambar. The sale is made, but for naming the price."

Halambar bowed. "For you, twelve hundred silver pieces."

The lute was worth that and more, but Danilo shook his head and reluctantly held the lute out to the guildmaster. "I'm afraid I haven't that amount with me, and I need to purchase a lute tonight. Have you a lesser instrument?"

"Please don't consider such a thing. I'd be pleased to extend credit."

That was a first, but Dan was not inclined to debate his good fortune. He also purchased extra strings, a weatherproof leather covering for the lute, and a sheaf of tablature paper on which to scribble new songs. If the Harpers required him to play the role of a bard, Danilo supposed he ought to oblige with a few original works.

While Halambar's clerk tallied the purchase, Danilo strode over to the register and began to flip through the pages, with a solicitous Halambar at his heels. "Do you know the whereabouts of a riddlemaster by the name of Vartain? He was in Waterdeep when I left several months past."

Halambar harumphed. "Vartain has been here and gone

more times than a lyre has strings. His services are prized, yet his employers tire of him quickly."

"Oh?"

"Vartain has a most annoying habit," the guildmaster explained. "It would seem that he is always right."

"I can see how that could become exasperating, but that is precisely what I need. If he is not available, can you recommend someone else as good?"

"I wish I could," Halambar replied, leafing through the book. "Riddlemasters are few these days, and fewer still can match Vartain's skill or knowledge. Certainly, there's none in Waterdeep right now. Perhaps you might seek out Vartain's current employer and bid for the riddlemaster's services. There is an excellent chance that the employer has repented of the hire and will welcome the chance to rid himself of Vartain. Ah, here is the entry."

A grim smile touched Halambar's lips, and he tapped the page with one finger. "Perhaps there is justice in the world, after all. If anyone deserves Vartain, it's this rogue!"

Danilo glanced over the guildmaster's shoulder and groaned. In slanted, spidery writing were the words:

Vartain of Calimport, Riddlemaster.
Hired this twenty-eighth day of Mirtul.
Employer: Elaith Craulnober.

Three

Elaith Craulnober's black cape flowed behind him like an angry shadow as he stalked through the village once known as Taskerleigh, a small cluster of buildings in the midst of fields and forest. The town was completely deserted, but for a few old corpses rotting in some of the houses. Strangely enough, only one building, a small cottage by the edge of the forest, showed any damage whatsoever. There was no sign of a fight, no evidence of a plague, and so far, no sign of the treasure.

Elaith hurried to the ruined cottage and began to kick through the rubble. Behind him strolled a middle-aged man, bronze of skin and completely bald, whose slightly protruding eyes took in the scene with an expression of detached interest. The elf's hired men, a dozen hard and tested mercenaries, muttered and made surreptitious warding signs as they wandered through the ghost town. They were careful to hide their discomfort from their elven employer, who had little tolerance for superstition and even less for cowardice.

A glint of silver caught Elaith's eye, and he hurled aside a fallen timber to get at the object. He stooped and picked up a curling length of silver wire. His fist clenched around the wire in pure frustration.

"It was here," muttered the elf. For almost a year, he had searched for a rare and priceless treasure, and he had spent a small fortune tracing it to this remote village. He rose slowly to his feet and turned to face Vartain of Calimport.

"We're too late," he said, showing Vartain what he had found.

The riddlemaster nodded calmly, as if he had anticipated this turn of events. "Let us hope that does not occur again today." He turned and walked toward the overgrown garden of a nearby farmhouse.

Elaith gritted his teeth and followed. He recognized Vartain's worth: the riddlemaster was brilliant and resourceful, an asset to any quest. Vartain was always thinking, watching, weighing the facts, considering and calculating the odds. When questioned, he shared his observations freely and expressed his opinions honestly, and he never seemed to be wrong about anything. In short, he was a colossal pain.

The elf's irritation shifted focus abruptly when he got to the garden's wall. His amber eyes narrowed at the frivolous scene before him. Two of his highly paid men were digging at a peppergum tree with their daggers. The tree was commonly cultivated in the Northlands for its summer shade and brilliant autumn foliage, and each spring it yielded thick, pliant sap that tasted faintly of peppermint. One of the malingerers, a black-bearded bear of a man named Balindar, had worked for Elaith before and should have known better than to risk his ire. It was the elf's custom to purchase his mercenaries' efforts with generous payment in gold, and to ensure their loyalty with cold steel.

Elaith drew a throwing knife from his sleeve and flicked it at the tree. The blade bit deep into the soft wood, just inches from Balindar's head. The mercenary spun about, a hand on his blade and a startled oath on his lips. His eyes widened at the sight of his employer's cold face. He eased his hand away from his weapon and raised it slowly in a conciliatory gesture. Although more than a handsbreadth taller and a good fifty pounds heavier than the elf, Balindar was clearly not interested in fighting his employer.

"This is your concept of treasure?" Elaith asked in tones of silky menace as he leaped nimbly over the garden wall. "This? A child's treat?"

"Wasn't my idea," Balindar grumbled. "The riddle-master told Mange and me to gather peppergum sap." The other mercenary—a whip-thin archer whose mottled blend of naked scalp and short-cropped brown fuzz gave birth to his apt nickname—bobbed his head in nervous agreement.

His temper near to burning, Elaith rounded on the man behind him. Vartain had just finished his laborious climb over the garden wall. He stood eyeing the distant hills, his hands resting on his paunch in a meditative pose. Something about the man's bulging black eyes, large hooked nose, and bald pate reminded Elaith of a buzzard. Vartain looked over, as if drawn by the heat of the elf's glare.

"The terrain about a league to the northwest suggests the presence of caves," Vartain said mildly, pointing toward the rock-strewn hills beyond the village. "Considering the proximity of potential lairs, prudence demands that we have earplugs available."

Elaith stared at the riddlemaster for a moment, waiting for the man to come to the point. Vartain, however, seldom explained what seemed obvious to him unless he was asked direct, specific questions. It was the riddlemaster's custom to put forth a fact or two, then allow others the opportunity to work their way to the logical conclusion. The elf was in no mood to appreciate such generosity, and in three quick strides he had the riddlemaster by the throat.

"Save your games for Lady Raventree's parties," Elaith hissed from between clenched teeth. He gave the man a sharp shake. "A straight answer. Now!"

Vartain gurgled and pointed a finger toward the hills in the northwest. Elaith glanced, and immediately released the riddlemaster's throat.

On the horizon, several winged, gray creatures were emerging from a rocky outcrop. The avian beasts rose into the sky with the distinctive looping flight of vultures, but the elf's sharp eyes noted the human torsos and the hair streaming behind the heads. They were harpies, monsters whose song was a magical weapon that could charm a listener into immobility, allowing the evil beasts leisure for torture and feasting.

"Harpies attacking from the north!" the elf shouted. "Men, to me!"

The men bolted toward the garden. Vartain had already appropriated the sap Balindar had collected and was rolling it into small cylinders. Elaith snatched Mange's dagger, scraped off a bit of sap and pressed some into each of his ears. He passed the dagger to Balindar, the group's best fighter. There would not be enough for everyone.

As it happened, time ran out before the sap did. When the first note of the harpies' song reached the men, four of them simply froze. Four living statues faced Vartain with entreating hands, threatening snarls, and terror-filled eyes. Then, despite his ear protection, Elaith caught the unearthly song and could spare the men no more thought.

The broken stone wall was as good a line of defense as

any. Elaith plucked his bow from its place on his shoulder, gesturing for his men to arm themselves as well. He drew six arrows from his quiver—he'd be lucky to get off that many—and then dropped to one knee. The elf nocked the first arrow and waited for the creatures to come within range.

Despite his many adventures and his fearsome reputation as a fighter, Elaith felt uneasy as he watched the approach of the avian horrors. There was a bitter, metallic taste in his mouth. With a touch of surprise, he identified it as fear. The outcome of this battle was by no means certain, and the elf was flooded with momentary panic at the thought of dying before he found the treasure he'd sought for so long. He patted the ancient sword at his hip, as if to remind himself what was at stake in this battle.

Swiftly the harpies approached, and the sight of them sent a shudder through the row of waiting archers. A dozen of them, Elaith noted, against the ten men left unaffected by the spell. The odds were by no means favorable, and the men eyed their foes with naked dread.

The monsters' wings and lower bodies were those of enormous vultures, and the talons on their feet flexed in cruel anticipation. From the waist up, the creatures resembled gray-skinned women with youthful bodies and the faces of hideous hags. Thick, gray hair writhed in tangled ropes around each harpy's face, and their fang-filled mouths strained and contorted as they sang their enticing, wordless song.

As soon as the lead harpy came into range, Elaith loosed his arrow. The silver-tipped shaft streaked toward the monster, piercing it through the shoulder and tearing into its wing. Feathers flew, and the creature shrieked as it spiraled to the ground. The wounded harpy landed hard but was on its feet immediately, one wiry arm dripping blood and the other brandishing a bone club. Foul odor roiled off the creature as it rushed with a birdlike, hopping gait toward Elaith. Again the elf shot, and this time the arrow buried itself below the harpy's breast. The beast collapsed with a hiss, flopping about for several moments before conceding to death.

The sight of the fallen harpy drove the other monsters into a frenzy, for they realized that most of their prey was immune to the musical charm. They waved clenched fists and tore at their wild hair, and the tempo of their deadly song began to quicken. Down they came, singing all the while, their talons spread wide as they swooped toward the fighters. The men got off a single volley of arrows before the harpies closed in. Ignoring the men who'd already succumbed to their song, the harpies fell upon those still fighting.

Like an owl closing on a rabbit, one of the monsters dove toward a half-orc mercenary. The half-orc ducked, but not before the harpy's wicked talons raked his back, scoring it deeply across the shoulders. Almost immediately a second harpy plummeted into the wounded mercenary, and the impact sent them both tumbling to the ground. The half-orc's massive hands instinctively closed around his assailant, an instant before the poison from the first harpy's talons took effect. The captured harpy writhed and shrieked as it struggled to break free, but it was securely pinned under the mercenary. Trapped and furious, the harpy bared its fangs and ripped open the half-orc's throat.

Roaring an oath to his god of vengeance, a Northman sell-sword thrust his blade through his dead comrade and into the harpy's chest. The creature's struggles slowed, and black blood oozed from the corners of its hideous mouth. Satisfied that he'd finished the harpy, the Northman leaned down to tug his sword free. The dying harpy spat in his face.

The Northman stumbled back, screaming with pain and clawing at his blinded eyes with both hands. Within seconds, he, too, was immobilized.

Meanwhile, another harpy swooped down at the riddlemaster. Vartain dropped to the ground and rolled aside with surprising agility. The harpy missed its target and landed a few feet away. Wings arched, it lurched toward Vartain with outstretched, grasping hands.

The riddlemaster put a hollow wooden pipe to his lips and blew. A dart flew toward the harpy's face. The beast let out a shrilling cry and pawed at its cheek, leaving its feathered belly unprotected. Elaith stepped in and delivered a vicious backhanded slash with his sword. The harpy crashed to the ground with a spray of gore and feathers.

Two of the creatures came in low to circle the elf, each wielding a stout club fashioned from an ogre's leg bone. Fighting with sword and dirk, Elaith held the pair of harpies off. The harpies' wheeling flight kept them out of reach of a killing strike, but Elaith slipped past their guard again and again. The monsters were each bleeding from a dozen hits.

Others of his band were not so fortunate. To the far side of the battlefield, three creatures hunched over a disemboweled body, cackling and arguing over the entrails. The man's outflung hands spasmed repeatedly, indicating that he was—if but for a short time—still alive. Nearby, Balindar faced off in a hideous duel with a large harpy, bristling with arrows but still full of fight and fury and wielding a bone club as handily as a swordsman uses a rapier.

When his two opponents finally lay dead, Elaith snatched up his bow and sighted one of the three harpies still circling the battlefield. His first arrow flew directly into a harpy's open mouth, ending its song and sending it plummeting to the ground. The next shot was not as clean;

he brought his target down, but the harpy landed close to the forest edge. It was wounded but still singing. Elaith snatched an arrow from the quiver of one of the enspelled men, and prepared for a shot that would finish off the harpy. He nocked the arrow and sighted down his target. So odd was the scene playing out at the forest's edge that for an instant Elaith lowered his bow and stared.

Another fighter had joined their battle. A ragged hermit harried the wounded harpy, poking at it with a stout piece of wood as if he were playing with a chained and snarling puppy. To all appearances, the hermit seemed to be enjoying the battle; his shoulders shook, and his high-pitched giggle rang through the shrill harpy song and Elaith's protective barrier of peppergum sap. The hermit's rags flapped around emaciated limbs as he danced about, and a wild tangle of dirt-colored hair fell to the middle of his back. Glad for assistance of any kind, Elaith turned his attention back to the problem at hand. His final arrow took the last flying harpy through the heart.

Only one harpy still sang; the one fencing with Balindar. Eager to end the unearthly song, Elaith hurled his dirk toward Balindar's opponent. The weapon spun end over end, catching the harpy in the back, directly between the wings. The shock of impact threw its arms wide, and the creature's song exploded into a final shriek. Balindar grinned and finished the beast with a quick thrust. He and Elaith closed in on the three feasting harpies, swords leading.

Loathe to abandon their meal, the creatures bent protectively over the torn corpse and hissed at the approaching swordsmen. While the harpies watched the deadly elf and the huge black-bearded fighter, two of Elaith's men slipped in from behind and stabbed a pair of the monsters in the back. Before anyone could strike again, the third harpy lumbered into the darkening sky. It flapped toward the north, a length of dripping entrails hanging from its talons.

The silence that shrouded the battlefield felt as thick and heavy as a dense fog. After a long, tense moment, the survivors plucked the protective sap from their ears and faced their losses. Three men had been killed and five more stood frozen by the harpies' charm song or poison. They had killed eleven of the monsters, but Elaith did not consider the battle a victory. He was left with four able men, not counting himself or the riddlemaster. The number was not equal to the challenges of the road ahead.

The elf kicked over one of the dead monsters and bent to retrieve his dagger, holding his breath against the noxious odor. The high-pitched giggle rang out again, this time at his elbow, and Elaith whirled to face the hermit, who had finally dispatched the harpy Elaith had wounded earlier.

Beneath the tangled thatch of hair was a filthy, beardless face and wild eyes of a distinctive almond shape and violet hue. Violet eyes! Elaith recoiled in horror and disgust. The mad hermit was an elf! As if to confirm this discovery, the hermit grasped a handful of matted hair in each hand and raised it high. One ear was missing entirely, but the other was long, pointed, and definitely elven.

The hermit gazed down at the slain harpy, shaking his head sadly. "Smelly things to be sure, but dance to the harp they do!"

The sight of a fellow elf grieving over a harpy was too much for Elaith. "Get this creature out of my sight," he snarled at Balindar.

"Perhaps you should reconsider," Vartain interrupted. "This unfortunate fellow appears to be the sole survivor of Taskerleigh. We should question him, insane though he undoubtedly is. Perhaps he can tell us more about what happened here, so that we might plan the next step of our journey."

Elaith nodded, for something that hermit had said might be worth pursuing. Grasping him by one bony arm, Elaith pulled him upwind of the harpy's carcass. "You spoke of a harp. What about it?"

The wretched elf spread his fingers before him, staring down at them with an awe that suggested that he had just now acquired the bony digits. "I played it," he whispered. "I played the harp, and even the korreds crept from the forest to dance to its silver tones." The hermit's words sounded calm and measured, and Elaith began to hope that they could yet glean some useful information.

"Was there anything special about this harp? Does it have a name?"

"It has been called Morninglark, and it is more special than you could imagine," the ragged elf replied calmly.

"Where is it?" Elaith demanded.

Grief flooded the elf's wasted face. "Gone," he mourned. "Taken!"

"By whom?" Vartain asked.

The hermit turned his violet eyes to the riddlemaster. "A great green one. His breath killed the villagers where they stood."

Elaith and Vartain exchanged incredulous glances. The hermit was describing a dragon attack. "How did you survive?" Vartain asked.

"Magic." The hermit's bony arm traced a circle in the air around his head, obviously pantomiming some sort of protective sphere. He pressed his fingertips to his forehead. "I live, but the dragon's gaze shattered my . . ." His voice drifted off into silent despair.

Elaith was not feeling any too cheerful himself. Dragons of any sort were uncommon, and greens were both rare and reclusive. The hermit's dragon was most likely Grimnoshtadrano, a venerable wyrm who lived nearby in the High Forest. The dragon seldom ventured out of the forest, so he had apparently wanted the elven harp badly and would not be willingly separated from it. Not, of course, that it would be easy to take from a full-grown green dragon something of which he was only moderately fond.

"Grimnosh," muttered Balindar in disbelief, and then he shook his massive dark head. "I'm for heading back to Waterdeep. I've no notion to end up like these folk," he said defensively.

"Farmers," Elaith pointed out. "And judging by the number of dead, not enough to give the dragon a fight."

"There were many more than we found," Vartain corrected, drawing an exasperated look from his employer. "I suspect that they were—"

"Eaten," the hermit broke in, speaking in sepulchral tones. Once again he broke into shrill laughter. This time his giggle held an edge of hysteria, and he hurled himself into a wild dance, spinning and leaping amid the corpses that littered the ruined garden.

Elaith turned away, his face unreadable. "Collect the survivors. We're moving out."

"What of these men?" Vartain asked, pointed to those who were frozen by the harpies' musical charm. Three were unharmed, but the Northman, if he lived, would no doubt be blinded. The fifth man bled profusely from four long, ragged gashes where claws had raked his upraised sword arm. His immobile features showed no acknowledgment of the wound, but his skin was pallid, and he would surely die if not treated soon. "We lost three fighters to the harpies and cannot reasonably afford the loss of five more."

The elf closed his eyes, rubbing his aching temples. "Tie them to their horses, if you must, but we're leaving this place!" he said, raising his voice to be heard over the hermit's insane giggling.

"We caught these three trying to sneak up on us," Mange's reedy voice announced from behind Elaith. "Bring 'em over, men!"

"More harpies?" the elf asked wearily, not bothering to turn around.

"Almost, but not quite," announced a familiar, irritating drawl. "And you know what they say—whoever the Nine Hells *they* are—*almost* only counts when you're throwing horseshoes or magic fireballs."

Disbelieving horror flooded Elaith's face. "No," the elf whispered, silently cursing the gods for rewarding his misspent life in this manner. He turned around slowly. Sure enough, there stood Danilo Thann, wearing an indolent grin and apparently too foolish to be frightened by the four mercenaries who'd escorted him to their feared elven employer. The man flipped aside his tabard and waggled the harp-and-moon pin affixed to the shirt beneath.

"Not harpies," Danilo Thann amended cheerfully. "*Harpers*. Quite a difference, when you think about it."

"That may be so." The elf's eyes narrowed into amber slits. "My situation, however, has not noticeably improved."

Four

Lucia Thione gazed with great satisfaction at the ballroom of her Sea Ward villa. All was in readiness for the party, a lavish affair that would open the Midsummer season. Never had planning a party been so difficult, and she felt a sense of accomplishment as she viewed what weeks of toil had yielded.

Vases of fresh roses filled every alcove and graced the small tables. That in itself was a triumph, for a strange blight had fallen upon the crops and gardens of Waterdeep this year. Perhaps the working people experienced this as a hardship, but to Lucia it was merely an inconvenience that could be circumvented, provided one possessed the money and creativity. As a buyer for merchant caravans, Lucia knew where almost anything could be found. Roses had been rushed from Rassalantar, and vats of raspberries from the Korinn Archipelago north of the Moonshaes. Venison, quail, and partridges had been brought from the Misty Forest, a day's ride to the south. Lucia's steward had laid in a supply of smoked salmon from Gundarlun and barrels of Neverwinter's famed icewine. A small army of servants would be on hand to tend to the guests' needs, and in an hour the musicians would arrive for a final rehearsal under the critical eye of Faunadine, Master of Festivities. Faunadine was a plump, graying halfling whose skills were much in demand. Her attention to detail made the best and most elaborate parties seem effortless, and Lucia considered hiring the halfling away from Lady Raventree a personal and political triumph.

The silvery notes of a harp interrupted Lucia's complacent thoughts and filled her with indignation. Surely, her well-trained servants had not admitted a musician before the appointed time! She followed the sound to a window alcove, her purple velvet slippers whispering across the polished marble of the floor.

In the curve of a bay window, under a trellis covered with flowering vines, sat a drab half-elf woman, playing a small dark harp of ancient design. To a casual observer, the woman's fading hair and simple gray gown made her look like a plump and matronly goodwife, entirely out of place in the elegant room. Since it was Lucia's job to see what others missed, she noted the haughty, aristocratic tilt of the half-elf's head, the power and assurance in her long-fingered hands, and the intelligence in her vivid blue eyes. Although prudence demanded that she summon a servant to oust this intruder, instinct warned Lucia that this was something she should handle herself, and carefully.

"I have met all this evening's performers," Lucia began. "Despite your skill on the harp, lady, you are not one of them. May I know your name?"

The harpist did not look up from her playing. "You may call me Garnet. Since we have worked together before, I see no need for formality. Please, sit down."

Lucia sank onto the low, velvet-covered bench, as far

away from the strange half-elf as possible. "My memory is excellent, but I don't recall our association."

"Three nights ago, in the Street of Swords bazaar district. That ballad you heard was mine, and that bard is under my influence. By itself, the ballad is creating quite a stir, but I watched you at work afterward, and I must admit that you enhanced the situation admirably."

"You flatter me," the noblewoman said cautiously, distressed to learn that her actions had not escaped notice.

"Not at all. I've made some inquiries, and you are an astonishingly versatile woman. Your business interests make you an influential part of Waterdeep's web of commerce, and you pay membership dues to two guilds. You have also reached a high position in court society." Garnet finally stopped playing and looked up, locking her intense blue gaze with the noblewoman's wary eyes. "And, most important, you have managed to infiltrate the Lords of Waterdeep. No wonder the Knights of the Shield speak highly of you. I am told that you're their highest ranked agent in this city."

Lucia's heart thumped painfully, but she merely folded her hands in her silken lap. "I would be a fool to admit to any of this," she said.

"Yes, you would," Garnet agreed with a thin smile. "But since I am quite sure of my facts, I don't require verification."

The noblewoman's mind raced over the possibilities. Other than her trusted agents, no one in Waterdeep knew that she was a member of the Knights of the Shield, a secret organization from the south that gathered information and manipulated politics to whatever end suited them. Obviously, with this information, Garnet could threaten to ruin her in Waterdeep and demand whatever she liked. There was a second danger: the half-elf's words revealed to Lucia that this information had come directly from high officials

in the Knights of the Shield. Lucia had secured her position
with the Knights by *claiming* to be one of the secret Lords
of Waterdeep. Since the identity of the Lords was a closely
held secret, and since the Knights and the Lords were bitter
enemies and not known to exchange information, she had
little fear that either her superiors or the true Lords would
discover her ruse. If this half-elf—who clearly had the ear of
someone important among the Knights—was going to
demand favors that only a Lord of Waterdeep could accomplish, then Lucia had a serious problem.

"You seem to know a great deal about me, and therefore
you have me at a disadvantage," Lucia said sweetly, hoping
to draw more information from Garnet.

"What would you like to know?" the half-elf responded
bluntly.

"Well, you said that the bard was under your influence.
How was this done?"

Garnet plucked a large purple trumpet flower from the
vines overhead and handed it to the noblewoman. "I'll
show you how it was done," she said simply, and once
again she put her fingers to the harp strings. She began to
play a lilting dance tune, to which she sang a few lines of
cryptic verse.

The flower in Lucia's hand collapsed into a withered
brown thread. The noblewoman gasped and looked up at
the trellis. The vines were also blighted, and a dead leaf
drifted onto her upturned cheek. Lucia brushed it off and
took a deep, steadying breath. "You are a sorceress then,
as well as a bard."

"Whether those are two separate things or parts of one
talent is a matter for a later discussion. It will suffice to say
that, like you, I have many skills. We share a single purpose, however: to work against the Lords of Waterdeep."
Garnet gently removed the harp from her shoulder and
leaned toward the noblewoman. "May I speak frankly?"

"Please."

"Working from the inside, you can do much against Waterdeep's secret Lords. But can you strike against Khelben Arunsun?"

"Many have tried and failed. He is too powerful," Lucia hedged.

"That is my point precisely," Garnet said, stabbing the air with a slender finger. "Khelben is far too powerful. Many consider him the backbone of the Lords' power and influence. This offends me. I do not believe he should be in a position of political power, and I will see him removed."

Lucia doubted this, but she was in no position to argue. "What would you have me do?"

"Harass the other Lords. Keep them busy, off guard. Send them running about the city stamping out small fires."

"You hardly need my help for that. Waterdeep has many problems these days."

Garnet smiled and inclined her head in a slight bow. "Thank you."

The noblewoman absorbed this, studying the withered flower in her hand. If the blight on the local fields and crops was Garnet's doing, this woman was powerful indeed. "How will you remove Khelben from his position?"

"The archmage may be too formidable to attack, but no one is too powerful to discredit."

"But the Knights of the Shield have sought for many years for information we could use against him!"

"A thing need not be true to be damaging," Garnet pointed out. "An accusation need not be proven; ofttimes it is enough that words are said. Words have great power." She reached out and stroked the dark wood of her harp. "As does music."

After a few moments' reflection, the sorceress continued. "I control many bards. They will spread tales about

Khelben, and about his lady. As it happens, most of these
will be true. I know many things about Khelben, things
only a few of his closest friends suspect. My bards will
apply pressure, as you saw the other evening."

"And I?"

"You know who the Lords are. If enough of them are
kept out of the way, we increase the pressure on Khelben.
Eventually, even he will make a mistake, and you may be
assured that all the city will know of it."

"But doesn't that put you in a dangerous situation?
When these little-known tales are told, they may well be
traced to you."

"Very perceptive," Garnet said approvingly. "The
Knights were not wrong in their estimation of your talents.
But I have anticipated that, and I have prepared a distraction. Khelben's nephew, Danilo Thann, has bardic pretensions. I have improved many of the young man's songs,
and I have woven them into the memories of the bards I
control. You can be sure that these songs are widely and
often sung. As you know, Waterdeep is a city of passing
fashions, each pursued almost fanatically before being
abandoned for the next. Danilo Thann's songs are currently all the rage, and the Waterdhavians listen with close
attention and great interest. Thus shall I use Danilo Thann
to discredit his uncle, the archmage, while deflecting
attention that might have otherwise come my way. He will
accept the credit, and the blame."

Lucia shook her head adamantly. "I know Danilo. He is a
bit of a fool, but there is no malice in him. He will not stand
by to see his uncle discredited. Neither can I picture him
as a master bard, and I'm sure many others suffer from a
similar lack of imagination."

Garnet tucked a loose strand of graying brown hair
behind one slightly pointed ear. "Fair concerns, both of
them, but I assure you that neither will be a problem. The

young 'bard's' fame has become well established, and it will continue to grow—*posthumously*. Now, have we an agreement?"

It was clear to Lucia that she had little choice in the matter, but she saw that the scheme could redound to her own benefit. If they succeeded in removing Khelben Arunsun from power, she could name her reward, and the Knights would be delighted to grant it. As for her own deepest secret, she would handle Garnet the same way she had dealt with her superiors for years: pretend to be a Lord of Waterdeep, and pass along as privileged information things she garnered through business deals, social gossip, and her network of spies. And perhaps, if her suspicions were correct, her liaison with Caladorn might prove useful, as well as entertaining. The young man was besotted with her and trusted her completely. If he had any secrets, they were hers for the taking.

"I believe we can work together," Lucia agreed. "Now, tell me a little more about your plan."

"That is not necessary. We shall proceed one step at a time. When I require your services, I will detail what is expected."

That was more than a descendant of royalty could abide. Lucia rose slowly to her feet. Trembling with anger, she glared down at the half-elf. "I am servant to no one. Remember, you need my political power."

"Less than you need the magic I wield through music," Garnet returned. For a long moment their eyes held in silent challenge. Lucia was the first to look away.

"Then it is settled," Garnet said with a smile. "Bardcraft and politics will join forces once again, and that is as it should be. Now, let us show Khelben Arunsun what can be done when there is a proper balance between the two."

* * * * *

Now that he was face-to-face with Elaith Craulnober, Danilo began to doubt the wisdom of his decision to confront the elf and bargain for Vartain's services. When they'd first met, some two years earlier, Elaith had taken an instant dislike to Danilo and, for that reason alone, had ordered his death. Judging from the vexation on Elaith's handsome, angular face, Danilo supposed that the elf was regretting his decision to rescind that order.

A wild giggle shattered the tense silence, and a ragged elf capered through the garden. The setting sun cast a long, emaciated shadow behind him as he whirled and leaped. Danilo watched the elf disappear around a corner, then turned a bland smile toward Elaith. "Friend of yours?"

The moon elf ignored Danilo's needling and pointed to the Harper pin. "How did *you* come by one of those? I know many who would pay dearly to obtain it, should you choose to sell."

"One must earn a Harper pin," Danilo said quietly.

The elf chuckled. "And you have?"

"Let's just say that if I haven't already, I'm about to."

Elaith folded his arms and cocked a silver eyebrow. "You have my attention."

"The Harpers require the services of a bard. Since most of these have fallen under a spell that affects their music and memories, I was drafted to help."

"Really! Thank you for sharing such welcome news," the elf said with a cordial smile. "Many of my associates will be delighted to learn that the Harpers have fallen to such depths. I shall dine out on this tale for months to come."

"So glad to be of service. Now, if I may present my companions: Morgalla the Mirthful, a bard of astounding talents, and Wyn Ashgrove, a minstrel from Evermeet. Perhaps you've met him before?" Danilo's choice of words was not entirely without malice; he knew of Elaith's self-imposed exile from the island homeland of the elves.

Wyn greeted the moon elf with a polite ritual bow, which Elaith simply ignored. He shot an incredulous glance at the stout, short, brown-clad woman who'd come to stand at Danilo's side. "A dwarf, Lord Thann? Your taste in traveling companions has sadly deteriorated. Where is Arilyn these days?"

"Elsewhere," Danilo said curtly. "Now, if we've exhausted our present supply of verbal stilettos, I have a business proposal for you."

Elaith looked intrigued. "A deal that brought the son of a Waterdeep merchant this far afield might prove interesting."

"It's unusual, at the very least," the Harper said. "Sing him the ballad, Wyn."

The minstrel took his silver lyre from its shoulder strap and sang the *Ballad of Grimnoshtadrano*. Elaith seemed irritated by this development and gave the gold elf scant attention, but as Wyn sang, Vartain came to stand at his employer's side. The riddlemaster listened with deep interest, and his prominent black eyes were lively with intelligence and curiosity.

"I believe I see this path's destination," Vartain said when the song was done. "These three wish to answer the dragon's challenge, which means they must answer a riddle, read a scroll, and sing a song. Since the words 'reading a scroll' most likely indicate the casting of a spell, this young man is probably a mage. He travels with two bards. What he yet lacks is the talents of a riddlemaster, and he has come here to bid for my services. With all three skills, they have a chance at success, or, at the very least, survival."

"Well, you're not going," Elaith said flatly. "You signed on for the duration of this hunt, and you will remain in my service."

Vartain nodded, but he pulled Elaith aside. Turning his

back to the newcomers, he began to spell out his argument in the silent hand language of thieves' cant. "As a riddlemaster, I collect lore of many kinds. Recently I've noted that ballads by and about Harpers have changed. When I questioned the bards who sang them, they all insisted that the songs were as they had always been. It is likely that what this young man says is true. No available Harper bards were unaffected by this spell, yet the dragon's challenge specifies that a Harper must come. This would explain why the young man so openly touts his affiliation with this usually secret organization. Perhaps the Harpers are undergoing difficult times, but they are generally quite effective. If they have given assent to this quest, I believe it is because it has a fair chance of success."

"So?" Elaith asked aloud.

"So you can make his success your own," Vartain spelled out, his bony fingers gesticulating with fluid, practiced ease. "You were not listening to the ballad, but it stated that those who successfully challenge Grimnoshtadrano can choose their reward from the dragon's hoard."

Elaith glared at the riddlemaster for a moment, then a strange glint entered his amber eyes. He affixed Danilo and his bardic companions with a measuring, speculative gaze.

"Of course, I will recompense you for the loss of Vartain's services," Danilo said hastily, seeing the expression on the elf's face and eager to press any advantage. "You've little need for money, but rumor has it you've a fondness for magical items."

Danilo pushed up the full sleeve of his shirt, revealing a jeweled knife in an elaborately tooled leather wrist sheath. Turning away so that pulling the blade could not be construed as a threat, Danilo flicked the knife toward the peppergum tree. It quivered in the soft bark for five heartbeats. Then, suddenly, it was gone. Danilo held out his wrist for the elf's inspection. The knife had returned to the sheath.

"A very handy toy," Elaith agreed. "Very well, you may have Vartain and welcome. I will take the knife, as well as fifty pieces of platinum, standard trade weight. The former I will collect now; the latter is payable by you or your estate upon my return to Waterdeep. There is one other condition: my men and I will join forces with your formidable army." He paused and made an ironic bow to Wyn and Morgalla, then turned back to Dan with a small, tight smile. "From this day until the completion of the search, you and I will be partners."

Danilo stared at the elf, utterly dumbfounded. At length he found his tongue and said in a dazed tone, "Partners?"

"That's right."

"Buggering Beshaba!" Danilo swore fervently, evoking the goddess of bad luck. "I had not anticipated this turn of events!"

"Nor I," said Elaith dryly. "I can see that you're as pleased with the prospect as I am. Regardless, have we a deal?"

"I suppose we do," Dan agreed slowly. His eyed the elf dubiously, but he unstrapped the leather sheath and handed it to him. Elaith removed the magic knife from the sheath and examined it closely, tested its weight and balance, and then tossed it high into the air. He caught the descending knife by the tip and hurled it, all in one smooth movement, at the peppergum tree. The jeweled knife found the same spot Danilo had struck.

"I'm curious," Elaith said casually. "Say that I were to throw this knife at an enemy. The wound wouldn't heal once the knife magically withdrew, would it? The damage would remain?"

"That's right."

The elf held Danilo's eyes as he strapped the sheath onto his forearm, and his smile was not a pleasant one. "Splendid," he said.

*   *   *   *   *

The morning was still young when Larissa Neathal pulled herself from her bed. Sitting at a dressing table before a large triple mirror, she assessed her face for evidence of the all-night party. The laughter and music still echoed through her head, leaving it throbbing with dull pain, yet her gray eyes were clear and her white skin flawless. She pressed her fingertips delicately to the tiny puffs under her eyes, and with a shrug she reached for a jar of tinted unguent. Larissa disliked cosmetics and did not often resort to their use, but she had an appointment within the hour, and in her business she could ill afford to look less than her best.

Last night had been especially profitable for the beautiful courtesan. The socially prominent Lady Thione had opened the Midsummer season with an extravagant costume affair. During the long hours of revelry Larissa's legendary capacity for dancing and drinking had been stretched to the limit. From a courtesan's point of view—particularly a courtesan who also served as a Lord of Waterdeep—the party could hardly have been better. She had charmed some business secrets from a smitten Cormyrian merchant, gleaned some interesting news from a far-traveled bard named Garnet, and met a merchant nobleman visiting from Tethyr. Lord Hhune—a fat, black-haired man with small, unreadable eyes, thick black brows, and an abundant mustache—had engaged her to show him the city's sights. She did not like the man, but, since Tethyr was a constantly simmering caldron of political trouble, she would skim what knowledge she could from him.

Despite all these successes, Larissa had felt vaguely ill for most of the evening and had been glad to see the party end. Perhaps she had caught a chill, she mused, glancing at the costume she'd tossed over a velvet settee near the door, just before she'd fallen into bed. The form-fitting, richly embroidered gown of a Shou princess had attracted much admiration, but thin red satin offered little protection from the chill night winds that buffeted the Sea Ward. Or perhaps she had simply been working too hard. In recent weeks, the Lords of Waterdeep had been stretched to the limits of their various abilities. Larissa's talent was gathering information, and her sphere was the whirl of social events and court functions. She could not remember the last time she'd slept for more than two or three hours, and she was beginning to feel a kinship with the walking dead.

Whatever the case, Larissa was in no mood to play the part of a simpering courtesan, dancing to some stranger's whims. Usually she played her role with real pride and genuine enjoyment, but she had no heart for it today.

Well, there was no help for it. Larissa stifled a yawn and continued her preparations. First she unbraided her red hair. Since her luxuriant tresses were too long for her to brush herself, she rang the small brass bell that would summon her maid. She stripped off her rings and massaged scented ointment into her hands. Then she rose from the dressing table and glided over to a vast oak wardrobe. Her pale green nightgown, a marvel of translucent silk, swirled and floated about her legs as she moved. Throwing open the wardrobe door, she began to debate which gown her latest client might fancy.

Behind her, the bedchamber door creaked open. "Come in, Marta, and hurry. I must be dressed in an hour," Larissa said without turning.

"You need not bother, dear lady," said a deep, heavily

accented voice. "That green gown you are *almost* wearing pleases me well."

Startled, Larissa whirled in a cloud of floating silk. Lord Hhune of Tethyr was seated on the settee, insolently fingering the red satin of her Shou costume. In the doorway stood two dark-clad men, wielding curved daggers and holding captive between them a terrified Marta.

Larissa's right hand went instinctively to her left pinkie, reaching for the enspelled ring given to all Waterdeep's Lords. Her heart plummeted when she realized she'd inadvertently taken it off with her other rings and left it on the dressing table. The ring not only granted her immunity to poisons, but it would have allowed her to summon her powerful comrades. Her mind raced over other options. Screaming for help would be futile. She had several skilled and trusted fighters among her servants; if they were not already here defending her, they were dead. All her gowns were equipped with cunningly hidden stilettos, but her nearly transparent nightgowns afforded her no such protection. Larissa had but one weapon at hand—the art of a courtesan—and her maid's life depended upon her skill in wielding it.

With a delicate laugh, Larissa glided over to Hhune. "I am flattered by your impatience," she said in sultry tones. Looking up into his face, she gave him her most winsome smile and began to toy with the buttons on his coat.

"But my maid has little skill in such games as you and I might enjoy. Surely, your men would be better served at any one of our city's festhalls. Perhaps you could give them a day's holiday to taste the city's pleasures, so that we might spend the afternoon in . . . privacy?"

Larissa swayed closer, and Hhune's eyes darkened with an expression the courtesan knew well. She began to allow herself a bit of hope.

"You are most beautiful," the nobleman said in a thick

voice. He gathered up a handful of her gleaming red hair. "I almost regret what must come to pass."

Hhune gave Larissa's hair a brutal yank, jerking her head back. With the edge of his free hand, he struck her hard on the throat. Dazed by the pain, the courtesan fell to her knees. A word from Hhune brought three more men from the hall beyond. Two of the ruffians held her while the third man caught her flailing hands. The man systematically broke her fingers, one by one. When the task was completed, Hhune nodded and his men fell back. Still on her knees, Larissa rocked back and forth, cupping ruined hands to her breast as sobs bubbled from her shattered voice box.

"Now, Larissa, Lord of Waterdeep, you will not be able to communicate by voice or quill for many days to come," Hhune said coldly. "Do not fear for your life, dear lady. Far from it. This city reeks of barbarian magic, and too many could speak with your spirit. My men are too skilled to allow you to die, so you will live, lingering for many days as if in enchanted slumber. After that," he paused and shrugged, "you may awaken. Perhaps potions and prayers may restore your voice, your hands, and your beauty. Or perhaps not."

He turned to the waiting men. "See to it," he commanded. "As for the maid, kill her and remove her from this place. Our Waterdeep agent will see that the body disappears deep into the harbor."

Hhune whirled and stalked from the bedchamber, faintly repulsed by the eager gleam in the men's eyes as they closed on the sobbing courtesan. Torture was not an uncommon weapon for the Knights of the Shield, and these men been chosen for their skill in the art. Hhune had little taste for such things, but he supposed that a man should enjoy his work.

He nearly bumped into Garnet, who awaited him in the

hall. The look of blatant disapproval she sent him made
Hhune feel defensive of his methods.

"The courtesan is being dealt with," Hhune said, nodding toward the closed door. "Since you did not succeed in
poisoning her last night, we felt another approach was indicated."

The half-elf's eyes blazed. "Lady Thione neglected to tell
me that all Lords of Waterdeep are immune to poison. Had
I known such methods would fail, I would not have wasted
the night chatting with her and performing at the party
like some common minstrel."

"Thione said nothing of that, eh? This is most interesting," Hhune said thoughtfully.

Garnet noted that the southern nobleman was far from
displeased to learn of Lady Thione's omission. Since she
had little interest in the internal politics of the Knights of
the Shield, she merely shrugged and turned away. She
hurried down the hall to an arched doorway and stepped
out onto a balcony.

Hhune watched her, his black brows knit together in
puzzlement. What did the half-elf expect to do: fly? Curiosity got the better of him, and he crept down the hall with as
much stealth as his bulk could manage. He peered around
the edge of the drapery, and recoiled in surprise.

A milk-white horse stood on the balcony, two stories
above the quiet street. As Hhune watched, Garnet hoisted
herself onto the animal's back and gathered up the reins,
slapping them sharply against her steed's neck. The horse
hesitated, and Garnet's face hardened into a mask of concentration and anger. As if in response, the horse dipped
its head in a gesture that spoke eloquently of both sadness
and resignation. It lifted straight into the air, as lightly as a
hummingbird. Then, as quickly as that delicate bird, the
horse darted away into the clouds.

"Asperii," breathed Hhune in an awed tone. He had

heard of the rare and magical wind steeds, but never before had he seen one. Like pegasi, these horses could fly, but they had no wings. Their flight came from their natural powers of levitation, and they were uncommonly fast. An asperii formed a telepathic bond with a mage or priest of great power, and would remain with its master for life.

This discovery intrigued Hhune. He had arrived in Waterdeep the day before with a shipment of goods for the Midsummer Faire. Once his duties as a merchant had been discharged, he'd called on Lady Thione expecting a routine report. Instead, he'd discovered that she had made an alliance with a formidable sorceress, and that she had put a plan in action that would come to fruition in a matter of days. She would not tell him the details of this plan. In itself, this did not surprise Hhune, for he was not Lady Thione's superior, and the Knights of the Shield kept secrets even from their own. He got the impression, however, that Lady Thione herself did not know all that would happen.

To Hhune's eye, Garnet was firmly in control. The sorceress was using the Knights of the Shield as a personal tool, of that Hhune was fairly certain. He also suspected that she knew something that gave her power over Lady Thione. Hhune would dearly love to know what that was. Perhaps, he mused, a longer stay in Waterdeep would be most rewarding.

*   *   *   *   *

Morning light streamed in through the tall, slender windows that encircled the round bedchamber. Lucia Thione stretched, languid as a contented cat, and reached for her young lover. But the bed was empty, and only rumpled silk sheets and a broad depression in the down-filled mattress indicated that the evening before had been more than a pleasant dream.

"Ah, you're awake. Now it can truly be said that morning has come." Dressed in leathers and riding boots, Caladorn strode into the room, his auburn hair still damp from the baths. Lucia sat up and raised her face for a kiss. The young man bent over and greeted her tenderly.

"You are off so soon?" she asked, pouting a little. "But you have been working so hard of late. We've had so little time together."

"I have business," Caladorn said with a fond smile, tracing the delicate arch of her nose with a gloved finger. "Surely a merchant of your acumen knows the importance of that."

"What sort of business?"

"The city has engaged me to train those who wish to compete in the Midsummer Games. I shall be at the Field of Triumph all day."

After promising to meet her back at his townhouse that evening, Caladorn took leave of his lady. Left alone, Lucia smiled and flung herself back among the pillows. She waited until she heard the muffled thud of the front door. Although she would have enjoyed Caladorn's company this morning, she needed the time alone to find a path out of her dilemma.

By pretending to be one of the Lords of Waterdeep, she had placed herself in a favored position with the Knights of the Shield. Their support had allowed her to amass a great fortune, and all had been well, until Garnet entered her life. The sorceress's dangerous knowledge had placed Lucia in a position of virtual slavery. The arrival of Lord Hhune from Tethyr worsened matters considerably, for the Knights of the Shield would not be pleased to learn of her alliance with Garnet. This association had started out on a dangerous note: Garnet had assumed control of Hhune, his men, and Lucia's local agents. Worse, the sorceress had demanded that Lucia reveal the names of the Lords of Waterdeep.

Lucia could hardly admit she did not have this knowledge, so she'd compiled a short list for Garnet: Khelben Arunsun, Larissa Neathal, the moneylender Mirt, Durnan, and Texter the Paladin. These names were whispered in every tavern of Waterdeep, and they would suffice for now. Lucia knew she would have to do better, and soon.

The noblewoman flung aside the covers and left the bedchamber. If Caladorn did have connections to the Lords of Waterdeep, she would find no evidence of it here. She made her way down the spiral stairs to the next level, which held the bathing area and dressing rooms. One room was filled with chests and wardrobes, and it seemed like a good place to begin her search.

Moving quietly so as not to alert Caladorn's manservant, Lucia systematically went through each chest and every drawer, looking for anything that might link Caladorn to the Lords of Waterdeep. For almost an hour she combed the room, to no avail.

Frustrated but determined to persist, Lucia headed for her own closet. She planned to search the townhouse to the last nail and tile, but she could hardly do so clad in a diaphanous nightdress. Caladorn, who was in all things attentive and romantic, had filled a closet with several changes of clothing for such mornings, all of them in Lucia's trademark purple. With a deep sigh, Lucia drew a lavender robe from the closet. Perhaps, after a bath and a change of clothes—

Her thoughts came to an abrupt stop. For no reason that she could ascertain, the hem of the robe was stuck to the back of the wooden wardrobe. She gave the garment a sharp tug, but it held fast. She dropped to her knees for a closer look. The grain of the wood around the trapped fabric was even and uninterrupted, and when she ran her fingers over the smooth panel, she felt no ridge or gap. It was as if the lavender silk grew directly out of the wood.

Excited now, Lucia pushed the other garments aside and began to search the inside of the wardrobe. After several minutes, her seeking fingers found a tiny button hidden in the swirling pattern of the wood. She pressed it, and a small door on the back panel slid silently open, releasing the robe and revealing a hidden shelf. Lucia reached inside and drew out a black helmet covered with a thick veil.

She slipped the helm over her head and spun to view her reflection in a standing mirror. Though she could see with perfect clarity, her features were completely obscured by the veil. She sang a few notes of a Tethyrian folk song, and the voice was not recognizably her own. In fact, it was not recognizably anything. The voice could have been male or female, old or young. A peal of exultant laughter burst from her, and it, too, was magically disguised by the helm of a Lord of Waterdeep.

So! Her young lover actually held the place she had long pretended to! Caladorn could deny her nothing, and with knowledge gleaned from him she could easily placate Garnet. A smile curved her lips, and the burden of worry fell from her narrow shoulders.

Lucia removed the helm and replaced it in the cabinet. Before she shut the door, she carefully placed the hem of the lavender robe where it would again be caught in the hidden door. She arranged the other garments as she had found them, making it appear that the wardrobe had not been disturbed, and she dressed herself in the clothes she had worn the night before. When the room was in order, she sauntered out of Caladorn's home in the direction of Mother Tathlorn's House of Pleasure and Healing. With the morning's success behind her, she felt well justified in treating herself to a massage, a manicure, and perhaps a little something more.

Five

Taskerleigh lay two days' travel behind him, but Danilo had yet to come up with an explanation for his current predicament.

By Dan's reckoning, Elaith Craulnober would rather wed a troll than travel in his company, yet here they were. Danilo had ruefully dubbed their combined forces "Music and Mayhem," and the name stuck. That was not, in his opinion, a good omen.

Theirs was beyond doubt the most uneasy alliance the Harper had ever encountered. The elf held all the prejudices of his race and had no love of dwarves, but to Dan's surprise Elaith treated Wyn Ashgrove no better than he did Morgalla. The elven minstrel was spared the sharp edge of Elaith's tongue, but he pointedly ignored Wyn's presence among the travelers. Several times, though, Elaith's eyes rested on the gold elf, and the pure hatred in their amber depths chilled Danilo. For his part, Wyn treated everyone with the same distant courtesy, and he

seemed to take no notice of his fellow elf's bad manners. If
there was a common thread weaving together the disparate adventurers, it was Vartain. The riddlemaster
seemed to annoy everyone in equal measure.

But Elaith's mercenaries, especially the huge black-
bearded man known as Balindar, were quite taken with the
dwarf maid. When they learned that Morgalla was a veteran of the Alliance War, the men plied her with eager
questions. Waterdeep had not sent an army to help turn
back the barbarian invaders, and many sell-swords of the
Northlands felt they'd missed out on the greatest, most
glorious adventure of their lifetimes. The dwarf was hesitant at first, but she warmed to their interest, and by mid-
morning of the second day, she was helping to pass the
tedium of travel with one well-told tale after another. Dan
listened to snatches of their conversations, enjoying the
dwarf's mellow voice and skilled storytelling. He remembered Morgalla's gruff rejection of the title "dwarven
bard," but to his ears, she deserved to be accounted so
even if there was no music in her soul. And that lack, he
doubted. Every night since they'd left Waterdeep, Morgalla had persuaded him to play his lute and sing. Never
would she join him, but she listened to every air and ballad
with a rapt expression of mingled joy and longing on her
broad face.

Danilo glanced over at Elaith, who was riding apart from
the others, as alert and wary as the silver fox he resembled. He could not imagine what treasure induced the
elf to take to the road. It was widely rumored in Waterdeep
that the moon elf was wealthy almost beyond calculation.
Elaith often hired mercenary bands and sent them on trips
of exploration and adventure, but in recent years he had
remained in Waterdeep, making his dark deals and reap-
ing the reward from others' blood and toils. The Harper
didn't trust Elaith for a moment, and the sooner he knew

the elf's hidden purpose, the better his little band's chances of survival. Danilo reined his bay, a fast and sturdy horse he favored for long trips, over to the elf's fine-boned black steed.

"How does Cleddish?" the Harper asked, nodding toward a mercenary who had been wounded in the harpy attack. Cleddish was one of five men who had been turned into living statues by the harpy charm song. The effect had finally worn off this morning, and Danilo would long remember the man's horrible, keening screams when he awoke. Danilo carried a number of tiny vials containing potions that sped healing or countered poisons, and he'd given one of each to Cleddish. This precaution closed the gashes made by the harpy's filthy talons and would probably stave off putrefaction, but the man had lost a good deal of blood. Danilo suspected that Cleddish had sustained hidden wounds, as well. The mercenary sat his horse with grim, stoic determination, but he had spoken little since the attack, and his face was almost as gray as the single braid of hair that hung over his wounded shoulder. Still, Cleddish was more fortunate than his comrade, a Northman who had been blinded by the harpy's venom. At Elaith's order, the blinded man had been put out of his agony and his body left beside the trail.

"Cleddish seems rather subdued, and his color is poor," Danilo pointed out, "but I don't know him well enough to judge whether or not this is normal for him."

Elaith turned a long-suffering gaze to the human, his expression plainly indicating that he tolerated this interruption as but one indignity among many. "Cleddish is a hired sword, not some beloved cousin. You know him as well as I."

"Ah. Well, that exhausts that topic," Danilo said dryly.

"I should hope so."

After a moment's silence, the nobleman tried again. "In

all candor, I can't envision you joining forces with bards and Harpers."

The elf responded with an enigmatic smile. "Let's say that I've become a patron of the arts."

"Most commendable. I must say, it was a surprise to learn that you've taken up adventuring again. I trust your expedition to Taskerleigh was a success?"

"Perhaps you shouldn't be so trusting." The rejoinder was offered in silky, pleasant tones, but it was nonetheless a warning.

Danilo decided not to take it. "Hit a nerve there, did I?" he said cheerfully. "Well, if your men expected treasure and were disappointed, one way of keeping up morale would be offering them a green dragon's hoard." He left an unspoken question hanging in the air.

"A gracious offer." Elaith made the Harper a small, mock bow. "On behalf of my men, I accept. Now, if you'll excuse me, one of us should watch the road." The elf kicked his horse into a trot, putting several lengths' distance between himself and the Harper.

Danilo grimaced and rubbed the back of his neck with both hands. That went about as well as he'd expected. Still, the elf had a point. The terrain through which the adventurers rode was rugged and inhospitable, and caution was definitely in order. The village of Taskerleigh lay near Ganstar's Creek, in hilly and fertile land northwest of the Goldenfield temple farms. The roads through it had fallen into disrepair, for rumors of monsters and the disappearance of more than one adventuring party had discouraged resettlement. The main road that led westward from the deserted village was also lightly traveled, for only the heartiest travelers ventured into the High Forest, and even fewer emerged. The path that Music and Mayhem followed skirted the rock-strewn hills marking the grave of the Fallen Kingdom, a long-ago settlement of humans, elves, and dwarves. The land had long since become wild: fields had been reclaimed by scrub forest, buildings had been reduced to occasional heaps of stone, dwarven tunnels had either collapsed or become home to underground monsters. To Danilo, the scene was an ominous suggestion of what befell humans, elves, and dwarves who tried to cast their lots together.

The sun cast long shadows before them as they climbed a particularly high and rocky hill. At the summit, Elaith signaled a halt. The riders came together to survey the land before them. Near the bottom of the hill was a fork in the road. The southern branch, Danilo knew, led toward the town Secomber, where it connected with a major trade route. The northern fork was a narrow path into the High Forest. Far to the north Danilo could see the rapid waters of Unicorn Run, and beyond the river lay the dense green wilderness. A section of the road ahead went through marshlands, and the bed had been built up with soil and stone into a narrow causeway. This road had been built many years before by an adventuring party known as the Nine, and it ended at their famed stronghold in the southern part of the High Forest. But the Nine had retired long before Danilo's birth—some rumors had most of them rolling in wealth on another plane—and the causeway had crumbled.

Danilo considered the marshlands with a dubious expression. Sunset was hours away, yet already the songs of frogs and other, unknown swamp creatures drifted toward them. He had fought lizard men once in the dreaded Marsh of Chelimber, and it was not an experience he cared to repeat. "I, for one, am for making camp right here," Danilo said.

"There is no water here, nor fodder for the horses," Vartain pointed out, predictably enough. No matter what idea was presented, the riddlemaster usually had a better one.

"If would seem the best course to ride on. At a good pace, we could be past the wetlands before nightfall. The best and safest campsite would be near the river, but not in the forest itself."

Elaith gave a curt nod of agreement, and Danilo, despite misgivings, gave in.

They rode hard, reining their horses to a walk only when they reached the narrow causeway. Caution was needed, for though some parts of the path had room for two or three to ride abreast, large chunks of the road had been reclaimed by the marsh. They picked their way along, riding in silence.

The chirping of the frogs grew louder as they rode, with an unearthly, reverberating sound that made the marsh seem to close in around them. Danilo found it unnerving. When they were near the middle of the causeway, he leaned close to Morgalla and whispered, "Reminds me of the effect I get when singing Tantrasan opera in a small bathchamber."

"Yeah. I don't like it," the dwarf responded grimly.

"Tantrasan opera is an acquired taste," the Harper quipped.

Morgalla nodded absently. "That, too." Her brown eyes searched the shallow water for anything that might signal danger. After a moment she smacked Danilo's knee to get his attention, then pointed to their right. A stand of thick, oat-colored reeds swayed in the breeze. The tops of many had been partially severed, and they emitted a strange, hollow whistle as the wind blew across them. When the riders passed, the flow of air was interrupted and the mournful sound ceased. "An alarm?" the dwarf suggested.

Danilo was about to demur when he noticed a strange stand of reeds several yards ahead. A thick bank of these reeds seemed to have been arranged in several rows. Those in back were long and thick, and each successive

row was shorter. The reeds in each row tapered downward
to either side. Something about the arrangement struck
Danilo's memory. He reached down and tugged at one of
the reeds that grew near the path, but it would not give. He
took a hunting knife from his boot and hacked off the bent
top. It was hard and rigid. The tops of these water plants
had not broken by a passing breeze, of that much he was
certain. Danilo motioned for Wyn, and the elven minstrel
reined his horse over to the Harper's side.

"Look at that bank of reeds ahead," Danilo said softly.
"Is it my imagination, or does it remind you of something?"

The gold elf examined the plants politely, then his green
eyes widened in astonishment. "A pipe organ," he murmured. "Some being has fashioned a musical instrument
in this marsh!"

"Damn," Danilo said with feeling. "I was hoping it was
my imagination."

The Harper caught Morgalla's eye and rested his hand
on his sword hilt. She gave a barely perceptible nod, and
urged her pony over to Balindar's side. She whispered
something, and the huge fighter passed the hushed message down the line. The mercenaries readied their
weapons with a lack of subtlety that made Danilo wince.
The gold elf, however, took his lyre from its shoulder strap
and quickly checked the tuning of the strings.

Immediately, the "organ" began to play. At first, the
whistling tones were indistinguishable from the random,
hollow sounds of the windswept reeds around them. The
sounds quickened and became higher in pitch, tumbling
together into a dancelike melody that set the bank of reeds
ahead quivering merrily. There was something oddly like
speech in the music, Danilo noted. A moment later, the song
was echoed back from the far side of the marsh. He would
have given a great deal to know what the little tune said, and
even more to avoid learning *to whom* the music spoke.

Then the largest reeds began to sound. A deep, resonant call rang out over the marsh in macabre counterpoint
to the lilting dance tune. Despite his rising fear, Danilo listened to the marsh music as objectively as he could. The
sound was very like that of an enormous hunting horn.

"A call to battle," Wyn said softly, echoing Danilo's disconcerting thoughts.

Elaith wrapped his reins around the pommel of the
saddle and readied his bow. "What are we fighting?"

"I don't know," Wyn replied in a tense voice. "Something
new, perhaps."

The organ's music stopped abruptly. A grim silence
hung over the marsh, broken only by the gentle pop of
bubbles rising to the surface of the water. Vartain pointed
to bubbles on both sides of the causeway. "Whatever they
are, they're all around us," he observed.

That observation was too much for Cleddish, and his
long gray braid whipped from side to side as he frantically
tracked the marsh for the unseen musicians. His dappled
gray horse sensed the rider's rising panic, and it shied and
pitched. At that, Cleddish snapped. Dropping his sword
into the marsh, he flung both arms around his horse's
neck. This increased the horse's panic and it reared. Its
hoofs came too close to the causeway's edge. Stone gave
way, and horse and rider tumbled backward into the
marsh. The horse found its feet quickly and scrambled
back onto the path, its eyes wild and white-rimmed. Cleddish thrashed about in the shallow water, shrieking hyster-
ically.

"Pull him out!" Danilo called to those closest the fallen
man.

Morgalla leaped from her mount and snatched her
spear from its holder. Grasping it near the jester's-head
top, the dwarf held the other end out to the hysterical mercenary and planted her booted feet wide. "Grab ahold,"

she hollered, but Cleddish was apparently past hearing or reason.

Then the source of his panic became apparent. Green hands rose out of the weeds and water, closing around the frantic mercenary's throat. Danilo caught sight of long fingers ending in bulbous tips before Cleddish was pulled under. The water churned madly for several moments. Morgalla flipped her staff around and bared the spear's tip, dancing back and forth as she tried to decide where to stab.

"Ride on," Elaith commanded softly. "Stay as far away from the causeway's edge as possible. Maybe the creatures are like wolves, only attacking those who weaken and fall away from the herd."

Morgalla spun on her heel. "Yer gonna leave him?" she demanded.

"Yes," the elf said curtly. "And quickly, before whatever ate him decides to seek a second course."

As if on cue, a large green head broke the surface of the water several yards from where Cleddish had disappeared. The creature had the bulging yellow eyes and broad mouth of a frog, but as it rose from the water its body appeared to be roughly shaped like a man's. Its jowls suddenly bulged outward like those of a giant bullfrog, but with one difference: three long green appendages hung from the lower part of its giant air sack. A shrill, droning sound began to issue from the creature, an unmistakable call to battle that struck Dan as hideously similar to the skirl of bagpipes.

More of the creatures rose from the marsh in response to the summons, and the droning became a battle chorus. Elaith and his mercenaries fired again and again, but the agile frogs took cover under the surface of the water and few of the arrows found their marks. The frog creatures closed in, slowly and from all sides.

One of the pipers threw back his green arm and hurled a sharpened reed like a javelin. The rigid shaft sank deep into the flank of Balindar's horse. The animal screamed and reared, sending the huge mercenary into the marsh.

Again green hands reached out for their prey, but this time Morgalla was ready. She stabbed the creature through the wrist, then gave her spear a vicious tug back and up, pulling the frog creature partly onto the causeway. With its unharmed hand, it gripped her ankle, and its jowls bulged for another sort of attack: it shrieked. If a hurricane had been forced through a bagpipe, the sound could hardly have been less painful. Morgalla froze, her face contorted with agony.

Two streaks of silver flashed toward the dwarf. Elaith's first knife ripped into the creature's air chamber, and the shrieking collapsed into a flatulent gurgle. The second knife pierced the creature's wrist, pinning it to the causeway and freeing Morgalla. She danced back, yanking her spear out of the monstrous frog. Snatching the hand-axe from her belt, she struck deep between its yellow eyes. Morgalla yanked Elaith's knife free and kicked the dead monster back into the water. Still twitching, it sank, leaving a spreading pool of dark ichor. She nodded her thanks toward the elf, but he had turned aside, sword drawn in preparation for the next attack. Beside Morgalla, Balindar crawled onto the causeway, his shoulders heaving as he rid himself of the brackish water.

"They're not close enough," Wyn murmured as he clutched his lyre, his golden face creased with worry.

Danilo shot an incredulous look at the elf. In that moment of distraction, one of the creatures leaped onto the path and grabbed Danilo's ankle. The dwarf was at his side in an instant, and again her axe flashed. The giant frog bellowed and jumped back, clutching its severed and dripping stump. Danilo drew his long sword and slashed the creature's throat. Three more frogs climbed over the body of their fallen brother, and the hideous creatures began to swarm onto the causeway from both sides.

"Close enough for you now?" Danilo shouted at Wyn as he slashed at the closest frog.

The gold elf was beyond hearing. He strummed his lyre, singing in a voice as high and clear as a woman's, but unmistakably masculine. The elf's countertenor voice soared above the sounds of battle and the ghastly drone of amphibian pipes. Looking as calm as if he performed for friends in his own chambers, Wyn sang a gentle, lyric tune. The words were in the elven tongue, but a sense of peace filled Danilo's heart even as he continued to fight. Only once had Danilo heard such music: after the battle in Evereska, an elven priest had healed the Harper's seared hand with a song. He felt now the same power, the same awe, and the same humility before a beauty he could not begin to imitate or understand.

Wyn's music seemed to surround the elf and his horse in an invisible, protective sphere, and any frog who came near him fell back. Gradually the area of calm expanded, and the deadly frogs dropped their reed weapons. They ceased their raucous battle-skirl, as if the better to hear the elven song. Finally the pipers retreated into the marsh, sinking low in the water until all that could be seen of them was their bulging eyes. Still singing, Wyn began to ride forward along the causeway.

The others fell in behind him, and as they rode through the deepening twilight their path was brightened by the light of dozens of unblinking yellow eyes.

* * * * *

As vast and mysterious as Waterdeep might seem to a visitor, the city possessed layers of history and intrigue

that were beyond the imagination of most of its citizens.
Beneath the city's streets and buildings was a network of
secret tunnels and passages that defied efforts at mapping
or exploration. Even deeper were the mines of a long-
dead dwarven nation, and beneath that, it was rumored,
lay the cavernous lairs and abandoned hoards of dragons.
There were also stories of tunnels into other planes, but
most considered these tales best left untold. Waterdeep
was well run despite its secrets, or, perhaps, because of
them.

One of the most secure of these secret tunnels ran
between Piergeiron's Palace and Blackstaff Tower. Deeply
troubled, Khelben Arunsun made his way back through it
toward his tower home, trying without success to bring to
mind an image of Larissa Neathal's beautiful face, as it
once had been.

Mirt had found the courtesan in her home, barely alive
and battered almost past recognition. Rarely had Khelben
seen the former mercenary weep. Now, having seen
Larissa, Khelben felt near tears himself. She had been
taken to the palace as soon as the physicians felt it was
safe to move her, and there she remained under the best
care—and the best protection—the city could offer. Healing potions and clerical prayers seemed to have eased her
suffering, but nothing could touch her deathlike slumber.
She had been too badly hurt, and in too many ways, for
such methods to prevail. His friend's life was truly in the
hands of the gods, and for all his power, the archmage was
helpless to intervene.

Khelben climbed the stairs to his tower. The door was
flung open at his approach, and Laeral stood at the top of
the stairs. She was dressed as usual in a clinging, seductive gown, and her luxuriant silvery hair spilled over her
bared shoulders. For once, though, her face lacked merri-
ness, and her dimples were nowhere in evidence.

"How does Larissa?" she asked. Even through her concern, her voice was sultry as a summer breeze.

"She sleeps," Khelben muttered. "That is the best that can be said."

Laeral held out her arms, offering what comfort she could. For a long moment the powerful wizards clung to each other. Khelben drew back first, smoothing his lady's silver hair and giving her a small, grateful smile.

"A message came from the Lady of Berdusk while you were gone," Laeral said quietly, producing a small scrying globe from the folds of her gown. Such devices required powerful magic, and were used by the Harpers and their allies only in time of immediate need. "Asper has been captured by a band of brigands. They demand ransom, and will take it only from her father's hand."

Khelben drew in a long, steadying breath. Asper was a fighter currently working near Baldur's Gate as a caravan guard. She was a tiny young woman, pert and dark and merry, but none the less deadly for her happy nature. She was also the adopted daughter and the heart's-blood of his friend Mirt. Although Mirt was a retired mercenary who could still provide a respectable fight, he was getting on in years. Khelben feared what this news would do to his friend, coming as it did so close to Larissa's tragedy. Still, he must be told.

"I'll let Mirt know at once," he said.

"I'll come with you," Laeral offered, but the archmage shook his head.

"No, it's better that someone remain here in case there's more word on Asper. I was planning to meet Mirt at the tavern, anyway."

"Ah. I'd forgotten it was the Like-Minded Lords' night out," Laeral said with a tiny smile. These six Lords of Waterdeep met regularly, sometimes to plan strategies and share information, but often just to enjoy their friendship.

Again the archmage descended the stairs into the city-beneath-a-city, this time taking a tunnel that led toward the Yawning Portal, the tavern owned by his friend Durnan. Khelben quickly made his way through a labyrinth of doors and passages and ladders that led him into the secret back room of the tavern.

The gathering of Lords was small and somber tonight. Mirt, Durnan, and Kitten were waiting behind untouched mugs. Brian the Swordmaster arrived on Khelben's heels.

The archmage broke the news. Mirt listened in silence, then nodded and rose to him feet.

"Well, I'm off, then," he said simply.

Durnan grasped his friend's plump wrist. "Give me an hour to see to the tavern, lad. A lot of years have been washed downstream, but I'd be proud to ride with you again."

The retired mercenary shook his head, declining the offer of his friend and former comrade-in-arms. "Stay, Durnan, and see you to the city. There are too few of us left." With those words, Mirt disappeared down the ladder with an agility astonishing for a man of his size and years.

Mirt's words seemed to echo in the room. "He's right, you know," Kitten pointed out. "First Larissa. Now Mirt is called away. Texter is off riding again, and only the gods know where Sammer is." She took a swig of her ale and grimaced. "Though they can hold their peace as far as that one's concerned."

Durnan nodded in agreement. The traveling merchant Sammereza Salphontis brought valuable information from the surrounding kingdoms, but he was not well liked by his fellow Lords.

"Got more bad news," Brian said. "During the past ten-day, I've got near to thirty orders for scimitars."

"So business is good," Kitten observed, examining her formidable manicure. Although she usually appeared in public looking as tousled and unlaced as if she'd just risen from her bed—or, more to the point, someone else's—this evening she was as elegantly coifed and gowned as any Waterdhavian noblewoman. "What's your point?"

The Swordmaster produced a small curved knife from his leather pouch and slapped it down on the table in front of her. "Ever seen one of these?"

Kitten picked it up and examined it, frowning in puzzlement at the dozens of tiny marks carved into the blade. "Looks like someone's keeping score on this thing."

"That's precisely right," Khelben said, taking the knife from her hands, his face set in tight, grim lines. "Southern assassins often use such knives. The more marks, the more illustrious the career. How did you get this, Brian?"

The man shrugged. "Got me a new apprentice. The boy needed work. He can't swing a hammer worth a tin coin just yet, but he can pick pockets quicker'n a halfling. The man he lifted this off ordered six of those scimitars."

"Which are favored weapons in the southern lands," Khelben added wearily. "So we may have an influx of southern assassins. Someone should tell Piergeiron at once; he's the usual target."

Kitten chugged the rest of her ale, then rose to her feet with a rustle of brocade and lace. "I'll go; I dressed for the palace, since I planned to look in on Larissa." She disappeared through one of the room's four doors.

"That's it for tonight, then," the archmage said, rising from his chair.

"Before you go, Khelben, there's something you ought to hear," Durnan said. The innkeeper opened the door that led into the tavern's storeroom. Khelben and Brian exchanged puzzled glances, but followed him. They made their way past barrels and neatly stacked crates to the taproom. Durnan cracked open the door and beckoned the men closer.

"I say it be truth!" argued one drunken voice from beyond the door.

"Nay, how could it? That'd make the wizard more long-lived than a dragon," countered a second man.

"It's true, all right," stated a petulant female voice, "and Danilo ought to know. He's kin to Khelben, and he loves family history. He tells the most amusingly ribald story, don't you know, about his great aunt Clarinda Thann—"

"Shut up, Myrna." Galinda Raventree's distinctive husky voice was unusually sharp as she silenced her rival. "Khelben is always chastising Dan for those cute, harmless little spells, and this song is just Dan's way of tweaking the old man's beard."

"Well said, miss," agreed a rumbling voice with a touch of Cormyrian burr. "The young bard tells a good story, I'll grant you, but the song is nothing more or less than that."

"Let's have it again!" demanded another.

The sounds of a lute stilled the debate, and after a few rippling notes a woman began to sing in a deep, raw voice that was uniquely seductive and feminine. Khelben recognized the dark voice as that of the Masked Minstrel, a mysterious woman who wandered the Castle Ward, often giving open-air concerts in Jester's Court of a nice summer's eve. Her name and origin were matters of heated speculation in the city: she was variously thought to be a mad noblewoman, a Zhentish spy, or a Harper agent. Whatever else she might be, her song left no doubt in Khelben's mind that she had succumbed to the curse upon the bards.

In the Year of the Tomb a magical flight
Took the sage to a land where the shadows held
*   sway.*
And the Malaugrym, armed with their shapeshifting
*   might*

Followed him back to the light of the day.
The Harpers gathered to force the beasts back,
Using magic, and steel, and a staff strong and black."

Durnan probed Khelben's ribs with an elbow. "They say your nephew wrote that song, but I can't believe it of the lad. It has a lot to say about you, and Elminster as well, and it puts you both back some two hundred years. Who would do such a thing?"

"I wish I knew," Khelben muttered, gesturing for silence so that he might hear the words. The verses that followed were not reassuring. The song was indeed based on one of Danilo's, and the incident it referred to was the Harpstar Wars, a dark time that had occurred more that two centuries past. Khelben had seen to it that Danilo was versed in Harper history and lore, but the song Danilo had written was no more than veiled allegory; the words of *this* ballad went on to describe the battles, name many of the Harpers who'd fallen in the war, and warn of the continuing threat offered by the few shapeshifting Malaugrym that survived. Whoever had changed the words might well have been there, Khelben noted with a growing sense of dread.

The archmage searched his memory for the names of the Harpers who had survived those times, and those who might still live. Perhaps one survivor of that long-ago war had turned away from the Harpers' path, becoming so twisted that he or she outlived death as a lich. That would explain much, for an extremely powerful undead wizard might be able to command a spell that could change the minds and memories of the bards.

The ballad raised another concern as well. Khelben had done all he reasonably could to suppress the ballad about Laeral's misadventure with an evil artifact, but the song was everywhere, spreading speculation and distrust. There were many other things in Khelben's life that were best left untold, yet someone seemed determined to air them. Although Khelben's parentage was a matter of record and his genealogy open to all who cared to inquire, his history had in fact been borrowed from another. Few knew his true age, or the secrets of his past, or the extent of his power. In truth, Khelben controlled the affairs of Waterdeep much less than he was capable of doing, but few would believe this if all his secrets came to light.

The final stanza of the Masked Minstrel's ballad took Khelben's troubled thoughts and put them to music:

"Like a milkweed pod whose seeds wander far
On the breath of the wind, or the arms of the sea,
Magic can't be recalled once the gate is ajar,
And the pod can't be mended once all the seeds flee.
So beware of all those who could open such doors
And bring Hellgate Keep to our deepwater shores."

The tavern fell into deep, ominous silence. History and legend were full of tales that admonished vigilance against magic grown too proud and powerful, and the final line of the ballad contained a common watchword for disaster. All knew the story of Hellgate Keep, and the ambitious wizards who opened a door into the Abyss. Fiends, imps, and other fell denizens flooded into the light, destroying a kingdom and remaining even to this day, attacking travelers and waging occasional war on Silverymoon. The danger of powerful magic gone awry was real, the possibility soberingly close to home.

"It's true, I tell you," Myrna insisted. This time, no one contradicted her.

Durnan laid a hand on Khelben's shoulder. "If I were you, old friend, I'd be sure to leave by the back door."

* * * * *

Wyn Ashgrove continued singing the adventurers to safety until the causeway was far behind them and the first stars winked into light. Danilo was the first to break the awed silence.

"That was remarkable, whatever it was. Whatever was it?"

"Spellsong," Elaith whispered at his elbow. For once, the moon elf's silky composure seemed shaken, and he gazed at the minstrel with naked awe. "A rare elven magic that can charm any creature that draws breath. I see now why you dare to hunt dragons with an army of three! Few among the elves have such a gift, and never have I seen a feat to rival this one."

Danilo rode closer to Wyn and asked, "Can the art of spellsong magic be taught?"

"As in any other sort of magic, a certain aptitude is required," the elf replied. "Likewise, just as in all magic, spellsong is learned through practice and study."

Danilo nodded, taking this in. "So you're saying that humans could learn it, too?"

"No, he isn't!" Elaith snapped, his head held at a haughty angle. He drew a deep breath as if to say more, but his offended expression froze, then disappeared behind an expressionless mask. The moon elf wheeled his horse aside and rode hard toward the banks of the river. He stopped at a level clearing and called for the others to set up camp.

Strangely enough, Danilo understood Elaith's response. The elven distrust of humans and the desire to keep their culture intact and separate had been trained into him. Elaith Craulnober was the last of an ancient noble family, born on Evermeet and raised as a member of the royal court. Wyn's magic reminded Elaith what he was, and also mocked him for what he was not. Danilo understood, but he firmly believed that he could learn the elfsong magic, with no loss to the elves.

He turned to Wyn, who had been riding silently beside him. The gold elf slumped in his saddle, exhausted by the powerful spell he had cast. "I would like to learn more about such music," Danilo said wistfully. "Would you be willing to teach me?"

The minstrel did not answer for a long moment, so Danilo prodded. "I trust that you don't harbor the same hostilities and beliefs as our friend," he said, nodding toward Elaith, who was already directing the mercenaries at the work of building a circle of campfires to cook the evening meal and to ward off predators. The scene was one of busy cooperation. Morgalla worked beside Balindar, chips of firewood flying from her small axe.

"The hostilities, no," said Wyn quietly. "Please excuse me."

With these words, the elven minstrel slipped from his horse and walked toward the workers, calling out to Morgalla in a friendly tone. The dwarf paused in her labor and glanced up, suspicion etched on her broad features.

Left alone, Danilo blinked with openmouthed astonishment. Wyn had been nothing but courteous since their first meeting, but the meaning of his actions was startlingly clear. Given the choice of teaching elven magic to a human, or suffering—indeed, seeking out!—the company of a dwarf he had hitherto avoided, the minstrel did not need long to consider.

"Well, it's nice to be back on familiar terrain," Danilo said wryly to himself as he swung down from the saddle. "All that popularity, respect, and acclaim back in Waterdeep was starting to make me nervous."

Six

By the time the evening meal sizzled on the fire, the dangers of the marshlands seemed far away, eclipsed, perhaps, by the enormity of the task that lay ahead. As fearsome as the amphibious pipers had been, dragons were the most powerful creatures in the land, and green dragons were both evil and unpredictable. Perhaps in defiance of the danger that awaited them, the members of Music and Mayhem seemed determined that the night before the confrontation would be a celebration.

Fresh-caught fish sizzled on the fire, seasoned with herbs from Danilo's magic bag—"Never travel without certain amenities," he'd advised Yando, the group's cook—and the truffles that Vartain had located under a stand of young oaks had been added to the rice steaming in a travel kettle. As the travelers ate, Wyn sang songs he had gathered from years of travels among the Northmen, the Ffolk of the Moonshaes, and from a dozen lands of Faerun.

Morgalla sat on a log placed a few feet from the fire,

munching trail bread and fish as she listened to Wyn sing. Indeed, all seemed to be drawn by the elf's songs. As Danilo watched the circle of mercenaries, a suspicion entered his mind. Since Wyn was capable of charming the froglike monsters, what effect might his music have on people? Could the power of the elf's music bend them all to his will?

Wiping his fingers on a handkerchief, Danilo withdrew to the shadows beyond the circle of small fires that ringed the encampment. As much as he disliked his suspicions, he had to be sure that Wyn's magical ability was not endangering his mission. He began to cast a cantrip, a simple spell that would detect the use of magic.

Wyn stopped playing, and his keen night vision pierced the shadows that hid the mage. "The instrument is magical, the song is not," he said evenly. The elf rose and held out the silvery instrument. "Come. Try it yourself. This is a lyre of changing, and upon command it will take the form of any other instrument of its size, or smaller. But please, not bagpipes," he said with a tiny smile.

"That goes without saying," Danilo agreed as he came back over to the circle. He took the lyre with interest; he had heard of such instruments but had never handled one. "A rebec, please," he said, and the lyre immediately became a long, pear-shaped instrument that vaguely resembled a lute, but was played like a fiddle with a horsehair bow. Danilo spoke again, and the rebec became the most unusual lap harp he had ever seen. The instrument was the pale color of driftwood, and the wood had been intricately carved with tiny seascapes, complete with ships, mermaids, and wheeling gulls. Impressed, Danilo handed back the magic instrument.

"I am especially fond of the harp's music, but I cannot play," Wyn said wistfully, pressing the harp back into Danilo's hands. "Would you do the honors?"

"By all means," Elaith put in smoothly, his lips curved in an urbane smile. "A small task, for one who claims to be a Harper and aspires to confrontations with legendary dragons."

"Speaking o' legends, elf, I heared yer name a few times," Morgalla observed pleasantly. She jabbed at a bit of fish with a wicked-looking hunting knife. " 'Cept yer always called a snake in the tales. Why is that, do you suppose?"

"Serpent," Vartain corrected. "Named for his grace in battle and speed of strike."

"If'n it slithers, it's all the same to me," the dwarf said with a shrug.

"In answer to your question, Wyn," Danilo put in hastily, "the harp was my first instrument, although it's been years since I last played. My first teacher was a bard trained in the style of the MacFuirmidh school. He was adamant that the old songs had to be sung to the original instrument of composition."

Danilo tried the strings and found that the memory of the music was still in his fingers. After a moment's thought, he began the introduction to a dwarven ballad, an old song taught to him by a bard visiting from Utrumm's Conservatory in Silverymoon. It was a sad but dignified lament for a people and a way of life that was slowly fading from the land.

To Danilo's surprise, Wyn Ashgrove began to sing the dwarven song with genuine feeling. After a moment, Morgalla also joined in, singing harmony in a rich alto. The deep tones of the dwarf's voice encompassed about the same range as Wyn's soaring countertenor, and the two voices blended as well as any duo Danilo had ever heard. As he played, the Harper listened with awe to the singers. In the elf's silvery tones was the beauty of the sea and stars, while the rich, feminine strength of Morgalla's voice seemed to spring from the earth and the stone: opposites, perhaps, but together forming a whole.

The last notes of the harp faded away, leaving an invisible bond between the two singers that neither had considered. Their gazes clung for a moment, then slid away, a little self-conscious. Morgalla took a deep breath and raised her eyes to Danilo. Her expression was defiant, quickly becoming bewildered as the circle broke into applause.

"Beauty, brawn, *and* talent!" Balindar whooped, raising his tin traveling cup to the dwarf in a salute.

"Morgalla, my dear, your voice is remarkable," Danilo told her. She shrugged and looked away.

Wyn reclaimed his instrument from the Harper and held it out to the dwarf. "Do you play as well as sing?"

She snorted and held out her stubby-fingered hands for inspection. "With these?"

"There are instruments—even stringed instruments— that would suit you well," Wyn told her. "Have you never heard of a hammered dulcimer?"

"Hammers, you say?" The dwarf looked interested despite herself.

The elf smiled faintly. "More like spoons than hammers, and wielded with more delicacy than one would employ at a forge, but the idea is the same. Let me show you."

A word from the elf changed the lap harp into a small wooden box, wider at one end than the other and crisscrossed with strings. Wyn took two small beaters and began to tap the strings, showing Morgalla how the notes were arranged and then playing a snatch of the melody that they had just shared.

"Now you," Wyn said, and handed her the beaters.

The dwarf began to play, hesitantly at first but with growing delight as she picked out one tune after another. The instrument was uniquely suited to her, combining the dwarven love of percussion instruments with Morgalla's craving for melody. The tiny beaters fit in her hands as if made to order.

Danilo listened to Morgalla's music with pleasure and more than a little guilt. The dwarf had come to him wanting to learn more of bardcraft, and he'd done little to fulfill her expectations or to earn her loyalty. Granted, he'd invited her to sing a couple of times, but he was quick to accept her refusal and too preoccupied to wonder what might be behind her hesitation. Wyn Ashgrove had proven to be more perceptive and thoughtful, and Danilo was grateful to the gold elf.

Dan leaned closer to Wyn and murmured, "That was kindly done. You seem to have made a conquest."

The elf let the teasing remark pass. "Morgalla's love of music was plain to see; her talent you can judge for yourself. She needed but the means and a little encouragement. As for the others"—Wyn nodded toward the mercenaries—"this music will help keep their minds from the dangers ahead."

Morgalla finally stopped, heaving a sigh of deep satisfaction. So absorbed in the music had she been that she'd forgotten about the others, and at the applause she looked up, flushed and flustered.

"Take a bow," Danilo advised her, smiling. "Surely one with your gifts knows how to acknowledge an appreciative audience."

"It's been awhile," the dwarf said wryly. "You play, bard."

Sensing it best not to push her, Danilo got out his lute and regaled the adventurers with a ribald tale about a priestess of Sune—the goddess of love and beauty—who aspired to become the most infamous and popular hostess in Faerun. The priestess was well satisfied with her success until a visiting ranger, unimpressed by her wild party, advised her to seek out the satyrs and take a few lessons on debauchery. She did so on a Midsummer night, and the rest of the song told about the competition of priestess and satyrs to outdo each other in merriment. It was, without doubt, the most obscene song in Dan's considerable repertoire of off-color tales.

After the laughter and bawdy comments had died away, Danilo played a very different ballad. This was a historical tale about a long-ago battle between the Harpers and a drow elf queen who enslaved humans to work her mines. He sang the old song as it had been passed down in to him in strict bardic tradition, and doing so was an act of defiance against the power that had enspelled the bards and altered their record of the past. Wyn nodded slowly, understanding the Harper's gesture and approving.

When the tale was told, Danilo put aside the lute and motioned for Vartain, who sat just beyond the circle of firelight, gnawing at a bit of dried meat. "Your turn, riddlemaster. Give us a story."

Vartain wiped his fingers on his tunic and came into the circle. His bald pate reflected the firelight like some small, bronze moon, and the play of light and shadows across his face exaggerated the gaunt angles and prominent features. Morgalla nudged Danilo and handed him a scrap of paper. Sometime during the trip, she'd sketched Vartain as a potbellied vulture. Danilo swallowed a chuckle.

"There is an ancient tale from my homeland," Vartain began in a rich, carefully modulated bass voice, "about a wealthy man who was blessed with two sons. As do we all, the man grew old, and he knew his time was short. He called his sons to him, saying he could not decide which of them would be his heir. This they would determine by a race. The sons were to set forth the next morning for Kaddisht, a town some twenty miles away. The son whose camel was the *last* to arrive would be accounted his father's heir.

"When the sun arose, it found the two men ready for the race, dressed for travel and mounted upon their best camels. Their father gave them his blessing and wished them well, and the race was on. Each son employed every method he could think of to remain behind the other, while the beasts grew restless and the sun sank low behind the dessert. By the end of the day, the two men had gone less than a hundred paces!

"Deeply troubled, the two brothers took shelter at an inn. There they shared wine and discussed their troubles. Each man was wealthy by his own labors, and each had business affairs and families to tend. The task their father had given them had no clear end in sight. In pursuing their inheritance, the men were in very real danger of perishing in the desert that lay between the inn and the town of Kaddisht. The men told the innkeeper their dilemma. After a moment's thought, the innkeeper gave them two words of advice.

"The next morning the brothers again set forth for Kaddisht, but this time they rode as fast as they could. Tell me, then, what advice did the innkeeper give them?"

There was a long silence around the campfire as the companions thought this over. One after another, they shrugged their defeat.

"The two words where these: *Change camels*," Vartain said. "The father specified that the son whose *camel* arrived last would become heir. Therefore, whoever won the race would now win the fortune as well."

"Good tale," Mange admitted. The scrawny mercenary took a swig from a tin flask and then wiped the back of his hand across his mouth. "Me, I've always liked riddles. Second best way to pass the time of a cold winter night!"

"Riddles are far more than that," Vartain countered severely. "In ancient times, battles were fought through riddle challenges, and heirs to kingdoms selected. Magic can be cast through the giving or the solving of riddles." His cleared his throat, and continued in a pedantic tone. "There are many types of riddles, conundrums, puzzles, and mysteries. All of these challenge the mind, develop the character, and train one to observe keenly and to think with clarity and precision."

"Here's a good one," Mange continued as if Vartain had not spoken at all. "How many halflings can a troll eat on an empty stomach?" He punctuated the question with a resounding belch.

Several guesses ensued, and Mange shook his head at each. Finally he turned to Vartain with a smug grin. "You wanna take a stab, riddlemaster?"

Vartain lifted his beaky nose. "Base jests have nothing to do with a riddlemaster's art."

"One!" Mange answered gleefully. "A troll can eat *one* halfling on an empty stomach. After the first, his stomach ain't empty!"

"I got a good one!" put in Orcsarmor, a thin archer named for the rusty hue of his graying whiskers. "Whaddaya call a contest between two wizards?"

"That one, I know," Danilo said. "A *spelling* bee."

Every member of the circle groaned, and several of the men pelted the would-be riddler with travel biscuits. Orcsarmor ducked the good-natured missiles and grinned.

Vartain looked far less happy. "If you'll excuse me, I believe I shall retire," he said in a stony voice. The riddlemaster stalked over to his bedroll and lay down, his back to the revelers.

"*Retire*, eh? He don't take competition real well," Morgalla quipped. The mercenaries guffawed, all too happy to share a laugh at the riddlemaster's expense.

"Time for a song," Danilo said to Wyn, nodding toward Vartain's rigid back. As intelligent as the riddlemaster was, he seemed to have no idea how he was perceived by others. This, Danilo mused, was definitely not the time to enlighten him. Perhaps he would speak to Vartain about it someday, but the riddlemaster needed all his confidence and concentration focused for the challenge ahead.

So the minstrel took his lyre and sang an air about the elven homeland, an island of beauty and magic and peace. During the first part of the song, Elaith leaned against a tree at the edge of the encampment, with practiced ease twirling a small jeweled knife through and around his fingers. As Wyn sang on, the moon elf's angular face softened, taking on an almost wistful expression. At the song's end, Elaith came into the circle of firelight.

"I notice you carry a crystal flute, of the sort that is grown in the caves of Evermeet's wild elves," he said quietly, pointing to the translucent green flute that hung from the minstrel's belt. "Do you, by chance, know any of the sword dances famous on the north shore of the island? *The Ghost of Elmtree*, perhaps?"

In response, Wyn took the gemlike flute from its protective bag and played a few notes. "Yes, that's the one," Elaith said, pleased.

The elf turned to his men. "I'll need your swords. Dirks and daggers as well, if you please."

Puzzled, the mercenaries handed over their weapons.

"Considering the company I'm keeping these days, I prefer to keep both of my swords within reach," Danilo said cheerfully. "If it's all the same to you."

"By all means," Elaith returned just as pleasantly. "Much good may they do you, of course."

Morgalla's brown eyes narrowed at the insult to Danilo. "That elf is startin' to wear a hole in the sole of my boot," she muttered, watching as Elaith arranged the weapons in an intricate pattern of crosses and circles.

When that was done, he nodded to the elven minstrel

and took his place in the center of the design. Wyn began to play a slow, lyrical tune. The moon elf went into the dance, stepping lightly between the crossed swords, alternating heel and toe.

As Danilo admired the elf's fluid grace, he noted that Elaith had not added one of his own weapons to the arrangement. As did Danilo, the elf wore a sword at each hip. Something about Elaith's second blade was familiar.

The Harper's eyes narrowed as he realized the nature of the weapon worn by the rogue elf. It was a moonblade, an ancient elven sword that was passed from one generation to the next. A moonblade could judge character, and it would become dormant rather than trust its magic to an unworthy heir. Danilo had known that Elaith owned such a sword, and that the sword's rejection of the elf had been the seed that bore fruit in a life of treachery and evil. Why would the elf wear it now?

Danilo puzzled over this question as the music moved faster and faster. A strange mixture of elegance and menace, the elven dance was compelling to watch. The moon elf's pale face was rapt and intent as he whirled and leaped in time to the crystal flute's song. His silver hair glinted in the firelight, and he himself seemed transformed into a beautiful and deadly weapon. Then the elf flicked one booted foot, sending a dagger high into the air. It spiraled down like a falling star, catching the firelight as it tumbled. Effortlessly he caught it and sent it spinning upward again. The pace became more frenzied now, and one by one Elaith kicked the weapons into flight. Leaping and ducking, he avoided the falling blades, catching some and allowing others to land in an ever-shifting pattern before sending them up again with a deft flick of wrist or boot. It was an amazing display of artistry and agility, and Danilo found himself watching with bated breath and rapid heart. Elaith was as sinuous and graceful as the serpent for which he was named, and as quick.

The flute soared to a final, lingering note, and the dance stopped. Elaith stood in a perfect circle of blades, his arms raised to the stars, his silver hair gleaming and his angular face suffused with ecstasy. Magic lingered about the elf, and every blade seemed to gleam with an intensity that the fading firelight could not explain. With uncanny certainty, Danilo knew that the elf's dance held the power of rite. Elaith himself was a conduit for some mystical link between stars and steel. The insight flickered in his mind, gone before he could grasp and examine it. Danilo realized afresh how little he understood of the elves. With the knowledge came a stab of sadness and a longing he could not name.

The company released its collective breath in a sigh of awe and relief. Hushed conversations sprang up between small groups, and no one made a move to reclaim his weapons. It was plain that no one else would perform this night.

Elaith walked from the circle, his chest rising and falling quickly from the effort of his mystical elven dance. He picked up a waterskin and shook it. It was nearly empty. The elf drained it and looked around for another.

Danilo reached into his bag and removed a small silver flask. "Elverquisst," he said quietly, and handed it to the elf. Elaith looked sharply at the Harper, as if wondering how well the human understood his own gesture. The rare elven spirits formed a part of many an elven ritual and celebration, and the offer of it now, after the elven dance, was a tribute as well as a gift. This Danilo had learned from Arilyn, for she had shared with him the ritual farewell to summer and described some of the other rites that made the elverquisst a celebration as well as a libation. Elaith accepted the flask with a nod. He poured a few drops onto the earth and then drank slowly, savoring the distilled essence of summer fruit and elven magic.

"Fancy footwork, elf," Morgalla complimented him.

The dwarf's words seemed to pop the aura of content-
ment and mystery that surrounded the moon elf. He sat
down across from Morgalla and studied her as one would
a strange animal that had mysteriously appeared in one's
back yard.

"How does it happen that you venture so far from clan
and hearth?" he asked. "With your numbers dwindling
and dwarven females so few, I would think you'd be home
doing your duty by breeding little miners."

"Have a care how you speak," Danilo said in a low voice.
"The lady dwarf is not some dairy animal."

Morgalla leveled her brown eyes at Elaith. "Elves don't
seem to be doing so good in that regard, neither. Lotta
half-elves around, but I notice most of 'em got elf dames
and human sires. Ain't nothing wrong with your women,
that much we know." Something flickered in Elaith's eyes
in response to the insult, and the battle-savvy dwarf saw
this and went in for the kill. "Yer a fine one to talk. I don't
see no pointy-eared brats followin' you around."

"Actually," Elaith said mildly, "the People keep their children away from dwarves and goblins until such time as
they learn to tell these creatures apart. Elves being a
highly intelligent race, we're able to discern these minor
differences after, say, twenty or thirty years of practice."

Morgalla rose slowly to her feet. Firelight gleamed off
the two-edged blade and polished wood handle of the axe
prominently displayed on her belt. "Yer pushin' me, elf,
and you shouldn't ought to do that. We who mine the earth
have a saying: 'Be careful what you take for granite.'"

"Or ye shale regret it," Danilo murmured, hoping to
break the tension building between the two fighters. Neither Morgalla nor Elaith paid him any heed.

"Very pretty," Elaith said, nodding at Morgalla's axe. His

tone dismissed both the weapon and the wielder.

The dwarf's eyes hardened. "First *and* last pretty thing a lot o' orcs ever seed, if'n you get my meaning."

"Actually, I find that dwarven subtlety usually eludes me," the elf returned with knife-edged sarcasm.

Danilo dropped a hand on the angry woman's shoulder. "Chopping the elf into fish bait is a tempting notion—I'd be the first to admit that. Here's a better idea: draw his picture, instead."

Morgalla nodded slowly, staring at Elaith for a long moment. A glint entered her brown eyes, and she reached for her other weapon: her charcoal pencils. The dwarf plunked herself down on a log several paces away and began to sketch.

"Becoming quite the diplomat, aren't you?" Elaith said coldly. "If you're waiting for me to thank you for diverting a fight, you're in for a long, quiet evening. I need no protection from a mere dwarf."

Danilo's answering smile held a touch of irony. "Morgalla is more than mere, but we'll let that slide for the moment. Your fighting prowess is legendary; I have too much regard for you to see you waste your talents against such an unworthy weapon as Morgalla's axe." After a few moments, the Harper walked over to Morgalla and extended his hand. She gave him the paper.

On it was a quickly sketched design that suggested the art of an ancient Moonshae people, in which circles were entwined in such a way that no beginning or end could be discerned. Morgalla's design, however, was different from any Dan had ever seen in an illuminated text. Intrinsically woven together in interlocking circles were two things: a long, slender serpent with elven ears and Elaith's features, and a lifeless, flaccid sword with a dull moonstone in its hilt.

The Harper lifted his eyes from the paper, gazing at the

dwarf in pure astonishment. Once again, she had seen more than her eyes could possibly have told her. Danilo handed the sketch to Elaith without comment.

The elf regarded it in silence, his expressionless face as pale as death.

"As you can see," Dan said quietly, "her art has a keener edge than her axe."

"Eh?" piped in Morgalla, clearly miffed at the suggestion. She pulled the maligned weapon from her belt and brandished it. "You could *shave* with this axe, bard!"

In response, Danilo stroked the nearly invisible red down on her cheek. "So could you, lady dwarf, so could you."

"Hee, hee," she chortled, as pleased as any adolescent human lad contemplating his first beard.

In the shared laughter that rippled through the company, no one but Danilo noticed Elaith slip away from the campfire. Although the Harper had won this round, his gray eyes held not triumph, but puzzlement.

* * * * *

Stars sprinkled the sky above Lady Thione's villa, and in the fully enclosed courtyard, rare, night-blooming flowers scented the warm summer night. A fountain played softly in the center of the courtyard, the secluded arch of a grape arbor suggested a stolen kiss, and the soft-pillowed gazebo invited longer trysts. The music of a harp filled the air. Yet the woman bent over the strings had no room in her heart for romance. The one passion left to her was for justice.

Pain cramped her hands, and Garnet broke off the song with a frustrated oath. Since the day she had acquired the Morninglark harp from the dragon, she had struggled to harness its powers. She was an accomplished mage, and she could wield magic through both spells and song. An

artifact such as the elven harp possessed much magic of
its own, and she had devised a spell that would grant her
up to seven powers. So far, she had been able to gain only
four, and those four she wielded with uncertainty. The fault
was not in her sorcery, but in her faded musicianship.

Once again she cursed the Harpers for what they had
become, for what she had become in their service, and
Khelben Arunsun for his part in both. No longer were the
Heralds, the far-traveling keepers of history and tradition,
part of the Harper organization. They had split away many
years ago, not wishing to compromise their neutrality by
pursuing the Harpers' increasingly political objectives.
Then the barding colleges, once bastions of excellence,
had fallen into decline and faded into memory. The
Harpers had done little to reverse this course. They were
kept busy by Elminster and Khelben, fighting wars and
guarding trade routes.

Yes, many Harpers were bards still, but these bards
were for the most part fighters and informants who happened to play or sing. The once-honored title of "bard" was
given to any dolt who could warble a tavern song. The
prestige and power of bardcraft had declined, and many
people considered bards to be little more than traveling
rogues. Bards, once counselors to kings and queens, were
likely to be treated like servants who took their dinner in
the kitchen between dance sets. This Garnet could not forgive.

Nor could she forget it, not when her own hands had
been stiffened by years of fighting and spellcasting in the
name of the Harpers. Her final battle for the Harpers had
been in the Harpstar Wars against creatures from another
plane. Gravely wounded and left for dead in the confusion
of battle, she'd been found and nursed to health by an
elderly druid. When Garnet recovered and began once
again to sing and play, the druid recognized her gift for

spellsong and introduced her to a small band of wood elves. Even though she was a half-elf, the forest elves had taken her in and trained her gift. For almost two hundred years Garnet had lived among them, and as her power increased, so did her determination to prove to the Harpers that music was not a force to be lightly regarded.

The whisper of silk interrupted the sorceress's dark thoughts. Garnet looked up. Lady Thione was poised in the arch of a trellis. This evening the noblewoman was clad in a gown of clinging violet silk, covered with an overdress of quilted satin. Her hair was bound with a velvet snood, and her delicate aquiline features were composed and self-satisfied.

"How does the city?" Garnet demanded, massaging her aching hands.

"Poorly, thanks to you," Lucia Thione responded cheerfully. "Your musically inclined monsters have been preying on farmerfolk and travelers. The merchants' guilds have hired mercenary bands to go out against these monsters, as have the Lords of Waterdeep. Even with these precautions, a smaller crowd is expected for the Midsummer Faire. This is matter of much speculation and discontent among the tradespeople and merchants. The crop failures have created a hardship, but for those who can afford the high prices, produce and goods are coming in by sea."

"A *hardship*?" the half-elf repeated. "What then would constitute a catastrophe?"

Lucia hesitated. "A disruption of commerce."

"Ah, Waterdeep." Garnet's smile was hard. "Well then, see to it."

"Have a care how you speak," the noblewoman said in a tight voice. "I do not take orders like some serving wench."

"Of course you do. You serve the Knights of the Shield, and they have assured me that you will cooperate in my plan to remove Khelben Arunsun from power."

"So you have said. How do I know this to be true?" Lucia demanded.

Garnet spoke a name, and the woman paled. The sorceress had named a Knight of high position and dark power, the man to whom Lucia herself reported. "He sends his regards," Garnet added casually.

"We will increase our activities against the city," she continued. "I have some influence with the local merfolk—you'd be amazed at how much music and discontent lies under the sea. We will also remove more of the Lords of Waterdeep to increase the demands on Khelben Arunsun and his powerful associates. Give Lord Hhune the names of three lesser-known Lords. Although Hhune's methods are crude, he has the resources needed to handle the matter quickly."

"Hhune is still in the city?" Lucia asked, unable to keep the concern from her voice. Hhune made no secret of his ambition, and nothing would please the Tethyrian merchant more than taking Lucia's place in Waterdeep.

Garnet shot a sidelong glance at the noblewoman. "What of it? Your superior said I might use any resources at his command. Hhune is a guildmaster in his native land, and he is adept at organizing and recruiting. I have him trying to establish local guilds for Waterdeep's thieves and assassins. He is unlikely to succeed, but it gives the Lords of Waterdeep one more thing to worry about. Now, which Lords' names are you giving to Hhune?"

Without hesitation, Lucia Thione named three business rivals, not knowing or caring whether any of them sat among the Lords of Waterdeep.

"Good." Garnet nodded with satisfaction and rose from her seat. Her horse came cantering from a remote corner of Lucia's garden, in response to a summons the noblewoman could not hear. The sorceress secured her harp to the saddle and hoisted herself onto the horse's back. "I must travel north for a few days. There I will gain an additional power to use against Khelben Arunsun, and on the way I shall dispatch another of Waterdeep's Lords. I leave the city in your capable hands, and expect to find all in order upon my return."

Lucia caught her breath as the white steed rose straight into the sky. Like a tiny comet, it streaked away toward the north. "An asperii," she whispered, realizing anew the extent of the sorceress's power. Suddenly Garnet's last words to her seemed less a compliment than a warning.

* * * * *

The cookfire burned low, and one by one the members of Music and Mayhem drew away from the central fire, wrapping themselves in cloaks or travel blankets. Soon the only sounds were the crackle of the outer fires, the distant chirping of insects, and the rustle of leaves as Orcsarmor climbed a nearby oak to take first watch. Morgalla, also on watch, slipped off into the shadows.

Left alone, Danilo idly tossed acorn caps into the dying fire, trying not to remember other nights spent under the stars, his only companion a stubborn, unreasonable, taciturn half-elven assassin. Those, he mused with a wistful smile, were the best times he'd ever known.

Never had the young man felt so alone as he did at this moment, surrounded as he was by snoring mercenaries. For the first time, he understood Khelben's concern over the close partnership Danilo and Arilyn had forged. One way or another, Harpers usually ended up working alone.

With a sigh, Danilo reached into the bag of holding at his belt and rummaged around for the spellbook his uncle had prepared for him. If all went as planned, they would face the dragon Grimnoshtadrano the following afternoon, and he wanted to be as prepared as possible. A green dragon's breath weapon was a cloud of noxious gas. He hoped Khelben had armed him with a spell that could create protective spheres.

Actually the book contained but one spell, and it was like none other he'd encountered. Danilo examined it with growing excitement. On the left side was a page of neatly written music: a simple, soaring melody and the basic notation for lute accompaniment. On the right side were a few lines of explanation, then the words to the songs, written in arcane runes. This spell used music as the speech component, and the lute accompaniment formed the necessary hand gestures. The result was a charm spell, very much like the elven spellsong Wyn had used. Beyond its application in the morrow's encounter, the spell fascinated Danilo, for it suggested a way to meld his training in the art of magic to his genuine love for music and lore, and his current role as bard.

Like all his Harper assignments, the task of recovering the dragon's scroll had been placed upon Danilo by his uncle. For more than two years, the young mage had worked closely with Arilyn, enjoying the challenges she offered and the knowledge that their disparate skills combined into a unique whole, but for the most part he had followed her lead and reacted to situations of her choosing. He would always treasure his time with the half-elf, and some part of him would continue to hope that it had not come to an end. For the first time, however, Danilo began to see a path that he might follow on his own, a path of his own devising. If this spell were not unique, perhaps he could learn the elfsong magic that Wyn had wielded!

Danilo rose, taking the spellbook to the far side of the campsite where Wyn Ashgrove sat gazing into the trees and wrapped in his own thoughts. Despite the minstrel's abrupt dismissal of him earlier, Danilo felt he had to pursue the matter of spellsong.

"Elaith said that few elves have your magical skills. Is the aptitude lacking, or are the teachers?"

Wyn looked surprised by the abrupt question, but he thought it over. "I imagine that many more elves possess the ability than are trained. I come from a family of musical scholars, so my talents were recognized early, and the means to develop them were at hand. It may be that others are not so fortunate."

"If such spells could be written down, perhaps many more of your people could learn this art," Danilo argued, tapping the spellbook. He held it out to the elf for inspection. "In this way, magical arts and bardic training could be combined."

"The two types of magic are not compatible," Wyn said firmly, pressing the book back into the Harper's hands. He rose, signaling plainly that the conversation was at an end.

At that moment Morgalla emerged from behind a clump of bushes, brushing bits of leaves off her shoulders with an expression of glum distaste. The dwarf seemed not at all embarrassed to be revealed as an eavesdropper. "Hate to disagree with you, bard, but I'm with the elf. Magic is fine and well for weapons and clerical prayers, but don't go mucking up music with it," she said firmly.

Danilo knew better than to argue with a dwarf, and, since her words brought an unanswered question to mind, he turned to other matters. "Speaking of magical weapons, how did you know what Elaith Craulnober's sword was, that you could draw such a picture?"

Morgalla shrugged. "I heared yer tale of the elfwoman's moonblade, remember? It told how the sword is linked to the elf that wears it." She pointed with her jester's staff to a spot behind Danilo. "If that be true, yon elf's got hisself a problem: he can't use the sword, can't get rid of it."

Danilo spun, finding himself almost face-to-face with Elaith. The elf cast a glance at the open spellbook in the

Harper's hands. "More parlor tricks?" he said disparagingly.

"Preparing for tomorrow," Danilo said quietly. "It might be well to have a plan in case our large green friend chooses not to honor his side of the bargain."

"Just so," Elaith agreed, crossing his arms and rocking back on his heels as if reconsidering the human before him. "You realize, of course, that if your dragon wishes to be found, it will find *you*. Green dragons blend with the forest in more ways than mere appearance. They are difficult to find and nearly impossible to ambush. We can't split up and search for it, for if the dragon were to first encounter a group unable to play this riddle game, the beast might be less kindly disposed to hearing a riddle challenge from another."

Danilo nodded slowly. "What do you suggest?"

"Make the dragon come to you. We'll break camp early and travel north toward the hills. The dragon's lair is there, hidden somewhere in the Endless Caverns. I know a small clearing nearby. Send out a challenge to the thing —sing that damned ballad, perhaps. If the dragon doesn't hear you, the forest is full of creatures that will carry your message fast enough. Ask the dragon for the scroll, as well as something to make the exercise worthwhile to the men. A cask of emeralds would do nicely."

"I should say," murmured Danilo.

"It would be better to meet Grimnoshtadrano with a small group. The dragon might not take kindly to being approached by our entire party."

"I had thought to go alone, but for Vartain."

"You now have a partner to consider," Elaith reminded him. "If you wish to kill yourself, kindly do so on your own time. Yes, Vartain will go to answer the riddle, but you should at least take the minstrel. Spellsong is a powerful weapon."

"Not Wyn," Danilo said firmly. "No elves, absolutely. Green dragons consider you folk a delicacy, and for all we know Grimnoshtadrano might be in the mood for a snack."

"Point taken," the moon elf said grudgingly. "We will hold the spellsinger back, out of sight." His eyes fell on Morgalla, who listened with the mien of one well accustomed to councils of war. "You might take the dwarf with you, though, in case the dragon requires feeding."

"I doubt I could keep her back," Danilo said, noting the battle-gleam in the dwarven warrior's eyes, "and I don't envy anything that might try to eat her."

"You got that right." Morgalla agreed. "But what if the beast don't hold up his side of the bargain?"

"If our large green friend defaults," Danilo responded, "I'll challenge it to a second riddle. The riddle is actually a spell, and it will hold the dragon long enough for us to make an escape."

Elaith looked dubious. "You'd be better off taking the spellsinger."

"Maybe. I'm curious, Wyn," Danilo said casually. "Those marsh pipers were on the small side. Have you ever tried to charm something larger than a tavern wench?"

"A dragon, no," Wyn admitted, a slight twinkle in the green depths of his eyes, "but I did live among the Northmen for a time, and I found their women quite susceptible. Will that do?"

"Close enough," Danilo admitted with a surprised grin. He'd learned from his time with Arilyn that elven humor tended to be dry and subtle; Wyn's remark seemed uncharacteristically bawdy, but the elf's assessment of Northwomen—whose ample charms were much prized by the ambitious and the athletic—was remarkably apt.

"If the spell doesn't work—and frankly, Lord Thann, we've got to consider that as a possibility—I've a powder that ignites the dragon's poisonous gas," Elaith said, holding up a small cylinder. "If the beast opens its mouth in preparation for attack, we toss this inside. The result is like rather like setting an alchemist's shop on fire. The explosion will daze the creature and give us time to be away."

"Who'll get close enough to do the tossing? You got that good an arm, elf?" Morgalla asked.

"Vartain will handle it," Elaith responded. "He is a master of the blowgun."

"Now why am I not surprised," Danilo commented dryly. "That one's got more air than the north wind."

"Indeed," the rogue elf said in rare agreement.

The dwarf responded with a derisive sniff. "When *you* two start singing the same tune, it's past time to get some sleep. Maybe come morning, you'll have come to yer senses and be back to scrapping."

"It is late," Wyn agreed, and the two made their way to the far side of the encampment, leaving Dan and Elaith alone with their uneasy alliance.

"How did you come to have this explosive powder?" the Harper asked cautiously. The elf's path paralleled his own too closely for comfort, and what he knew of Elaith did not inspire peace of mind under any circumstances. "Did you plan to encounter the dragon?"

"No, but my travels took me close to its lair. Vartain felt it was a possibility and suggested I prepare for it," the elf answered in apparent candor.

"Farsighted fellow, isn't he?" Danilo said admiringly, pretending to take the elf's response at face value. "Does he truly live up to his reputation?"

"He's as good as you've heard, and just as annoying," Elaith grumbled. "Never have I seen him wrong, and he doesn't hesitate to herald this fact."

"Modest sort."

"You heard him at the campfire. Vartain is firmly convinced of his superiority and inordinately proud of his traditions."

"Yes," Danilo said in a dry tone. "For a moment, he reminded me of an elf."

Elaith's brows shot up in surprise. "Quite so," he admitted, not without humor.

Since the elf seemed unusually mellow, Danilo decided to press him for information. He wasn't entirely sure whether his motive was to exploit the unexpected camaraderie, or to destroy it.

"Speaking of elves and traditions and so forth, that sword dance was remarkable. During the dance I noticed that you carry your hereditary sword. Since this is not your usual habit, I couldn't help but wonder why you brought the moonblade along."

The cautious truce dissolved instantly. "That is not your concern," Elaith said coldly. He spun away, and with silent grace he disappeared into the darkness.

* * * * *

When night faded to the first silver of morning, Texter the Paladin resumed his solitary journey. Although Texter was devoted to the city of Waterdeep and devout in his duties as one of its secret Lords, he could not long abide within walls. He often rode alone into the wilderness to renew his commitment to Tyr, the god of justice whom he served. The silence cleared his mind and allowed him to reach inside himself for strength, and the austere challenges of the road tested and honed his skills as a knight. His rides also enabled him to serve the city by seeing with his own eyes how things in the Northlands fared.

Conditions north of Waterdeep were every bit as grim as Texter had feared.

From high astride his huge war-horse, the paladin surveyed the ruined fields around him. At this time of year, the second crop of hay should have been more than hock-high, but his horse stood amid stunted sprouts and brambles. This field, lying as it did near the edges of the wilderness, had been planted to fodder, but the same tale could be told of the food crops nearer the safety of the farming villages. For many days, Texter had ridden through scenes of desolation, and he had noticed a peculiar pattern. Crops had been blighted all around the city, but as he rode north the area of damage narrowed. Whatever—or whoever—caused the blight had left a clear and apparently deliberate path.

Leaving the stunted field behind, Texter headed north toward the first scrubby trees that marked the beginning of the forest. As he rode toward the River Dessarin, he noted that even the woodlands had been blighted along this mysterious path. Ferns withered, mosses turned black on fallen logs, and the nearby trees were eerily silent of birds or small game.

A woman's scream rang out from behind a small hill. Texter nudged his horse into a gallop and raced in the direction of the sound. As he urged the horse over the hillock, he saw below both the river and the source of the scream.

Near the riverbank, two gray-green orcs were toying with a young woman. They had laid their weapons aside, and were spinning her from one to the other in a cruel game of catch. Their eyes glowed red with the reflected first rays of sun, and tusklike teeth gleamed in perverse delight at the woman's terror.

Texter drew his sword and charged down the hill. The thunder of the mighty horse's hooves shook the ground, and the startled orcs shoved the woman aside and dove for their weapons. The first orc grabbed its axe and rolled to its feet just in time to meet Texter's first swing. With that one stroke, the paladin decapitated the orc. Its head flew into the river and was swept downstream by the rushing current.

The second orc charged forward over the body of its fallen brother, holding high a spiked mace. Texter's battle-trained steed nimbly sidestepped the downward smash. The paladin delivered a backhanded stroke with the blunt side of his blade, catching the orc on the snout and sending the beast reeling away. Texter's sword cut back, slashing the gray hide of the orc's chest and sending tufts of coarse hair flying. His final thrust found the creature's heart, and the orc crashed backward onto the bloodied ground.

Texter dismounted and strode to where the woman lay, crumpled and sobbing. "Be at ease, lady," he said gently. "You are safe now."

Tears streaming down her cheeks, the woman raised sea-green eyes to his. She was surprisingly young, not more than fifteen winters, and fair despite her tears. The girl had thick brown braids and a sweet face with apple cheeks and a scattering of freckles.

A farm lass, Texter noted, probably from the village near Yartar, but far from home. The reason for her travels lay beside her; a basket was half full of the fiddlehead ferns that grew in the calmer water at the river's edge. These greens were a delicacy, steamed and served with a bit of butter, and all the more needed because of the failed crops.

"I will take you back to your home," Texter offered, holding out his hand. "Galadin is strong and can carry us both with ease."

The girl let the paladin pull her to her feet. "First, I must thank you for saving my life," she said in a voice that was sweet, clear, and remarkably composed. "I regret I have no reward to offer you but a song."

Clasping her hands demurely before her, the girl began
to sing. In her voice was the music of the wind and water,
and the lure of an almost-remembered dream. As she
sang, her form shifted from that of a farm lass to a rare and
magical creature. Before Texter's dazzled eyes, her face
became fair enough to ensnare a man's soul. Abundant
hair the color of kelp flowed over her shoulders, and slender, webbed hands gestured gracefully in time to the
music. Only the color of her eyes remained unchanged:
the vivid sea green of a lorelei.

As Texter listened with rapt attention to the lorelei's
voice, the landscape that surrounded them began to blur,
the shapes and colors melting together like a painting left
in the rain. Soon he was aware of nothing but the enchant-
ing, wordless song, and the soul-deep longing that it
stirred in his breast.

Not realizing he did so, Texter again mounted his horse.
The lorelei beckoned the paladin to follow, and then she
dove into the river. Swimming effortlessly against the fast-
moving stream, she began to head north, singing all the
while.

Entranced by the lorelei's siren song, Texter rode along
the river's edge, unaware that the creature was leading
him ever deeper into the wilderness.

Seven

 The members of Music and Mayhem rose before dawn, and by first light they were well into the High Forest. As they traveled north, the path narrowed until it was completely sheltered by a deep, leafy canopy. On either side grew thick banks of ferns, and the tangle of exposed roots around the ancient trees were shod with velvety moss. From time to time, the road followed near the course of Unicorn Run, whose vivid blue-green waters ran laughing over polished stones. Even the air itself seemed green, for the light filtered through layers of trees and the breeze was scented with the wild mint reputed to be a unicorn's favorite fodder. Danilo scanned the shadows in search of unicorns, but the morning passed without such a blessing. Perhaps, he mused, the magical creatures sensed the danger the travelers courted, and so kept a wise distance.

Danilo did not for a moment forget that the dragon was just one of the hazards of this mission. Although he had slept but little the night before—memorizing the difficult spell had taken him almost until dawn—the Harper kept alert for danger from any quarter.

His moon elf partner was not to be trusted under any circumstances, and the revelation that Elaith carried a moonblade added to Danilo's uncertainty. He could not fathom why Elaith carried a reminder of his failure. Actually, very little about the elf's motives made sense. Danilo could not understand why Elaith would request only a cask of gems from the dragon. The elf had a legendary fondness for magical items, and surely a dragon's hoard would contain something a bit more compelling than jewelry. Danilo added to this conjecture the very real possibility that Elaith would prove treacherous once he had secured whatever it was he sought.

The riders reached a small clearing before highsun and set to work at Elaith's direction. Two of the mercenaries built a campfire, while Orcsarmor, their best archer, shot several of the squirrels who chattered and scampered among the ancient oaks. A pot of over-seasoned stew was soon simmering, and the firewood doused with water and strewn with herbs so that the scented smoke might confuse the dragon's keen nose. This precaution, Elaith explained, was to ensure that no sign of his or Wyn's presence lingered in the clearing. Since elves were a favorite meal of green dragons, the wyrms were particularly adept at scenting and tracking them, and the urge to do just that might distract the dragon from the riddle challenge. The elf then sent the mercenaries down a narrow path lined with young birch, through a section of forest that Elaith claimed was too densely grown to allow passage to a full-grown dragon. To Danilo's surprise, Elaith gave the lead reins of his black stallion to Mange, and ordered Orcsarmor to take Wyn and Balindar's horses, as well.

"We three will remain nearby," Elaith announced,

"Balindar and me to protect my interests, and the minstrel to provide spellsong magic if the need arises."

Danilo faced down the elf, his gray eyes cold. "That's not what we agreed. You'll not put Wyn at risk."

"By standing here quibbling instead of announcing your intentions to the dragon, you risk us all," Elaith countered, pointing to the campfire. "How long do you think it will take the dragon to realize that there are travelers in the forest?"

"It's best to do as he says," Wyn told Danilo. "He's quite right about the dragon. We will do whatever we must to retrieve that scroll."

The Harper conceded with a terse nod, and Balindar and the two elves took cover downwind in a nearby copse of young birch and giant ferns. Morgalla loosely tied the three remaining horses near the escape trail, and Vartain cut a branch of pine and quickly swept the sandy clearing free of footprints.

Then they joined Danilo at the cookfire. To all appearances, they were the only three who had come in the clearing. When all was in readiness, Danilo took his place on a moss-covered rock and began to adjust his lute's tuning pegs.

"Get on with it!" Elaith hissed from the nearby copse.

"This dragon of yers is gonna be a nice change o' pace," Morgalla muttered to Danilo, glaring at the moon elf's hiding place.

Danilo took a deep breath and began to sing the words to the *Ballad of Grimnoshtadrano*, adding a new stanza that outlined his demands.

"Now what?" the dwarf asked when the song was done.

"We wait," the Harper responded. "In a few minutes, I'll sing it again."

They waited for nearly an hour, and Danilo sang the challenge several times, before their patience was rewarded.

A huge, winged creature came into view over the clearing. Grimnoshtadrano swooped down along the bank of Unicorn Run, his enormous batlike wings curved to catch the play of sun-warmed air rising from the river. With astonishing grace, the dragon landed lightly on the bank nearby, and he walked toward the clearing on all fours. The three terrified horses tore free of their bindings and raced off down the path. Their riders scarcely noticed.

Danilo watched the dragon's approach with awe. He had never seen a dragon before, and Grimnoshtadrano was not the creature of legend he'd expected. Danilo had always pictured a dragon as a hulking monster, an imposing presence, deadly but rather ponderous. Rather like his Uncle Khelben, now that he thought of it. Grimnosh was certainly huge—Dan guessed that the dragon was a good eighty feet from snout to tail tip—but he was beautiful and exceedingly graceful, and his long slender tail twirled in the air above him in constant, sinuous motion. The dragon moved through the underbrush as silently as any other forest creature. His scales didn't clank like some reptilian version of plate armor, and their surfaces reflected every shade of green in the forest. As the dragon approached, Danilo noted that his coloring changed to match the foliage around him. Apparently Grimnosh could change color at will also, for when the dragon fully entered the clearing his scales took on the brilliant, gemlike shades of emerald, jade, and malachite. Crown jewels, Danilo noted, and the analogy fit the regal creature.

When Grimnoshtadrano was fully in the clearing, he began to circle the three adventurers like a wolf closing in, studying them all the while. His eyes were golden green, slashed by vertical pupils and bright with a cold, alien intelligence.

"Well?" the dragon inquired. His voice was a deep, inhuman rumble that reminded Danilo of the reverberation of a kettledrum. Setting aside his lute, the Harper rose to his feet and bowed deeply to the dragon.

"Well met, noble Grimnoshtadrano. I am Danilo Thann of Waterdeep, Harper and bard, and these are my companions, bards both. You know what we seek from the words of my song."

"This little trifle, I believe?" Grimnosh sat back on his haunches, and with a forepaw he removed a large bag slung over one of his horns. From it he pulled a roll of parchment. He laid it on the ground in front of him, and then placed beside it a small golden cask. With the tip of his tail he flicked open the latch and lifted the lid to reveal a hoard of sparkling gems. "You are prepared to earn this?"

"My talents do not run to riddles," Danilo said. "I have brought you a more worthy opponent."

Vartain rose, his bald head held high. "I am Vartain of Calimport, a riddlemaster trained in the Mulhorand tradition. I have traveled from southern Shaar to Waterdeep, from the western Moonshaes to the eastern lands of Rashemen, collecting riddles and stories from a hundred kingdoms. From these, I have compiled a three-volume collection of riddles housed with honor in the libraries of Candlekeep. I am a scholar of languages both modern and forgotten, the latter so that I might plumb the wealth of earlier ages. Since an active life offers puzzles as well, I have aided the cause of many a famed explorer and adventurer. Modesty forbids that I name or number them."

"I can see that it would," the dragon agreed with a touch of sarcasm in his rumbling voice. "Welcome to the forest, Vartain of Calimport. It isn't often that I'm gifted with such a challenge. You must give me a minute to think, that I might put forth a riddle worthy of your talents."

"First, great Grimnoshtadrano, permit me to name my own reward," Vartain added, earning an incredulous stare from Danilo and Morgalla. "I wish to recover a certain elven artifact, last seen in the village of Taskerleigh."

The dragon snorted. "You're too late. I traded it for a song, you might say, and not a particularly successful one at that, considering that you three are the first to respond to it."

"To whom, if I might ask?"

"One matter at a time, if you please," Grimnosh returned. "I will give you that information as a reward if you can answer my riddle. Agreed?"

Vartain inclined his head graciously. The dragon tapped at his fang-studded jaw as he reflected, and the metallic click of talon against tooth was a discomfiting sound. Finally, Grimnosh cleared his throat—emitting as he did a small puff of gas redolent of overripe eggs—and gave this puzzle:

> *King Khalzol's kingdom is long gone.*
> *Take five steps to the site of his grave:*
> *The first means to think over,*
> *The second is over your thoughts,*
> *The third means one of something,*
> *The last must be stronger than anything,*
> *The whole reveals everything.*

"Now tell me, why did King Khalzol's subjects bury him in a copper coffin?"

Silence hung over the clearing for a long moment. Danilo nudged the riddlemaster and leaned close to his ear. "Because he was dead?" the Harper suggested, sotto voce.

Vartain shot a scathing glance at the young man. "Leave these matters to me," he hissed in a fierce whisper, and he turned to face the dragon.

"This is a classic conundrum, in which a one-word answer is given, piece by piece, in several related riddles," he announced aloud. "It is an elegant conundrum, to be sure, and unfamiliar to me. Nevertheless, here is its solution:

"What is to *mull* but to think over? Speaking quite literally, what lies over men's thoughts but their *hair*? The word 'a' means one of something, as in 'a pomegranate.' A *hold*, or fortress, must be stronger than any force brought against it. Put together, one obtains the site of King Khalzol's grave: *Mulharahold*, a city to the south of the Mountains of Copper. The copper coffin, of course, is the clue that confirms the conundrum's answer." Vartain fell silent, his chin lifted in a expectant pose.

The dragon examined his claws with a satisfied air. "I rather thought you'd say that," he rumbled.

Vartain reached out to claim the scroll, but the dragon batted the man's hand away with a flick of his tail. "Humans are always in such a rush," he purred. "The answer to the question 'Why did his subjects bury King Khalzol in a copper coffin?' is far simpler that you would make it, and I regret to say that the reason had nothing to do with his grave site. They buried him, dear riddlemaster, *because he was dead!*"

"He ain't the only one," muttered the dwarf.

"But strictly speaking, your puzzle was not a simple riddle," Vartain protested in an aggrieved tone. "It was a conundrum!"

Morgalla huffed, exasperated. "But it was a conundrum," she mimicked softly. "*That'll* look good on yer headstone, if'n a mason alive can spell it!"

With two claws, the dragon picked up Vartain by the back of his tunic. He examined the dangling riddlemaster thoughtfully, then with the knuckles of his free paw he shined the man's bald pate as if polishing an apple. The effect was chilling, the intention obvious.

"Wait!" Danilo shouted. He quickly offered Grimnosh

the second challenge. "If you fail to answer the riddle I put to you, we go free, with the scroll our only treasure. But if you succeed, I will remain here in your employ for the remainder of my life."

"Hmmm. It would be nice to have a musician on hand," Grimnoshtadrano mused. He held Vartain out at arm's length and considered him. The dangling riddlemaster's pot belly and bowed, skinny legs lent him all the dignity and appeal of a captured frog. "And on the whole, this one looks rather unpalatable." The dragon dropped Vartain, who disappeared with a grunt into a thick bank of ferns.

"The riddle is in song form," Danilo began, picking up his lute.

"Really! How droll." Grimnosh settled down like a watchful cat, propping his massive head up on one fore-paw. "Riddle away, by all means."

Danilo began to play the opening chords to the musical spell Khelben had given him, hoping that it would take effect before the dragon recognized the ploy. Hoping, indeed, that it would work at all! He had practiced the lute accompaniment, learned the melody, and memorized the arcane words, but he had not dared to combine them until this moment.

When he sang the first note, a wave of power surged through him and seemed to flow out with the melody. Although Danilo could not say exactly where it came from, the magic felt oddly familiar. He had the peculiar feeling that it had always been there in his favorite songs, like a shadow he had glimpsed from the corner of his eye. Exhilaration filled him as he sang and played, and a sense of fulfillment deeper than anything he had every known.

The effect on the dragon was equally profound. His enormous golden eyes grew dreamy and vacant. The long green tail continued to twirl, but the elaborate pattern of movement simplified until just the tip swayed from side to side, moving in time to the music and looking like a languid cobra dancing to the horn of a Calashite snake charmer.

When Danilo thought the dragon safely ensorcelled, he nodded to Morgalla. She eased forward, brown eyes shining with excitement, and tugged the parchment roll out from under the dragon's elbow.

Too soon! A low rumble came from the dragon's throat as he struggled to free himself from the charm. Morgalla eased away slowly, and Danilo sang on. For a moment he thought the dragon would subside.

Then the rumpled fern bed rustled wildly, and Vartain poked his head out. The riddlemaster looked dazed, and he swayed like a sapling in a gale. Grimnosh began to stir and twitch, as if shaking off a deep slumber. His tail stopped its rhythmic swaying and started an agitated churning motion.

"Get away, you fools," snapped Elaith from his hiding place.

Before they could respond, Grimnosh's eyes focused, then filled with malevolence. The creature's armored chest rose; he drew in a deep breath. Vartain placed the blowpipe to his lips and puffed out his cheeks. A tiny canister flew unerringly toward the dragon. It disappeared into the terrible maw just as the dragon opened his mouth to attack.

The result was immediate and spectacular. An explosion ripped through the clearing, extinguishing the cookfire and stripping leaves from trees. The force of it tore Danilo's lute from his arms and sent him tumbling to the ground. He struggled to his feet, unable to hear anything but the painful ringing in his ears. When his vision cleared, he saw the stunned dragon lying on his back near the remains of the cookfire. His tongue lolled from his blackened mouth, and the golden-green plates that covered his abdomen gleamed through the dissipating wisps of smoke. Coughing and batting at the foul-scented smoke, the Harper looked around for his companions.

His first thought was for Morgalla; she'd been the closest to the dragon. He needn't have worried. Morgalla was already up, the scroll gripped triumphantly in one small hand and a broad grin on her face. Legs pumping, she sprinted from the clearing with Elaith and Wyn close on her heels. Balindar moved slower, stumbling a bit and clutching at his ears.

Danilo looked around for Vartain. The riddlemaster had fallen facedown into the ferns, and the bronze dome of his head was barely visible above the battered foliage. The Harper grabbed Balindar's arm and pointed to the unconscious riddlemaster. The burly man glanced at Vartain. His lip curled, and he shook his head. Danilo stripped an onyx ring from his hand and held it out to the mercenary, then pointed again. With a grin, Balindar pocketed the ring. He slung Vartain over his shoulder and followed the others.

Danilo was the last to leave the clearing. He snatched up his lute and slid the strap over his shoulder, then glanced at the stunned dragon. Grimnosh's mighty chest rose and fell in a shallow but regular rhythm. Every instinct warned Danilo to flee at once. The bargain he'd just struck with Balindar raised certain practical considerations, however, so he edged closer to the dragon and snatched up the cask, dropping it into his magic bag. The hoard disappeared without a trace, and he jogged down the path, his lute bobbing lightly on his shoulder as he ran.

Music and Mayhem regrouped nearly a mile away. The three spooked horses had been captured and calmed by the time Dan arrived. Vartain had been revived, thanks to repeated doses from Mange's flask of rivengut. Morgalla's face was dusty and bruised from the tumble she'd taken, but the tough little woman seemed otherwise unhurt.

Dan shook his head in astonishment and sank down on a large stone beside her. He wrapped an arm around her sturdy shoulders and gave her a quick hug. "Thank the Eternal Forge you're a dwarf," he murmured, borrowing a term from the mythology of her people.

"You can bet I do," Morgalla replied with a wink. "Loud and offen."

* * * * *

The last silver of twilight faded from the Sea of Swords, and in the Dock Ward district of Waterdeep, business dealings became as dark and mysterious as the sea beyond. Those who knew the city and who wished to see the sun rise the next morning knew what alleys to avoid and which taverns served danger along with watered ale. The watch patrol assigned to the southern tip of the ward was therefore surprised to find a large and vocal group of merchants gathered at the corner of Dock Street and Wharf Street.

"Is there a problem?" the watch commander inquired as politely as possible, considering that she was shouting over the din of some three dozen angry voices.

"I should say!" The speaker was Zelderan Guthel, the head of the Council of Farmer-Grocers, and at his words the crowd quieted somewhat. Among its other responsibilities, the guild rented warehouse space to merchants of all kinds. The angry crowd was gathered in front of a large stone and timber warehouse built to provide winter grain storage. In off seasons, it was used to store the exotic goods specially made or imported for sale at the Midsummer Faire.

"This is a common facility, and protecting it is the city's responsibility! Just what do you intend to do?" An angry chorus of mutters echoed the guildmaster's question.

The captain scratched her chin. "Do? This area is well

patrolled. We check this warehouse every twenty minutes!"

"Then whoever emptied the place went through us faster'n tainted stew," groused a dwarf in an ale-stained apron. "My tavern had over a hunnerd kegs o' mead stored here. The city better make good on it, is all I got to say!"

"It always has." The captain took a small book and a quill from her bag. "I'll make a full report." She said, jotting down the dwarf's name and losses.

Others came forward, shouting out lists of missing goods and demanding action. Within minutes the four members of the watch patrol were hidden from sight, surrounded by irate merchants jostling each other to give their reports. To all appearances, the crowd not been noticeably appeased.

Hoof beats echoed down the nearby alleys as reinforcements rushed in from other beats. The first mounted guardsman to arrive noted the glint of green and gold chain mail in the midst of the angry crowd, and he came to what seemed a reasonable conclusion. Brandishing a stout rod, he rode into the angry crowd, laying about briskly as he cleared a path that would free the beleaguered watch.

The merchants reeled back, revealing the four members of the regular patrol. The "rescued" watch captain stared up at the guardsman in horror and disbelief. In her hands she held not a weapon, but a report book and a quill.

The silence that fell over the crowd was deep and uneasy. The dwarven tavern-keeper was the first to break it. Massaging a knot on his head from the guardsman's rod, he muttered, "The city better make good for this, is all I got to say."

* * * * *

Waves lapped at the wooden platform, sending a spray of salty water into the air. Lucia Thione leaped back, pulling her silken skirts away from certain ruin. "Where could this Hodatar be?" she fretted.

"He's very reliable," Zzundar Thul assured her, casting a surreptitious glance at the slender ankles revealed by the woman's quick movement. Sun-bronzed and heavily muscled from his labors, Zzundar was a waterman and the son of the same, but he was as quick as any to recognize and appreciate a lady of quality. In Zzundar's opinion, of all the privileges he'd enjoyed as master of the watermen's guild, this meeting with Lady Thione ranked highest. A successful merchant and caravan organizer, she was a guild member and had just become their liaison with the mermen who helped keep the harbor clean. For this purpose she came to the guild hall. Zzundar was grateful for an excuse to accompany her down to the merdock, even though it was not the romantic setting he would have chosen.

Actually, the merdock was little more than a large cistern. It opened to a passage that led from the basement of the dockside guildhall into the sea. The reclusive mermen preferred to deal with as few humans as possible, and this particular arrangement suited them well.

The surface of the water dimpled and broke, revealing a gleaming, clean-shaven head. The merman pulled himself partway out of the water, resting his weight on his elbows and leveling an insolent stare at the noblewoman.

"I've news," he said bluntly. "Several ships bound for Waterdeep were attacked this afternoon. One fell to pirates, two more to monsters of the sea. There were no survivors on any of these vessels." The merman quickly gave the names, owners, and ports of origin of each ship, information his people had gleaned from the logs of the sunken ships.

"And the cargoes?" Lady Thione demanded.

"Lost."

Zzundar paled beneath his tan. "The vessels you named carried goods for Midsummer Faire! You're telling me that nothing could be salvaged?"

"We did what we could," Hodatar said coldly. The gills on his neck flared, betraying his anger.

"I'm sure you did," Lucia hastened to assure him. In truth, she was disturbed by the merman's demeanor. Garnet had described him as cooperative, if not exactly respectful, but Lucia disliked the bold and calculating expression in his narrow, sea-green eyes. She paused as if suddenly distracted. "Whatever is that noise from the street, Zzundar? Ah, I was a fool to come to this ward, alone and at such an hour!" she lamented, raising her enormous dark eyes to his.

The guildmaster's brow creased as he strained to catch the sounds that had distressed the lady. Finally, he made out the faint noise of voices and horsemen. "You needn't worry. I'll check it out and be back directly," he said, patting her arm as if to reassure her. Her protector hastened up the narrow spiral of wooden steps that led toward the street. After a few minutes, the clunk of the heavy wooden trapdoor echoed through the basement chamber.

"Finally," Lucia said in acid tones. When she turned back to the merman, all the softness had disappeared from her face. "What news of the goods?"

"They'll be safely stored on Whalebones," Hodatar said. "Minus the pirates' share, of course."

"I told you to take them to Orlumbor!" she protested. "I have agents on that island who can fence the goods. Whalebones is nothing but seal colonies and rock!"

The merman shrugged, unimpressed by her outburst. "What I can't sell to the Ruathym, I'll send south in small shipments to Alaron. I have contacts with Moonshae

merchants there. Your share should be at least a third of
the goods' Waterdeep market value."

"It should be considerably more than that," Lucia
snapped. "Without the information I gave you, your pirates
wouldn't have known the trade routes and could not have
overcome those ships!"

"Information is very valuable," the merman agreed slyly.
"I wonder, for example, what Zzundar might pay to learn
that these ships disappeared at your command."

Lucia's dark eyes narrowed. "You're very ambitious,
Hodatar," she observed softly. She took a small silk bag
from her bodice and dangled it before the merman. "It is
not enough that you take payment both from me and the
city of Waterdeep?"

Hodatar snatched the bag from her and eagerly jerked
open the purse strings. He smiled with satisfaction and fin-
gered the rare spell components that he'd demanded as
payment. "Magic is not inexpensive, and it is rare under
the sea. Once I learn to use it, I'll rule kingdoms that surpass those of your most ambitious conquerors!"

Lucia yawned delicately, patting at her parted lips with
the tips of her fingers. "Don't be tiresome, Hodatar. Future
fish kings shouldn't stoop to blackmail," she chided him,
her derision cloaked in genteel tones. "But Garnet tells me
that you've been a good ally, and she would like to see you
succeed in your study of magic. As a wizard, you'd be even
more useful to our cause. I've a talisman that will increase
the power of your spells." She slipped a hand into a pocket
of her gown, then she paused and bit her lower lip, acting
if she'd spoken before thinking and was now reconsidering her action. "Of course, it might be dangerous to one
who lacked knowledge," she added hastily.

"A risk I will gladly take!" the merman said. He sank low
into the water, and then with a quick thrust of his tail
sprang out at the noblewoman.

Lucia Thione was ready for him. She yanked a curved dagger from her pocket and sank it deep into his underbelly, ripping downward through scales and flesh as if she were gutting a trout. Hodatar fell heavily onto the wooden floor, his mouth gaping in shock and pain as he clutched at his spilling entrails.

The noblewoman watched the merman's death throes with an impassive face. When the treacherous Hodatar lay still, she stooped by the water and splashed some of the briny liquid over her dress. Standing, she raked her fingers through her hair repeatedly, reducing the elegant ringlets to a tousled mass of chestnut curls. Finally she took her money purse and scattered a handful of coins on the floor to make it appear that the merman had tried to rob her and had died in the struggle.

When Zzundar returned, the noblewoman threw herself into his arms, babbling helplessly that she hadn't meant to kill Hodatar. She sobbed against the guildmaster's broad chest, allowing him to smooth her hair and murmur inane platitudes about the gods, the fates, and the right of any woman to protect herself from thieves and scoundrels. After a suitable interval she looked up at Zzundar, giving him a small grateful smile and declaring through her tears that she couldn't bear to be alone that night.

As Lucia had anticipated, the guildmaster was too entranced by this turn of events to question her story. Nor did he think to ask how she knew that a strong undercurrent caused by the morning tides would carry the body far into the harbor.

Hodatar himself had told this to Garnet, and Lucia had tested the theory with the body of Larissa Neathal's maid. Zzundar was not the only guildmember enchanted by Lucia's elegant beauty, and it had been a small matter to arrange access to the merdock for two agents of the Knights of the Shield. Of course, she had paid that man in a coin far less personal than that she was using to purchase Zzundar.

She cast a sidelong glance at the guildmaster and repressed a sigh. She was not adverse to using her charm and beauty to serve her own ends, but she bitterly resented doing so to further Garnet's vendetta against Khelben Arunsun. As she accompanied Zzundar out of the guildhall, Lucia wondered what more the half-elven sorceress might demand of her.

Eight

Astride her magical asperii, Garnet sped through the sunrise clouds on her swift journey northward. Far below, she could see the spires of Silverymoon gleaming in the soft pink light, and the sight filled her with dark satisfaction. More than three moons had passed since she had last visited the wondrous city and cast the spell that bound the bards to her will. They had done their part admirably, and would soon prove the power of bardcraft.

From the vantage point of her wind-riding mount, Garnet spotted a narrow brown ribbon, the main trade route leading east from Silverymoon to Sundabar. She sent a silent command to her horse. The asperii followed the command without comment or complaint, but the telepathic creature's thoughts were tightly closed to her. For a moment this irritated Garnet, but she had far too much on her mind to concern herself overmuch with her surly steed's mood.

Before highsun the bard saw below her the stout gray walls that surrounded Sundabar. The city had been built long ago by dwarves and was still a heavily armed fortress. Once the site of the barding college known as Anstruth, it was still renowned for the fine wooden instruments crafted there. The city sat at the crossroad of the River Rauvin and the trade road, and beyond it were the thick forests that yielded lumber for the city's craftspeople. More exotic woods were carried on the barges that traveled the busy river. From Garnet's height, the cargo boats looked to be about the size of water bugs.

Another command from the bard sent the asperii into a spiraling descent. Garnet landed openly on the trade road and entered the city without challenge, for bards were welcomed almost anywhere for their music and the news they carried.

As she traveled down the narrow cobblestone roads past the homes and shops of busy tradespeople, she found that Sundabar was greatly changed since she had last walked its streets, almost three hundred years before. As a very young noblewoman she had studied at Anstruth on her path toward the degree of Magnum Alumnus, the highest honor afforded a bard. Her years of study did not bring her to that goal, however, for a charismatic young bard had persuaded her to join the Harpers. While she ran about the Northlands doing the bidding of politicians such as Khelben, the barding colleges began their final slide into decline.

That Garnet could never forgive. The Harpers had originally been created, at least in part, to sustain tradition and preserve history, yet their efforts were ever directed to this or that political end. She would repay the lords and rulers in their own coin. Let Khelben and his ilk see what happened when music and history no longer served them and furthered their political games!

Finding her way through Sundabar was more difficult than Garnet had anticipated. The city through which she rode was now more concerned with commerce than art, and to her dismay she found that only one of Anstruth's original buildings still stood: a concert hall whose stone walls had survived the passage of time. Rage coursed through the bard when she realized that the once-beautiful building had been gutted and turned into a common warehouse.

Nevertheless, she tied her horse outside and made her way to a door at the back of the building. Within she found stacks of lumber, and at one end of the vast room was a workshop equipped with lathes and bores that transformed wood into the fine musical instruments for which Sundabar was famed. A number of unfinished recorders, shawms, and wooden flutes lay on various work tables, but she was alone in the vast room.

The workers had just left, probably to take a highsun meal. Garnet's sharp eyes—part of her inheritance from her elven mother—perceived the blurred and quickly fading shadows of warmth they had left behind. She had little time to complete her task. Garnet pulled up a low stool and seated herself in the midst of the workshop. Once again, she began to play the melody that bound magic and music together, singing the interwoven riddles that formed the words of the spell.

When the spell was complete, Garnet picked up her harp and hurried into the back alley. Impatient to test her new power, she set down the harp on the cobblestones and with her right hand plucked a single string. Her left hand she flung upward. Lightning sizzled *upward*, disappearing into a low-hanging bank of clouds.

The rain began immediately. Garnet closed her eyes and raised her face to the soft shower, smiling as she imagined the reaction another such storm would cause in

Waterdeep. Rain on Midsummer's Day was such a rare event that it was considered a dire omen. She would use this superstition to fuel the growing discontent in Waterdeep, and she would spread rumors that the freak weather was due to the twisted wizardry of Khelben Arunsun. A small thing, perhaps, but Garnet knew that rulers had lost favor for less than this.

A stinging blow slapped Garnet's cheek, and then another. Her eyes snapped open, then widened in disbelief. The rain had turned to hail! She ducked back into the doorway of the warehouse, out of the way of increasingly larger pieces of ice. As the appalled half-elf watched, the sky darkened to the color of slate and hail began to accumulate on the stone-paved alley.

Garnet hurried through the warehouse to the front post where she had left her asperii. She quickly untied the frightened, battered horse and drew it into the building, soothing it as best she could with soft words and projected mental assurances. The asperii quieted, and it fixed its liquid brown eyes on its mistress. For an instant the veil that the asperii had cast up between their two minds parted, and Garnet caught a glimpse of the horse's fear and indecision.

For the first time, Garnet understood the significance of the asperii's withdrawal; each magical horse only formed its telepathic, lifelong bond with a mage or priest of great power, and the asperii would not serve anyone whose goals or motives were evil. Garnet had never before doubted the rightness of her plan, and the quiet accusation in the asperii's eyes struck her like a physical blow. Pain flashed in the half-elf's chest and down her arm, and she sank gasping onto a nearby crate.

"I seek justice, not vengeance," Garnet whispered to herself when the waves of pain had subsided. She looked up into the asperii's eyes, and saw her twin reflections there as if in a dark mirror. "In all things, there must be a balance," she said earnestly.

The horse merely blinked and turned its gaze toward the open door. After a moment Garnet also looked out at the plummeting hail. The silence between them was complete as they waited for the storm to play itself out.

* * * * *

It was uncanny, mused Jannaxil Serpentil, but sooner or later every scrap of stolen paper in Waterdeep seemed to come across his desk. The proprietor of Serpentil Books and Folios sold everything from spellbooks to love letters, but this latest find was something quite new.

Deftly sketched on the paper was a picture of Khelben Arunsun. The archmage stood before an easel, dabbing at the canvas with an oversized brush while the faceless, black-robed Lords of Waterdeep stood by, holding his palettes and brushes. By Deneir, it was clever! The artist had caught perfectly the mood and fears of the cityfolk, condensing much gossip and speculation into a single, vivid image.

Jannaxil scratched his thin black beard thoughtfully. The first secret of being a good fence—and he was very good indeed—was to have a buyer for nearly anything. No one in Waterdeep would be so foolish as to attempt to blackmail the archmage, but the fence could think of several people who might have an interest in this sketch.

He affixed the would-be seller, an apprentice instrument builder whose gambling debts far outstripped his earnings, with his most intimidating scowl. "Where did you find this?"

The young man licked his lips nervously. "One of Halambar's patrons dropped it in the shop. I thought that, perhaps—"

"I doubt that you thought at all!" Jannaxil glanced at the sketch again and sniffed disdainfully. The second secret of success was knowing the value of an object, and then convincing the seller to accept far less. "Who would have a use for such a thing? I can give you three copper pieces, no more."

Jannaxil pushed the coins toward the young man. "You have brought me a few interesting pieces in the past. These coppers are an investment, for I hope that you might do better in the future."

"Yes, sir." Halambar's apprentice looked disappointed, but he gathered up the coins and left the shop.

Alone is his dusty, book-lined kingdom, Jannaxil finally gave vent to a dry chuckle. He was tempted to keep the sketch himself, although he was certain that the sorcerer Maaril would be delighted by the satirical jab at his more powerful colleague, and that the wizard would pay many pieces of silver to possess it.

The challenge in this transaction, Jannaxil mused, was finding a carrier foolhardy enough to take the drawing to the Dragon Tower. Maaril's tower was actually shaped like a dragon, standing upright on its haunches with its mouth flung open as if ready to attack. Although the odd tower was a landmark that held great appeal for children and visitors—especially at night when the light within made the dragon's eyes and mouth glow with a crimson fire—only the most intrepid ventured close enough for more than a peek. The tower was steeped in sinister magic, and even the streets surrounding it were dangerous.

Jannaxil pondered the matter for a long moment, then he smiled. A certain thief of his acquaintance had recently married into a clan of wealthy North End merchants. This family was newly come to wealth and were very conscious of their social position. Jannaxil knew the clan matriarch; she prized respectability above all and would not be accepting of her son-in-law's colorful past. Jannaxil was certain the erstwhile thief would do him this little favor, in exchange for continued discretion.

As Jannaxil had noted before, the secret to a fence's success was knowing the right price of everything.

* * * * *

Music and Mayhem rode hard throughout the rest of the day, for they wanted to put as many miles as possible between themselves and the High Forest. The afternoon fled, and by sunset they had left the marshlands behind.

The moon was high before they found a campsite that Elaith considered reasonably safe and defensible. While the elf and Balindar directed the care of horses and the making of camp, Danilo settled down by the campfire and removed the hard-won scroll of parchment from his magic bag. When Wyn Ashgrove saw what was in the Harper's hands, he hurried over, with Morgalla close on his heels.

"Open it!" the elf urged, impatience and excitement in his dark green eyes. "Perhaps it will reveal who enspelled the bards!"

Danilo shook his head and pointed to the blob of dark red wax sealing the scroll. "Many spell scrolls are protected. Breaking this seal could set off something lethal: a fireball, a mind-blank spell, an irate redhead. . . ." Danilo illustrated the last possibility by tugging at one of the dwarf's long auburn braids, teasing the fierce warrior as if she were a favorite younger sister. Morgalla rolled her eyes skyward and tried not to look pleased.

"So now what, bard?" she asked.

"There are tiny runes pressed into the wax," Danilo said, holding the scroll close and squinting at it. "The writing itself isn't arcane, but that doesn't mean it's not a spell of some sort. I don't recognize the language."

"Let me see." Vartain strode over, extending one hand in a peremptory fashion. "Riddlemasters are of necessity students of linguistics and lore."

Danilo gave him the scroll. "Read it if you can, but don't disturb the seal," he said firmly. "I like to limit myself to one explosion a day."

The riddlemaster glanced at the runes. "This is a contrived dialect of middle Sespechian, a court language developed some three centuries past but long since fallen into disuse," he announced in dry, didactic tones. "Upon the death of the ruling Baron of Sespech, the baroness took a young consort from Turmish. The man was reputed to be handsome beyond compare, but lacking facility in language. This bastardized dialect of Sespechian, which every member of court was required to learn, was the queen's attempt to draw her new consort into the social and diplomatic concerns of court life."

"The nice thing about dwarves and elves," Morgalla interrupted plaintively, "is that generally we come to the point after an hour or two."

"The words on this seal appear to be a riddle, and its title suggests that it is the key to the scroll," Vartain continued in a stiff tone. "Translated into the Common tongue, making the necessary allowances for rhyme and meter, it would read something like this:

The beginning of eternity.
The end of time and space.
The start of every end,
And the end of every place."

Wyn and Danilo exchanged puzzled glances. "Unriddling can be yet another form of magic," Vartain informed them. "Solve the riddle, and you will very likely unseal the scroll."

"By all means," the Harper urged him.

"The answer," Vartain said without hesitation, "is the letter *E*."

Even as the riddlemaster spoke, the wax dissolved into red mist and disappeared. Vartain unrolled the scroll. After a moment's study, he laid it out before the Harper.

The scroll contained only a few lines, written in the Common trade language. Danilo scanned the words. "This seems to be a single stanza of an unrhymed tale or ballad," the Harper noted. "The meter has a definite pattern. I have absolutely no idea what the words mean."

"The meaning has been carefully obscured," Vartain said. "These lines contain several small riddles, woven warp and weft like a cloth. If I am not mistaken, this verse is but a part of the entire puzzle." He read aloud several of the lines:

"First of seven now begins:
Tread anew the forgotten path.
Silent strings send out silvery webs
To the music all will bend."

The riddlemaster stopped and looked up from the scroll. "The phrase 'first of seven' suggests that this stanza is but a part of a larger puzzle. 'Silent strings' is, I believe, another way of referring to a Harper pin, is it not?"

"Yes," Danilo agreed quietly. "That is not widely known."

"Indeed. I would therefore surmise that the author of this is either a scholar, such as myself, or more likely a Harper. Or perhaps both, although that combination is exceedingly rare."

"No offense intended, of course," Morgalla said pleasantly.

The riddlemaster pointed to the third line of text and continued with his explanation, showing a remarkable immunity to sarcasm. "Magic is oft referred to as a weave or a web. Perhaps the author is also a mage of some sort."

Danilo reclaimed the scroll and rolled it up. "I agree. I'm taking this to Khelben Arunsun at once, so that he can trace the spellcaster. Wyn, Morgalla, let's be off."

"The horses need rest," the dwarf pointed out, "and it's a mite far to walk."

The Harper touched a plain silver ring on his left hand. "This can magically transport up to three people and their mounts—quickly and painlessly, I assure you—to the courtyard of Blackstaff Tower."

Morgalla blanched. "Did I say it was too far to walk?"

"Take ease, dwarf. You're not leaving yet." Elaith's cold voice cut short Morgalla's protest.

Danilo turned, recoiling at the sight of the armed and ready mercenaries who had formed a close ring around them. Firelight glinted from their bared weapons. The Harper stood and confronted the grim-faced moon elf. "What is this about?"

"You and I had an agreement," Elaith said. "Until the end of the search, we are partners and will work together."

"But my search is complete; we have the scroll we sought."

"Maybe so. But our original agreement was that I would get a share of the dragon's hoard. According to Vartain, the author of that scroll possesses the treasure I seek."

"How do you come to that conclusion?" Wyn demanded.

"I think I can tell you that," Dan said slowly. "When we challenged Grimnosh, Vartain requested that the dragon turn over an elven artifact he'd taken from Taskerleigh. Grimnosh said that he'd already traded the item 'for a song,' and commented that we were the first to respond to it. Vartain has evidently concluded that the song the dragon mentioned was the *Ballad of Grimnoshtadrano*, the one that brought us to the High Forest. Since this ballad first appeared after the Silverymoon Spring Faire, I assume it was the handiwork of the spellcaster we seek."

"That is the logic behind my assumption," Vartain agreed.

"Obviously," Danilo continued, nodding toward Elaith, "our well-armed partner here does not wish us to take the scroll to Waterdeep. If Khelben tracks down the spell-caster, Elaith would not be likely to retrieve this mysterious treasure. He no doubt wishes to find the spellcaster himself." Danilo turned to the watchful moon elf. "My question is this: why do you need us? You needed a Harper to get the scroll from the dragon, but why now?"

Elaith was silent for a long moment. He studied Danilo with a measuring gaze. "You are truly a Harper? This is not some ridiculous game of the sort you Waterdhavian nobles like to play?"

"A *game*? If I start having fun on this quest," Danilo assured the elf gravely, "I'll certainly let you know."

"And your pretensions to bardcraft? They are genuine as well?"

The nobleman sighed. "You've got me there. It's hard to say yes or no. I've trained, certainly, but not in the traditional or even conventional ways. I haven't attended the barding schools, obviously—they closed before my time—nor apprenticed to a bard of note. But my mother, the Lady Cassandra, is a gifted musician, and she insisted on the best teachers. They were all private, of course. I was much given to mischief as a lad, and several of Waterdeep's finest schools repented of their decision to accept me as a scholar. In despair, Lady Cassandra took it upon herself to hire an army of tutors, including bards trained in the styles of each of the seven elder barding colleges. None of them stayed long, but I managed to learn a bit here and there."

Danilo smiled engagingly. "And now that you know my life story, perhaps you'll tell me more about this elven artifact you seek. I'd love to hear that tale."

"After your life story? Hardly! It is said that there are some acts one should never attempt to follow. Dogs, children, jesters, and the like." The moon elf's amber eyes revealed nothing but a touch of mocking amusement.

"Not going to admit to anything, eh? Well, I can understand that. You've got to preserve the elven mystique, and so forth. What puzzles me, though," the young man added thoughtfully, "is what place your moonblade has in all of this."

Elaith's pleasant expression evaporated. "That is not your concern."

"It is if we're going to be partners."

"We *are* partners. I require the services of a mage and a bard. You are not altogether without credentials." Elaith's lips thinned in a smile. "As a bard, you are no immediate threat to Storm Silverhand. You are, however, the best we can come up with under the circumstances."

"The story of my life," Danilo murmured.

"You've shown yourself capable of wielding a considerable amount of magic. A dragon has a powerful resistance to charm spells, yet you held him."

"So?"

"The scroll is a riddle of sorts. Vartain can no doubt decipher it, but I have reason to believe that a knowledge of both magic and music might prove helpful to my search. I will spell out the terms of our partnership so that there is no further misunderstanding. We will combine our resources and talents until the scroll is deciphered and the spellcaster found. You may have whatever is necessary to undo the spell upon the bards, but I will take possession of the artifact. When that is accomplished, we part ways. This seems more than reasonable."

It didn't, but Danilo considered his options. He could see no other way to achieve his purpose, yet agreeing meant

putting a powerful artifact in the evil elf's hands. He had no
idea what Elaith would do with it, except perhaps . . .

The moonblade. Somehow, the elf had learned of a way
to restore the dormant magic of his elven sword! That had
to be the answer; Danilo could see no other connection.
This prospect was daunting, for he knew that each moonblade had unique and formidable powers. If this was
indeed Elaith's motive, one mystery remained: why would
the elf go to such trouble to restore a sword he could
never wield? He was the last of his line, and the sword
would simply return to dormancy in his hand. What did
the elf possibly have to gain? Of one thing Danilo was quite
certain: Elaith had far too much power already without the
added threat of either a restored moonblade or this mysterious elven artifact.

"Unfortunately, I have a previous commitment. The
archmage of Waterdeep is expecting me, and he's not one
to be put off. So if you'll excuse me?"

"No. We have an agreement." The elf's amber eyes narrowed. "I'm holding you to your word and your honor."

Danilo paused, and the struggle of conflicting pledges
was clearly written on his face.

"I'll make it easier for you," Elaith offered, and he
turned to Balindar. "You seem fond of the dwarf's company, so I'm placing her in your charge. If Lord Thann
proves treacherous, kill her." The black-bearded mercenary hesitated, then gave a terse nod.

"This is how you honor your agreements?" Danilo
protested.

"My agreement is with you, not her. If you like, I will
swear by whatever oath you choose that I will not raise a
hand or weapon against you personally."

"That's vastly comforting."

"Whatever else might be said of me, my word is still a
pledge of honor," the moon elf said with quiet dignity.

Danilo glanced toward Morgalla. She stood with arms crossed, glaring up at the huge mercenary who guarded her. Balindar had a rather sheepish expression on his black-bearded face, but he held a sword on the dwarf and would probably not hesitate to use it. The Harper had little choice.

"Well?" the elf prompted. One silvery eyebrow quirked at a sardonic angle. "Have we a deal?"

"Agreed. I suppose."

Elaith chuckled. "Such enthusiasm! Perhaps you are the sort who listens to rumors, that you fear to share the supposed fate of my former partners?" he taunted.

"A bard, listen to rumors? What a notion," Dan marveled. "But now that you mention it, *partner*, should I be concerned?"

The elf thought that over. "Probably," he agreed pleasantly.

After instructing Danilo to hand the scroll over to Vartain, Elaith told Balindar to stand down. The mercenary sheathed his sword with a profound sigh of relief, and nodded apologetically to Morgalla. Wyn Ashgrove, pale with fury and outrage, drew the dwarf safely away from the fighters, then he stalked off alone into the shadows. Danilo followed, fearing what the elven spellsinger might have in mind and hoping to calm him. Morgalla took a place at the far side of the camp and began to sketch furiously.

Left alone with his men, Elaith beckoned them close. "We take no chances," the elf said in a cold voice. "Balindar, your order is not rescinded. If Lord Thann attempts to go his own way, the dwarf dies. The Harper understands that; see that you remember it, as well. And you," he said, pointing to another of his men, "at first opportunity, steal Thann's magic ring and give it to me. We don't want him grabbing his precious dwarf and blinking out of here."

"I?" balked the man.

"Don't be coy," Elaith snapped. "All of us here know that you're a skilled thief. Use your skills as I command, and there should be no reason for others to share this knowledge. You would hardly be welcomed into the salons of Waterdeep or featured at Lady Raventree's parties if it became known that you started life as a street urchin. Am I making myself clear?"

"Quite," his victim replied with uncharacteristic brevity.

"Good. Mange, you and Tzadick take first watch. Balindar, guard the dwarf. Vartain, you and Thann start working on that scroll. The rest of you get what rest you can. I fear we've a hard road ahead."

* * * * *

In the privacy of his rented villa, Lord Hhune of Tethyr savored a late supper with a few of the higher-ranking agents of the Knights of the Shield. He was almost jovial this evening, delighted with the unusual turn his trip to Waterdeep had taken. His initial dislike of Garnet had been set aside, for the role the half-elven sorceress had given him to play dovetailed beautifully with his own ambitions. Hhune was a guildmaster in his own land, and this splendid northern city had real potential. It lacked guilds for thieves and assassins, and these he was busily putting in place. Waterdeep was in some ways too well run for its own good: there were few powerful crime organizations to challenge Hhune's activities.

Even Hhune's immediate prospects were pleasant, for he was enjoying a thick oyster stew and the report of one of his best agents. The thin, furtive Amnite who was known only as Chachim always seemed to surpass expectations.

"As you ordered, the merchant named by Lady Thione as a Lord of Waterdeep is dead by my hand," Chachim announced, predictably enough. "I followed him to the home of the wizard Maaril and slew him nearby. None saw the deed, for few venture near the Dragon Tower. I left the merchant's body nearby in Blue Alley. If it is ever recovered, all will assume that he fell to one of the magical traps that guard the wizard's tower."

The agent paused and took a folded piece of paper from his sleeve. "This was taken from the merchant's person. I thought you might find it interesting."

Hhune unfolded the paper and burst into belly-shaking laughter. "Oh, but this is priceless! Who is the artist? I could use a hundred like this one!"

Chachim bowed. "I have anticipated your wish, Lord Hhune. There is a signmaker in the trade ward who will carve this drawing onto a block of wood for the small price of twenty gold pieces. After the block is carved, it is a simple matter to stamp as many copies as you would like."

"Good, good!" Hhune nodded to his steward, who counted out the amount and handed it to Chachim. For good measure, Hhune handed the agent one of his own specially minted coins, commonly given as tribute to an agent who'd rendered a notable service. Chachim bowed again and left the chamber with the sketch and the gold.

The guildmaster chuckled. Although his assigned task was harrying the Lords of Waterdeep through increased criminal activity, he saw only benefit in furthering Garnet's personal goal: deposing the archmage Khelben Arunsun. Circulating a sketch that poked fun at the archmage and stirred controversy could only secure the favor of the powerful half-elven sorceress.

"Let us drink to Waterdeep, my friends," the guildmaster said expansively to his cohorts as he hoisted his tankard, "and to the day when the city will become truly ours."

Nine

Late into the night, Vartain and Danilo huddled over the scroll, holding conference amid a circle of sleeping mercenaries. Wyn sat silently nearby, listening to all that was said with an increasingly troubled expression in his large green eyes.

"The first stanza is solved," Vartain said at last. "As we surmised, it refers to the spell placed on the bards at Silverymoon."

"Why do you keep referring to those lines as the first stanza?" Danilo demanded. "There's nothing else on the scroll!"

"Not yet." The riddlemaster pointed to a faint smudge on the parchment, like the shadow of words. As the incredulous Harper watched, a second stanza began to take form beneath the first. "This is not uncommon for a riddle spell of such complexity. The first line of the verse refers to one of seven. As each is solved, the next will appear. This is a device to keep the entire riddle from being solved too easily."

"Rather like using a remote dialect of Sespechian to hide the key to the riddle," Danilo observed.

"Precisely. All these obscure details, however, tell us something about the spellcaster. He or she—or it, for that matter—is well versed in the riddlemaster's art. The spellcaster is either a linguist or a native speaker of Sespechian. If the latter is true, that would make our foe at least three hundred years old."

"Which makes sense, considering that the spellcaster has an interest in an elven artifact. Three hundred years is not so old for an elf," the Harper said. He squinted at the text dawning on the page. "What do you make of this?"

Vartain tipped the parchment to catch more of the dancing light of the campfire. "The answer to the first two lines is 'mother.' Many riddles have to do with family relationships. The mention of woodruff puzzles me," he admitted.

"I can explain that," Danilo said with a tight smile. "My family deals in wines, and a large part of our wealth is due to that herb. It is grown in the Moonshaes and is used to make the famous spring wine that lubricates the Midsummer festivities."

"Fascinating. I would therefore suppose that the mother named here is the Earthmother, the goddess who is synonymous with the Moonshae Isles themselves. Where is the herb grown, precisely?"

"Where? In the ground, I would imagine. Granted, I'm no expert. . . ."

"That is not what I meant," Vartain broke in impatiently. "Where is this herb-flavored wine produced? This could be important!"

Danilo thought it over. "Now that you mention it, my teacher from MacFuirmidh spoke of the vast herb gardens and vineyards that surrounded the college. The school has fallen into decline, of course, but the wineries are a thriving business. At least, they were until this very season,"

Danilo added slowly. "Nearly three moon cycles past, there were severe crop failures, and the herb gardens and vineyards were almost destroyed. I was in Tethyr at the time, working among the wine merchants there. The southern vintners were delighted by this development, as you can well imagine."

"You know what this means, of course." Vartain's tone contradicted his words, and he waited for the young Harper to admit his ignorance.

"Sorry to disappoint you," Danilo said evenly, "but I'm afraid I do." The riddlemaster's brows flew upward in surprise, earning a half-smile from the Harper. "At the height of bardcraft, there were seven elder barding colleges, ranked in order of honor and importance. An aspiring bard would attend them all in a specific order, working his way toward the status of master bard. Our mysterious foe seems to be enacting a bizarre parody of this. The first of these barding colleges was Foclucan, which was located in Silverymoon. There a spell was cast on the bards and ballads. I have no idea how it was done. You were there, Wyn; care to hazard a guess?"

"Not quite yet," the elf replied in a tight voice.

"The crops failed abruptly and mysteriously, not long after the events at Silverymoon's Spring Faire. The event is described in the second stanza, which makes reference to MacFuirmidh, the second of the barding colleges."

Danilo paused and took a deep breath. "Two is a coincidence, three forms a pattern. If the third stanza"—he paused and pointed to the spot on the blank page where the words would appear—"if this names the town of Berdusk and the barding college known as Doss, then we will know to expect a total of seven spells. We will also know the path our foe will take."

"Well done," Vartain said grudgingly.

"There is more," Danilo added. "I began this quest

thinking only to remove the curse on the bards. This is clearly only one part of the problem. Finally, I doubt that these curses were chosen randomly; they all probably contribute to some ultimate goal. This we must discover, so that we can find and stop the spellcaster before that goal is accomplished. It's imperative that you solve the riddles as quickly as possible, so that we know what form the other spells take."

The riddlemaster seemed taken aback by the command in Danilo's tone. "I am in the employ of Elaith Craulnober," he reminded the Harper.

"Elaith and I seem to be partners in this effort," Danilo countered. "You work for both of us now. Think about this, before you limit your allegiance: Elaith wants to possess the artifact, but I want the person behind all this. Can you honestly tell me you wouldn't relish the chance to match wits with the author of this riddle scroll?"

That thought flickered in the riddlemaster's large black eyes, then caught fire. Danilo noted the gleam of dawning obsession and was satisfied. He rose to his feet and walked off to waken the camp, and to give Vartain time to assimilate the Harper's goal as his own.

Music and Mayhem were on their way by sunrise. At Danilo's insistence—and for the price of another gem from the dragon's hoard—Balindar guided Vartain's horse with a leading rein, so that the riddlemaster could devote himself to the study of the scroll as he rode.

Wyn and Morgalla rode side by side, as was becoming their custom. It was clear to Danilo that the dwarf had found in Wyn the musical mentor she craved, but, as much as he hated to disturb their camaraderie, he needed time to convince Wyn to share elfsong magic. So soon after his conversation with Vartain, broaching this subject made Danilo feel as if he were a juggler trying to keep a few too many balls in the air.

"Ride with me a while," he requested of the elf. Morgalla took the hint and reined her stout pony over to Balindar's side. The mercenary looked a bit sheepish when the dwarf approached, but she made some comment that got him laughing and seemed to ease his conscience.

Danilo reached into the magic bag at his belt and withdrew the spellbook Khelben had prepared for him. "This is the spell I used on Grimnosh. Be careful not to look at the runes—that can be dangerous to the untrained. It's a charm spell, very like the one you cast in the marshlands. It suggests that wizard magic and elven spellsong are compatible."

"After what occurred in the High Forest, I cannot deny that," the elf said with obvious reluctance. "Morgalla told me all that happened. She sang me the melody you used, and it is identical to a powerful elven charm spell. This is what you were trying to tell me last night: an elven spellsong had been written in arcane notation."

"Actually, no. I had no idea it was an elfsong spell. I'd never seen anything like this, and I had no idea what it was or even, for that matter, whether it would work. Khelben gave me this spellbook, but I've never heard him cast such magic." Danilo paused, and his brow furrowed. "Come to think of it, I can see why. Uncle Khelben has a voice reminiscent of an amorous cat on an alley fence.

"But I'm wandering from the point," he continued, giving himself a little shake. "As the good archmage often admonishes me, I ought not to let my mind wander, as it's too small to go off by itself."

"You were saying?" Wyn prodded politely.

"Indeed I was. The point is, I'm not an elf, yet I was able to cast magic through music. Consider the possibilities!" Danilo waited for the elf to reply, but Wyn kept his eyes on the path ahead. "Don't you see what this could mean for the Harpers? After the Time of Trouble passed and the gods returned to their own planes, magic was changed in many important ways. Bardic magic was stolen from humans. If some bards could learn the magic of elfsong, think what we could become!"

"I have considered that."

"And?"

The elven minstrel rode in silence for several moments before he turned to the Harper. "Please listen to my explanation before you pass judgment. Keep in mind that I mean no offense, and that my hesitation does not reflect upon you personally."

"I think I've heard this speech before, from at least a dozen Waterdhavian maidens," Danilo said warily.

Wyn's answering smile was faint. "Elfsong, as you have so aptly named the spellsong magic, is a power that when learned is easily accessed. But consider this: power is more easily acquired than wisdom. The elven people live for many human lifetimes, and this gives us a different perspective and a patience that humans tend to lack. We are guided by rich and ancient traditions, and we are prone to consider many solutions before resorting to the use of magic. If humans could resolve their difficulties by the singing of a song, the temptation to abuse—or at least overuse—this power would surely be too great to bear."

"That argument can be made for any kind of magic," Danilo countered. "Yet many humans wield magic with honor."

"And there are many who do not. At least with wizard magic, one must take the time to study and memorize a spell before each casting. That guarantees time for deliberation and reflection, and surely keeps many mages from acting in haste. Elfsong lacks any such safeguard; once a spellsong is learned, it can be cast at will." Wyn shook his head. "I'm sorry, but I have spent many years among human musicians, and there are none I would entrust with such a power. Your ways and elven ways are simply too different."

"I have the next two stanzas!" announced Vartain.

The riddlemaster's words forestalled the protest Danilo had ready. "Can we discuss this at a later time?" he asked the elf.

"It would do no good," Wyn said with quiet finality.

Although he was deeply disappointed, Danilo saw no option but to accept the elf's decision. He inclined his head in a small, formal bow and rode to Vartain's side.

"You were correct," the riddlemaster said, and his voice was less patronizing than usual. "The third and fourth sites were also barding colleges. The riddles name Doss in Berdusk, and Canaith, located near Zazesspur in the land of Tethyr."

"I have recently come from Tethyr," Danilo said thoughtfully, remembering the ballad that had driven him north. He'd tried to put that night from his mind, but he quickly reviewed the event now in search of something that might yield a clue. He wished he had asked Arilyn for more details about the bard who had spread this ballad. Perhaps such information would help them now.

"What powers did the caster gain?" Danilo asked, returning to the matter at hand.

"In Berdusk, the ability to call up or control monsters who use music as a weapon. That would perhaps explain the frog pipers we met in the marshlands near the High Forest. It is interesting to note that there has recently been a marked increase of monster attacks on travelers and farmers to the south of Waterdeep. In many cases, the victims were slain before they could raise weapons in their own defense. These incidents seem to fall along a path between Berdusk and Waterdeep." The riddlemaster paused and considered. "For that matter, the failure of crops around Waterdeep has been profound this year, and unmatched elsewhere in the Northlands but for that one area in the Moonshaes."

"Marvelous," Danilo muttered. "And what happened at Canaith?"

"The caster regained the power to influence crowds through song. Once a common type of bardic magic, it fell dormant during the Time of Trouble."

Danilo fell silent, moving the pieces of this puzzle around in his mind and trying to fit them into a pattern. After a moment he abandoned the exercise. "What's going to happen in Sundabar? The old college Anstruth was there."

"I've haven't gotten that far."

The Harper scratched his chin thoughtfully. "It is possible that the sorcerer hasn't, either. Our foe can obviously travel fast, but we might yet precede him."

Danilo kicked his horse into a trot and rode to the front of the group. The moon elf was riding point guard, as usual, and his silvery hair gleamed in the bright morning light. "You'll have to live without me for a short time," the Harper announced. "I'm leaving for Sundabar at once. Upon my honor, I will return at daybreak."

"Upon the dwarf's life, I believe you," Elaith said pointedly, then he smiled at the Harper. "I shall strive to withhold my tears during your absence. What benevolent god should I thank for this turn of events?"

"Khelben Arunsun, but don't refer to him as such. As deities go, he isn't much for ceremony. Now, all jesting aside. The archmage gave me a ring of teleportation that can transport up to three persons to a site of my choice. I'm going to Sundabar, for there may be a chance of catching up with our spellcaster there."

"Then let us be off at once," Elaith said.

"*Us?* As in, you and me?"

"Of course." The elf smiled pleasantly and produced a

plain silver ring from a pouch at his belt. "Your magic ring, I believe."

Danilo's jaw dropped. He glanced down at his hands. Sure enough, one of his rings was missing. "How?"

"Let us tend to more important matters," the elf said, returning the ring to its owner. "If it would make you feel more comfortable, by all means bring someone else along with us."

The Harper nodded reluctant agreement as he slid the ring back onto his finger. "It's either Wyn or Morgalla. The others are in your employ, and I trust none of them." He raised his voice to hail the dwarf. "Morgalla, how would you like to teleport to Sundabar with me?"

"How'd you like to kiss an orc?" the dwarf responded sweetly. Dwarves were notoriously leery of magical travel, and Morgalla was no exception.

"Wyn it is," Danilo said in a matter-of-fact tone. "One problem: I can use the ring but once in any given day or night. We will not be able to return until after sunset, and I can only teleport to a place I have been before. We're about a day's travel from Taskerleigh: we could meet up with the others there tomorrow morning."

Elaith agreed. He called a halt and quickly explained the plan to the others, putting Balindar in charge and giving them strict orders to make camp at the nearby creek, away from both the ruins of Taskerleigh and the harpy-infested hills.

When all was in readiness, Danilo twisted the ring. The white whirl of the teleportation spell began to encompass him, and he grasped each of the elves by the wrist to bring them along. There was a long moment of nothing but swirling wind and white light, and then they were in Sundabar.

They were also ankle-deep in slush. Danilo stared agape at the devastation around them. The air was warm, but melting ice flooded the streets, and water flowed in rivulets down the gutters. He stooped and fished a chunk of ice from the slush, partly melted but still nearly the size of a hen's egg. It must have been quite a hailstorm, he noted, watching the industrious cityfolk as they set about righting the damage. A small army of workers replaced shattered glass windows, physicians and healers scurried about with herbs and amulets, and city workers dragged off dead and battered animals. Only the children seemed pleased by the novelty, and they darted about, shrieking and tossing balls of hard-packed slush.

For a moment, Danilo wondered if his transportation spell had misfired and taken them to a city farther to the north: perhaps Sossal or some other cold land.

Elaith apparently harbored similar misgivings. "Where the Nine Hells are we?" he demanded.

The Harper turned to the building behind them and squinted up at the heavy wooden sign. The Lusty Wench. Yes, that was the name of the inn he'd patronized on several occasions, and it was the site he had chosen as the destination for his teleportation spell.

"This is definitely Sundabar," he said.

"In that case," Elaith said smoothly, "I think it's safe to assume that we're a bit too late."

* * * * *

When Garnet awoke that morning, the sun was already well into the sky above Sundabar. Exhausted from her long flight and drained by the miscast spell, she had taken a room at an inn not far from the warehouse. Her asperii needed rest as well, for the return trip to Waterdeep would take two days of almost constant flight.

The sorceress dragged herself to the window of her bedchamber and looked down at the street. Almost a day had passed since the freak hailstorm, but the streets were still clogged with slush. Garnet heaved a profound sigh and glanced at the elven harp. It was proving more difficult to control than she had imagined.

She quickly dressed and made her way down to the taproom. As she ate a breakfast of fruit and oatcakes, she noted absently that the other patrons could speak of nothing but the storm. It was widely regarded as a portent of disaster, coming so close to Midsummer. Garnet observed this with satisfaction. At least her spell had succeeded at that much!

Three of the inn's patrons seemed unusually curious about the storm. Two of them were elves, the third a tall young man with long blond hair and an engaging smile. This he turned upon a servant girl, flirting extravagantly while he gently extracted information about the freak storm.

"Try to remember why we're here, Lord Thann!" grumbled the silver-haired elf when the girl left to fetch their order. His voice was soft, but Garnet's sharp elven hearing picked up the words. "While you waste your charm on a serving wench, our sorcerer is long gone."

Thann! Could it be? Garnet studied the young man with growing trepidation, noting the lute on his shoulder and the travel-worn state of his clothes. If this was Khelben Arunsun's nephew, what was he doing in Sundabar? Even such a fool as Danilo Thann was reputed to be should have found his way to Grimnoshtadrano by now. The possibility that he could have survived the dragon encounter was too ludicrous to consider. After all, Garnet had studied and altered Danilo's songs, and she knew what the young "bard" was capable of doing. He was hardly the musician and mage needed to outwit wily Grimnosh.

"Tavern servants hear a great deal," the young man told his elven companion. "Many people speak freely in front of them, as if they were invisible or deaf, or at the very least of no consequence. You would be surprised, my dear Elaith, at how much information they usually possess."

"Spoken like a true Harper," Elaith replied, and the moon elf's tone made clear that this was not a compliment.

"What do you propose we do now, Danilo?" asked the gold elf.

Garnet caught her breath. It was indeed Danilo Thann, and he was counted among Those Who Harped! Somehow the young man she had thought to use as a tool had become an adversary. She leaned forward and listened intently.

The young Harper paused to consider. "We cannot return to Ganstar's Creek until after sunset, and the others will not reach that site until well after dark, anyway. I propose that we spend the day and most of the night in Sundabar and return just before daybreak. That will give Vartain time to work on old Grimnosh's scroll, and us time to glean some information from the townspeople. Our sorcerer struck recently, and perhaps we can get some idea of his identity. Perhaps he is still in the city."

Not for long, Garnet added silently. She rose from the chair and tossed some coins onto the table. Her heart thudded painfully in her chest as she moved through the taproom.

Vartain, the young Harper had said. That could only be Vartain of Calimport, a riddlemaster of well-deserved fame. And he had in his possession her riddle scroll! Her situation could only be worse if one of Danilo Thann's elven companions was a spellsinger.

The sorceress hurried up to her room. She snatched up the Morninglark harp and took the back stairs out of the inn, then she ran across the courtyard to the stables. Her asperii looked up with a question in its sleepy eyes as Garnet cinched on the saddle with shaking hands.

"We're leaving at once. We fly to Ganstar's Creek with all haste, throughout the whole night if we must. It is imperative that we make it there before tomorrow's dawn!"

* * * * *

The early show at the Three Pearls theater opened to a large crowd. Outside the large stone and mud-brick building, a queue of people stretched down Pearl Alley. Several troupe members strolled along the narrow street, entertaining those who waited. Vendors hawked oranges and sweets, and there was a hum of curious anticipation.

"Lucia, I really haven't time for this," Caladorn told his lady, an uncustomary touch of impatience in his voice as they edged closer to the entrance. "The Midsummer Festival is almost upon us, and the practice sessions have been plagued by mishaps and injuries. I should be at the arena."

"I would not keep you from your work, but for something important," Lady Thione said in soft tones. "You know that guilds or other groups sometimes hire the theater for private performances. A private party is paying for this show, yet the performance is open to all who care to come."

"So?"

"The person behind this performance is Lord Hhune, a merchant visiting from Tethyr. The city's bards are unhappy about attempts to censor their songs, and Hhune is paying them to air their discontent at a concert satirizing the Lords of Waterdeep, particularly the archmage."

Caladorn stared at Lucia. "How did you come to know of this?"

The noblewoman shrugged. "Some of my servants understand the language of Tethyr. I have done business with Hhune in the past, and I trust him not, so I had him followed and watched. My servant overheard Hhune talking to one of his men. What Hhune hopes to gain from this, I cannot begin to imagine." She lifted enormous, haunted dark eyes to her lover's face and whispered, "You know what became of the royal family when men such as Hhune took power in Tethyr. There are many in the south who would see me dead, although my connection to the royal family is admittedly distant. Now that Hhune seeks to influence affairs in Waterdeep, I cannot help but fear."

Caladorn's stern expression melted, and he drew the tiny noblewoman away from the crowds. "Lucia, you are safe in Waterdeep, and with me."

"You're right, of course," she said, and cast a rueful smile up at him. "I suppose I'm being foolish."

"Your concern is easy to understand," the young man said, and he bent and kissed her forehead. "Now, let's leave Hhune to the city's Lords. You can be sure they know of his activities."

They do now, Lucia thought with dark satisfaction.

* * * * *

As soon as Caladorn had seen his lady safely to her villa, he hurried to the palace of Piergeiron, Waterdeep's only acknowledged ruler. The young man was not particularly surprised to find Khelben Arunsun in council with Piergeiron. The Lords of Waterdeep met often these days, in full council and in small groups, to deal with the city's seemingly unending problems.

"Did you enjoy the performance at the Three Pearls?" the archmage asked with a touch of wry amusement.

"I didn't stay," the young Lord responded. He had long ago ceased to be surprised at the extent of Khelben's knowledge; among the Lords of Waterdeep, it was often said that no one could sneeze in his bedchamber but that the archmage inquired after his health the following morning.

"I have some information about a merchant from Tethyr," Caladorn continued.

"That would be Lord Hhune," Piergeiron said, glancing at Khelben.

"You two know of him?"

"Oh, yes," the archmage said dryly. He handed Caladorn a piece of paper. "This is an example of Hhune's brand of diplomacy. He has papered the city with these."

Caladorn glanced at a satirical sketch of Khelben Arunsun painting stick figures, while the disguised Lords of Waterdeep looked on. He shook his head in deep puzzlement and handed it back. "What does this Hhune want?"

"That is not entirely clear. He is a guildmaster in his native Tethyr, the head of the merchant shipping guild. To all appearances, he came to Waterdeep with goods for the Midsummer Faire. His crew, however, seem to have unusual talents. Some of them have been busy in the Dock Ward, recruiting thieves and assassins in an attempt to organize secret guilds in Waterdeep," Piergeiron said, rubbing one red-rimmed eye as he spoke. The strain of the last few weeks showed plainly on the First Lord's face.

"We believe that Hhune may be a member of the Knights of the Shield," Khelben continued, and he handed the young Lord a large, gold coin. "These are tokens given to Knights who have performed notable services. Several of these have been recovered from Hhune's men, including some who entered the city before Hhune showed up. That suggests a larger problem," the archmage said. "While Hhune is not exactly subtle, the influx of agents prior to his arrival suggests that he has another, more canny partner in Waterdeep."

"None of our sources has been able to discern the identity of this agent," Piergeiron added. "But it seems clear that the Knights of the Shield have become extremely active in Waterdeep. You know that three merchant ships were recently lost."

"Yes," Caladorn said quietly. "I knew the captain on one of them, and a better sailor I never met. It struck me as odd that she would fall to a pirate ambush."

"The ships sailed from Baldur's Gate. Harper agents there are investigating the situation. It appears that the harbormaster is an agent of the Knights of the Shield, and he has been passing information on shipping routes and schedules to an unknown source in Waterdeep. This is not the Knights' first attempt at disrupting shipping," Piergeiron concluded with a sigh. "It just comes at a particularly inopportune time."

"What are you doing about Hhune?" Caladorn pressed.

"Frankly, Hhune is small fish. He is being watched in the hope that he will lead us to the Waterdeep agent."

Caladorn seemed less than happy with that conclusion, but he bowed and hurried away to his duties at the arena.

When they were alone, Piergeiron nodded at the paper in Khelben's hand.

"Subtle or not, Hhune's tactics are taking a toll, my friend. I am beginning to understand your concern about the changed ballads, for they are also proving to be highly effective. Many of them seem to be aimed at you personally. Does it seem likely that the Knights of the Shield are also responsible for the spell on the bards?"

"If not, they are certainly exploiting it," Khelben said in a weary voice. "I have a contact who may yield some information. I'll seek her out at once."

He murmured the words of a spell. In a moment, the tall archmage was gone, and in his place stood a young man of medium height and build. His features were pleasant, and shaded by a broad-brimmed hat. Simple, well-made clothing of dark gray linen would be deemed equally at home in

the marketplace or a North Ward parlor. In short, he was
unremarkable and could pass unnoticed through most of
the city. Thus disguised, Khelben took his leave of Piergeiron and headed toward the nearby Jester's Court. It
was time for the archmage of Waterdeep to pay a call on a
certain lady of the evening.

* * * * *

Imzeel Coopercan had heard too much in the last several days for his peace of mind. Yet the half-dwarven proprietor of the Mighty Manticore listened carefully to the
talk of the early supper crowd, picking out bits from the
hum of conversation as he endlessly polished the bar with
a rag.

"At the rate you're going, you'll wear clear through the
wood before moonrise," teased Ginalee, a plump, merry
lass who'd been Imzeel's barmaid long enough for him to
permit such familiarity. She was more than passing fond of
her employer, despite his dour personality and barrel-
shaped torso, and therefore she tried to distract him from
whatever woes now absorbed his attention. Resting her
elbows on the shining wood of the bar, she propped her
head in her hands and dimpled up at him. This posture
yielded Imzeel a view of cleavage that should have rallied a
dying man; he gave Ginalee a mere glance and went back
to polishing the bar.

The offended barmaid snatched the rag away and
draped it from the fang of the stuffed and mounted lion
head that hung over the bar. That trophy, with a little cre-
ative taxidermy and a great deal of wishful thinking, had
inspired the tavern's imposing name. For a moment,
Ginalee toyed with the idea of telling Imzeel his establishment was more commonly known as "the *Mangy* Manticore." With a sigh, she decided that it wouldn't matter to

him, as long as business continued to thrive.

And thrive it did. The Mighty Manticore was located in the heart of the Castle Ward, at the busy crossroads of Selduth and Silver streets. Those who spent their days in commerce and diplomacy often stopped by the tavern to share news and to make deals over a no-nonsense supper of thick, flavorful stew, sharp cheese, fresh black bread, and hearty ale. Just as important, the back of the tavern opened into Jester's Court. Something interesting always seemed to be happening there, and therefore those whose business was best conducted in shadows also found their way into the tavern through the back door. The result was a nice blend of information and intrigue that Imzeel found to be as satisfying as profit; the proprietor sought and hoarded knowledge as avidly as his dwarven forebears had mined for mithril.

Yet Imzeel found the day's talk troubling. He reclaimed his rag from the "manticore" and resumed his endless circling as he listened in. There were the usual complaints about problems with shipping and theft, but such things seemed to be occurring on a larger scale than normal. Entire ships and the full contents of warehouses were vanishing, right under the noses of city officials. Even more distressing were the whispers suggesting that the Lords of Waterdeep were disappearing. Tavern talk made the odds-on culprit Waterdeep's resident archmage.

It was widely accepted that Khelben Arunsun was one of the secret Lords of Waterdeep. There were some who felt the archmage had a bit too much power of his own without such a position, but most Waterdhavians had nothing against wizard rule. In fact, Ahghairon's Tower stood nearby, a monument to the powerful mage who'd established the Lords of Waterdeep several centuries past. The city had prospered under Ahghairon's long rule, and the consensus seemed to be that, as long as the Blackstaff could do as well, may the gods be with him! Waterdhavians weren't inclined to grease a cart until it squeaked. As trouble in the city increased, however, many feared that Khelben Arunsun was spending too much time dispatching his rival Lords, and not enough tending to the city and its concerns.

Imzeel noted with satisfaction that his own business seemed unaffected by the city's troubles. The supper hour had just started, and already the barkeep was tapping a third keg of ale. The patrons even had music with their dinner, for the Masked Minstrel had wandered in from her customary place in Jester's Court and was playing a plaintive tune on her lute. Usually the mysterious woman's appearance engendered much interest and speculation, but this evening other matters took precedence. Few bothered to listen to her songs, and Imzeel was not sorry to see her put aside her lute in response to a whispered invitation. She and a young customer disappeared through the back door into Jester's Court, no doubt bound for the privacy of the woods that covered the slopes of Waterdeep Mountain. Business as usual, Imzeel repeated silently, taking comfort from the thought.

"The wizards you ordered are here," Ginalee announced. She plunked a tray of empty mugs down on the counter, and tossed her head in the direction of three newcomers. "Should I tell them to go ahead?"

Imzeel nodded, and relief eased his countenance into something approaching a smile. He was a prudent man of business, and like many others he had contracted the wizards' guild to place magical wards about his establishment.

The Watchful Order of Magists and Protectors was Waterdeep's youngest guild, and they tended to matters ranging from policing visiting sorcerers to serving on the fire watch. The guild also sought to influence and—to whatever extent they could—monitor the magical activities of powerful, independent wizards. The bizarre occurrences in the city of late suggested that magic of some sort was at work, and this created an imperative demand for the guild's services. All over the city guild mages were busy setting up magical wards to detect and dispel magic. This gave Imzeel a sense of security, and his patrons also murmured their approval as they watched the proceedings.

As the guild mage finished the complex gestures of a spell to rid the room of magical illusions, the Masked Minstrel came back into the taproom on the arm of her latest client. A sharp blue light flared around the pair, drawing a startled scream from the woman. The room fell into silence, and every eye was drawn to the magical light. As the patrons watched, the young man's features melted and flowed together, in an instant crystallizing into a new and familiar shape.

Standing next to the mysterious masked woman was a tall, well-muscled man, clad in somber magnificence. His features were sharp, his expression grave, and his usually keen black eyes betrayed a touch of uncertainty. The wedge-shaped streak of silver in the center of his beard confirmed his identity to those who would not have known him from his face alone.

The Masked Minstrel fell away from him, one hand clasped to her painted lips. She backed off several paces, and then turned and fled toward Jester's Court. Whether she was surprised by the transformation, or just unwilling to be linked with Khelben Arunsun under such adverse circumstances, was impossible to say.

"So this is how the archmage of Waterdeep spends a summer evening," Ginalee murmured to Imzeel. "And the city going down to Cyric in a cistern, and all."

"Hush, girl," the man whispered fiercely, making a warding sign to stave off the ill luck said to follow when the god of strife's name was invoked.

One of the patrons broke the tense silence. A cleric of Tymora, perhaps trusting to the legendary luck his goddess was said to grant, rose from his dinner and faced the archmage.

"Perhaps no one in the city can stand against you and your ambitions," the cleric said quietly, "but that doesn't mean we have to drink with you."

The man turned and strode from the room. One by one, chairs scraped across the wooden floor as the other patrons followed suit. The taproom emptied quickly. Only Imzeel and his employees remained, eyeing the archmage with fear and uncertainty.

Khelben Arunsun came over to the bar, and his footsteps seemed to echo through the deserted room. He placed a small leather bag on the polished wood. "My apologies, Imzeel," he said in a voice devoid of expression. "Please accept this purse; the gold within should cover your lost business."

The next instant, he was gone.

"Well, I never," Ginalee huffed in mock indignation, her voice slightly unsteady but her sense of fun fully intact. "He just upped and disappeared! No flash of light, no puffs of colored smoke, not even a whiff of brimstone! They've got more interesting wizards over in Thay, or so I hear."

"Ginalee," Imzeel said in a weary voice, "why don't you take the rest of the night off."

Ten

Danilo and his elven companions lingered in the Lusty Wench through the evening hours and long into the night. When the black night sky began to fade to indigo and the last of the stars disappeared, many patrons of the Lusty Wench festhall and tavern were still enjoying the justly famed fortified wine, the exotic entertainment, and the company of the tavern's resident escorts. The Harper and his associates walked out into the dark and silent streets of Sundabar considerably poorer of coin, but with a good deal of information.

The freak summer storm had covered only a part of Sundabar. The trades district was hardest hit—Danilo privately noted that the site of the barding college was located in the very center of this area—with violent thunderstorms and hail. Various explanations were offered, but most of the tavern's patrons considered the strange Midsummer weather to be an evil omen.

More important, sentries had spoken of a bard who had

entered the city that morning, carrying a small dark harp and riding a snow-white asperii. No one could give details of her appearance, except that she was small and swathed in a light cloak.

"A sorceress of power could command an asperii," Danilo mused as they walked down the dark street, "but an asperii will not willingly serve one who embraces evil. It's hard to believe that our foe has the benefit of the Northlands in mind!"

"We've learned all we can here," Wyn said impatiently. "Let's return at once. I need to have a look at the riddle scroll."

Danilo stopped and studied the minstrel. "What do you expect to find?"

"I'm not sure. I just feel that we may have been missing something important," was all that the elf would say, shooting a pointed glance in Elaith's direction. Danilo took the hint and left the matter for a later discussion.

The Harper led the elves into a nearby alley and again called upon the magic of his ring. When the whirling light faded, they found themselves in the ruined garden where they'd met up days before.

The signs of battle were still visible in the faint light that preceded dawn. Three mounds of soft earth marked the places where they'd buried the fallen mercenaries, and at the far corner of the garden a bonfire had reduced the dead harpies to a pile of foul-smelling bones and ashes.

"Why have you brought us here?" Elaith snarled, taking in the scene with distaste. "We were supposed to meet the others near Ganstar's Creek!"

"Magical travel is reliable only if the destination is known. I could have tried for the creek, but at the risk of ending up being a permanent part of the landscape. Imagine a tree wearing your ears for knotholes, and you've got the general idea."

The elf hissed with exasperation and turned to leave.

"Wait!" shrieked a voice behind them, edged with hysteria. The elven hermit came loping from an abandoned building, his tattered rags fluttering around him. "Coming along I be," he said, casting a pleading look at Elaith. "You be seeking the Morninglark, and dance to the harp I do."

Wyn Ashgrove looked sharply at the disheveled elf. "The Morninglark! What have you do to with the Harp of Ingrival?"

The hermit's ravaged face suddenly appeared very sane, and his violet eyes held a lifetime of sadness. "I have nothing more to do with the harp, but it has everything to do with me. Played it I did."

Wyn looked closer. His lips moved in a silent oath, and his eyes widened in awe. "*You* are Ingrival, are you not?" he asked the hermit in a tone of great respect.

"It may be that I am. I remember not my name," came the sad response.

"What's going on, Wyn?" Danilo asked softly.

"The Morninglark is an ancient elven harp, an artifact crafted in the early days of Myth Drannor," the elf said in an aside. "It is considered too powerful to be played by any but the most skilled spellsingers. For centuries it has been safe in the possession of Ingrival, a famous musician. He went into seclusion and has not been heard from for many years. The harp was thought to be lost."

Wyn turned to Elaith, who had been standing by listening impassively. "This is what you seek, isn't it? The Morninglark?" he demanded in an accusing voice.

"What is that to you?"

"The harp is sacred to the People. It is not a treasure, and it is not a tool. Its power is not to be used for gain!"

"My motives are not your concern," Elaith said with icy finality.

"But your actions are." Shaking with indignation, Wyn

faced down the moon elf. "You knew, or at least suspected, the identity of this elf. He is exiled not by choice, but by misfortune. That you would abandon anyone—especially a fellow elf—to a life of solitude and madness! That is vile enough, but you turned away from a hero of the People!"

The minstrel spun away from Elaith and spoke to Danilo. "We must take this unfortunate elf with us to Waterdeep. The priests at the pantheon temple will care for him, and perhaps bring him a measure of healing. They are holy elves, and they take in the infirm and the outcast."

From the corner of his eye, Danilo saw Elaith recoil at Wyn's words. For an instant the rogue elf looked deeply stricken, then his usual expression of mocking humor came down over his pained face like a curtain. Danilo tucked this strange reaction away for future reflection, and he nodded his approval of Wyn's plan.

"You are welcome in our midst, friend elf," the Harper said to the one Wyn had called Ingrival. "As it turns out, the patriarch of the elven temple owes me a favor, but I'm sure the good priest would accept you for your own sake."

The hermit's face lit up beneath its crust of dirt. Then he let out a shriek of pure terror and dove into a thicket of bushes.

Danilo was the first to see the gigantic shadow approach, cast long by the slanting rays of early morning. Instinctively he ducked, then twisted to look up into the sky. Circling high above the abandoned village was an enormous winged creature. Although it looked like a harmless—if huge—lark, it was clearly a bird of prey, for it carried a deer in its talons as easily as a hawk would a field mouse.

"What now?" Elaith muttered as he readied an arrow.

"Hold your fire," Danilo commanded. He took the lute strap off his shoulder and quickly checked the instrument's tuning. "Whatever that thing is, it's too big to be brought down like that."

He began to play the introduction to the song that had lulled the dragon, hoping it would have the same effect on this creature. Wyn took his lyre and joined in with the musical spell. From far above, the magic-bearing melody bounced back to them, echoed by a trilling, avian voice. The eerie sound raised the hair on the back of Danilo's neck and sent a shiver of fear down his back. Nevertheless, he continued to sing.

As if drawn by the music, the enormous creature dove down into the clearing and landed on the sagging roof of the abandoned farmhouse. Leaving its torn prey draped over a gable, the monstrous songbird swooped into the garden and landed a few paces from the spellsingers.

Roughly the size of a war-horse, the beast had the form and the distinctive gray-and-white-speckled feathers of a mockinglark, a morning lark who imitated the song of other birds. But this creature also had the lethal talons and hooked beak of an eagle, and in the center of its head was a single enormous eye, as glossy and black as obsidian.

It made no move to attack, and it cocked its head quizzically as it listened to the magical song. Again it joined in, warbling along in perfect imitation of Wyn's soaring countertenor. As the bizarre trio continued, Danilo noticed that the bird was blinking more and more frequently, its enormous eyelids meeting in the center of the shining black orb. The blinking became more languid as the creature sang itself to sleep. Finally the eye stayed closed, and the bird's song faded into a regular, prolonged chirruping. The avian version of a snore, Danilo noted with deep relief. He ended the song and ran his shaking fingers through his hair.

"The power of elfsong at work," he said with quiet emphasis, nodding toward the slumbering monster. "This is how it could be used."

Wyn lowered his instrument and took a deep breath.

Before he could speak, Elaith walked up to enormous songbird. The moon elf drew his sword and slashed the sleeping creature once across the throat.

Indignation flooded the minstrel's face. "That was wanton and unnecessary! The creature was no danger to us, and no elf ever willingly kills a songbird!"

"I am an elf, the bird sang, and it is dead," Elaith pointed out coldly. "Perhaps you should review the facts and reconsider your conclusion. Now, if you two wish to linger in this charnel house, that is your concern. I'm joining the others at the creek." With that, the elf leaped nimbly over a broken stone wall and ran lightly toward the south.

Wyn's green eyes burned with wrath, and he looked as if he did not quite trust himself to speak.

"In this particular matter, I wouldn't be too hard on our silver-haired friend," Danilo said. "I've learned enough about elven traditions to know how you folk feel about the destruction of living trees and harmless creatures, but you've got to admit that this was no ordinary songbird. Perhaps Elaith's reaction was extreme, but it was not entirely unwarranted."

"It's not that alone. Elaith Craulnober violates elven mores and traditions at every turn. He is lawless and amoral."

"Really! Just picking up on that, are we?"

"But he is an elf!" The protest burst from Wyn with the force of a shattered icon.

Danilo sighed heavily. "You left Evermeet when you were very young, did you not? Since then you have traveled exclusively among mankind."

"Yes, that is so."

"The eyes of youth perceive only sunshine and shadows. A thing is right and good, or it isn't." The Harper smiled ruefully. "I am prone to that sort of thinking myself, so I do not judge you. As I am fast learning, sometimes one must simply do the best thing possible under the circumstances. If humans have a strength that sets us apart from elves, it is that knowledge. Of course, that is also our weakness," he added in a wry tone. "You'd do well not to trust the moon elf, but perhaps you should understand why he is what he is."

In a few words, Danilo told the story of Elaith's dormant moonblade and his self-imposed exile from Evermeet. "What drives him now I do not know, but of one thing I'm sure: in his heart Elaith Craulnober is as deeply and fully elven as you are. No one who saw him dance the magic linking star and steel could doubt that. Unfortunately, being an elf and being virtuous are not necessarily one and the same. Most people tend to forget that, and this is one reason why Elaith's career has been so successful."

"You have made your point." Wyn studied the Harper. "You seem to know and understand a good deal about the elven people."

"I ought to. For two years, I traveled with a half-elf who was raised in Evereska, amid elven people and customs. She considers herself more elf than human, although in my opinion she embodies the superlatives of both races."

"I see." Wyn smiled faintly. "It can be difficult to love someone so different from oneself."

"Wait a minute. Did I say that?"

"You didn't need to. Your loss is recent and deep, and it is in your eyes whenever you sing. Perhaps that accounts in part for your wisdom."

"If I were all that wise, I wouldn't be standing around in a place like this, blathering on like a five-copper sage," Danilo said, distinctly uncomfortable with the direction the conversation was taking. "Let's get back to the others. Come with us, friend elf," he called, and at his summons the hermit promptly crawled out from his hiding place in the bushes.

The three of them walked in silence for some time, each deep in his own thoughts. At the crest of a large hill, the camp came into sight, nestled in a clearing bounded by Ganstar's Creek to the west, and thick woodland to the east. Apparently Elaith was impatient to be off, for the horses were saddled and the gear packed. The cookfire had been doused, but the scent of woodsmoke and roasted fish lingered in the air.

Wyn paused at the crest of the hill and laid a hand on the Harper's shoulder. "Elaith Craulnober was correct about one thing: it is time for me to reconsider my thinking about elves and humans. You would wield the Morninglark with more honor than either Elaith or the elf who now possesses it. I will do all I can to help you recover the artifact. And if you still desire to learn elfsong, Danilo Thann, then it would be my honor to teach you."

Before the startled Harper could answer, Wyn's face turned ashen, and he pointed to the sky. "The asperii! There it is!"

Danilo squinted in the direction Wyn was pointing, but his eyes were not as keen as the elf's. He thought that the small moving spot could just as well have been a bird. "You're sure?"

"He's sure," the elven hermit said, peering up at the sky. "Flying horse, no wings. See you later!" He scampered off into the woods nearby.

Wyn's golden face clouded with concern. "The campsite below is surrounded with trees. From this hillside we can see much farther than the others! If this is an attack, they'll never see it coming."

"Maybe the sorceress is just passing by on her way to Waterdeep?"

Wyn shook his head and ran one hand through his ebony curls in an uncharacteristically nervous gesture. "Look. The asperii is circling."

* * * * *

High above Ganstar's Creek, Garnet ordered her exhausted asperii to circle the camp. From her vantage point in the sky, the adventurers looked like so many ants as they moved busily about the clearing. The half-elf's blue eyes narrowed as she considered the site. The camp was surrounded by verdant woodland. She smiled slowly, and silently bid the asperii to begin a spiraling descent.

The bard took the Morninglark harp into her arms and began to play, singing the words that had laid waste the Moonshaes' vineyards and the farmlands around Waterdeep. In response to her song, the trees surrounding the encampment shuddered and died. It was as if autumn came in the span of two heartbeats, and a hundred trees cast their leaves.

Next, Garnet struck a single string on her harp and pointed a finger at the camp. A stream of air spiraled downward toward the clearing.

* * * * *

"Damn," Danilo said emphatically, as he and Wyn squinted up at the circling asperii. "If you know an elfsong suitable for the occasion, I suggest you sing it!"

Wyn looked dubious, but he took up the lyre. The first blast of wind tore the magical instrument from his hands and knocked his feet out from under him. Danilo threw himself flat and gripped the elf's ankle. He barely had time to lock his own ankles around a young birch before the maelstrom began in earnest.

Howling as if in torment, the wind tore through the trees, growing in volume and speed until it threatened to suck the slight elf into its vortex. Danilo closed his eyes against the churning dust and debris, and he held on to the airborne minstrel with all his strength.

"As Mielikki is my witness, I hope this elf has a competent cobbler," Danilo muttered as he clung to Wyn's boot with both hands.

* * * * *

Flying high above the wind, Garnet watched as the giant whirlwind engulfed the clearing. The tiny figures huddled together in the eye of the magical storm, while the tunnel of air around them sucked in leaves and broken branches. The sorceress waited until the whirling debris formed a massive wall. Then, with a quick snapping motion, she clenched her outstretched hand. The wind tunnel collapsed, burying the dangerous riddlemaster and his traveling companions in a pile of rotting foliage.

Garnet commanded the asperii to swoop down closer, and she nodded in satisfaction at the size of the pile. No one could survive in there for more than a few minutes. She urged the asperii away from the clearing, and as they flew she sang the song that twisted living creatures into music-wielding monsters. A cricket the size of a moor hound crawled out of the blighted woodlands, burrowing into the pile of debris in search of food.

Not yet satisfied, Garnet flew northwest toward the hills that hid the harpy lair. She could command musical monsters as well as create them. If someone managed to crawl out of the pile, it wouldn't hurt to have a flock of vengeful harpies guarding the perimeter. When Danilo Thann and his elven companions arrived, they would have more than one surprise awaiting them. With that thought, the sorceress turned her path toward Waterdeep.

* * * * *

The windstorm ended as abruptly as it began, and Wyn and Danilo fell face-forward onto the hillside. The Harper groaned and spat dust. Every joint and muscle ached from his struggle against the buffeting wind. He rose slowly and painfully to his feet, flexing stiff fingers. He gave his birch tree anchor a grateful pat, and then offered a hand to the gold elf, who looked as dusty and battered as Dan felt.

"By the sea and stars!" Wyn spoke the oath softly as Dan pulled him to his feet.

Danilo followed the line of the elf's gaze. "Moander's mountain," he swore in turn, for the heap of rotting, steaming vegetation that covered the clearing looked like the handiwork of the erstwhile god of corruption.

The moment of shock passed quickly. "Morgalla's in there," Wyn said in a hollow voice. He took off after Danilo, who was already hurtling down the hillside, half running, half sliding.

When they reached the camp they began frantically tossing aside the branches that covered the pile, then they dug into the rotting leaves. Danilo's hand closed on something soft, and he held up Morgalla's jester doll in triumph. He and Wyn tore at the loamy mass with their hands, and in seconds they'd uncovered a pair of small, iron-shod boots. They each grabbed an ankle and tugged. Morgalla slid out of the pile gagging and choking, but still holding fast to the oak staff of her spear. She wiped slime from her face and waved Wyn aside, motioning for him to keep digging. As soon as she could stand, she started working beside them.

A high-pitched giggle momentarily distracted the workers. Standing by the pile was the elven hermit of Taskerleigh. He regarded their labors with a wide, mocking grin on his emaciated face, and his bony hands settled on his hips.

"That be not the way," the mad elf insisted. He darted

forward and deftly snatched the dwarf's spear from her. Before Morgalla could protest, the hermit climbed the pile and began poking experimentally into the rubbish.

"Use the blunt end, you daft, orc-sired scarecrow," she shouted.

"Oops!" The hermit giggled again and flipped the spear around. He jabbed a few more times and then nodded with satisfaction. "Soft," he proclaimed. "Squirmy! Dig here."

It took all four of them to pull Balindar out of the sludge. "Elaith's in there, real close," the huge mercenary gasped out, raking hunks of rotting foliage from his beard.

Morgalla huffed and folded her arms over her chest. "Can we pretend we didn't hear that, bard?"

"Stop tempting me, and dig!"

They found the moon elf, who came out sputtering curses in Elvish. Wyn gritted his teeth at this latest outrage and kept digging, the hermit working close at his side. Mange was recovered, and then Vartain. The riddlemaster was dragged, senseless, from the pile. While the others continued to dig, Danilo bent over Vartain. He put his ear against the riddlemaster's filthy tunic and heard the faint beating of Vartain's heart.

"Use this," Mange suggested, thrusting a flask of cheap whiskey into Danilo's hands. "Should bring him right around. It worked on 'im before, anyways."

The Harper took out the stopper and sniffed. "Cure or kill," he muttered as he poured some of the fluid into Vartain's slack mouth. With one hand he held the riddlemaster's mouth shut, and with the other he massaged the man's throat until finally he swallowed. After several tense seconds, the riddlemaster coughed.

Danilo's relief was short-lived. Two thrumming booms tore through the ravaged clearing, rattling the dead trees and sending bone-deep agony through the Harper with each blast. Incongruously, Dan thought of the musical

parlor trick in which glass was shattered by a high, clear
note. The explosive pain in his teeth and bones made him
certain that this sound, in time, could yield similar results.
Struggling against the pain, Danilo drew his sword and
whirled to face their latest attacker.

Crawling from the rotting pile was an enormous black
cricket, roughly the size of a hunting dog. The monster
chittered, its antennae twitching furiously this way and
that, and it turned its incurious, multiple eyes on the filthy
travelers. Its hind legs, notched like a washboard, rose and
moved together like a bow against a fiddle. Again the
killing blasts tore through the clearing. The waves of sear-
ing pain seemed to melt Danilo's strength; his knees
buckled and his hand lost its grip on the sword. All around
him, the fighters fell helpless to the ground. The giant
cricket skittered toward its prey.

Elaith was on his feet first. The elf drew his sword and
slashed at the monster. His strike severed an antenna, but
the creature continued to advance. Elaith struck again and
again, but the cricket's hard shell deflected any blow to its
body. He shouted for the others to help. The fighters
ringed the cricket and hacked at it from all sides. The
insect whirled and lunged with jerky movements, seemingly unhurt by the repeated blows.

Leveling her spear and bellowing a cry to the dwarven
god of battle, Morgalla charged. The tip of her spear found
a vulnerable spot between the plated armor of the cricket's
head and thorax, and it sank deep. The cricket reared up,
yanking the dwarf off her feet.

Morgalla held on to her staff and swung herself hard
toward the monstrous insect. The momentum drove the
spear deeper still. Grimly she held on as the cricket
thrashed and twisted, vainly trying to rid itself of its dwarven tormenter. Using each bruising tumble to her advantage, the dwarf dug and twisted her spear in search of a

vital spot. Danilo and the others circled with drawn swords, but they could not strike the cricket without harming Morgalla.

The monster dropped its weight onto its front four legs and marshaled its last defense. Again its hind legs rubbed together, and again its thrumming song boomed through the clearing.

Morgalla shrieked in anguish and clapped her hands over her ears. She flung herself away from the cricket and rolled several times, putting as much space as possible between herself and the killing song. The cricket leaped after her and seized her boot in its pincherlike mandible. It backed away toward the pile, dragging the dwarf along. Morgalla grabbed at the fallen branches that littered the ground, trying to find a handhold. Both Wyn and Danilo instinctively reached for their instruments and found no help there: the elf's had been carried away in the windstorm, and two strings on Danilo's lute had snapped. Balindar rose and staggered after the dwarf, shouting and slashing at the monster. Even his vast strength could not stop the cricket's retreat.

A remembered image flashed into Danilo's mind as he cast aside the worthless lute and rose to his feet: Arilyn slicing through the inch-thick skull of an ogre with her moonblade. Even without magic, the elf-forged swords were stronger than any steel. Not thinking of the consequences, he turned and snatched Elaith's dormant moonblade from its sheath. Raising it high overhead with both hands, he raced forward and slammed the sword down on one of the creature's deadly hind legs. The elven blade bit deep and severed the limb at the joint. The monster released Morgalla and lurched away, listing to one side like a sinking ship.

Balindar pulled Morgalla to her feet. The single-minded dwarf brushed him aside and charged after the cricket. She grabbed her spear and jerked it free, and with a second quick movement she plunged it into the cricket's eye. Using the spear like a lever, she flung herself forward. Under the force of her assault, the hard shell gave way with a sickening crack. Morgalla leaped back, wiping a splash of gore from her face as the cricket toppled over onto its side. It twitched a few more times, then finally lay still.

As soon as the immediate danger was past, Danilo dropped the moonblade and turned to Elaith, his hands raised in a gesture of surrender. The moon elf took no notice. His face was set in a mask of fury, and he sprang silently at the Harper.

Danilo dropped to the ground and rolled left, hearing as he did the swish of a dagger dangerously close to his right ear. He leaped to his feet and drew his own sword, crouching in a defensive stance. Elaith was already up, the dagger in one hand and a long silver dirk in the other.

Wyn Ashgrove stepped between the fighters. Although nearly a half foot shorter than either Dan or Elaith, the slight elf had a commanding mien that neither could ignore. The fighters involuntarily lowered their weapons.

"In what way, Lord Craulnober, has this human defiled the elven sword?" he demanded, his cool green eyes fixed upon the angry moon elf. "Were not the moonblades forged for great deeds? The Harper saved a life, perhaps all our lives. If his task was unworthy, even a dormant sword would have struck him down. Do not judge where the moonblade did not, for in doing so you dishonor the sword." The unspoken words *more than you have already* hung in the air.

Elaith sheathed his weapons and picked up the ancient blade. Without a word, he turned and strode from the camp into the blighted forest.

"You'll fight that one yet," Morgalla observed. She wrenched her spear free of the monster and came to stand at Danilo's side. "I owe you, bard."

"Repay me, then, by letting me fight him alone when the time comes."

The Harper's voice was quiet and uncharacteristically grim, and the dwarf nodded once in understanding. With a deep sigh, Danilo turned back to the pile.

They dug until all the men had been recovered. Orcsarmor was not found in time, and several other mercenaries —whose names Danilo had never learned—had been slain and partially eaten by the giant cricket. After the survivors laid the men in shallow graves, Wyn went in search of the runaway hermit, and the others bathed in the cold, deep waters of the creek.

Following a cursory dip in the stream, Vartain pulled the scroll out of his leather pouch and resumed his study. Danilo came out of the creek dripping and chilly. He discarded his wet tunic and began to remove dry clothing from his magic bag. The others watched agape as he took from the bag a fine linen shirt, a dark green tabard, leggings, linens, and stockings, even a spare pair of boots. The Harper looked up and noted his audience.

"It's a bag of holding," he commented, and continued to rummage. "An especially roomy one. You wouldn't believe all the stuff that's in here. I've got something that should suit you, Morgalla, at least until Wyn gets back with your pony and your travel bag. It's fortunate that you folks had readied the horses and supplies before the sorceress struck. Ah, here it is."

Danilo drew forth a loose shirt of pale green silk. "This is hardly the gown I would have chosen for you, but it should serve for the time. Here's a scarf, too, and a gold clasp with a rather nice cluster of peridots—"

"Fancy stuff like this don't hold up to the road," Morgalla pointed out, but she took the luxurious garments and headed for the privacy of a cluster of rocks.

The Harper dressed quickly and passed out what articles of clothing he thought might fit the others. Mange looked almost a gentleman in a fine shirt and leggings, with his patchwork scalp covered by a rakish bandanna. Balindar teased his friend unmercifully, and Mange's self-conscious grin sat oddly on his weathered and battle-scarred face. The riddlemaster, however, absently waved away Danilo's offer of a fresh tunic.

"The next of the barding colleges is in Waterdeep. I know of no such site," Vartain said, looking up at last.

"The school was called Ollamn. There is no barding college now, but as you know most people involved in the bardic arts register at Halambar's Lute Shop. Halambar is the master of the musicians' guild, and this practice gives local and visiting bards a service once provided by the college. What will happen in Waterdeep?"

"According to the riddle, a lord will fall on the field of triumph, on a day that is not a day."

Morgalla emerged from the rock cluster, clad in green silk. The shirt hung past her knees, and she'd girded it at the waist with the sash and the gold and peridot pin. With her damp, unbraided auburn hair curling about her face and her feet bare, she looked a bit like a very stocky wood nymph.

"You look lovely, my dear," Danilo said solemnly, and the circle of mercenaries nodded in avid agreement.

"I have a question," the unimpressed Vartain broke in. "Waterdeep is a big town."

"That's a question?"

"Enough, Lord Thann!" the riddlemaster snapped. "I am not a man who appreciates levity. During the Midsummer Faire, every traveling entertainer in the north heads for the city. I'm assuming that the sorceress will not flaunt her asperii, and nearly every singer in Waterdeep has a harp of some sort, so how are we to recognize her?"

"Midsummer Faire," Danilo repeated in a distracted voice. " 'The lord falls on a field of triumph, on a day that is not a day. . . .' " The Harper smacked his forehead with the flat of his hand. "Shieldmeet. That's it!"

Vartain nodded, his black eyes shining as he followed the Harper's logic. "Your reasoning is sound. Shieldmeet is not part of any mooncycle, or counted as a day in the roll of the years. It is a day that is not a day."

"Am I missing something important?" Morgalla asked.

"Shieldmeet is an extra day that occurs once every four years, right after Midsummer. After the tournaments of Midsummer Day, contracts are renewed, betrothals announced, allegiances sworn. Even the Lords of Waterdeep are reaffirmed every four years," Vartain explained.

"Maybe, maybe not," Danilo added. "You notice that each of these curses has been brought to bear on Waterdeep. Between crop failures and monster attacks on merchant caravans, Midsummer Faire will be a rather dismal event. A storm on Midsummer Day will play into the people's fears and superstitions, and a bard who can influence crowds might be able to convince them that the Lords of Waterdeep are no longer able to govern. Rightly done, it could be a near-bloodless coup!"

"But why fuss around with Harpers and dragons? What do the Lords of Waterdeep have to do with a bunch o' bards?"

"Enough," Danilo said succinctly. "The two groups work together. Bardcraft and politics are intrinsically enjoined. We must leave for Waterdeep at once! Where is Wyn?"

"Here." The elf minstrel called, striding quickly down the hilltop holding the leading reins of three horses. The elven hermit followed close by Wyn's side. "We recovered only three horses, but I found my lyre of changing."

At that moment, Elaith crested the hill behind Wyn at a run. "Then use it!" he shouted as he dashed toward the others. "A flock of harpies, coming from the north!"

Eleven

Wyn shaded his eyes against the sun and scanned the skies. As Elaith had said, far to the north were several dark shapes. The minstrel looked helplessly at Danilo. "There are no harpies on Evermeet. I've learned no spellsong to combat them!"

Danilo patted the sword at his right side. "Not to worry. I carry a singing sword whose music will negate the effect of the harpies' song. This shouldn't be any more difficult than fighting any other flying monster. Teeth, talons, that sort of thing."

The adventurers' relief was palpable, and even Elaith's grim visage relaxed somewhat. Seeing that, a seed of mischief took root in Danilo's fertile mind. He drew the magic weapon and with a solemn face handed it to the elf.

"If I were to be killed or disarmed during the battle, the sword's music would cease at once, and all would be lost. You're by far the best swordsman among us. You'd better use this."

Elaith's silver brows rose in a skeptical arc, but he accepted the magic weapon. "Very sensible of you," he said, question and sarcasm blending in his words.

Danilo shrugged. "First time for everything." The thin, outer edge of the keening waves of sound began to reach them. "The sword will sing as soon as you take your first strike. Mind that you don't put it down once it begins, though. It can be touchy, and it might not start up again."

The elf made a few experimental passes to test the sword's balance and to activate the song. Immediately a rollicking baritone voice began to sing:

> *"There was a knight who longed to wield*
> *A more impressive lance*
> *To carry into battle*
> *And to aid him in romance."*

Elaith turned an incredulous stare toward the Harper. Danilo responded with a bland smile and drew his own blade. "Here they come," he said, pointing with the sword in the direction of the approaching monsters. There were nine of them, granting the fighters below one-to-one odds.

The harpies were close enough now that their hideous faces were clearly visible, fangs gleaming from mouths flung wide open with their magical song. Although the unearthly music chilled the adventurers, the harpies' fell magic could not compete with the enchantment of the singing sword. Meanwhile, the sword rolled on through the chorus.

> *"Hey, there! Ho, there!*
> *A lesson's here for you:*
> *Be careful what you ask for,*
> *For your wishes might come true."*

Elaith held the sword at arm's length, glaring as if it were an ill-trained puppy that had just puddled his best boots. He had little choice but to continue wielding the weapon, though, and he slashed viciously at the first harpy to venture within range. The stroke cut deep into the creature's arm, nearly severing the filthy gray limb. Shrieking with pain and rage, the harpy flapped out of the elf's reach and circled back for a second attack. Its teeth bared, it dove, screaming, toward the elf. Elaith pulled a knife from the sleeve of his sword arm and threw it at the oncoming monster. It caught the harpy in the throat, abruptly cutting off its screams. The creature plummeted straight toward its killer. Elaith threw himself to one side and rolled, taking care not to lose his hold on the magical sword.

> *"A wizard overheard the knight*
> *And granted his request.*
> *The knight at first was overjoyed*
> *To see how he was blessed."*

Again the sword went into the chorus, admonishing the fighters in jovial tones to beware of wishes lightly made. The harpies, too, seemed to take this advice to heart. Perhaps the creatures recalled their last battle with these fighters, or at least had learned to be wary of prey who wouldn't obligingly hold still. The harpies circled the clearing, keeping carefully out of reach of the flashing swords as they sang their deadly, beautiful song. Clearly audible above the harpies' charm song was the sword's cheerful baritone:

> *"The knight went to a party*
> *With his weapon thus enhanced.*
> *The lance made dining difficult*
> *And tripped him when he danced."*

Morgalla chuckled briefly, then her brow furrowed in frustration. This fight was not going to the dwarf's liking, for her opponents stayed out of reach. Using her spear like a javelin, she hurled the weapon at a low-flying harpy. The point tore through the creature, and the sheer force of the dwarf's throw carried it along for the flight. The spear struck a tree trunk and bit deep. Impaled upon the spear, the dying harpy writhed and shrieked. Morgalla nodded with satisfaction and drew her axe in readiness for the next attack.

"Shoot them down!" Danilo shouted, taking the dwarf's lead. He put away his sword and snatched up a bow. The Harper's first arrow missed. He grimaced and nocked another, noting that Elaith gritted his teeth in helpless frustration as he continued to slash ineffectually at any monster that came close. Elaith's mercenaries sent volley after volley of arrows into the sky. By the end of the chorus all of the remaining harpies had been downed, some of them still alive despite the arrows jutting from their rank bodies.

One of the wounded harpies flung itself at Mange. The canny mercenary grabbed the creature's flailing wrists, knowing that a scratch from its talons would render him immobile. At the same moment he kicked its hideous face with a heavy-booted foot. The creature reeled backward, pawing at its shattered nose.

The furious Elaith dove at the wounded harpy, burying the magical sword up to the hilt in its throat. The expression on the elf's face suggested that he strove to quench the sword's song with blood. Undaunted, the sword sang on:

"The next day at the tournament,
He won the jousting meets,
For all who faced his fearsome lance
Fell laughing from their seats."

Morgalla's axe flashed as she battled a club-wielding harpy. She feigned a stumble, going down onto one knee. The harpy raised its bone club and flung itself forward for a killing blow. At the last moment, the nimble dwarf dove to the side. She leaped up, coming behind the off-balance harpy and burying her axe deep into the back of the creature's neck. Dark blood spurted through the thick mat of tangled hair, and the creature dropped onto its face. At that moment, Elaith gutted the final monster. With the death of the last harpy, the deadly song charm faded into silence. The singing sword, however, continued merrily:

"Hey, there! Ho, there!
A lesson's here for you:
Be careful what you ask for,
For your wishes might come tru—"

Elaith hurled the sword to the ground; its song broke off with a choked "Erp!" that suggested the magical singer had been throttled by unseen hands. The moon elf stalked over to Danilo. Shaking with barely contained rage, he thrust a finger into the Harper's chest.

"You *fool!*" he thundered. "No one, *no one* but you would wield such a ridiculous weapon!"

Danilo crossed his arms and leaned back against a tree. "Oh, I don't know. I thought you did rather well."

A silver dagger flashed in the elf's hand. With a quicksilver motion, Elaith lunged forward and held the point against the Harper's throat. Danilo merely cocked an eyebrow.

"Now really, my dear Elaith. I should hate to see you change your methods at this late hour. Wouldn't you rather I turned my back first?"

"Might I remind you both that we have business in Waterdeep?" Vartain's emotionless voice broke in. "Our foe is bound there and will strike on Shieldmeet. That is three days from now."

The elf glared at Danilo with undisguised hatred, but with a visible effort he eased the dagger away. "We made an adventurer's pact. I will honor it. Once the harp is recovered, though, I make no guarantees."

"I'll bear that in mind." Danilo picked up his singing sword and tucked it back into its scabbard. "I'm off for Waterdeep. I can take two people with me now and return after sunset for two more. Vartain, you should come now. Perhaps if you and Khelben Arunsun were to put your resources together, you might be able to come up with the identity of our bardic foe."

The riddlemaster bowed. "It would be my honor."

"I'm coming, too," Elaith stated. "I have information sources in Waterdeep that the archmage himself would envy."

"Modestly put," Danilo said dryly. He studied those who would remain behind. There were Wyn and Morgalla, the elven hermit, Balindar, Mange, and Cory, a dark-skinned youth who was the youngest of Elaith's sell-swords. "First off, try to find the other horses, then head toward the Goldenfield temple farms. Once you find the stream, follow it to a calm, deep pool and set up camp. I'll meet you there shortly after sunset."

Danilo motioned Vartain and Elaith to his side and set in motion the spell of teleportation. Swirling white light filled their vision, solidifying into solid black granite.

The trio stood in a courtyard before the tall, smooth cone of Blackstaff Tower. A twenty-foot wall loomed behind them. Neither structure had any visible doors, gates, or windows. Both of the Harper's companions surveyed the archmage's home with intense interest.

The solid wall of the tower blurred for a moment, and the archmage stepped out to greet his visitors. Danilo sped through the introductions. Khelben Arunsun proved himself a master of diplomacy when he received the news that the rogue elf Elaith Craulnober was his nephew's partner.

"Welcome to Blackstaff Tower. Please join my lady and me for midday meal. We have much to discuss, and can talk while we eat."

Elaith responded with a cryptic smile. "A pleasure deferred, Lord Arunsun. If you'll show me the way out, I have inquiries to make." After promising to meet Danilo at a tavern the following day at highsun, Elaith slipped through the wall's invisible door.

"It's a long story," Danilo said dryly, nodding his head in the direction the elf had taken.

"It'll wait. Now, what have you two got?"

Over a midday meal of lentil stew and smoky cheese, Danilo filled his uncle in on the events of the last several days. Vartain gave the archmage a brief summary of the encounter with the dragon, and he went over the scroll's contents in detail. He then offered his profile of the sorceress.

"Our enemy is a bard and a mage of considerable power. She is a speaker of Middle Sespechian, which means she is either a specialist in obscure dialects, or a native of Sespech who is at least three hundred years old. She is also a skilled riddlemaster, and the wording of the riddle suggests that she is—or at least was at one point—a Harper."

Khelben nodded, his face grim. "Some of the altered ballads suggest that you are right about the last point. This bard was seen in Sundabar, you say? Is she an elf?"

Danilo shook his head. "No one who saw her could say one way or another, but the age Vartain suggests makes it seem likely. Wyn seems to think she is, too. Why do you ask?"

"I can think of one person who might fit this pattern. Iriador Wintermist was the daughter of a famous elven

minstrel and a human baron of Sespech. She was a noted
mage and an up-and-coming bard. She joined forces with
Finder Wyvernspur's band and traveled with him for a
time. By all reports, she fell in battle during the Harpstar
Wars."

"A half-elf, eh? What did she look like?"

"Iriador was a famed beauty with brilliant red hair and
vivid blue eyes. She was very slender, not much over five
feet in height, and delicate of feature. If she is alive today,
even with a potion of longevity she would no doubt appear
ancient. Three hundred years is very old for a half-elf."

"That's not much to go on," Danilo said ruefully, rising
from the table. "We've got to alert Kriios Halambar. If we
can keep this sorceress from entering the site of the barding college Ollamn, perhaps we can purchase a little more
time. At the very least, we can have the shop watched for
someone who fits that description. Vartain, you're the one
to handle this. Come, I'll see you out."

The riddlemaster walked with him in silence out of the
tower and onto the street. "If I may ask, why do you entrust this mission to me?" he asked.

"You see things most men miss," Danilo said with no
thought of flattery.

"In recent days, I seem to have missed a great deal," the
riddlemaster in a glum voice.

Danilo looked at him sharply, for such introspection
seemed uncharacteristic of Vartain. "Actually, your accu-
racy is astounding. You've a remarkable mind. Never have
I seen anyone with your breadth of knowledge or attention
to detail. I've noticed that when you do miss something, it
is because you are too involved with sorting through facts
and fitting things together. If I may ask, how would you
define 'humor'?"

Vartain looked puzzled by the apparent change in topic.
"Levity, that which is lighthearted and amusing."

"Well, that's good, as far as it goes. I've got another definition: humor is looking at the broad picture, and then finding the incongruous detail. Humor is another word for looking at life from a slightly different angle. It means not taking yourself too seriously. In addition to all that, it adds a bit of fun to the process of living."

"Fun?"

Danilo slapped the riddlemaster on the back. "Fun," he repeated. "When all this is over, I suggest you look into it."

Vartain seemed unconvinced, but he bowed and hurried off in the direction of Halambar's Lute Shop. The Harper retraced his steps into the tower's reception hall.

"Let's see the scroll," Khelben demanded at once.

Danilo reached into his magic bag. His eyebrows met in a puzzled frown. "That's odd," he mused as he rummaged around. "It was right here on top." The Harper began to remove one item after another from his bag, until the pile on the floor was nearly knee-deep.

"Enough!" Khelben said in exasperation. "The scroll is obviously gone."

His nephew nodded to concede defeat. "Elaith Craulnober has struck again. I've no idea how he does it, but he got a ring off my finger without my noticing."

"What does he want with the scroll?"

"He wants to keep it away from you, for fear that you'll find the sorceress before he does. That's why I didn't return at once with the scroll," Danilo admitted. "Apparently our sorceress possesses an elven artifact, a powerful magic harp known as the Morninglark, and Elaith would very much like to possess it."

The archmage received this news in silence. "So Elaith Craulnober will be searching the city, making inquiries about this magic harp."

"Most likely. Can you have him picked up?"

"I'll see to the elf," Khelben said firmly. "Why don't you

go to Halambar's and see if Vartain is coming up with any useful information."

The Harper hurried to the guildmaster's shop. Kriios Halambar received Danilo politely but looked puzzled when Dan asked for Vartain. "The riddlemaster has not been here since he was hired by Elaith Craulnober, many days ago. Why?"

"You answered my question, I'm afraid," the Harper said ruefully. "Vartain is still working for Elaith." He told Halambar an abbreviated version of the story, and asked if the shop could be closed and guarded so that the sorceress could not cast a spell at the site of the college of Ollamn.

"Visiting bards come here to sign the register, but the actual college stood on the site of the guildhall," Halambar corrected him. He reflected on that possibility. "It would be unprecedented to close the guildhall during the Midsummer festivities. Many visiting bards take lodgings there."

"But it could be done?"

"Oh, yes. I admit to having placed magical wards around the hall. In addition to normal precautions, events in Waterdeep have made such seem prudent."

"Our bard packs a good deal of magical muscle," Danilo said, and reached into his bag for the dragon's cask. It held fewer jewels that he remembered, but he selected several nice gems and handed them to Halambar. "Augment the guard on your shop and the guildhall with as much magic and steel as these stones will purchase. Have the place watched for anyone who fits the description I gave you."

The guildmaster bowed. "All will be done as you say. Lift the curse on the bards, Lord Thann, and your name will be remembered as foremost among us."

Danilo had reason to believe otherwise. Once the magical delusion was lifted, he would again be regarded as an

amusing and inept dabbler, a typical idle nobleman of great
wealth and little substance. At the moment, Danilo truly
regretted the role he had lived for years. If he had not
played the fool, if he had taken Khelben's advice and
served openly as a mage of promise, he would have been
able to share his vision of elfsong's importance. As Khelben's acknowledged apprentice, he could have accomplished much. But who would listen seriously to Danilo
Thann, dandy and dilettante? Now knowing what else to
do, the Harper politely returned Halambar's respectful
bow.

* * * * *

Even during the bright summer afternoon, in the basement tavern known as the Crawling Spider it was dark as
night. The plaster walls had been molded to look like the
hewn stone of underground tunnels, and glowing mosses
and lichen gave a faint green light to the room. Stuffed
spiders hung from the ceiling, and realistic sculptures of
more frightening deep-dwelling beasts decorated the odd
taproom. In one corner stood a wooden illithid, holding
the hat some waggish customer had hung on a purple ten-
tacle. The tavern catered to those who missed their sub-
terranean homes—mostly dwarves, half-orcs, and a few
gnomes—as well as clerics who enjoyed an occasional
respite from respectability. The servants were dressed to
resemble drow elves, wearing tight black leggings topped
with the briefest of chain mail, black masks with pointed
ears, and flowing white wigs. These servants were exclusively beautiful human women. No elf, Elaith Craulnober
noted with disdain, would submit to such an indignity.
The moon elf found this tavern abhorrent, but one of the
serving wenches was a former employee and a reliable
source of information.

Elaith came in through the back entrance and slipped into one of the tavern's curtained booths. Although the servants were all dressed alike, he recognized Winnifer, a former thief and a diverting companion, by her undulating walk and tiny red mouth. He caught the woman by the wrist as she passed, and he pulled her into the booth.

Winnifer plopped onto his lap, and her lips parted in a delighted smile. "Elaith! How wonderful to see you again." She curled up against him like a contented kitten, and her slim, black-gloved hands ran down his arms. "When you pulled me in here like that, I was afraid you were another naughty cleric!"

He captured the hand roaming his chest and gave it a warning squeeze. "I need some information, Winnifer."

The woman pouted until she checked her hand and noted the small red gem in her palm. "I got a job offer yesterday," she purred, stroking his face, "and this time, it was *not* from a cleric! Someone is trying to get a thieves' guild going."

It was not the first time Elaith had heard this rumor. It troubled him, as did the influx of foreign talent in the city. Imported thieves at the festival and market seasons were nothing new, but the sheer number of thieves currently in Waterdeep could not be explained by Midsummer Faire alone. Even more disturbing was the plentiful supply of assassins, and the vigor with which both these groups sought converts. Assassins as a rule were not concerned with winning friends and influencing people. They were far more likely to attempt to thin their own ranks than to deliberately enlarge them. This trend indicated the hidden hand of some powerful organization.

"Who is behind this?"

Winnifer shrugged and wriggled her fingers under the tight black leather of her knee-high boots. She dug out a large gold coin and handed it to the elf. "I want it back,"

she warned as she twined her hands around his waist and
began to nuzzle at his neck. Elaith blew aside a lock of her
white hair and examined the coin.

"Much good may it do you," Elaith responded. "Spend
this in Waterdeep, and you'll most likely end up hanging
from the city walls. This coin bears the symbol of the
Knights of the Shield."

Winnifer swore and sat up straight. "Buy it from me,
won't you? You can pass it more easily than I could."

"Thank you, no," the elf responded, slipping the coin
back into her boot. "You haven't seen more of these
around, have you?"

"Not me. But you know my sister, Flowna? She dances
at the Three Pearls? Well, she said that coins like this one
paid for a concert. A lot of visiting bards sang stories about
the Blackstaff and that witch wench he lives with. It was
pretty funny, Flowna said."

"Really."

"Uh-huh. What I can't see is what the Knights—this spy
group—expect to do using a bunch of bards and thieves."

"A temporary alliance, perhaps." Elaith eased the
woman off his lap and slipped out of the booth, promising
to meet her soon.

Winnifer waited in the curtained booth for several minutes. When she felt certain that the elf was gone, she hurried to the dressing room, pulled off the drow mask and
wig, and wrapped herself in a loose cloak to cover her costume. Leaving the underground tavern behind, she hurried to a nearby shop.

Magda, a dark-eyed crone who sold fanciful wooden toys
and small statues, was alone in the shop. She ushered the
beautiful thief into a back room, which was furnished only
with a small table that held a low, round basin of water.

The old woman tossed a handful of herbs into the water
and spoke the words of a spell. Winnifer stepped back as

the water roiled and steamed. In minutes, the herbs had dissolved into a smooth, dark surface. Reflected in it was the face of the mage Laeral.

"Greetings, Magda. Someone has located the elf for us?"

"I have Winnifer Fleetfingers with me," the crone said, and stepped back to make room for the thief.

Winnifer leaned over the scrying bowl. "I told Elaith everything I was supposed to say," she reported. "He identified the Knights' mark on that coin, and from what he said, I think he believes that the Knights and your sorceress may be in alliance."

"Good work," Laeral said. "Elaith Craulnober knows the dark side of Waterdeep better than anyone. If the elf can't ferret out the Knights' agent, no one can."

"That spell scroll you're looking for? He doesn't have it on him," Winnifer added.

Laeral's silver brows flew up. "You're certain?"

The beautifully thief sniffed scornfully, and Laeral acceded to Winnifer's expertise with a nod.

"All right. He doesn't have it. Magda, get in touch with all those in the network and change their instructions. Elaith Craulnober is not to be stopped. He must be observed, but allowed to go wherever he will. Make note of everyone he contacts. As for the scroll, start looking for one Vartain of Calimport."

Twelve

As soon as the sun set over Waterdeep, Danilo again twisted his ring of teleportation, picturing in his mind the site he had mentioned to Wyn and the others.

He found the party camped beside the pool, in a scene of incongruous peace and beauty. The glowing sunset clouds were reflected in the still water, and in the clearing surrounding the pool, fireflies blinked in and out of view. The elven hermit was off to one side, playing tunelessly upon Wyn's lyre of changing. Morgalla greeted Danilo with her usual nod, but Wyn rushed toward him. The elf was more excited that Danilo had ever seen him.

"I know how the spell must be undone!"

"You do?"

"Well, almost," the elf admitted. "I made a copy of the riddle on the scroll. Vartain has been looking at it solely as a puzzle, and I thought that a musician's eye might find something he overlooked."

"And?" Danilo found that the elf's excitement was contagious.

"The ballad on the scroll is a ballad indeed, and it is meant to be sung. Look at the meter: every stanza is regular despite the lack of rhyme."

A possibility occurred to Danilo, and he sank down on a moss-covered stone. "You're an expert in Harper lore. Does the name Iriador Wintermist mean anything to you?"

"Oh, yes. She was a Harper who traveled for some time with Finder Wyvernspur's band. Her name, Iriador, is derived from the Elvish word for 'ruby,' and she was so named for her brilliant red hair. She was a notable beauty, and a gifted mage and bard."

"According to Khelben Arunsun, this woman was half-elven, and the daughter of a famous elven musician. Is it possible that she knew the art of elfsong?"

Wyn recoiled. He stared at the Harper in dismay. "Are you saying that Iriador Wintermist is our elusive sorceress? A *half*-elf?"

"Yes, in my own inimitable fashion. Now, are you telling me that all this turmoil has been the result of elfsong magic?"

"I'm afraid so," the minstrel admitted. "I have suspected it for some time, and my suspicions were confirmed when I learned that our enemy possesses the Morninglark. Only a powerful spellsinger can use the harp, so I assumed that the sorceress would be an elf."

"What can this harp do?"

"It allows the musician to create new spellsongs. This is not an easy matter. Our foe has created a complex spell with several layers. First, as Vartain said, there is magic in the making and solving of riddles. She also drew power from *place magic*; the sites of the elder barding colleges are steeped in the collective magic of the music played there over the ages. At each site, she gains another power toward her ultimate goal."

"Which is?"

"To restore the honor to bardcraft."

"Strange way to go about it," Danilo observed. "Her concept of honor requires a good deal of preliminary destruction. How can these spells of hers be undone?"

"By singing the ballad in its entirety. Throughout the riddle are sprinkled hints to its performance. Many of these are hidden in other clues."

Danilo thought this over, nodding as something occurred to him. "The key to the spell," he repeated softly. He looked up at Wyn. "Remember the riddle that opened the scroll?

"The beginning of eternity,
The end of time and space,
It is the start of every end
And the end of every place."

The Harper spoke the riddle quickly, and shook his head in astonishment at his own shortsightedness. "The *key* to the spell was the letter *E*, right? Answering the riddle opened the scroll, but it also gives the *key* in which the spell must be sung."

"I hadn't noticed that particular double riddle," Wyn admitted, "but there are several others."

"By Milil," Danilo swore, invoking the god of music, "this bard of ours has a twisted mind. We'll have to look at every phrase and line from three different angles just to put the pieces of this spell together."

"That is so. But I'm afraid this puts you in a great deal of danger, my friend."

"This whole adventure has not been lacking in danger," Danilo observed. "But why me, specifically?"

"You probably know the legend of Heward's Mystical

Organ. If this artifact could be found, one could theoretically cast an infinite number of spells by playing tunes upon its keys."

"If one survived the effort," Danilo said dryly. "Also according to legend, those whose research is faulty or whose musicianship is not up to the task will end up dead or mad."

The elven minstrel nodded gravely. "That danger is present in the casting of any powerful spell, and this one will be no exception. This spell was cast by wedding elfsong to the power of the Morninglark. The magic is therefore doubly powerful, and it must be undone by singing the entire ballad and playing upon the Morninglark itself."

"Which only a spellsinger can do. That's you."

"I'm afraid not," Wyn countered. "Remember, I do not play the harp. The task therefore falls to you."

Danilo took a deep breath. He had no choice but to attempt the spell, yet he was not a spellsinger like Wyn, or even much of a bard! His eyes drifted toward the elven hermit, who had set aside the lyre and was now dancing to wild music only he could hear. The Harper knew that if his voice faltered or his fingers stumbled on the strings, the mad elf's fate could be his. As soon as he trusted himself to speak, he raised his eyes to Wyn's.

"You promised me a lesson in elfsong," he said casually. "I believe this would be a good time to start."

* * * * *

Silent as a shadow, Elaith Craulnober picked his way through the debris that littered Twoflask Alley. But for the elf, the lane was deserted; local wisdom had it that no one who'd imbibed less than two flasks of something much stronger than ale would chance the dangerous passage after sunset. Raised planks paved the center of the narrow throughway, allowing the foolish, the inebriated, or the intrepid to walk above most of the garbage and sewage that was tossed into the alley from the seedy taverns and storehouses on either side.

The elf's boots made no sound on the wide boards, and beneath his feet the rats scuttled and snarled undisturbed, busily foraging before the daily sluicing washed much of the garbage—and many of the rats—into the large sewer gratings that dotted either side of the path. There were no gaslights or torches to dispel the darkness of Twoflask Alley, and the elf made his way quickly toward the back entrance of the infamous Thirsty Sailor Tavern in darkness. The patrons of this tavern favored the dark, and they tended to vanish at first light like so many vampires.

The Thirsty Sailor was a dive frequented by brawlers and heavy drinkers, and the deals made and information exchanged in its squalid upper rooms were invariably small, inept exchanges among the dregs of Waterdeep. To Elaith, however, the tavern's owner was an excellent source of dark information. The elf had spent a long day traveling from one tavern and meeting place to another, gathering news from his vast network of informants. He had learned a great deal, but he had yet to fit all the pieces together. He hurried past the last building on the alley, a low-eaved warehouse stocked with barrels of whiskey and ale for the tavern.

The elf was a few paces from the tavern's back door when a solid thud sounded behind him, resounding through the wooden planks that paved the alley. From the corner of his eye, Elaith caught the glint of high-held steel.

With fluid, practiced grace, he spun about and caught the assailant's upraised arm by the wrist. He threw himself into a backward roll, using the force of the intended knife-stroke to help bring the much larger man down with him. As they fell, he planted both booted feet in the thug's midsection, and at the precise moment, he kicked out hard. The man soared over Elaith, flipped, and landed heavily on his back.

Before the startled "Oof!" died away, the elf was on his feet, a knife in each hand. With two quick throws, the thug's outflung arms were pinned securely to the boards by the coarse linen of his shirt cuffs.

Elaith drew a larger knife from his boot and walked slowly to stand over the man. This was a favored technique of the elf's, for he'd learned that men—and women, for that matter—were more prone to part with information under such intimidating circumstances.

"As ambushes go, that was rather clumsy," the elf observed mildly.

Sweat beaded on the trapped man's face, but he didn't attempt to move or cry out. "I swear by the Mother of Mask, Craulnober, I didn't know it was you! It was just a quick cutpurse job, nothing personal."

The would-be thief had a familiar voice, but the elf's memory connected the slurred, whining tones with a heavily bearded man who wore his long brown hair in three thick braids. This man was cropped and clean-shaven. Elaith peered closer.

"Is that you, Kornith? Good gods, man, what an appalling excuse for a chin! Were I you, I would grow that beard back at once. Whatever possessed you to molt in the first place?"

"Guild rules," he muttered. "Can't stand out in a crowd." The thief glanced meaningfully at one of the knives that held him immobile. His elven tormenter took no notice of the hint.

"*Guild* rules?" Elaith's amber eyes narrowed. There were already rules in place? "Since when is there a Loyal Order of Cutpurses in this town?"

"It's coming," the thief asserted. "Assassins' guild, too.

Word's been put out."

"By?" The elf took a step closer and stroked the blade of his knife.

"Don't know." Kornith licked his lips nervously. "I'd tell you if I knew. Word's out, that's all."

Winnifer Fleetfingers's revelation about the Knights of the Shield was gaining credibility by the moment, and this deeply concerned Elaith. For all its intrigue, Waterdeep had no single, truly organized crime network, and it was in the rogue elf's interests to keep things that way.

Yet he would get no more information from Kornith, of that he was certain. Elaith hooked the toe of his boot under the hilt of one of the knives that held the thief immobile, kicking it up and easily catching it as it fell. Kornith rolled to the side and tugged the other knife free. He leaped to his feet and backed away, his face suffused with a mixture of relief and apprehension.

"Thought I was a stinkin' corpse, Craulnober," he said, as he continued to put distance between himself and the deadly elf. "Never supposed you'd show a man mercy, but I'm grateful and I owe you."

Elaith froze. The very sincerity of the thief's words stirred the confusion brewing in the elf's heart. Kornith had every reason to fear him, for no one who had threatened Elaith Craulnober's life still drew breath. The elf had built a fortune on his dark reputation, yet here he was, prepared to let this thug walk away. Indeed, a year earlier he would have not have been content to ruin the man's shirtsleeves, but would rather have pinned him to the walkway through the palms of his hands. The elf's fury turned quickly inward, and he cursed himself for the uncharacteristic lapse. At the same moment, he swung back his hand and with a deft underhand toss sent the knife he held spinning upward.

The weapon sank deep, just below Kornith's rib cage.

The thief slumped against the wall of the warehouse, grasping the hilt with both hands. Bubbles of blood formed at the corner of his mouth, and he slid slowly to the filthy walkway. His lips twisted into an expression of self-contempt, and he sought the elf's face with eyes that were rapidly glazing over. "I shoulda run. Forgot what . . . you was," he gasped out.

Elaith stepped closer, and with a vicious kick he drove the knife still deeper. Kornith's last breath was swallowed in a blood-drenched gurgle.

The elf stood over the fallen man, eyeing his handiwork in silence. "For a moment," he said softly, "so did I."

* * * * *

At Morgalla's request, Balindar, Mange, and Cory dragged a log into the circle of light cast by a roaring campfire. Bribing the burly mercenary captain had put a considerable dent in Danilo's supply of gems, and the Harper had learned it was more economical to channel his requests through Morgalla. Balindar had grown so fond of the dwarf—and he was so guilt-ridden over Elaith's order to hold her hostage to ensure Danilo's cooperation—that Dan had little doubt that the mercenary would dive into the pond and catch fish with his teeth if Morgalla expressed a desire for seafood. For her part, Morgalla lingered with the three surviving sell-swords, repaying the favor with a tale of battle waged against a horde of orc invaders. Left alone, Danilo and Wyn studied the copy of the ballad by the dancing firelight.

"The final stanza gives more hints about the song's performance," the elf noted. "Here, for example. 'First the harp, then the singer circles twice.' Does that make sense to you?"

"I think so," Danilo said thoughtfully. "That would

indicate that the ballad must be sung as a round, with the harp beginning the melody. The entire song must be sung twice."

"What's a round?" Morgalla put in, coming to sit beside Wyn.

"It's a type of simple harmony," Wyn told her. "One person begins a song, the second begins at a certain point, and so on. Dwarven music is not much given to such devices, as I understand."

"So how d'you know where to join in?"

"I can answer that one," Danilo broke in. "The melody determines that, but usually the round begins after the first line of verse. For example." Danilo cleared his throat and began to sing:

"He who would an alehouse keep
Must have three things in store:
A chamber with a feather bed,
A pillow and a . . . hey-nony-nony,
Hey-nony-nony, hey-nony-nony nay."

The Harper paused. "Then the second time through, you would join in after I sing the first line. Now then, altogether!"

The dwarf eyed him with a dour expression. "Yer gittin' a mite punchy, bard."

Wyn nodded in agreement. "This discussion does raise a valid point, though. We must know the melody to which these words were set."

"I think the riddle gives that, as well," Danilo said, getting back to the scroll with reluctance. "Look at the final line of the ballad. It says the song must be sung to the armed man of Canaith."

"Who's that?" Morgalla demanded.

"That is not a who. That's a what. If I'm not mistaken,

this refers to an old song, *L'homme arme*—the armed man —which is attributed to Finder Wyvernspur. He was sentenced by his fellow Harpers to centuries of isolation on another plane of existence, and his music was wiped from the land by powerful spells. Our bardic foe used this particular melody as another safeguard."

"That fits everything we suspect to be true," Wyn said. "Iriador Wintermist traveled with Finder Wyvernspur and would be familiar with his fate. In fact, his sentence probably gave our foe the inspiration for her own spell against the bards! But how is it, Danilo, that you know this song?"

"In my travels, I ran into Olive Ruskettle, a halfling bard and fellow Harper. Don't call her that to her face, though, as she has mixed feelings toward the Harpers. When Finder returned to Faerun, they became friends. Now that the sentence against him has been lifted, she is making a point of singing his music everywhere she goes."

"And the reference to Canaith?"

"The barding college, of course. The tune was quite popular and was often borrowed as the foundation for other music. I'm assuming that the spell is set to whatever version was popular at Canaith."

"And you're sure the halfling sang that particular version?" Wyn asked.

"Wouldn't that be nice! I'll be sure after I attempt to cast the spell," Danilo said with a grim smile. He studied the words of the ballad, humming as he read. He nodded slowly. "The meter fits the melody, that much we know. Apparently I'm to play the first line of the song on the harp, then start to sing in harmony with the harp's continuing melody."

"Hmmph. Sounds like yer trying to dig one tunnel east and another west, hopin' to meet in the middle."

"Indeed it does, lady dwarf. If I might borrow your lyre of changing, Wyn, I suppose I ought to start practicing,"

Danilo said with no discernible enthusiasm as he rose to
leave the campfire.

"Hold on, bard. I'll walk with you a bit," Morgalla said,
hopping down from her perch beside Wyn.

Danilo turned, ready to decline her offer. Something in
the set of her face held him back, and he motioned for her
to join him. They left the campfire and walked in silence
for several minutes. A small path cut through a wooded
area on its way toward the travel route, and here Morgalla
paused.

"Got a story to tell you," the dwarf began, keeping her
eyes averted. "I come from the Earthfast Mountains, far to
the east o' here. Since my great-grandsire's time, orc wars
have whittled my clan down to so much kindling. My
mother was Thendara Spearsinger, a captain in the hearth
guard and as fierce a fighter as ever you'd see. Soon as I
was old enough to stand up on my own, she put a staff in
my hand and teached me to use it. My clan is Chistlesmith, an' I learnt the clan trade of carving wood into useful stuff. That was my life: I fought an' I carved, like folks
expected, but in me was a wantin' for more. Had me a taste
for adventure, and for the learning of new tales and songs.
Dwarves like these things well, but with troubles like ours,
there wasn't much daylight to spare to 'em.

"Times was grim, but of a night folks gathered in the
great clan hall for song and stories. I was knowed throughout Earthfast for my singing and stories—and my dancing." The dwarf cast a sidelong glance at Danilo as if
daring him to smirk. The Harper nodded gravely, and she
took a deep breath to continue.

"You may know that Princess Alusair—King Azoun's
girl—tarried in the Earthfast, fighting orcs and just generally hiding out. She could spin a good tale, and after the
war with the horselords, I took me to Cormyr to see with
my own eyes the wonders of her father's kingdom. My

craft apprenticeship was almost up, you see, and my fifty-year celebration right around the bend. When that passes, I gotta choose me a mate and set up my own hearth. My time for music and adventure was running short. So I thought to go to the cities of Cormyr, and there make me a name big enough to earn me a place alongside a bard who could learn me what I couldn't get in Earthfast.

"Full of myself, I was," Morgalla said with a grim smile, "and sure that all o' Cormyr would soon know my name. Didn't work out that way. Tall people can't picture a dwarf doing aught but swingin' a hammer or a weapon. Decided I was funny, they did, without takin' time to listen and watch."

The dwarf shrugged away the sting of the memory. "Humans got no patience. Tall folk won't sit still for a story, but they can look at a picture well enough. I took to drawin', and learnt I could hide a whole lot of words and ideas in one picture. I carved 'em on blocks of wood, stamping out enough copies to make folks mad enough to spit." Morgalla chuckled, and the music she'd long denied echoed in her low-pitched laughter.

"I've wondered why you were so hesitant to sing," Danilo said. "You are a gifted musician, Morgalla, as all of Cormyr would have realized in time. Even with your artwork you've risen above your detractors. Your work is nothing short of inspired."

"Maybe," she admitted. "But that ain't the point. I lost faith in myself. I fergot who I was, and what I was made to do."

The dwarf reached high and slapped Danilo on the back. "We who mine the earth have a saying: If someone's walked a tunnel, and he tells you where it ends up, you already been to the end without taking a single step, so you might as well save yerself the time and trouble of walking it yerself."

"Ouch! No offense, my dear, but I've heard snappier sayings."

Morgalla shrugged. "As long as you get the point. Yer a damn fine bard, and you'd do yerself a favor to keep that in mind." She turned and sauntered back to the cheery comfort of the fire.

Danilo watched her go, wishing that he could find it in his heart to take the dwarf's advice. However highly Morgalla might regard him, the fact remained that he'd taken a role that was beyond him, and the demands were greater than his ability to meet them. Unfortunately, he was as short on time was as he was talent, so with a deep sigh he turned his attention to the task ahead.

He found the lyre beside the elven hermit, who had been overcome by his wild dancing and had fallen asleep in the long grass that ringed the pool. Danilo gazed down at the mad elf for a long moment, noting the tear that slipped down the ravaged face. He wondered what sort of dreams tormented the hermit.

The Harper quickly stooped and picked up the lyre of changing. With a word, he transformed it into the driftwood-colored lap harp. He made his way into the wood, seeking a quiet place to prepare and reflect. Not far from the camp, he found a small natural clearing in the shadow of a giant oak. Seating himself on the ground, he began to play a lilting dance tune on the harp.

Twilight had deepened into night, but Danilo needed no light beyond that provided by the full moon and the flickering courtship of the fireflies. He had already committed the words of the spellsong to memory. It had long been his gift to retain what he read and heard, and his bardic tutors had worked to foster and strengthen this ability. The music came quickly, too, and after several passes through the melody he joined the harp in a duet. His strong, clear tenor rang out, projecting much more assurance than he actually felt.

If there was magic in the ancient music and the arcane riddles, Danilo couldn't sense it. Perhaps Wyn had been right: perhaps elfsong magic rightly belonged only to the elves. Magic seemed to flow from and through them without effort or artifice. Humans *used* the weave of magic that surrounds all things, Khelben had once explained, but elves were *part* of the weave.

Danilo pushed aside his doubts and threw himself into the music, marshaling the intense concentration he had learned in his years of magical studies.

Drawn by the sound of the young man's voice, Wyn made his way into the woods. Earlier that evening he had taught the Harper some of the principles of elfsong, but one important lesson remained. Danilo had proven himself a worthy pupil, and Wyn had little doubt that the Harper could master and cast the difficult spell. At first the elf had doubted the possibility of explaining elfsong to someone who'd been trained to consider magic a laborious, arcane art, who dealt in chants and runes and elaborate gestures and ridiculous spell components. What he himself had forgotten was this: The magic was in the music itself, and in the heart of the musician. That is what Danilo must understand and remember.

And so Wyn reached into the pouch at his belt and drew forth a tightly folded piece of paper, the sketch Morgalla had drawn of Danilo days earlier in Waterdeep. The archmage had entrusted it to Wyn, understanding that his nephew was not yet ready to see himself through the canny dwarf's eyes.

Wyn drew near the giant oak. Danilo was utterly absorbed in his task, his gray eyes closed in concentration as he played and sang.

"Despite all that has happened, despite all the arguments you yourself have put forth, you do not believe that elfsong can be yours," Wyn said softly, breaking into the song.

The Harper jumped and fell silent, startled by the unexpected interruption. Wyn handed him the sketch. "Perhaps you will accept Morgalla's vision, if not your own."

Danilo looked down at the paper. The dwarf usually relied on a few telling, exaggerated details to get her point across, but this drawing was a careful and realistic rendering. As Morgalla depicted him, he was dressed in an adventurer's weathered and practical gear, but the tilt of his head somehow gave the impression that he was a lord traveling in disguise. There was a bit of humor lurking at the corners of his lips, but the eyes were serious, touched with sadness. He played a lute, but surrounding him was an aureole of tiny motes and stars that suggested magic as well as music. Most startling of all was the way Morgalla had managed to portray a man in command of his powers, at peace with his own contradictions. It was captioned only "The Bard."

"The magic is in the music, and also in the heart of the bard. The lady dwarf got the instrument wrong," Wyn said quietly as he pointed to the harp at Danilo's side, "but I believe she's right in all other particulars."

Danilo said nothing, and after a moment the elf added, "The night grows late. You should try to get some rest, for we must leave for Waterdeep at sunrise."

Thirteen

On the day of Midsummer Eve, Khelben Arunsun was up before the sun. The archmage paced the courtyard between Blackstaff Tower and the surrounding wall as he awaited his nephew's return.

The day before, Danilo had reconstructed the scroll from memory and had left a copy at the tower. Khelben had studied the scroll well into the night, but finally it had been Laeral who recognized it as a variant of elven spellsong. She was one of the few humans welcome on Evermeet, and she was familiar with the ways of elves. Khelben had never paid much attention to spellsong magic, for there was no music in his hands, and far less in his voice. Laeral was not a musician, either, and neither of the wizards knew a spellsinger.

The task of casting the spell would of necessity fall to Danilo. Whether the lad was up to it, Khelben could not say. His own knowledge of music was insufficient to the challenges of the riddle, and he had no way of evaluating what Danilo and Wyn might be able to discern between them.

"Good morning, Uncle!"

The archmage spun. Danilo stood behind him, an insouciant smile on his face and a rather battered lute slung over his shoulder. With him were Wyn Ashgrove and Morgalla. Khelben noted absently that the dwarf had not taken well to magical travel: her face was set and pallid, and she gripped her staff with one white-knuckled hand and clung to the elf's arm with the other.

"So you made it," the archmage observed, hiding his relief behind a scowl of stern disapproval.

"As usual, you've got a firm grip on the obvious," Danilo quipped lightly. "Bless you, Uncle, are those sweet rolls I smell?"

"Porridge," Khelben said absently, heading toward the tower. "Well, come in, all of you."

"With a welcome such as that before us?" Danilo sniffed. "I think not. Had I known that porridge was on the horizon, I would have teleported to Ackrieg's Bakery, instead."

"We can all discuss the spell while you eat," Khelben said, taking no notice of the young man's teasing.

Danilo elbowed the dwarf. "What would you say to a nice gobbet of roasted venison and a mug of ale for breakfast? There's an inn near the tournament field that understands hospitality and serves a splendid morning feast. Raspberry pastries are a specialty, and the almond cakes are also very good."

"Make it three mugs, and you got yerself a deal."

"Done!"

Morgalla loosed her grip on Wyn's arm, and she and Danilo headed toward the black granite wall. As inconspicuously as possible, the elven minstrel flexed his fingers to aid the return of feeling to his hand.

The archmage stared after the retreating Harper.

"You're not serious."

"Actually, I am. Quite a surprise, isn't it?" Danilo tossed
the words cheerfully over his shoulder. "Wyn can tell you
all about elfsong, and why we need the Morninglark harp.
Since we've got less than two days to find it, I'm off. Hot on
the trail, as they say. Right after breakfast." So saying, the
Harper dragged the dwarf through the invisible door, and
they both disappeared into the city.

"What now?" Khelben muttered, shaking his head.

"The scroll claims that a lord would fall on the field of
triumph. The young bard is doubtless headed to the city's
tournament field to seek clues that will lead him to the
elven harp," Wyn said softly.

The archmage met the elf's steady, green-eyed gaze.
"The young bard, eh? So Morgalla's sketch came close to
the truth?"

"If anything, it fell short of the mark."

Khelben digested this news in silence. "I see," he said
finally. "Well, that's settled, then."

"Whatever path is given him to walk, your nephew does
you credit," Wyn said in a quiet tone. "You have trained
him well; his memory is remarkable and his discipline
impressive. I assume his command of magic is equally
strong."

"It had better be," the archmage said darkly. "Wizard or
no, there's Nine Hells of a spell to be cast. And now, what
is this elfsong that my boy was talking about?"

* * * * *

The early morning sun sent slanting rays across the
farmlands east of Waterdeep, making the scattered whitewashed buildings gleam like so many nesting doves. It
was the day before Midsummer, and the fields and
orchards should have been lush with fruit and jeweled in

the deepest green of the year. From her perch on the asperii, high above the farmlands, Garnet could see that vegetation was sparse. Yet some crops grew, despite her spells and as if in testament to the stubborn resilience necessary to survival in the Northlands. A few farmers were headed toward Waterdeep, their carts laden with produce for sale in the markets there.

Garnet guided her wind steed toward the River Gate, the eastern entrance to Waterdeep's trade district. They landed out of sight of the city-bound travelers and the wall sentries, then joined the other early morning arrivals on the road to the city. She felt more secure once the asperii was on firm ground. The magical horse was becoming increasingly skittish, and Garnet feared that the horse would soon go into open revolt. This would result in the asperii's death, for the creature was bound to Garnet for life. She did not wish to go through the trouble of obtaining and training another mount, for asperii were hard to come by. She brushed aside the niggling doubt that no other asperii would accept her as master.

The Trade Ward bustled with activity as Garnet rode down the streets. A stout dairy farmer dipped a large pewter ladle into a barrel of foaming milk, filling the pitchers and jugs held out to him by a small crowd, while a bright-cheeked lass cut wedges to order from wheels of cheese. Nearby, a potter, bare to the waist against the glowing heat and already daubed with the red-brown clay from his morning's work, fired up a kiln. Vendors set up shop at street corners, and tradespeople readied their wares in preparation for the merchants who came to purchase goods for the shops located in the city's vast, open-air market. Those who sold their wares themselves were loading carts bound for the marketplace. Taverns dealt a brisk business in morning ale and oatcakes. As Garnet took in scene after scene, she began to wonder if the much-touted Lady Thione had done her part. Commerce seemed to be going on apace.

Yet closer scrutiny showed the signs of distress. The wares displayed were of quality far below the usual standards of the proud Waterdhavians. There were shortages; in particular she noted that the produce sold by fruit or flower vendors was sparse and dearly priced. Inns served small portions, and the breakfast customers were almost universally clad in the simple homespun of local tradespeople. The early morning bustle soon flagged, and Garnet realized that what she had taken to be business as usual was merely the local residents going about their daily routine as dictated by a lifetime of industrious habits. They soon settled down to tend their businesses, their faces showing varying degrees of resignation and hopeful expectancy. Garnet encountered a few meandering customers and merchant buyers, but on the whole the streets and shops were far too quiet.

This state of affairs changed as Garnet turned onto Rivon Street. She saw a crowd of people gathered around the House of Song, a large complex that served as guild headquarters for the Council of Musicians, Instrumentmakers, and Choristers. Her brow furrowed in puzzlement, and she absently tucked a strand of drab brown hair behind one slightly pointed ear.

Garnet urged her magic steed closer. There was an inn across the way, and she tied the asperii's reins to the rail outside so that she might pass on foot through the crowd that surrounded the guildhall.

This proved to be more difficult than the bard had anticipated, for what she first took to be a crowd was in effect a small army. The distinctive green and black uniforms of the city guard first caught her eye. She estimated nearly a full battalion. The guard was augmented by several dozen sell-swords, including a detachment of lizard men—very rare in the city and highly regarded as fierce mercenaries. One of the creatures, a seven-foot lizard armed with a spiked mace, returned her glare with incurious golden eyes. Its tongue flicked out as if to taste her scent, and she turned away with a shudder. There were several men and women garbed in street clothes, unarmed but for the occasional staff or wand. Wizards! The guild hall was well and thoroughly guarded. Someone had funded an impressive amount of magic and muscle. Well, so be it. She was not without resources of her own.

Head held high, she marched toward the broad double doors of the guildhouse entrance. A pair of crossed pikes barred the way.

"The guild hall is closed."

"On Midsummer Eve? I highly doubt that." She sniffed and walked around the two guards. Again her path was blocked, this time by a well-muscled, ruddy woman who wore the insignia of a guard captain.

"No one may pass," she said firmly. "We have our orders."

"Oh? From whence came these 'orders'?" Garnet's noble birth and her upbringing in the courts of Sespech lent her tones and her face a degree of patronizing disdain that could not be learned under lesser circumstances.

The captain was not suitably quelled, although she did bow before answering. "By order of the guildmaster, Kriios Halambar, and the Lords of Waterdeep."

Anger coursed through Garnet like a dark tide. She spun and stalked back to her asperii. Mounting the horse, she sped toward the west.

"A bard down on her luck, looking for a free place to stay," opined the guard captain. "Crazy, maybe, but no harm in her." A murmur of agreement came from the other guards.

From the vantage point of his window in the inn across

from the guild hall, Vartain had to disagree with this assessment of the matter. In many ways, the woman did not fit the template he had fashioned, yet he had little doubt that she was indeed the author of the scroll he carried.

The riddlemaster's fingers sought the parchment roll tucked into his belt. He had stolen it from Danilo just before he'd left the Harper outside Blackstaff Tower. Vartain did not like to remember his ignoble past, and he was loathe to use the skills he'd learned as a child on the streets of Calimport. It was, however, the only way he could think of to ensure that no one found the sorceress but himself.

This plot had been formulating in his mind for some time. He'd deliberately disavowed knowledge of the barding college in Waterdeep, and Danilo Thann apparently held the popular misconception that Halambar's Lute Shop stood on the original site. No doubt the Harper had learned differently by now and had probably sought Vartain around the musicians' guild hall. Vartain had come to this inn directly from the archmage's tower, and he felt secure that his presence there would be kept secret. Discretion was the watchword at this inn, and the proprietor would not stay in business long if he started to reveal his patrons' secrets.

Vartain pulled the embroidered sash that hung over the bed, ringing the bell that summoned the chamber servant. When the young man appeared, Vartain requested that a private, closed coach be sent to the back alley immediately. The matter was tended to swiftly, for some of Lord Thann's pilfered emeralds had gone to ensure that Vartain's every desire would be tended.

The riddlemaster made his way to the rear of the inn. He climbed into the coach and instructed the driver to take him to Halambar's Lute Shop. He also suggested a route that, if not the most direct, would be sure to take them to their destination in the least possible time, should certain anticipated conditions exist. The driver listened to Vartain's precise, detailed instructions and then, to the riddlemaster's utter bewilderment, he burst out laughing.

Vartain flopped back against the plushly padded seat of the coach, and for some reason he recalled young Thann's definition of humor: looking at a situation from a new and different perspective. But was that not what he himself did? Was not his art the consideration of all possibilities, and the combination of observed facts into a logical whole? Yet Vartain often found himself puzzled while others laughed, and he took no pleasure in the telling of amusing tales for the sake of levity alone. Nor, apparently, did he tell them well. "Great material, but your delivery could stink up a stockyard," a jester of casual acquaintance had once advised him. These thoughts presented a paradox to the riddlemaster.

As Vartain predicted, his coach did arrive at the music shop in short order. Even so, they were too late; Vartain saw the flick of a dove-white tail as the bard's horse rounded a corner at a brisk trot. He was not overly concerned; there was much he could garner from the bard's registration. Vartain climbed down from the coach and entered the shop.

He made a perfunctory bow to the haughty guildmaster and then went immediately to the table upon which the register was displayed. Ignoring the stool placed there for the comfort of the shop's patrons, he opened the book and thumbed through to the last entry. It read simply:

Garnet, a bard.
Entered Waterdeep the final day of Flamerule.

That was today, Vartain noted.

The riddlemaster sank slowly down on the stool, staring with unseeing eyes at a display of unique magical instruments. Khelben Arunsun's suspicions about the sorceress's true name and nature were almost certainly correct. The name Iriador was derived from the Elvish word for "ruby," and it seemed fitting that the proud woman would take another precious stone as her name.

He pulled the scroll from his belt and unrolled it, looking over the possibilities and fitting together the pieces in a way that reflected this understanding. As he read, the details of her plot became clear to him. He knew exactly where Garnet would strike, who would be the target of her harp-given power, and what weapons she would employ.

Vartain scratched his chin, troubled by the dilemma this presented. By all accounts, he should hurry to the designated meeting place and tell his employers, Elaith Craulnober and Danilo Thann, all that he had learned. He was bound in honor to serve them with all his powers. That the two clearly had different goals in mind was of no concern to Vartain and did not enter into his internal debate. Something more basic and compelling guided the riddlemaster's hesitation.

Once before on this quest he had failed. In missing the dragon's riddle, he for the first time had fallen short of expectations. As Danilo Thann had so intuitively noted, Vartain longed for the chance to match wits with the person who had devised the riddle spell. Not only would it exonerate him of this failure, but it presented a challenge such that he might never again encounter. Could he bear to cast aside such an opportunity? Confiding in his employers would be doing precisely that: Danilo Thann was determined to overcome the sorceress with magic, and Elaith Craulnober would certainly attempt to kill her, that he might obtain the valuable artifact needed to purchase his child's inheritance. No, this opportunity Vartain must have for himself.

Then doubt, an emotion almost unknown to the riddle-master, edged into his mind. In many ways, he and this Garnet were much alike: she was a riddlemaster, a master of lore and language, a traveler and a teller of tales. Yet she was also a mage, and she wielded an artifact of great power. In addition, she had lived more than six of his life-times, and although he had learned and accomplished much, he could not be sure that it would be enough. If he kept the knowledge of her identity to himself, and met the bard Garnet on the field of intellectual combat, what was to say he would fare better against her than he had against the wily Grimnoshtadrano?

A notion entered Vartain's mind, an idea so unexpected and droll that he blinked in astonishment. He would over-come *Garnet* the same way that the dragon had deceived *him*! If he and Garnet were as much alike as he suspected, she would also be hampered by an abundance of intellec-tual pride and a dearth of humor.

A chuckle escaped him, a rusty and experimental sound that drew stares from the shop's other patrons. Then, for the first time in his adult life, Vartain burst into unre-strained laughter.

By the glyphs of Deneir, it was worth a try! thought Var-tain as he laughed, holding his sides against the unaccus-tomed twinge in his shaking ribs.

* * * * *

Garnet rode up to Lady Thione's Sea Ward villa and threw the reins of her horse to a servant. Unannounced, she walked into the parlor where the noblewoman held conference with several merchants.

Lucia looked up at the interruption, imperious anger in her dark eyes. When she saw Garnet, however, her face instantly become a calm, expressionless mask. She rose and politely greeted the sorceress. She drew her out of the room, carefully closing the heavy oak door behind them.

"Get rid of them," demanded Garnet. "We have much to discuss." She thrust a handful of papers at the noblewoman.

Lucia glanced at the top page and grimaced. She quickly leafed through the papers: all were identical. "Lord Hhune's work. He was acting on his own initiative, I assure you."

"Good." The sorceress nodded. "I would not want this traced back to you. On the other hand, I am glad he did this. This drawing of the archmage is another type of bardcraft, a new way of telling a story. It is fitting that such a weapon be brought against Khelben Arunsun. Hhune will most likely be found out, but he is expendable. Now, we must move on to other things.

"Midsummer Day will be a disaster," Garnet continued. "You have played your part well in the disruption of commerce. Other agents of the Knights of the Shield have ensured that the traditional tournament games will go badly. Above all this, there will be a violent storm of rain— and possibly hail—on Midsummer Day. These northern barbarians will take the storm as an evil omen."

"But the weather has been fine all week," Lucia said, a question in her voice.

"All the better! The wizard weather will be blamed on the archmage, and when Shieldmeet begins, the people will be ready to listen to your suggestion."

"*My* suggestion?" Lucia hedged.

"Oh, yes. Shieldmeet begins at sunset with a vast meeting open to all the citizens of Waterdeep. At this time the Lords of Waterdeep are reaffirmed by popular acclamation. When the meeting begins, you will reveal yourself as one of the Lords, argue that the city's woes are due to the

ambitions of Khelben Arunsun, and demand that he resign
from the Council of Lords."

Lucia paled.

"You are well connected with the guilds, popular with
the nobility, and beloved of the tradespeople. The only
major faction in Waterdeep that is not in your pocket is the
collective clergy." Garnet paused for a hard smile. "How
fortunate for us that Waterdeep is not a deeply devout
city."

Lucia Thione stared at the sorceress, her eyes enormous with shock. She licked her lips nervously and tried
to speak, but the words would not come.

The half-elf noted this with growing suspicion. "Is there
a problem?"

"Yes! That is, you realize of course that Lord Piergeiron
will deny that I am one of the Lords of Waterdeep. This is
standard practice whenever a Lord is unmasked, much as
the Knights of the Shield disavow any of our members
who are caught."

Garnet did not look convinced. "I wonder," she said
softly, her sapphire eyes searching the noblewoman's pale
face. She smiled suddenly. "You know, I have always been
curious about the magical properties of those helms that
you Lords of Waterdeep wear in public. Might I examine
yours?"

Lucia's heart thudded painfully, and she struggled to
keep her panic from her face. "I do not keep it in my Sea
Ward villa. It is safely locked away, but I will be happy to
retrieve it for you later in the day."

"You do that," Garnet said, pushing past Lucia and making her way up the stairs. "I will be staying here until
Shieldmeet is past. Kindly send some of your servants to
attend me," she called over her shoulder.

The noblewoman slumped against the wall. Her worse
fears had come to fruition. Garnet's demands had placed

her in an impossible situation. She could not openly claim to be a Lord of Waterdeep, for the penalty for impersonating a Lord was death. Yet if she refused, Garnet would make sure that the Knights of the Shield learned of Lucia's deception. The best she could do was stall for time and hope that a solution would come to her. Always before, Lucia had been able to untie the Gordian knots that came with her life of intrigue, but this time there seemed to be no way out.

"Lady Thione? Are you ill, madame?"

The question snapped her back into the present. She recognized the deep, charmingly accented voice of Bergand, a merchant lord of the faraway island of Nimbral. A possible solution presented itself to Lucia. Nimbral lay southwest of the Jungle of Chult, and it was far beyond the reach of the Knights of the Shield. The land was rich, and trade was busy and diverse. Bergand himself had vast holdings and a thriving business, and he was not immune to her charm.

Lucia turned to her client and gave him her most dazzling smile.

Fourteen

"If'n I knowed yer friend would be late abed, I'd've had me another mug of that ale," Morgalla said wistfully.

Danilo grinned, not taking the dwarf at all seriously. They'd been waiting for Caladorn at the Field of Triumph for well over an hour, and Danilo noticed that Morgalla watched the morning's practice with an interested and critical eye. A fighter to the core, she was having a fine time appraising the styles and skills displayed on the practice fields.

The Harper also made good use of the time. He noted the poor turnout, the dispirited air of the contestants, and the number of clerics on hand to heal injuries. The horses in the arena's stables—supposedly the best horses in all the Northlands—looked dull and lethargic. A number of them had suffered injuries, and for the price of a silver coin one of the grooms confided that several horses had been hurt so badly that they'd been put down.

Danilo also learned that many of the renowned fighters

who'd expected to be in the contests had suffered injury or met with troubles of one sort or another. Most of the contestants who trained this morning were youths and visitors, eager for the fame that victory at the Midsummer Games would bring them and willing to take the all-too-apparent risks involved.

"If this be the best fighters you got in Waterdeep, I can't figger out why the city ain't overrun with trolls," Morgalla commented. With the jester-head of her staff, she pointed toward two young men battling with staffs. Even to Danilo, it seemed a clumsy and halfhearted meet.

"Jarun hurt his shoulder yesterday," explained a deep voice behind them. "He's favoring one side too much."

Morgalla snorted, not bothering to turn around. "He'd do both sides a favor if'n he put down his staff and took up tapestry."

Danilo turned at the familiar, hearty laughter that the dwarf's comment evoked. Behind them stood Caladorn, dressed for the practice field in leggings and a linen shirt, which was unlaced nearly to the waist. The short red curls on his head and on his well-muscled chest glistened in the bright midday sun.

"Sweet Sune!" Danilo exclaimed, casting an arch glance at Caladorn's state of half-dress. "What sort of events are you preparing for, and where can I sign up?"

Caladorn laughed again and patted the sword at his hip. "It's hot work, Dan, swinging seven pounds of steel in the midday sun."

When Danilo responded with a delicate shudder, the swordsman chuckled and clapped him on the back. "You'll not take me in with that act, lad! If I recall aright, you had the same swordmaster as did your brother Randor, and he's a fine hand with a sword. Would you care for a match? I could use a bit of a challenge."

"If you would for one moment consider me a challenge,

things here must be in a sorry state," Danilo said lightly.

Caladorn's handsome face turned grim, and he raised a hand in the gesture of a fencer acknowledging a hit. "I'll tell you all about it some time over a few tankards."

"How about now?"

"I wish I could, but I had to stop by the palace on tournament business, and I can't afford to take any more time from the training. The games are tomorrow, and there remains much to do. I've got to put these boys and girls through their paces," Caladorn said, eyeing the field with a resigned expression.

The firm manner in which Caladorn spoke, not to mention the indisputable evidence in the contestants around them, gave Danilo little hope of changing the fighter's mind. He was about to take his leave when Caladorn spoke again.

"The stableboy said you've been waiting for me an hour and more. I'm sorry for that, Dan, but I ran into Khelben on my way to the field, and he kept me talking for some time. You know how the good archmage can run on."

"Only too well," Danilo replied with a rueful grin. In truth, he thought Caladorn's comment rather odd. His Uncle Khelben was not given to idle, social chitchat. The Harper decided to probe for a bit more information. "Don't tell me, Caladorn: you tried to talk the archmage into giving you a love potion to slip into Lady Thione's wine!"

The fighter good-naturedly shrugged away Danilo's teasing.

"I knew it!" Danilo crowed. "I've been wondering how a pitiful specimen such as yourself managed to hold the lovely lady's interest."

A wistful expression crossed Caladorn's face. "To tell you the truth, there is little I wouldn't do to win the lady's heart, barring that," he said, his voice suddenly serious. "I have asked Lucia for her hand, but she is not yet ready to entrust it. When that day comes, I am determined to be worthy of the honor."

The words were put forth simply, with a dignity and an old-fashioned courtliness that reminded Danilo of the knights of an earlier time. The love and reverence in Caladorn's eyes when he spoke of his lady made Danilo feel vaguely ashamed of his earlier jest. After promising Caladorn a match at a later time, he and Morgalla left the tournament field.

"Where to?" the dwarf asked.

"We're to meet the others at the Broken Lance, a tavern not far from here," Danilo said, leading the way down a side street. "Let's hope that one of them has fared better than we have!"

* * * * *

While her troublesome houseguest took a midday nap, Lucia Thione slipped away from her villa and hurried to Caladorn's townhouse in the Castle Ward. To her dismay, she found all the cupboards locked. Her young lover was not at home. His manservant did not have the keys, but he informed her that Caladorn had left early, and that he'd had business with the archmage.

Although society deemed the hour far too early to be making calls, the noblewoman went at once to Blackstaff Tower. She was greeted at the wall by the Lady Arunsun and graciously received. Lucia felt uneasy in the beautiful mage's presence—the noblewoman often had the feeling that those wicked silver eyes saw far too much—but she entered the tower with Laeral and accepted a goblet of iced pomegranate nectar. After the usual exchange of social amenities, Lucia asked for the archmage.

"He is not here, I'm afraid," Laeral said, and her bare shoulders—at this time of the day!—lifted in a graceful, apologetic shrug.

Despite the mage's polite words, Lucia got the distinct impression that Laeral was not at all displeased with the situation. The noblewoman's tiny chin firmed and lifted to an imperious angle. "Would you be so good as to tell me where I might find him? Or Caladorn, for that matter?"

Silver eyes twinkled, and a dimple flashed briefly on the mage's face. "I regret that such goodness is beyond me," Laeral murmured. "Khelben left the tower early this morning, and he did not mention his destination."

Before the frustrated noblewoman could respond, a young gold elf entered the reception hall, a silver lyre in his arms. He paused when he noted Lady Thione and made her a deep bow. The irrepressible Laeral dimpled and winked at the newcomer.

"Lady Thione, may I present Wyn Ashgrove. He is a minstrel and our guest at the tower. Wyn, Lady Thione is of the old royal family of Tethyr. Perhaps you might honor her with a song from her homeland?"

The elf agreed. He promptly seated himself and began to play a familiar melody on his silver lyre. His voice was high and sweet, and his skill remarkable, yet Lucia Thione had difficulty sitting through the elf's well-meaning performance. For one thing, she'd had entirely too much to do with bards of late! Even more exasperating was the amused gleam in Laeral's silver eyes. The mage was clearly aware of Lucia's eagerness to be off, and she was deliberately detaining her guest in a fashion that the noblewoman could not dismiss without displaying an appalling lack of breeding. Angry at being toyed with in such a fashion, Lucia Thione seethed throughout the elf's song. Despite Laeral's power, beauty, charm, and social position as Khelben Arunsun's lady, the mage remained somewhat of a rogue. With such a base trick, Lucia thought with a touch of malice, Laeral revealed herself as the common wench that she was!

As soon as the last silvery chord faded into silence, Lucia Thione rose to her feet. "Thank you for your lovely tribute, Master Ashgrove," she said, using her most regal tones to hide how flustered she truly felt. "Please accept in return this small tribute to your skills." She reached into her money purse and selected one of several small coin bags. She handed it to the elf. He rose and accepted it with a polite bow.

The noblewoman's farewell to the lady mage was as frosty as propriety allowed. Although Laeral did not appear to realize that she had been put in her place, at least she had the decency to escort Lady Thione to the street without further mockery.

Lucia settled into her carriage, deeply troubled by the morning's events. Bergand would not be leaving for Nimbral until after the Midsummer Faire, and Garnet could not be put off. She would not wait that long for a helm of a Lord of Waterdeep, and the only one Lucia had a hope of procuring was Caladorn's. Unless she got it quickly, she stood the risk of being unveiled before Garnet and the Knights of the Shield. The helm she must have, right away, and at any cost.

With a deep sigh, she resolved herself to the necessary course of action. Tapping briskly on the carriage glass, she got the driver's attention and instructed him to take her to Diloontier's Apothecary. The posh shop, located in the heart of the Castle Ward, catered to the needs of wealthy ladies and dandies who required herbal and magical balms, perfumes, and potions, and it possessed a sterling reputation and a clientele that included many of those whose names were featured on society's first-choice guest lists. Diloontier also had a startling array of poisons and potions, which he secretly sold to those who had the appropriate credentials and the right amount of gold. Unfortunately for Caladorn, Lucia possessed both.

* * * * *

When Danilo and Morgalla arrived at the Broken Lance, Wyn Ashgrove was waiting for them, looking strangely out of place amid the athletes and fighters who frequented the tavern. The elf waved them over to his table. "Khelben Arunsun could not come. He sends his regrets. Do you have any news?"

"Less than I'd like," Danilo replied, taking a seat at the large circular table. The Harper ordered wine and sipped at it absently while Wyn told them about the recent events in Waterdeep. The rumored disappearances of the Lords of Waterdeep concerned the Harper deeply, not only for the city, but because his uncle and mentor was among that group. Not that Khelben had ever admitted to these disappearances, but Danilo had no doubt that the rumors at least in this instance were accurate. Wyn's news also cast a sinister light on the prophecy in the spell scroll: the lord to fall on the field of triumph would most likely be one of the Lords of Waterdeep.

"Ready to order?" The serving woman, a former city champion in both jousting and swordplay, gave the question an inflection that suggested the talkative party would be advised to either order immediately, vacate the tavern, or draw weapons.

"Another round of drinks," Danilo suggested, "some bread and cheese for the table, a bowl of bitter greens with summer herbs, and three servings of the eel pie. You must try it; it's a house specialty," he informed Morgalla and Wyn.

"Bring four servings," corrected Elaith Craulnober, coming to the table with a silent grace that startled everyone there.

"You!" Danilo leaped to his feet. "I don't believe you actually showed up! You've got more nerve than a drunken ogre."

The moon elf rocked back on his heels, surprised by the Harper's vehemence. "Have I missed something? We did agree to meet here at highsun."

"That was before you stole the spell scroll."

"Wait a minute," Elaith demanded, taking a step toward the angry Harper. "The spell scroll is gone?"

"What? Is there an echo in here?"

Elaith let out a long hiss of exasperation and sank into a chair. "Vartain!" he said with disgust.

"Vartain?" echoed Morgalla and Wyn, in unison and disbelief.

"You heard me. He's a better thief than a riddlemaster, although he doesn't like to advertise the fact. By the way, Lord Thann, it was he who separated you from your magic ring."

"He *is* good," Danilo muttered as he resumed his seat.

The servant came back with their meal. "Anything to drink?" she asked the moon elf.

"A large bottle of your best gold firewine."

Danilo's eyebrows rose. The wine was both potent and expensive. "Are we celebrating or drowning our sorrows?" he asked.

"Do whatever pleases you," the rogue elf responded, leaning back in his chair. "The firewine is for me."

"Ah." The Harper nodded sagely.

"Who's paying?" the server demanded bluntly.

Before Danilo could reach for his purse, Wyn produced a large gold coin and held it out to the impatient woman. "This should more than cover the cost of the meal and the wine," he said.

Elaith's amber eyes narrowed, and he snatched the coin from the gold elf's hand. After a moment's scrutiny, he demanded, "Where did you get this?"

"It was given in tribute for an impromptu performance," Wyn replied, looking both surprised and defensive. "Many of the People make their living with music, and there is no shame in my accepting payment. The gold was rightly earned."

"Only if you've taken up work as a thief or assassin," Elaith retorted.

"Look, I don't care how you make the money. Just pass some of it over," the server demanded.

Danilo handed the woman several silver pieces and waved her on her way. The rogue elf's words, combined with the size of the coin, reminded him of the coin Arilyn had given him in Tethyr. "How do you know all this?" he asked Elaith. "Seriously," he added, before the rogue elf could put him off by stating the obvious.

Elaith held out the coin and traced a finger around the circular pattern of runes along the edge. "See these markings? And this shield in the middle of the coin? This is the symbol of the Knights of the Shield, a secret society active mostly in the Southlands—"

"I know who they are," Danilo interrupted.

"Then you also knew they are sworn enemies of the Lords of Waterdeep. These coins are used for several purposes: as payment, as a tribute for work well done, as a warning when given to an uncooperative lord or merchant, as a means of claiming responsibility for certain violent acts. Some coins even give the name of the agent."

"How do you know so much?" Danilo asked.

"Agents of the Knights show up in Waterdeep from time to time, and I've been forced to remove those who get too active," Elaith admitted freely. "Although I bear little love for the Lords of Waterdeep, the present system works well for me, and it's in my own best interest to help sustain it."

"Big o' him," muttered Morgalla.

"You have reason to believe the Knights of the Shield threaten Waterdeep and her Lords?" Danilo asked.

Elaith nodded. "I've spent the night being bombarded

with rumors that two new guilds are being organized for thieves and assassins." When the Harper looked skeptical, Elaith added, "This has been verified by one of my best informants: a highly placed agent of the Kraken Society. His organization is not involved, but they do not disapprove."

"It must be nice to have friends in low places," Danilo murmured absently. He claimed Wyn's coin from the rogue elf and studied it. In the center of the Knights' distinctive shield was a familiar rune. "I know this symbol!" he exclaimed. "This is the mark of one Lord Hhune of Tethyr. He's master of the shipping guild there, and I managed to annoy him repeatedly during my sojourn in that land."

"That I can well imagine," Elaith said. He looked at the Harper with a touch of amusement. "You may be interested to know that Lord Hhune is now in Waterdeep. By all accounts, he is organizing the city's thieves and assassins, but he may have time to spare for you. Is he the persistent type, do you think?"

"I can see that your day is made," Danilo said dryly. He turned to the gold elf. "Who gave you this coin, Wyn?"

"A lady of Tethyr, who came to Blackstaff Tower early this morning seeking the archmage. Her name escapes me, I'm afraid." The minstrel smiled apologetically. "I was contemplating Lady Laeral's smile and did not take notice."

"I won't pass that on to my uncle. What did this visitor look like?"

Wyn considered. "She was small and slender, with olive skin and large dark eyes. Her nose was narrow and slightly aquiline, and her hair was a gleaming dark chestnut hue, elegantly dressed in coils and ringlets. I found her decolletage a bit extreme, but this is after all Waterdeep."

"Mercy! I'd love to know what you'd see if you *were* taking notice. Remind me to ask you about the special

properties of your elven heat vision at some later time.
Was the lady wearing purple?"

"I believe so. If this is any help, she was seeking the
archmage and someone else, as well. I believe the name
was—"

"Caladorn?"

"Yes, that's it. The Lady Laeral said that he and Khelben
had an appointment to meet this morning. Is that important?"

The Harper nodded slowly as he put together the pieces
of information, then he buried his head in his hands. He
had to warn Caladorn, but in light of their earlier conversation, the situation was extremely delicate. Before he could
confront the lovestruck young lord, he would have to confirm his suspicions.

"What is it?" Morgalla demanded, elbowing Danilo
sharply.

He raised weary eyes to his dwarven friend. "You can
have my portion of eel pie, Morgalla. I must return to
Blackstaff Tower."

"That ain't the place to be at mealtime, lessen yer prepared to do the cookin' yerself," the dwarf observed.

"Yes. My sentiments precisely, but it can't be helped.
After you eat, Morgalla, why don't you head down to Vir-
gin's Square and see what more you can find out about
these proposed guilds. Find old Blazidon One-Eye and
claim to be looking for work. He knows who's hiring
whom. Also, his bodyguard is a dwarf. Think he might be
susceptible to your charm?"

"Never met me a dwarf who wasn't," Morgalla replied
with a twinkle in her brown eyes. "I'll meet you back at yer
townhouse at sunset."

"What would you like the rest of us to do?" Wyn asked
softly.

"Keep looking for the Morninglark harp, of course. It

wouldn't hurt to keep an eye out for Vartain, as well."

"Rest assured, I'll find that treacherous buzzard," Elaith said.

Danilo gazed thoughtfully at the moon elf. If Elaith were to find the sorceress first, the elf would no doubt abscond with the harp, and he would have no hope of reversing the spell. "Why don't you go along with our partner, Wyn, just to keep things rolling along on the right path?"

Elaith's silver brows rose, and he nodded approvingly at the Harper. "Very good, young man. There may yet be hope for you."

"I live for your approval," Dan said as he rose from his chair. "Now, if you will all excuse me, I must attend to a most unpleasant task."

"One moment," Elaith said. The moon elf paused and cast his eyes toward the ceiling, as if he could not believe what he was about to do. "I recognized Lady Thione from the minstrel's description. Perhaps you should know that one of her servants secretly paid for a satirical performance at the Three Pearls club. The payment was made with Hhune's marked coin."

Danilo stared at the elf for a moment, then he nodded his thanks. He left the tavern and made his way quickly to Blackstaff Tower. He found Khelben and Laeral at midday meal, eating more of the lentil stew of which the archmage was so perversely fond.

"Caladorn said he met with you this morning," Danilo said without preamble. "Is that true?"

Khelben laid down his spoon and fixed keen black eyes on his nephew. "Why do you ask?"

Danilo took a deep breath and threw diplomacy down the cistern. "I need to know whether Caladorn is one of the Lords of Waterdeep."

"The identities of the Lords are secret. You know that."

"There's no time to hedge! To whom do you think that

spell scroll was referring when it spoke of a lord falling on the field of triumph?"

"I have already considered that," Khelben told him, "and it was for that reason that I met with young Caladorn this morning. He is in charge of the tournament, and he is of noble birth. I advised him to withdraw from the games; barring that, I warned him to take whatever precautions he could."

Danilo placed both hands on the table and leaned down to glare into his uncle's eyes. "What would you say if I told you that Caladorn's ladylove, Lucia Thione, is an agent of the Knights of the Shield?"

The archmage's eyes widened, and an uncharacteristically earthy expletive burst from him.

"Well!" Danilo straightened up. "That's not what I thought you'd say, to be sure, but apt nonetheless. May I take that as a confirmation?"

When Khelben again hesitated, Laeral broke in. "Lucia Thione was here earlier looking for Caladorn. She seemed anxious, almost distraught. I agree with Danilo. Someone has to warn Caladorn at once. If you'd seen that woman's face, you'd know that the dangers arrayed against him are not limited to the arena. Go, Dan."

The archmage conceded with a grim nod.

"Unless you'd rather speak to him yourself?" Danilo asked, hope in his voice.

"Go!"

After receiving Khelben's assurance that the city officials would take care of Lady Thione and Lord Hhune, Danilo went. He retraced his way to the tournament field, and the memory of the love shining in Caladorn's eyes haunted him as he went.

Fifteen

Caladorn was hard at work when Danilo arrived at the Field of Triumph. When the young lord saw Dan, he sheathed his sword and dismissed his opponent with a nod. He strode over to the entrance and greeted the younger man with enthusiasm.

"Here to give me that match you promised, are you?"

"Well, not exactly."

"I won't hear otherwise! You've a sword already; shed your cloak and let's have a go."

"Caladorn, I really must speak with you. It's most important."

"So is sword practice. We can talk while we work."

With a sigh, Danilo did as he was bid. Ideally, he preferred not to break bad news to an armed man. Yet he had little time to spare with arguments, and Caladorn was adamant. The Harper drew his sword and mirrored his friend's salute, then blocked the first ringing blow. He retreated and then feinted to the left. Caladorn blocked easily and riposted.

"The Knights of the Shield are active in Waterdeep," Danilo began as he blocked.

Caladorn chuckled and made a flamboyant advance, his right foot stamping. He danced back before the Harper could retreat. "And how would a bard know of such things? Oh, yes, I know of your rapidly growing fame. You are planning a new ballad about these infamous spies, is that it?"

"Not immediately, no." Dan again blocked, riposted, retreated. "I don't know how to tell you this, so I'll be blunt. Lady Thione is one of their agents."

Caladorn's face darkened, and for a moment he lowered his sword. "You're right, lad, you don't know how to tell me anything of the sort."

The Harper brought his sword up in time to fend off a high, downward strike. "She paid my associate with a coin bearing the Knights' mark."

"So? It was passed to her!"

"By whom?"

"How would I know!" Caladorn slammed his sword back into its scabbard and folded his arms.

"I can tell you that," Danilo said softly as he sheathed his own blade. "Lord Hhune, a guildmaster of Tethyr and an agent of the Knights, is now here in Waterdeep, working to establish guilds for thieves and assassins."

"So? This has nothing to do with Lucia! She is a merchant, and she has done business with Hhune in the past. He must have given the coin to her during a business transaction. She probably never knew she had it!"

"For your sake, I hope you're right. It's interesting, though, that one of Lucia Thione's servants paid for a performance at the Three Pearls theater, using some of Hhune's marked coins."

Caladorn's face went very still.

"I'm sorry about this, my friend, but can you afford to dismiss all suspicion?"

The fighter shook his head in astonishment. "Why are you doing this, Dan? What could you possibly know of such matters?"

"I'm a Harper, Caladorn. It's my job to know what's going on."

The young lord's laughter was harsh. "I'm still trying to absorb the concept of your bardhood! Don't stretch my credulity to the breaking point."

"Nevertheless, all I've told you is true."

"I'll not hear another word against Lucia." Caladorn glared at the younger man, controlling himself with visible effort. At long last he whirled and stalked away, leaving Danilo standing alone in the middle of the arena.

"Well," the Harper said wryly, "that went better than I expected. Things could be worse."

His words were met by a boom of thunder. Dark purple clouds began to gather over the Field of Triumph, and a flash of lightning ripped across the livid sky.

"You'd think I'd learn not to say things like that," Danilo muttered to himself as he sprinted through the first streaks of rain.

* * * * *

After Danilo left Blackstaff Tower, Khelben Arunsun strode quickly through the underground passages that led to Piergeiron's palace. The unmasked Lord commanded the combined forces of the guard and the watch, and his command would be needed to arrest important persons such as Hhune and Lady Thione.

Hhune's presence in Waterdeep had been noted, and he would have been carefully watched under any circumstances. As a guildmaster, Hhune was a powerful force in

Tethyr. This made his connection with the Knights of the
Shield all the more disturbing, for it combined two powers
hostile to Waterdeep and to her Lords. But he was also a
wealthy, traveling merchant, and these were always welcome in Waterdeep. By rescinding this welcome, Piergeiron risked endangering trade between Waterdeep and
Tethyr. It was a delicate matter, and no decision that the
First Lord made would be entirely correct.

Khelben's entrance to the palace was hidden in a small
anteroom. He strode quickly through the halls toward the
council room, noting as he went that the careful eyes of
Piergeiron's guard were upon him. Even here, he noted
wearily, he could not escape the burden of suspicion that
the bards' songs had placed upon him.

"I will do what I can," Piergeiron said once Khelben had
related the story, "but it's hard to believe that Lucia Thione
is connected with Knights of the Shield. We will need more
proof of guilt before taking steps against someone so powerful and popular. A quick sentence by the Lords of Waterdeep could bring about a good deal of resentment and
unrest. Our decision to censor the bards was notoriously
unpopular, and it backfired most decisively."

"At least have Lady Thione followed," the archmage
insisted.

Piergeiron grimaced and pointed to the arched window
of the audience chamber. "That will be difficult at present.
I doubt that she, or anyone else for that matter, will be
going anywhere until that storm passes."

Khelben glanced toward the window. Blue lightning
flared against roiling purple clouds. "Wizard weather," he
muttered. A roll of thunder punctuated his words.

"In that case, can you undo it?" the First Lord asked anx-
iously.

"Not without a certain elven harp."

"Really! I didn't know you played."

The archmage responded with a grim smile. "I don't, but I'm beginning to think that perhaps I should have learned."

* * * * *

By midafternoon the sky was as dark as night. Rain pelted the outdoor market, sending merchants and shoppers, street performers and pickpockets scurrying for cover. Taverns, festhalls, and shops filled to capacity and beyond as the townspeople and visitors sought shelter from the violent thunderstorm. On and on the rain went, past the time of sunset and the official beginning of Midsummer. In every tavern and festhall in the city, bards and performers recited to their captive audiences tales of past evil that had been foretold by Midsummer storms.

Danilo was alone on the street as he dashed through the rain toward the Elfstone Tavern. It seemed a likely place for a half-elven bard to go. At the very least, perhaps he could get some information about the Morninglark harp. He entered the crowded taproom—for once, the tavern had opened its doors to member of all races—and handed his sodden cloak to an elven servant.

Danilo made his way through the crowds to the hearth. He was soaked to the skin, tired to the point of exhaustion, and becoming increasingly uncertain of his success. All efforts to find Vartain had met with failure. Danilo and his friends had searched every likely place and made inquiries throughout the city. It was as if the riddlemaster had been snatched into another plane of existence. Finally, Danilo had left the exhausted Wyn at his townhouse to rest. Morgalla had elected to stay behind, as well, not sure of her welcome in the elven tavern. With a profound sigh, Dan stretched his hands toward the hearth fire, hoping that the heat would restore a measure of feeling to his numb fingers.

"Well met, young bard," said a dry, ancient voice at his elbow. Danilo looked down into the thin, patrician face of the elven priest Evindal Duirsar. "I would rise to greet you, but I fear that someone would steal my place from under me," the elf said with a touch of humor as he regarded the mixed crowd. The tavern was strictly standing room only, and few of the surly, sodden patrons would respect the patriarch's age or position. At the elf's invitation, Danilo upended a log of firewood and made it into an impromptu chair at the small table.

"Your fame has multiplied since last we met," the patriarch noted.

"Not as fast as the challenges," Danilo murmured. He remembered another of his responsibilities: the rest of Elaith's mercenaries would be arriving in Waterdeep in a few days, and with them would be the mad elven hermit of Taskerleigh. Dan asked Evindal if the temple would accept the elf as a ward. The patriarch listened to the story with keen interest.

"By all means, the unfortunate soul is welcome in the temple. Now, tell me more about your recent journey."

To the wise and sympathetic elf, Danilo poured out the tale of a quest gone terribly awry, from the encounter with the dragon to the partnership with Elaith to the growing outcry against his uncle the archmage. He told Evindal of his personal quest to learn the art of elfsong, and he told of the spell scroll and the plot against the city. Finally, he spoke of the Morninglark harp, its power and its challenges.

"And I have pledged to hand the harp over to Elaith Craulnober when this is done," Danilo concluded.

"Given all that is said of him, it is reasonable for you to assume that he will put the artifact's power to evil purpose," the patriarch said thoughtfully. After a moment of silence, he rose from the table. "There is nothing more you can do here, and you may find some of the answers you seek at the temple. Come, let us go at once."

Despite his surprise, the Harper's manners brought him to his feet. "Humans are permitted?"

"Under certain circumstances, yes. You are a friend of the People, and you strive to reclaim an elven artifact from one who wields it with dishonor. We must aid you in this quest. Also, you have remanded an elven ward to our care. It is only fitting that you meet another ward of the temple, so that you may know how we will honor the trust you have placed in us." The patriarch led the way to the front door.

"The rain is still coming down in sheets," Danilo observed.

"Yes," the elf agreed, and then strode out into the storm.

The Harper followed. In time they came to a sweeping stairway of white marble, leading to a building complex defined by curving lines and surrounded by flowering plants. They hurried up the steps and into the corridor, where an elven servant took their cloaks. Evindal took Danilo down a corridor lined with doors. He tapped gently on one and cracked it open for a peek.

"Come in quietly," the elf said, disappearing into the room.

Curious, Danilo followed. The room was softly lit by several floating, glowing balls of white light, and was furnished with comfortable chairs, a low table and a tiny stool, and a small bed. No expense had been spared in the room, for the furnishings were fine and costly, and wondrous toys were scattered about. On a velvet cushion near the bed curled a yellow kitten, and in the corner sat a white-robed elven woman. She smiled at Danilo and pointed toward the bed.

The Harper took a step closer and peered down. Sleeping there was an elven toddler, perhaps the most beautiful child he had ever seen. Tousled silvery curls clustered about her face, and a tiny golden thumb nestled in her mouth. The points of her little elven ears were still soft, folding over slightly at the tips. Her features were tiny and delicate, and her skin in the soft light appeared both rosy and golden.

"Who is she?" Danilo whispered.

"May I present the Lady Azariah Craulnober," Evindal said softly.

Danilo looked up sharply. "Elaith's daughter?"

"That is so. Last spring, his elven mistress bore him a child. It was a most unexpected pregnancy, troubled from the first. The mother died at childbirth, leaving our mutual friend with an heir. As time went on, it became important to him that his daughter should receive her birthright, and he came to me asking what might be done to restore magic to his moonblade. I bid him recover an artifact and bring it to the temple. He carries the sword now by elven law and tradition. I will not burden you with the particulars."

"I see," Danilo said slowly. He recalled Elaith's stricken face when Wyn Ashgrove mentioned that the elven temple took in the ill and the outcast. Although it was hard to imagine this beautiful child as a social outcast, by Elaith's actions she was without honor or heritage. Suddenly the elf's actions made perfect sense to the Harper. He wondered if the true purpose of the quest was as clear to Elaith.

"I suppose he thinks that the artifact is to be rendered in payment, as one would pay a wizard or cleric for a powerful spell," Danilo said.

Evindal smiled sadly. "You know him well. To find an artifact is a difficult task, and such a quest inevitably changes all who undertake it. It was my hope that as Elaith Craulnober sought the elven harp, he would come to remember who he is. From all you have told me, that seems unlikely."

They quietly left the elfling's room. "You should get some rest, my friend," the patriarch told him. "There is little more you can do this night. You are welcome to stay here in the temple complex for the night."

The elf smiled suddenly. "It suddenly occurred to me that it has been some time since the temple was graced by the presence of a spellsinger."

"Life is full of these little ironies," Danilo murmured.

Evindal's soft chuckle echoed down the silent halls.

* * * * *

Later that night, a chill easterly wind drove the storm out to sea, and the captive Waterdhavians ventured out of their shelters. The quiet that the storm left behind felt unnatural, and to Caladorn's eyes and ears the city seemed as dispirited and demoralized as his own fighters.

As he made his way home through the puddles and the swirling mist, Caladorn's thoughts turned to his seafaring cronies, and he wondered how their ships would fare in the approaching storm. He almost envied them a peril as straightforward as Umberlee's wrath, for at least the goddess of sea and storm was a force that could be understood and appeased. The threats to his beloved Waterdeep, and to his own peace of mind, were far more complex.

To his surprise, Lucia met him at the door of his townhouse. She greeted him with a warm embrace and a goblet of his favorite wine.

"Where is Antony?" Caladorn asked, looked over her dark head toward the kitchens. The lower level of the townhouse was unusually chill and unwelcoming, not at all what he had come to expect from his competent manservant. Caladorn was tired and hungry and disgruntled with life; in short, he was in no mood to endure domestic incompetence.

"Oh, I gave him the night off," the noblewoman said airily. "Tonight I will see to all your wants personally." After giving him another kiss, she drifted off toward the kitchen to see to dinner.

As Caladorn watched her go, Danilo Thann's accusations rang in his head. He did not want to believe this of Lucia—he did not believe!—but neither could he dismiss the notion entirely. It occurred to him, suddenly, that there were no cooking odors emanating from the kitchen. The lower hall was usually redolent with the scent of roasts, steaming vegetables, and fresh bread.

Caladorn looked down at the goblet in his hand. After a moment of indecision, he poured the wine into a potted plant.

Following a decent interval in the cold darkness of the kitchen, Lucia returned to the front hall to find Caladorn lying on the floor, facedown. Quickly she picked up the goblet. It had been drained. Antony had died from half the dose, and the twisted, tormented posture in which her lover lay suggested that he had suffered from the corrosive acid as painfully as had his manservant. Regrettable, but it could not be helped. This was the quickest acting of all Diloontier's poisons, and Lucia was painfully short of time.

With quick, expert movements she patted Caladorn down for his keys. When she found the small ring of keys, she turned and ran lightly up two flights of stairs. After a few moments, she hurried back down to the front hall, a large square box in her arms and a dark, hooded traveling coat obscuring her face and form. Thus garbed, Lucia Thione left her lover's home for the last time without a backward glance.

So intent was she on her purpose that she did not notice

the quickly withering plant beside the body of her lover.

Silence filled the hall for a long moment. When he was certain that Lucia was gone, Caladorn rose to his feet. The pain in his heart and the bleak emptiness in his soul dimmed the memory of any battle wound he'd ever received.

What, then, was he to do? His heart and his hopes were not the only casualties of Lucia's treachery. Should he treat her like a wily trout, and give her enough line to maneuver, so that she would give proof to her evil intentions? Or should he bring her to instant and immediate justice? As a spy, she would no doubt be tried and executed. Caladorn doubted he had the strength to bring his lady to her death regardless of what she had tried to do to him, or her reasons for doing it.

With a ragged sigh, Caladorn turned and mounted the stairs toward the third floor. If he was to uncover Lucia's plot, he would have to know what object she considered worth the price of his life.

* * * * *

Clutching the box containing the magical helm, Lucia Thione fled through the quiet street. She had left one of Hhune's coins beside Caladorn's body, hoping to place the blame for the murders on the Tethyrian merchant. It was important, however, that no one see her out and abroad this night. She made her way quickly to a well-guarded home she owned nearby. Armed servants stood watch at every entrance, and several fierce moor hounds patrolled the walled grounds surrounding the house.

She brushed past one of the silent sentinels and made her way quickly up to her private chamber. She placed the box on her bed and shrugged off her cloak.

"Good evening, Lady Thione."

The noblewoman screamed and spun around, one hand at her throat. A tall, slender moon elf clad in unrelieved black rose gracefully from a chair. She recognized Elaith Craulnober, and her terror increased fourfold. Backing away, she lunged for the bellpull that would summon her armed servants.

"Don't bother your servants at this hour on my behalf," the elf said with a polite smile. "I gave them the night off."

The echo of words she had recently spoken to Caladorn chilled Lucia, and an image of Antony's body flashed into her mind. "They are all dead," she stated in a dull voice.

"Quite," Elaith agreed pleasantly. He resumed his seat and began to toy with a jeweled dagger. "Sit down, won't you? We have a shared problem to discuss."

Lucia sank down onto the edge of her bed. "How did you get past the magical wards around this house?" she demanded.

"Collecting magical toys is a hobby of mine," the elf said. "I've become rather good at identifying and dispatching them. Now, about this problem. We both have allies who have outlived their usefulness. I will remove yours, if you would be so kind as to have your agents tend to a partner of mine."

"I do not need to make such arrangements. The Lords of Waterdeep will see to Hhune," she said.

"No doubt. I was speaking of the other, the bard who carries an elven harp."

The noblewoman stared. "How do you know of this?"

"That is not important. Just tell me where she is—or *who* she is, for that matter—and I assure you she'll not trouble you further."

Lucia's mind whirled as she considered this possibility. The elf had proven himself capable of dispatching armed men and powerful magic. Perhaps he might be a match for the sorceress. That, however, raised another question.

"If you can do this, why do you not remove this unwanted partner yourself?"

The elf's smile held a bit of self-mockery. "Let's just say it's a matter of honor. Now, have we a deal?"

"Garnet is a half-elf woman of middle years. She is staying at my Sea Ward villa. Kill her, and I will grant you anything in my power to give," she said in a hard voice.

"I see that we shall get along fine," Elaith observed. "Now, there is something else you should know. Khelben Arunsun will soon be informed that you are an agent of the Knights of the Shield. All is not lost," the elf said, holding up a hand at her cry of dismay. "I have a network of safe houses throughout the city. I will be happy to hide you and smuggle you safely out of Waterdeep. I will ensure that an armed escort will see you to an appropriate destination."

The elf smiled pleasantly. "Of course, I will do all this for you *after* you have ordered your agents to rid the world of one Danilo Thann."

Sixteen

Throughout the night, the wall surrounding Blackstaff Tower was ringed by an assortment of unhappy people. Mages from the Watchful Order stood guard, ready with spells and wands to counter another attack of wizard weather. A circle of bards took turns singing the ballads that had changed the respect many Waterdhavians held for Khelben Arunsun into fear and distrust. The bards' audience, frightened by the strange Midsummer storm and the reputed disappearances of some of the Lords of Waterdeep, feared that the city's troubles were examples of anarchy to come. Khelben Arunsun was being blamed for events as varied as the attack upon the courtesan Larissa Neathal and the death of a caravan master from Baldur's Gate by the hands of overeager cutpurses. Several watch patrols stood by the tower in case the crowd's emotions spilled over into violence.

Inside the tower, Khelben paced his private chamber. "You should try to get some rest, my love," Laeral told him, laying aside the book she was vainly trying to read. "You have not slept for days now."

"Who could sleep with all that noise outside?" he retorted, flinging a hand toward the window. Like all the windows and doors of the tower and the surrounding wall, this one was visible only from the inside, and it shifted location constantly, yielding the wizards an ever-changing view of the crowd outside.

"While Piergeiron pondered matters of diplomacy and trade, Lucia Thione went into hiding," Khelben fumed. "I sent Harper agents to check all the properties she owns in the city. No one has found a trace of her. That was hours ago, and two agents have failed to report back at all."

In the corner of the room, a large crystal globe began to pulse with light. Khelben strode over to the scrying crystal and passed a hand over it. The face of a well-known shopkeeper came into view.

"Well?" the archmage demanded.

"Greetings, Blackstaff. Ariadne and Rix have been found," the woman said in a voice raw with unshed tears. "They were outside the walls of Lucia Thione's estate in the Sea Ward. Both died by garotte, and the bodies were left as if in warning." She stopped and cleared her throat several times before she could proceed. "Their eyes had been closed, and a large gold coin placed on each eyelid."

"Hhune's mark?" Khelben asked, his voice low.

"Yes."

The shopkeeper's face faded from view, but the archmage did not move or speak. As the minutes ticked by, Laeral studied her love with growing concern. Always he was hard hit by the death of Harpers who acted at his bidding, but this time she feared that Khelben's broad shoulders could not bear another such burden. He was overextended and exhausted, frustrated by his inability to control this situation or solve the city's problems.

With a sudden fierce swing, Khelben backhanded the scrying crystal. The globe flew across the room and shattered against the wall. He snatched up a cloak and the black wooden staff for which he was famed and feared. Before Laeral could respond to the uncharacteristic outburst, the archmage vanished.

Khelben materialized in the ballroom where Lucia Thione had recently held her lavish party. The room looked quite different at this hour of the night, almost austere without its crowd of merry revelers. It was lit only by the moonlight that filtered in from the garden beyond, casting silvery shadows upon the pale marble of the floor. The night air was scented by flowering vines that climbed trellises over each window alcove and arched door, and the silence was heavy with the memory of gay laughter and rollicking music. The archmage stood there a long moment, trying to collect his thoughts and to decide how to follow through on his impulsive action.

Like the ghost of a forgotten melody, a thread of silvery harp music reached out to him from the shadows at the far side of the ballroom. The archmage followed the sound, and his footsteps echoed in a somber counterpoint to the lilting little song.

The music seemed to come from everywhere and nowhere, and as Khelben drifted through the ballroom in search of its source, he felt as if he were moving in a dream, or trying to grasp a shadow. Finally he came to a large arched door that led out into the garden. There sat a small woman, clad in an elegant gown the color of sapphires. Her graying hair was tucked behind slightly pointed ears, and she played a small harp of dark wood.

"It has been many years, Iriador," he said softly.

The half-elf continued to play. "Much has changed, Khelben, and not for the better," she said. She looked up at him and smiled. "Attack me," she suggested. "Or try. If you do, you will not be able to move. Nor will you be able to speak, although there is little you could say that would matter now."

Magic, with the full force of the power he had wielded for centuries, welled up within the archmage in response to his silent command. Khelben willed his fingers to shape the spell, but his mortal frame proved to be less obedient than his magic. With astonishment and growing rage, he realized that the former Harper had spoken the truth.

The air around the archmage might as well have been solid stone, for he could neither move nor speak. The magic he had summoned had no place to go and it coursed through his body like captured lightning.

Only once before had Khelben known such pain. It circled endlessly through the conduits of power in his mind and body; it burned him as if molten steel filled his veins. With each pulse of anguish, the room dissolved into white light, and even his formidable will began to lose its grip upon consciousness.

Iriador Wintermist saw this, and triumph flared in her brilliant blue eyes. She rose with the harp in her arms and walked over to the man who was imprisoned by her magic and tortured by his own.

"You did not recognize the spell in my song, Khelben Arunsun, or you would have fled from this place. Always you have held bardcraft in little regard, and in your ignorance you prepared no defense against the power of spellsong."

She moved a step closer. "You deserted the bards, Khelben, and if you do not know your error by now, you soon shall. This I will prove, not by destroying you outright, but by removing you from power through the very force you scorned."

The woman spun toward the window. A white horse came galloping from the garden in response to her silent command. Quickly she mounted the asperii, and horse and rider disappeared through the arched doorway into the night.

A snatch of melody floated back into the room. Khelben fell to the floor, partially released from the powerful song charm. His release set free the remnants of his own spell, and magic exploded like an alchemist's nightmare. Pulse after pulse of unchanneled magical energy rocked the ballroom, sending multicolored light streaking into the garden beyond.

From the roof of a nearby mansion, Elaith Craulnober witnessed the light show with growing rage and frustration. He peered down the Street of Whispers. Already, members of the vigilant watch were approaching in response to the disturbance. With a smothered oath, he ran across the roof and leaped into the night, landing lightly on the next building.

With grace and balance that an acrobat might envy, he ran across a high wooden fence and leaped onto the triangular roof that topped the steam house of the Urmbrusk family's sybaritic villa. He raced across the roof, then summoned all his strength and threw himself into flight. The elf soared over Diamond Street, tucked at the last moment, and rolled onto the roof of a low building across the way. Within minutes he had made his way to Lady Thione's enclosed villa.

Elaith dropped over the wall and rushed through the garden. An armed guard came threateningly toward him. The elf tossed a knife into the man's throat without breaking stride. He followed the curling, glowing wisps of smoke into the ballroom. The fumes roiled through the room and stung his eyes, but he could see well enough to know that the room was empty but for himself and the man slumped nearby.

He was too late! The sorceress Garnet had gone, and with her was his hope of restoring his child's birthright.

The elf snatched a throwing knife from his sleeve, thinking to vent his frustration by hurling it into the body. At the last moment, he recognized the fallen man and sent his knife skittering harmlessly across the blackened marble floor.

Elaith knelt beside Khelben Arunsun and turned the wizard onto his back. The man yet lived, but his heart beat faintly. As the elf debated his course, the archmage's black eyes opened and fixed upon him. The archmage did not speak or move, but he seemed dimly aware of his surroundings.

"A charm spell," the elf muttered. He rocked back on his heels and ran his hand through his hair. The best person in the city to tend the wizard would be the mage Laeral. He should take the fallen man to Blackstaff Tower at once. A delay, however, could cost Elaith the harp he had sought for so long.

The elf decided. He reached into the bag at his belt and took out a plain silver ring. Vartain was not the only skilled thief in Music and Mayhem, and Elaith had once again relieved his Harper partner of the magic ring when they'd met at the Broken Lance tavern. He quickly slipped the ring on his own hand and twisted it as he'd seen Danilo do.

As the watch patrol burst into the room, they saw the fading outline of a tall slender elf and the archmage of Waterdeep.

* * * * *

In the hours before dawn, clerics of Mystra gathered at Blackstaff Tower to pray for the favor of the goddess of magic. Under their care and through the favor of his goddess, Khelben Arunsun's battered body began to heal. Nothing could touch the charm spell that held him, though, and after several hours the weary and heartsick

Laeral made her way down to the reception hall. After bringing Khelben to her, Elaith Craulnober had left the tower. He'd recently returned and sent up word that he wished to see her as soon as circumstances permitted.

The elf stood when Laeral entered the room. "How is the archmage?"

"He will live," the beautiful wizard replied.

Elaith nodded, a look of profound relief on his face. He handed Laeral a large, square box. "You may consider this a gift, a wish for Lord Arunsun's recovery."

Puzzled, Laeral peered inside. Within the box was one of the magical helms worn by the Lords of Waterdeep.

"I recovered the helm from Lady Thione. Perhaps you would see that it is returned to its rightful owner."

"Indeed we will," the mage said. She affixed Elaith with a penetrating gaze. "Forgive me, but—"

"This seems to be out of character?" the elf finished with an amused smile. "Not at all, dear lady. My own business interests are best served by preserving the status quo in Waterdeep."

"And Lady Thione?"

"She is in hiding, and under my protection," Elaith said. "My men will help her escape from Waterdeep." He smiled pleasantly. "Of course, I have not bothered to mention to her the destination. I've arranged to have her escorted back to Tethyr to face the locals."

Laeral's eyes flashed silver fire, and she nodded grim agreement with the justice that the elf's treachery meted out. "Elaith Craulnober, under different circumstances I believe we could have become very good friends."

* * * * *

High above the canopy of the High Forest, the sky faded to the pale silver that preceded dawn. It was still dark in the Endless Caverns, but the green dragon Grimnosh-tadrano felt the coming of day. He eased himself up onto his haunches and flexed his wings experimentally. The stiffness caused by the explosion and the smoke had finally eased, and at last he would be able to fly again. Never would he forget the indignity of crawling back to his cavern after he awoke in the clearing. He was determined that someone would pay dearly for the insults dealt him.

Grimnosh inhaled deeply and blew a long blast of air into his cave. A satisfying stench filled the chamber as poisonous chlorine gas flowed from his fanged maw. For days, he had been unable to muster his breath weapon. Now, it was back and ready to bring to bear on the treacherous bard. The dragon threw back his head and let out a roar of satisfaction.

Dropping down onto all fours, Grimnosh made his way through the labyrinth of caves and passages that led out of his lair. He emerged into the forest clearing where this misadventure had begun, exactly half a year ago, on the shortest day of winter. It seemed fitting that he would end it today on the summer solstice. His enormous green wings beat the air, and the dragon rose steadily into the sky.

With grim determination, the dragon set course for Waterdeep. Dragonflight was faster than lesser creatures could imagine, and his mighty wings and magic would bring him to the city before the day—the longest of the year—came to a close.

* * * * *

Midsummer morning dawned bright and clear over Waterdeep, and the tournament games began as scheduled. To the hundreds of people gathered to watch the meets, it seemed as if the hand of Beshaba, the goddess of bad luck, was over the Field of Triumph.

The grassy plain had been turned into a marshland by
the previous night's rain, and before long the field had
become a muddy, slippery mess. Many fighters and several mounts fell, and some of accidents were serious. The
magefair contests, always a favorite with the crowd, were if
possible even more dispirited than the games. Many of the
city's most powerful mages were at Blackstaff Tower, trying to remove the charm spell that held the archmage.
Rumors about what had happened to Khelben Arunsun
were whispered throughout the city. It was widely believed
that he had fallen due to his own miscast spell, and fear
was a more common response to this news than sympathy.

When Danilo heard of his uncle's accident, he went
directly to Blackstaff Tower. He couldn't get near the
tower for all the people around it, and when he tried to
teleport in, he realized that his magic ring had once again
been stolen.

"Dan."

Laeral's musical voice broke into his colorful spate of
self-recriminations. He spun to find the mage standing
behind him, her lovely face worn with worry and lack of
sleep. She took his arm and drew him away from the
crowd. "Khelben is held in some sort of charm spell. I
believe it is part of the Morninglark's elfsong spell. You've
got to find the harp, Dan."

The Harper was startled by the pleading note in the
powerful wizard's voice. Quickly covering his own distress, he took her hand and bowed low over it. "I never
could refuse a beautiful woman anything. I also have a celebrated imagination and season tickets for two to Mother
Tathlorn's festhall. Please bear all those things in mind
next time you ask something of me."

A dimple flashed briefly on the woman's face. "By Mystra, how you remind me of your uncle! He was very like
you when he was younger."

Danilo recoiled and dropped her hand. "I'll find the damn harp," he said in an aggrieved voice. "There's no need to insult me." He stalked away, and was gratified to hear the mage's laughter follow him.

Danilo met Wyn and Morgalla at the gate to the Field of Triumph, and they split between them the task of searching the huge arena for any who might fit the description of their bardic foe.

As they searched, Danilo kept an anxious eye on the field. By highsun, Caladorn had yet to show up. Danilo was surprised and more than a little worried. Perhaps his friend had taken his warning to heart and confronted Lady Thione. The Harper made inquiries of the fighters and stable hands, but no one seemed to know where the swordmaster had gone. First Vartain had disappeared, and now Caladorn!

The afternoon was nearing its close when Danilo finally caught a glimpse of Vartain, several stands away and very close to the raised dais used for announcements and awards.

"What could that blasted riddlemaster be up to?" he murmured aloud.

"I've no idea, but you can rest assured he'll suffer for it," announced a familiar voice behind him.

Danilo turned to face Elaith Craulnober. "No harp, I see. It would appear you've done no better than I have."

The elf pretended to wince. "What a concept! I shall remember those words, and use them whenever I need to express utter and abject failure."

"Now then, there's no need to take that tone. Save your venom for our mystery bard."

"I assure you, I've plenty to spare."

The Harper shrugged. "Much as I'd like to exchange pleasantries with you, I've got to get that scroll from Vartain."

Before Danilo could move away, Elaith's hand closed on
his arm like a vise, and the elf nodded toward the dais.
"The time for that has passed. You might as well stay for
the festivities."

Lord Piergeiron walked to the center of the platform,
raising his hands for attention. Two mages stepped forward, casting the spells that would send the First Lord's
voice throughout the arena. The crowd fell silent, for no
other individual in Waterdeep could command their attention as could Piergeiron. The First Lord was not given to
oratory, but he had a simple direct way about him to which
people responded.

"I declare that the tournament games are over, and that
the Midsummer festivities are at an end. We will begin
Shieldmeet with the traditional affirmation of the Lords of
Waterdeep."

"I sincerely doubt that," Elaith murmured, gazing
intently into the clouds.

Danilo followed the elf's gaze. "Don't tell me: it's an
asperii."

"I'm afraid so. With Lady Thione out of the way, the sorceress will no doubt try to depose Khelben herself."

"The sorceress has the power to influence crowds
through song," Danilo murmured, remembering the
riddle spell. "Let's get down there." He began to elbow his
way through the crowd.

Elaith followed him, but he looked doubtful. "What do
you propose to do?"

"Don't know, but I'll think of something."

The asperii swooped down over the arena, drawing
gasps of wonder from the crowd and diverting all attention
from Piergeiron. The noble wind steeds were rare and
considered a blessing from the gods. No one thought of
attacking the horse and its rider any more than they would
have fired upon a unicorn that suddenly appeared in their

midst. Even on the dais, the city dignitaries fell back to give the magical horse room to land.

The white horse landed lightly on the dais. Its rider dismounted and took her harp from its fastenings.

"With your leave, Lord Piergeiron," she said in a clear voice that carried to the farthest corner of the arena, "by law and by custom, until sunset the day is to be given to contests, festivity, and song. Shieldmeet does not begin until that time, and any contracts and agreements made before that time do not bear the force of law."

"That is true, lady bard," Piergeiron responded, and bowed to the half-elven woman. "We await your song."

"We've got to stop that song!" Danilo exclaimed, pushing aside a pair of rough looking half-orcs. One of the thugs bared his tusks in a scowl, then quickly subsided when he caught sight of the silver-haired elf at the human's side.

"I challenge the bard!" demanded a resonant bass voice.

The afternoon sun glinted off Vartain's bald pate as the riddlemaster pushed his way toward the platform. He spoke to the guards and was allowed to come forward.

"I challenge the mage and riddlemaster Iriador Wintermist of Sespech, who is currently known as Garnet the bard, to a challenge of riddles."

"That orc-sired buzzard!" Elaith muttered as he and Danilo pushed forward. "What in the Nine Hells is he doing?"

"Don't complain. He's stopping the song," Danilo retorted.

While the two made their way toward the stage, Vartain announced his terms: he would put forth a riddle, and if Garnet failed to guess it she would forfeit her harp. After a moment's hesitation, the bard agreed.

Morgalla fought her way over to Danilo's side, with Wyn in her wake. "What's that fool up to?" she demanded as they continued their struggle toward the dais.

"Saving face. We four will have to get the harp if Vartain fails, or if the bard does not honor the terms of the challenge."

"What four?" Morgalla demanded. "That silver serpent o' yers took off afore we got over to you."

Danilo scanned the crowd. There was no sign of Elaith. At that moment, Vartain cleared his throat and gave the riddle challenge:

King Khalzol's kingdom is long gone.
Take five steps to the site of his grave:
The first means to think over,
The second is over your thoughts,
The third means one of something,
The last must be stronger than anything,
The whole reveals everything.

"Now tell me, why did King Khalzol's subjects bury him in a copper coffin?"

"He's daft to try that one agin!" Morgalla exploded.

"Wait a minute," Danilo said, noting the thoughtful absorption on the sorceress's face. She was doing precisely what Vartain had done: she was giving the complex riddle all the consideration that a traditional conundrum required. Sure enough, she gave the same intelligent and incorrect answer that Vartain had given the dragon.

Vartain smiled broadly, vastly increasing his resemblance to a buzzard. "The answer to the question, 'Why was King Khalzol buried in a copper coffin?' is far simpler that you would make it, and I regret that it has nothing to do with the site of his grave. They buried him *because he was dead.*"

Garnet snatched up the harp. She struck a single ringing note and flung a hand toward the sky. Instantly the clouds began to gather, and a familiar rumbling sounded over the arena. The people nearest the exits fled at once in search of cover.

Suddenly a vast, green form burst from the roiling purple clouds. With a roar, a full-grown green dragon swooped down upon the city. Pandemonium struck the arena. People shrieked, shoving and pushing for the exits.

In the confusion that followed, Danilo caught sight of the rogue elf. Elaith was at the head of a band of rough-looking fighters. The mercenaries pushed toward the platform where the bard stood. Piergeiron's personal guard moved forward to protect the First Lord. Within moments, a nasty gutter-fight melee surrounded the platform, obscuring the bard and her harp from view.

"Now this is a proper fight," the dwarf announced with relish. She bared her spear and charged into the fray. Dan and Wyn exchanged a dismayed glance and then drew their swords, guarding the dwarf's back as she plowed a path toward the center of the battle. Morgalla worked her way forward, yelling colorful dwarven insults as she clobbered a brawling tough with the blunt end of her spear.

Before they could reach the platform, the sorceress mounted her steed and urged it into the sky. With a roar of rage, the dragon bore down. The asperii darted to the side like a huge white hummingbird, barely evading the dragon's lunge. The horse rose straight up into the air, away from the dragon, but into the midst of the gathering storm.

A streak of lightning flashed past the wind steed. The horse went into a panic-stricken dive, with the half-elf clinging to its neck. Hail began to pelt the frightened wind steed, and the horse's whinny of fear and protest shrilled through the screams of the people and the regular, thumping whoosh of the dragon's beating wings.

The asperii reared in midair, sending the sorceress and

her harp falling toward the crowd. As she tumbled toward death, Garnet flailed helplessly in a futile attempt to regain the enchanted instrument.

With the precision of a bat snatching a flying insect from the air, Grimnosh swooped down and grabbed the sorceress in his talons. The dragon's laughter rolled over the city like thunder as he flapped off toward the east with his prey. The harp plummeted to the ground and was lost int the brawl beside the dais.

Garnet was gone, but her spell raged on. Hail bounced off the platform and pelted those who still remained in the arena.

"We've got to get the harp!" Danilo said, pressing toward the dais. Their process was easier now, for the crowd was rapidly dissipating. Clerics and healers carried off those who had been trampled in the first rush to escape. Most of Elaith's ruffians had been subdued, and members of the guard were dragging off those who still showed an inclination to fight. Vartain remained near the platform, his hands folded over his paunch in a triumphant pose and a smile on his bronze face.

Morgalla shoved her way through and leveled her spear at Vartain's throat. "Where's the harp, you over-grown halfling sneak-thief?" she demanded.

"It's not Vartain this time," Danilo said. "Elaith has the harp."

Seventeen

The sun was setting as Danilo raced toward the elven temple. Wyn and Morgalla followed close on his heels. Huge gray and indigo clouds continued to rove the sky, pelting parts of the city with rain and hail. The western horizon was streaked with spires of vivid purple and crimson, and the sun peered over the Sea of Swords like a single flaming red eye.

The three friends rounded the corner to the temple courtyard just as Elaith started up the broad, white marble steps of the main building. He was alone, and the Morninglark harp was tucked under one arm. Danilo pulled his sword and hailed the moon elf. Elaith spun about and fixed a look of pure malevolence upon the Harper.

"Do not hinder me, fool! Too much is at stake."

"My point precisely," Danilo said in a voice that was equally cold. "The Knights of the Shield are earning a foothold in the city, the archmage has been brought low by a charm spell, music-wielding monsters feed upon farmers

291

and travelers, and the bards have become unwitting tools of evil."

"That is a problem for you and yours, *Harper*. It has nothing to do with me."

Danilo advanced a step. "Really! Then you are content to rear the Lady Azariah in the type of world I've just described?"

The elf's face turned white with rage. "You must *never* speak that name," he commanded. "No one in Waterdeep can know of her. I have many enemies who would pay dearly for such information. Many of my associates, for that matter, would not hesitate to seize her for ransom or harm her in revenge against me."

Elaith put down the harp and drew his own sword, advancing with menacing slowness down the steps. "I have the harp now. By the terms of our agreement, my search is over. Our partnership is at an end."

"No, it isn't," Danilo responded, taking a battle stance and raising his sword in guard position. "By your word, I was to undo the spell before turning over the harp to you. Or doesn't your word matter?"

"Azariah is all that matters."

The Harper brought his sword up in time to meet Elaith's first lightning-fast strike. "So she'll be our little secret, is that what you're saying?"

"In a manner of speaking." The elf's smile was grim, and he advanced with a flurry of blows that stretched Danilo's swordsmanship to its limit and beyond. The Harper had little doubt that Elaith could kill him at will, but the elf was not content with a fast strike. The battle between them had been too long in coming.

"Why isn't your faithful dwarven guard dog coming to your aid?" the elf taunted, tossing his silver head in the direction of the grim and watchful warrior.

"This is between you and me. Morgalla understands the

concept of honor."

Elaith laughed unpleasantly. "If that allusion was intended to draw blood, you failed sadly, Harper." He drew a long dirk and advanced on the Harper, keeping his attacks deliberately slow so that Danilo could fend off both blades. The elf was openly, blatantly toying with his prey.

"Honor," Danilo repeated pointedly. "Consider the nature of your quest. Can your daughter's honor be won through dishonor?"

The elf recoiled, glaring at the Harper with naked hatred. He snapped his blades into their scabbards and pulled the magic knife from its wrist sheath. Slowly, he raised his arm for a killing throw.

Wyn wrapped a restraining arm around Morgalla's shoulders, and for a long moment all four stood frozen in tense indecision.

Elaith flung the blade at Danilo. It hit the street at the Harper's feet, embedding itself in the narrow crack between two large pieces of marble. The magic knife quivered there for the span of five heartbeats, then it disappeared.

"Take the accursed harp, then, and cast the spell—if you can." The elf stalked to the edge of the temple courtyard and folded his arms.

On a gusty sigh of relief, Morgalla released the breath she'd been holding, and Wyn's lips began to move in prayer to his elven gods.

The Harper sheathed his sword and walked slowly up the stairs to the ancient harp. He sat down on the step and tentatively stroked the strings. With a quick intake of breath he snatched away his hand, unprepared for the shock of power that had coursed through the silent strings at his touch.

"Get on with it!" Elaith demanded.

The memory of Khelben's stern face filled Danilo's

mind, and the young bard immediately took the harp in his arms. Whatever became of him through the casting of this spell, Dan resolved to do whatever he could for his uncle and his mentor.

Danilo rested the Morninglark harp against his shoulder. Quickly he tried the strings, learning their arrangement and ensuring that all were in tune. One misplayed note, one out-of-tune string, and the powerful spell could fail. If that were to happen, the patriarch Evindal Duirsar might find the temple burdened with yet another mad ward.

"You can do it," Morgalla said softly.

He gave his dwarven friend a reassuring nod, and raised his hands to the strings. The lilting dance melody filled the courtyard. He played it through to the end, then began to sing the riddle-filled spell in harmony with the harp's melody. Once again, Danilo felt the full power of the music course through him, as it had in the High Forest.

From the corner of his eye, the Harper saw a flash of silver in the alley. Six men, clad in the light-eating black garments favored by the southern assassins, burst into the temple courtyard. Each man wielded a long, curved scimitar.

"Keep singing. We got 'em," Morgalla assured him. She tossed aside her spear and pulled her axe. Wyn, too, drew his long sword. The two took a stand at the foot of the stairs, determined that none would get past them.

Danilo's friends fought hard, but they were badly outnumbered, and the assassins were skilled fighters. Morgalla fought with an abandon that was at once grim and gleeful, but even the fierce dwarf was not equal to the assassins. Over to the side of the courtyard, Elaith stood with his arms crossed, watching the fight with apparent amusement.

"You could help out, you long-eared, orc-souled cur!"

Morgalla shouted at him. "Yer still partners 'til the spell is done!"

Her words struck home, and indecision shimmered over the elf's face. Elaith's chest rose and fell with a resigned sigh, and he drew his magic knife. A flick of the wrist, and the assassin battling Wyn fell to the ground clutching his chest. The moon elf then waded into the thickest part of the battle, his blades flashing in streaks of silver and streams of red.

Danilo sang on, and the spell coursed through him, stretching his mind and his skills to encompass the power of the elfsong. When the final notes of the spell rang over the courtyard, he felt the sorcery dissolve suddenly, pulling back in upon itself and sucking magic after it like a vortex. He collapsed, gasping from a force only he could feel.

The visible results of his spell were equally dramatic. The unnatural clouds simply disappeared, and the skies cleared to an even, placid shade of silver. The hail and rain stopped immediately. Most startling was this: the Morninglark harp disappeared from his hands. He rose, looking at his empty hands in disbelief.

Morgalla dispatched the final assassin, then flung herself at Danilo, wrapping her arms around his waist in a bone-crushing hug. "I knowed you could do it, bard!" she crowed, and her blood-streaked face was wreathed in a broad grin.

Danilo returned her embrace, looking over her head at Wyn. "The harp itself was a component of the spell! Did you know that the harp would vanish?"

"I had an idea that it might. Your success was worth the sacrifice," Wyn said quietly.

"Doubt the elf thinks so," Morgalla observed, pulling away from Danilo and pointing toward Elaith.

With an oath, Danilo sprinted across the courtyard.

Elaith stood over the bodies of the four assassins he had downed, his face set in a grimace and one hand clasped to his shoulder. With a quick jerk, the elf pulled a small knife from the muscle of his upper arm. The Harper reached Elaith's side just in time to catch him as he collapsed.

Dan called for Wyn, and together they lifted the elf and began to carry him up the long flight of stairs to the temple. Morgalla picked up the knife and sniffed it. "Poison o' some sort," she said. "Better bring it along, so's the priests can figger out what best to do." She followed the men up toward the temple.

"Lord Thann," the elf said in a faint voice.

"Don't talk," Wyn advised him. "Stay as still as possible to slow the action of the poison."

"It is important. Listen well, Harper. In my bag is a key. It will admit you to my house on Selduth Street. See to it that my estate is settled and the means to raise Azariah directed to the temple." Elaith paused for a grim smile. "Solving that riddle spell will be good practice for unraveling my business affairs."

A spasm of pain crossed the elf's face, and beads of sweat began to collect on his upper lip. His amber eyes sought Danilo's, and the fierce gaze reminded the Harper of a dying hawk. The elf would not submit to the poison, however, until his mind was at ease. "Swear to it! Swear that you will see that my daughter receives her inheritance."

"There is no need for that," Danilo said quietly. He nodded to the faint blue glow emanating from Elaith's left side. The magic stone on the hilt of the moonblade was alight with inner fire. "You have accomplished that yourself."

Elaith reached over and touched the moonblade with awe. A look of utter peace crossed his face, and at last his eyes closed as darkness claimed him.

"In death, he has regained his honor," Wyn said, regarding the magic elven sword with wonder in his green eyes.

"He's won a second chance," the Harper corrected, noting that the elf still breathed. "How he chooses to use it remains to be seen."

* * * * *

Beneath the most dramatic sunset in living memory, the people of Waterdeep ventured out, heading to the marketplace for the Twilight Meeting that marked the official beginning of Shieldmeet.

All the portable booths had been removed from the open-air market, leaving ample room for the thousands who gathered in the vast area. A raised platform stood in the center of the marketplace, and a faint bowl of light surrounded it, providing illumination and amplifying the voices of those who would speak. There were sixteen thrones on the platform, one for each of the Lords of Waterdeep.

This was a matter of much speculation among the crowds, for the fate of the Lords seemed in no way certain. Most of the conversation, however, involved the events at the Field of Triumph. Dragon attacks were hardly common events.

The people recovered their equilibrium quickly, for Waterdhavians had seen it all and were as irrepressible and adaptable as any people in Faerun. Everywhere they were arguing about the identity of the strange bard, whether she or Khelben Arunsun was responsible for the wizard weather, and even whether they should confirm the rule of the Lords of Waterdeep or seek other solutions to their problems.

Vendors wove through the crowd, offering refreshments and—considering all that had transpired—herbs, simples, and potions to soothe the nerves and dull the pain of minor injuries. The wealthiest visitors and citizens settled into the raised, curtained seats that ringed the outer edge of the market, and servants tended to their needs and carried messages and wagers between the booths of various noble and wealthy families. Those of lesser station gathered in the middle of the marketplace, and soon the entire area resembled a living, closely woven tapestry.

In her hiding place over a nearby weapon shop, Lucia Thione could hear the sounds of the crowd as the throngs passed by on the way to the meeting. Elaith Craulnober had made all her travel arrangements, and had bid her to wait there for her armed escort. Lucia hated to leave Waterdeep, for she had lived in the city most of her life and had enjoyed her position here. Yet much of her wealth was secreted elsewhere, and she had substantial holdings outside Waterdeep. She would want for nothing, and she would start again.

As the twilight deepened into evening, there came a knock on the door in the elaborate code that the moon elf had prearranged.

Lucia nodded to her guard, and the man unlocked the door. A tall, red-haired man ducked to avoid hitting his head on the low lintel. He entered the room and affixed her with a sad, steady gaze. Lucia gasped and fell back from him.

"Your surprise is understandable, lady, considering the circumstances of our last meeting," said Caladorn. "I understand that you will be leaving our city, and I believe that you have already met your traveling companion."

A portly, dark-skinned man with a look of extreme satisfaction on his black-bearded face strolled into the room. The noblewoman's heart plummeted when her eyes settled on Lord Hhune.

Lucia threw herself into the young man's arms. "Caladorn, you love me! You cannot do this to me. If only you'll listen, you'll know that I—"

He broke off her despairing plea with a simple shake of his head, then took her shoulders and gently put her away from him. "No more. I am breaking the law by allowing you to go. You know as well as I the penalty for impersonating a Lord of Waterdeep." Caladorn took her hand and bowed deeply over it. "Farewell, Lucia."

The young man turned to Hhune, who was studying Lady Thione with an unreadable expression in his black eyes. "The Knights of the Shield are neither welcome nor tolerated in this city," Caladorn said. "I have been instructed to say that you must never return to Waterdeep. Shieldmeet is a time of truces: you would do well to be far from these gates when this day of peace is over. Remove your thieves and assassins, and the city is prepared to honor its trade agreements with your shipping guild."

"You are most generous, Lord Caladorn," Hhune said in inscrutable tones. "I accept your offer and will comply with its terms. And as the elf requested, I will see my countrywoman safely out of the city."

The young man bowed and turned away, quickly disappearing down the stairs and out into the market-bound crowd. With him went the last of Lucia's hopes. She wondered if he understood the sentence that his mercy had imposed upon her. She had no illusions about her fate in Hhune's hands, and she turned her gaze to the Tethyrian's face.

"Well, let us be off," he said evenly. "We've a long journey ahead."

Moving like one who slept, Lucia followed the guildmaster down the back stairs and into the carriage that waited there. Lord Hhune's mood—which was neither the gloating triumph nor the violent rage she would have expected, but a cynical and perverse amusement—terrified her.

"What will you do with me?" she asked in a low voice.

"I thought it might be entertaining to bring a member of the hated royal family back to Tethyr," Hhune mused, his black eyes glittering as he regarded her. "It is fitting, is it not? After all, you should be paid in coin of your own choosing."

With those words, the Tethyrian tapped the glass on the front of the carriage. The horses lurched forward on the long road southward.

* * * * *

As soon as the elven priests took Elaith into their care, Danilo and his friends hurried toward the marketplace. The Harper was relieved that his task was completed, but he could not be at ease until he learned the full extent of the elfsong spell's reversal. If Khelben had not recovered when the spell was lifted, the Harper's victory would be incomplete and empty.

There was little standing room left when the trio arrived. A firm hand settled on Danilo's shoulder, and the Harper looked up into the grave, handsome face of his friend Caladorn. Relief flooded him.

"Mystra be praised, you're all right! I can't tell you how glad I am that I was wrong, Caladorn."

"You were not wrong," the young man said softly. "I was, and I wish to make peace with you." Danilo took the hand offered him and clasped it briefly. "The Lady Laeral has told me all that has transpired, and your part in it," Caladorn concluded. He smiled faintly. "Finally, Dan, you have a bard's tale that is worthy of your talents!"

Before Dan could question him about Khelben, Caladorn hurried off into the crowd. With a deep sigh, Danilo turned his attention to the platform. Soon Lord Piergeiron and fifteen masked and robed Lords proceeded in and seated themselves on the raised platform. Murmurs rippled through the crowd, silencing immediately as Piergeiron rose to address the assembly.

"Good people of Waterdeep. It has been a long and troubling day, and much has happened in the last few weeks. Before the Shieldmeet alliances are made, many questions must be laid to rest about these strange events. One of the Lords of Waterdeep has related to me a wondrous tale. I am not an orator, though, and only a bard could do justice to this story."

The First Lord paused and smiled. "I call upon Danilo Thann."

This unexpected summons lifted Dan's heart. Surely this meant that Khelben had been released from his magical sleep, for only Khelben knew all that had occurred! Then he remembered Caladorn's knowledge of recent events, and this assumption wasn't good enough for him.

Beside him, Morgalla stamped and hooted, drawing attention to the bard at her side. The people around burst into loud huzzahs and enthusiastic applause, and they made way for Dan to pass.

The warmth and the acclaim strangely chilled the Harper, for it could only indicate that the elfsong spell had not been entirely banished. Shouldn't his reputation have perished along with the spell?

With Morgalla firmly pushing him from behind, Danilo made his way toward the middle of the marketplace. Seeing that he had no instrument, a beautiful, golden haired elf pressed her harp into his hands, bidding him with an inviting smile to return it whenever he wished.

As he looked at the instrument, inspiration struck Danilo, and he knew how he could ascertain Khelben's fate. He thanked the elf woman and ascended the platform.

The Harper began to play one of his favorite melodies, and to it he sang an improvised and almost-accurate account of the adventure. Danilo kept the facts in, but he deliberately embellished the tale, adding a comic twist and a ribald suggestion or two.

From the corner of his eye, Danilo saw one of the Lords raise a hand to his helmed forehead in a gesture of exasperation that the Harper knew very well. Joy flooded the young bard's heart, and the power of elfsong crept unbidden into his voice.

The people of Waterdeep listened to the ballad with deep attention, drawn into the music and the story in a way that, many of them said later, seemed almost magical.

Epilogue

Several days after Shieldmeet, Danilo visited Khelben at Blackstaff Tower. Although still weakened by his encounter with Garnet, the archmage insisted upon resuming his duties and sent for his nephew.

"How is he?" Dan whispered to Laeral as she showed him into Khelben's study.

"He's starting to get testy," the mage replied with a long-suffering sigh. "They say that's a good sign. *They*, of course, don't have to live with him."

Khelben motioned his nephew into the room. The archmage poured Danilo a cup of the steeped herbs he insisted upon drinking, and he seemed inclined to linger over bad tea and local gossip.

Things in Waterdeep, apparently, were looking up. The late crops were thriving. Monster attacks to the south had fallen off drastically, and small game was returning to the woods. Trouble in the harbor and fishing sites had ended.

"Most important, the ballads have returned to their

original form. Our past and our traditions have been restored," Khelben said with deep satisfaction.

"I understand Lady Thione has disappeared. How has Caladorn taken all this?" Danilo asked.

"He's put out to sea again," the archmage said.

"The change will do him good," Laeral said as she came into the room. "Although your uncle doesn't always remember this, there is a wide world outside the walls of Waterdeep."

"Hhune is gone as well," Khelben grumbled, ignoring his lady's teasing. "We wouldn't have let him go if we'd known he was responsible for what happened to Larissa."

"The courtesan?" Danilo asked.

"That and more. Larissa is a dear friend, and one of the Lords of Waterdeep. She was brutally attacked while you were gone and has lingered near death for many days. Just yesterday, she awoke and was able to tell us who did this to her. Clerics of Sune are praying for her full recovery. In time, she should regain her health and beauty."

Laeral nodded. "I saw her last night, and she already seems much better. She requested of the clerics to have her nose shortened slightly, if that tells you anything."

"Sounds like Larissa," the archmage agreed. "Texter is back in town, too. He's been out riding for days. The peculiar thing is, he has no idea where he's been."

"Not usual for Texter," Laeral noted.

"But he says he has the oddest feeling that he had a good time while he was gone."

"Now, that *is* strange," the beautiful mage said dryly. She turned to Danilo. "Texter is not one of the more fun-loving of the Lords of Waterdeep."

"All this city gossip is fascinating," the Harper said in a bemused tone, "but aren't these names supposed to be a dark secret?"

"Mirt's back, too," Khelben said as if he hadn't heard his

nephew, "and his daughter Asper is with him. You should meet Asper, by the way. She's our eyes and ears in Baldur's Gate."

"Wait a minute—she works for the Harpers?"

"I didn't say that." The archmage fell silent. "Now that your assignment is complete, Dan, we need to discuss the next step in your career."

Danilo nodded and leaned forward. "I've been meaning to speak with you about that. I've been talking to Halambar, and we're discussing the possibility of rebuilding the barding college in Waterdeep. A number of renowned bards have expressed an interest in the project. As you can imagine, many are none too happy about their recent role in the city's troubles. They wish to repay Waterdeep, and you as well, Uncle."

"I see. And what would your role be in all this?"

"For some time to come, very little. I will help fund the college—my ballad performances are quite the rage these days—but with the Harpers' permission I would like to devote most of my time to the study of elfsong. Perhaps when I have learned the art, I will teach it to others."

"You did well enough the other day," Khelben said. Despite his gruff tone, unmistakable pride shone on his face.

Danilo looked intently at the archmage. "You've worked with me for many years, Uncle, and you expected me to become a wizard. Tell me truly, are you disappointed that I did not chose to follow in your footsteps?"

The archmage shrugged. "What's another wizard, more or less?"

"Really," Danilo persisted.

"Really? All right then; I think that the only way you could follow me more closely would be to walk in my boots—while I'm wearing them. On the whole, I'm not in favor of that idea."

"I'm not sure I understand," Danilo faltered, puzzled by his uncle's uncharacteristic levity.

Khelben reached under his desk and took out a large, square box. "This ought to explain matters," he said, handing it to his nephew.

Danilo lifted the lid and took out the black, veiled helm of a Lord of Waterdeep. He stared at it in silence.

"Well, try it on!"

The Harper shook his head. "I don't want it," he said in a hollow voice.

"Who does?" Khelben said wryly.

"But I'm not fit for the task! What do I know about governing a city?"

The archmage's face turned serious. "More than you might think. Do you trust Elaith Craulnober?"

"Of course not," Danilo said, looking startled by the abrupt change of topic.

"But you worked together, and effectively. The ability to form an alliance between disparate individuals and groups is a rare and important one."

"So? Any festhall owner in Waterdeep can do as much. You'd be better seeking your spare Lord in the House of Purple Silks!"

"This is not the only reason for your induction. There's more," Khelben said, in the tone that signaled a lesson to come.

The Harper sighed. "There always seems to be."

"There is an old saying, 'Let me write a kingdom's songs, and I care not who writes its laws.' Of recent months we have seen how true this can be. Bardcraft and government cannot be separated, for without bards we forget our past and lack the perspective needed to evaluate our actions. Even the dark humor of Morgalla's art grants us an important new way to judge how our decisions are perceived."

"And likewise, were it not for the turmoil and intrigue of lords and kingdoms, and the heroic deeds that spring from these, we bards would soon be out of business," Danilo admitted.

"Except for love songs," Laeral said, batting her silver lashes in a parody of flirtation.

Danilo grinned at the roguish mage. "Even so."

"There is also the matter of Balance," Khelben added quietly. "Although her methods were misguided, Iriador—Garnet, if you will—was not entirely in the wrong. In our concern for the well-being and safety of Faerun, the Harpers have not tended and nurtured the bardic arts as we should have."

"Doesn't changing a bard into a politician continue that trend?"

"Not at all. You will still be a bard, but as a Lord of Waterdeep you will also have the power to ensure that this barding college becomes a reality."

The Harper thought for a long moment, staring at the black helm in his hands. "Now that I've finally chosen a path for myself," he said slowly, "I'd hoped to devote myself solely to bardcraft. Elfsong is demanding, and I've much to learn."

"So? What's to detain you? Every other Lord has a profession, ranging from tavern keeper to courtesan."

"Now that you mention it, this new role could yield some interesting material for new ballads," the Harper mused.

Khelben snorted. "Just see that you keep your facts straighter than you did in the Shieldmeet ballad!"

"Done." Danilo rose to his feet. "Now that my future's settled, I've got more frivolous things to tend to."

After a quick stop at his townhouse, he made his way, laden with gifts for a tiny elven lady, to the elven temple. Lady Azariah would soon be officially acknowledged as

Elaith's heir to the moonblade, and although Danilo would not be able to attend the exclusively elven ceremony, he wished to pay his respects betides. The elven toddler had stolen his heart at first sight.

Danilo nodded to the temple guards and made his way down the long corridor toward Azariah's nursery.

"What are you doing here?" demanded a familiar voice behind him.

The Harper turned, peering over the pile of gifts at Elaith Craulnober. Dan had not seen him since the day of their battle, for the elf had been long in recovering from the poison. Danilo noted that Elaith's angular face was even thinner, and that his skin was so pale that it nearly echoed the pale silver of his hair. The fighter was clad in the simple white robes of the temple elves, but Danilo did not doubt that a few weapons were hidden among the folds. The moonblade, however, was not at Elaith's hip.

"I'm not visiting you, that's for certain." Danilo glanced down at the elaborately carved and painted hobby horse in his arms. "This toy pegasus is a tribute for Patriarch Duirsar," he said solemnly.

The elf's face softened. "Azariah's nurse said you have visited her frequently during my convalescence. I hope she is not permanently warped by the association," he said, falling back into his customary acrid tone.

"I can see that you're back to normal," Dan replied. He resumed his walk toward the baby's room. Elaith fell in beside him, and the Harper cast a sidelong look at the elf. "Would it delay your recovery if I told you that your assistance against Lady Thione's thugs probably saved my life?"

"By several days, at least," the elf replied tartly.

"In that case, I'm so glad I mentioned it. If your recovery needs a boost, perhaps you should consider joining Vartain. He has more or less taken up residence in Mother

Tathlorn's House of Pleasure and Healing. Having discovered fun, he seems determined to make up for years of deprivation. By the time you get there, he'll probably need to avail himself of Mother Tathlorn's healing services at least as badly as you do."

Elaith grimaced. "I'll pass. Cavorting in Vartain's company is hardly an appealing prospect. What of the others? What is the spellsinger doing of late? I had hoped he would sing at the ceremony for Azariah."

"Wyn plans to travel east, to accompany Morgalla back to her people," Danilo explained with a sigh. "I shall miss her. She has been my houseguest since Shieldmeet. Now that she has overcome her aversion to singing and dancing, my townhouse has become a popular dwarven salon. The cost of mead has been staggering, but I've become acquainted with nearly every dwarf in Waterdeep. I'll definitely miss her," he repeated. "For a time, I thought she might join the Harpers."

"She has all the annoying, steadfast traits of the breed," Elaith agreed. "On the other hand, meddling is not something that comes naturally to the little diggers."

"Dwarves do seem to lack a certain requisite curiosity," Danilo agreed cheerfully. "I'm not troubled in that respect, so I'll just jump in and ask why you're not wearing your moonblade, after all the trouble you went through to awaken it."

Elaith was silent for a long moment. "By elven law, it is the right of any to decline the honor of bearing a moonblade. That honor will fall to Azariah, when she comes of age."

"I'm not sorry to hear that. Frankly, you're trouble enough without such a sword."

The elf's amber eyes glinted with the sharp humor he so often turned on others. "It's so comforting to be understood."

There was little Danilo could add to that. "So what is next for you?"

"As soon as my health permits, I will take Azariah to Evermeet. There she will be prepared to meet the magic sword's demands."

"She will be fostered there?" the Harper asked, wondering whether the lawful elves of Evermeet would allow the rogue to make his home among them.

"Yes, she will become a ward of the royal court. But I will spend as much time on the island as my affairs permit."

Elaith's amber eyes burned with longing as he said these words. Danilo was happy about the elf's homecoming, but he privately wondered whether someone on the island kingdom should be warned about the criminal element soon to be among them.

"And what of you? Now that all the excitement is over, I imagine you'll be getting back to the life of an idle young lord?" Elaith asked with silky sarcasm.

Danilo smiled wryly and dumped the pile of gifts into the elf's arms. "That cuts it fairly close."

Whistling the melody to one of his off-color songs, the Harper headed toward Blackstaff Tower. Before Morgalla left for the east, Danilo mused, he really should arrange to have his own secret tunnels dug connecting his townhouse with the meeting spots favored by the Lords of Waterdeep. As luck would have it, he had excellent connections among the dwarves.

The PRISM PENTAD
By Troy Denning

Searing drama in an unforgiving world . . .

The Obsidian Oracle Book Four

Power-hungry Tithian emerges as the new ruler of Tyr. When he pursues his dream of becoming a sorcerer-king, only the nobleman Agis stands between Tithian and his desire: possession of an ancient oracle that will lead to either the salvation of Athas – or its destruction.

ISBN 1-56076-603-4
Sug. Retail $4.95/CAN $5.95/£3.99 U.K.

The Cerulean Storm Book Five

Rajaat: The First Sorcerer – the only one who can return Athas to its former splendor – is imprisoned beyond space and time. When Tithian enlists the aid of his former slaves, Rikus, Neeva, and Sadira, to free the sorcerer, does he want to restore the world – or claim it as his own?

ISBN 1-56076-642-5
Sug. Retail $4.95/CAN $5.95/£3.99 U.K.

On Sale Now

The Verdant Passage Book One
ISBN 1-56076-121-0
Sug. Retail $4.95/CAN $5.95/£3.99 U.K.

The Amber Enchantress Book Three
ISBN 1-56076-236-5
Sug. Retail $4.95/CAN $5.95/£3.99 U.K.

The Crimson Legion
Book Two
ISBN 1-56076-260-8
Sug. Retail $4.95/
CAN $5.95/£3.99 U.K.

TALES OF GOTHIC HORROR
BEYOND YOUR WILDEST SCREAMS!

Tapestry of Dark Souls
Elaine Bergstrom
ISBN 1-56076-571-2
The monks' hold over the Gathering Cloth, containing some of the vilest evils in Ravenloft, is slipping. The only hope is a strange youth, who will become either the monks' champion . . . or their doom.

Heart of Midnight
J. Robert King
ISBN 1-56076-355-8
Even before he'd drawn his first breath, Casimir had inherited his father's lycanthropic curse. Now the young werewolf must embrace his powers to ward off his own murder and gain revenge.

MORE TALES OF TERROR

Vampire of the Mists
Christie Golden
ISBN 1-56076-155-5

Knight of the Black Rose
James Lowder
ISBN 1-56076-156-3

Dance of the Dead
Christie Golden
ISBN 1-56076-352-3

Available now at book and hobby stores everywhere!

Each $4.95/CAN $5.95/U.K. £3.99

Ravenloft
Books

The Penhaligon Trilogy

If you enjoyed *The Dragon's Tomb*, you'll want to read —